EMBERS OF FATE

DANI LOUGHARY

FOX HAVEN LLC

Book Cover by Gabriella Regina

Character Art by CamilleLouIllustration

Editing by Samantha Swart

Chapter Header Illustrations by vecteezy.com and canva.com

AUTHOR'S NOTE

Embers of Fate contains the following content warnings. Please be mindful of them, your mental health matters!

- Death of a parent

- Grief

- Threatened sexual assault

- Gendered Language/Bigotry (Though the book itself is LGBTQ+ friendly!)

- Adult Language

- Explicit Sexual Scenes

- Violence/Blood in fight scenes

If you prefer to skip over scenes with sexual content, these are mostly found in Chapters Twenty and Twenty-One, with a brief scene at the end of Chapter Twenty-Six.

DEDICATION

For my grandmother-
Who taught me to love reading and romance.

For Ethan and Ryan-
Who taught me the meaning of the truest love—a piece of my own heart living outside my body.

CHAPTER ONE

A few dark curls from Gwen's neat braids tickled her neck and framed her face as she urged the white-speckled horse forward. Akasha seemed to sense her rider's mood, galloping faster than ever before, her hooves thundering on the cobblestones below.

Gwen's heart pounded in her chest. She needed to get as far away from everyone and everything as possible. She burst through the cavernous wooden gate that separated the castle's inner guard wall from the village, racing past the small homes and shops that made up Thorncliff proper. The guards stationed in the towers of the massive outer wall were familiar with this routine. They had long since learned that the tongue-lashing they would receive for ignoring their princess's orders was far worse than the captain's reprimand for allowing her to leave. They opened the large iron gate ahead of her, revealing the road away from Thorncliff.

Akasha and Gwen veered off the main road, galloping through the long willow grass. Gwen glanced back over her shoulder towards the wall, where the guards were struggling to keep up. The small lead she had gained gave Gwen the upper hand. Akasha was one of the two fastest steeds in all of Thorncliff—perhaps even the entire district of Exester. Surefooted even on the most challenging terrain, Akasha served Gwen well on their chosen path. The guards were no match for them. Gwen twined her fingers in Akasha's mane and guided her further from the castle.

After a while, Gwen could no longer see the guards on the horizon. She slowed Akasha to a brisk trot and, as the small shady spring came into view, eased her mount into a walk. The setting sun from the west peeked around the large hill that partially concealed the spring, nearly blinding her with its brilliance. Akasha, familiar with the path, guided them down over the rocks towards the large tree that dominated the space. The pale bark of the gnarled, twisted branches rose high in the air, while the purple leaves trailed down and brushed the ground. Gwen slid off and looped Akasha's lead around a limb, her hands shaking as she did so, a tightening sensation settling into her chest, and her vision beginning to tunnel.

Gwen gasped for air and fell to her knees, her fingers digging into the rocky soil near the tree's roots. The water in the spring began to swirl and bubble as her control slipped, causing Akasha to nicker nervously and bump against her. Gwen counted softly under her breath, her chest heaving as she struggled to regain control and rein in her powers. She closed her eyes, focusing on the feel of the moist, velvety soil under her fingers. She took a deep breath, inhaling the earthy, musky scent of Akasha and the soil beneath her. She noted the way the cool wind against her sweaty skin made her shiver. Gwen stayed like that for several minutes, just breathing with her eyes closed.

Standing on shaky legs, she wrapped her arms around Akasha's neck. Burying her face in the horse's warm, silky mane, she surrendered to the emotions swirling inside her. Her sobs were painful, as if they had wrenched themselves from the depths of her soul and forced their way out.

The sound of approaching hoofbeats pierced through her turmoil. Realizing her vulnerability, she remained still, listening. The gods knew she could protect herself, but the aftermath would be messy, and she had sworn a blood oath to avoid such actions. She gripped the hilt of a small dagger hidden under her skirt. The rider approached with a confident pace. Chances were she knew this rider and would have little need for protection. Sure enough, a large black steed crested the rocky path and came into view, carrying the captain of her personal guard, dressed in his training uniform of straps crisscrossed over a leather chest plate layered over a blue under tunic.

Tyreal's stormy gray eyes scanned the cove before resting on her tear-streaked face. Worry etched deep lines between his brows, furrowing his chiseled forehead. His full lips, usually so expressive, were pressed into a thin, taut line, nearly vanishing into the rugged thickness of his beard. The tension in his face was palpable, every feature drawn tight. Gwen buried her face back into Akasha's neck, unwilling to meet his gaze. She released the dagger; she was in no danger from him.

"If you plan to chastise me for leaving my guards behind, Tyreal Blackbane, I am in no mood." Her words were muffled, but she knew he would understand. The damnable man had hearing unlike anyone she had ever met.

"I should, but no. I won't lecture you today. Though I also won't leave you unattended." Tyreal dismounted and tied his steed next to Akasha. Braken nuzzled the other side of the mare's neck and bumped Gwen's hand. She usually indulged him with a sugar cube from her pocket, and the horse never missed an opportunity to beg. Despite her mood, Gwen couldn't resist and reached into her pocket, producing two cubes for the pair. Finally, she felt brave enough to lift her face from Akasha and glance at Tyreal.

A mix of emotions crossed his face as their eyes met, emotions she wasn't in the mood to dissect. "Not a word about my unsightly appearance either," she said hoarsely. It felt as though the weight of a thousand stones was pressing down on her, her knees finally giving way to the flood of emotions.

Tyreal sat down beside her, aligning his shoulders with hers in a gesture of silent solidarity. It was far more forward than he would be if anyone else were present, but right now, she welcomed it. His other hand stayed on the hilt of his sword, ever vigilant, though it would be difficult to draw it in his current position. She sometimes wondered if he realized how often he grabbed it out of habit. Despite her turmoil, she felt much calmer with him beside her. For all of life's uncertainties, he was a constant.

"He's dying." Her voice startled her, as if she hadn't planned on speaking the words aloud.

"Aye."

"I don't want him to die." A sob threatened to escape again, her words cracking at the end. Tyreal's jaw tightened, and she watched his fists clench, the whites of his knuckles showing.

He sighed softly, releasing his sword hilt to wrap an arm around her shoulders, pulling her close as his other hand found hers. He didn't look at her, instead continuing to scan the horizon. His hand was warm and calloused in her own. "I don't think there are many in this kingdom who do, Gwennie."

She allowed herself to relax into his embrace, closing her eyes. Tears streamed from beneath her lashes, but she paid them no mind. She felt the warmth of him through the fabric of his tunic and smelled his distinctly male scent. It was familiar in a way it shouldn't have been, considering she was rarely this close to him. She listened to the steady sound of his heartbeat until her tears slowed and her own heartbeat steadied. "I'm so scared, Tyreal. I had to get out of there—I couldn't breathe."

He rubbed his thumb against hers. "I'm sorry. I'm no good with words in these situations. I can fight your enemies, but I can't protect you from this. It was hell when my own Papa died, and I didn't have to shoulder the weight of a kingdom on top of it," he said.

She ignored the kingdom comment; the very mention of it made the tight feeling in her chest return. "Aye, you were never good with words. Unless you were lecturing me on putting myself in harm's way."

"Well, I've had more practice with that one, haven't I? Damn insufferable woman."

"Is that any way to speak to your princess?" Her words held no bite, and she took a deep breath. Her next words were barely above a whisper. "I don't know if I can do it. I don't know how to be a queen. What if I'm horrible without him here to guide me?" Her fingers twisted at a long blade of willow grass as she spoke, watching it slip between her fingers and drift away.

He squeezed her hand gently, speaking gruffly. "You've been training to be queen your whole life. You're no longer a lass. Everything King Lorne could pass on to you, he already has. You're fair, kind, determined, beautiful, and more than capable of delivering the most terrifying of tongue-lashings to anyone who steps out of line. I know, I've seen it."

"I'm not my mother, Tyreal. I'll never be half the queen she was. I'm stubborn and I chafe under the weight of my crown now, and I'm just a princess. Sometimes I get angry and say awful things. The thought of marrying one of these royal men makes me want to run across the Baltecian Ocean. Anya got the only decent one I know of that's even close to our age." Her breathing hitched, coming in short, uneven breaths.

Tyreal turned towards her, grabbing her chin and tilting her face upwards. Their close proximity put her face just inches from his. "Gwendolyn Rosa Thorncrest, that's all true. Has been since I first met you when you were only four summers gone. You also forgot to add reckless, wild, and well... everything that makes you Gwen." She huffed, trying to pull away from him, but he held her in place. His stormy gray eyes bore into hers, forcing her to listen. "But you are the next in line for the Tavian throne. Everything you are is everything Tavia needs.

No one, and I mean no one, loves this land and its people as much as you. Our king is dying. Will you run and cast your people into chaos? Or will you take the role you've prepared for your whole life?"

"But what if I'm terrible? What if they write songs of the ice queen of Tavia who ended the era of peace?" She bit her bottom lip, horrified that she admitted that out loud.

"Ice queen? Be serious," he scoffed. "You burn hotter than the light of a thousand suns when you're angry or passionate about something. I've seen that too."

The air thickened between them. Her eyes dropped to his lips, but she forced herself to look away and turned back to the sparkling green spring. She wanted to respond but couldn't. So, she shoved her feelings down, as she always did. Tyreal seemed to take her silent cue and adjusted his body away from hers, dropping his hand back to his side.

She pulled her knees up, wrapping her arms around them and resting her chin on top. "I'm going to be all alone when he's gone. I don't know how to wrap my head around that."

He shook his head. "Nonsense. You have Pippen, friends who love you, and an entire kingdom that adores you."

Gwen let his words sink in. She thought back to her fourth summer when she first met Tyreal. She'd been hand in hand with her mama, happily picking wildflowers when Tommen Blackbane, captain of the armory, rode in to speak with her father, his son in tow. Gwen had been curious about the boy with the intense gray eyes and the mop of wavy dark hair that fell over his brow. There weren't many children in the castle, and her mother had lost two babes. So even though Tyreal was four summers older, she had relentlessly followed him around. He hadn't minded, solemnly declaring to her father and his that he would be her Captain of the Guard one day.

Tyreal's voice pulled her from her memories. "Gwen, he needs you now. I promise, you don't want him to go into the Everafter without you by his side. It still kills me that I was away when mine went."

She nodded, taking another deep breath as she stood. She brushed the leaves and grass from her skirt, which looked horribly rumpled. The light blue fabric was not designed for riding or sitting on the ground. It was just a simple day dress she had thrown on after learning of her father's deteriorating condition. She hadn't waited for Cora's help. "How much of a mess is my braid? I certainly don't look like a proper queen right now."

Tyreal stood as well. He raised his fingers, brushing them against her cheek as he plucked a leaf from her hair. Gwen's eyes fluttered closed for a moment, her cheeks flushing. "Just looks like you had a hard ride, Highness. And I don't think the king or your brother will mind much. Nor your people."

She winced at the return to their titles, but her moment of self-pity was over. It was time to return to the castle and face her fate. She moved towards the horses. "Come along, my Captain. Ride with me back to Thorncliff."

"Aye, Highness." Tyreal untied Akasha and Braken and handed her Akasha's reins.

"Tyreal... Thank you. I couldn't have—I mean, with anyone else—"

"My job is to protect you. From everything and everyone. You needed a moment to process. I provided it," he said.

She nodded and mounted Akasha. Gwen had never felt more reluctant to return home. "How did you find me, by the way?"

He looked towards the purple tree and the spring, shaking his head slightly. "It always comes back to this spring, doesn't it? It's where you go when you're trying to escape everything that comes with being princess."

"Never works though, does it?" Her voice was sad as she glanced at him. His jaw clenched as he turned back to Braken and swung his leg over the saddle.

"That's the thing about fate and stations in this life, Highness. They're the one thing you can never escape." Tyreal made a clicking sound with his tongue and moved Braken away so she could lead Akasha out. The two rode in silence over the large rocks surrounding the spring and the fairydew tree, and she resisted the urge to turn back and stare longingly at it.

CHAPTER TWO

The clatter of horses' hooves on the dirt path was the only sound as Gwen and Tyreal rounded the bend, coming into view of the guards. Each wore the red and gold uniform of the royal guard, a reminder of everything she'd been trying to escape. Gwen took a deep breath to steady herself. Tyreal must have instructed them to keep their distance, granting her a rare moment of solitude as she grappled with everything unfolding around her. She glanced at him and offered a small smile of gratitude. He responded with a slight incline of his head.

The guards saluted her with a fist over their hearts as she rode past, then fell into formation behind them. "So, who ratted on me for running?" she asked.

"Prince Pippen found me while I was training with Tensha in the yard. He said you tore out of the stables with Akasha as if the hounds of Ganderly were after you." Tyreal's frown deepened, and Gwen wondered how long it would be before he couldn't resist lecturing her.

She cursed under her breath, and although Tyreal's smirk returned briefly, he chose to remain silent. Gwen ignored it. "I didn't mean for him to see that. I've been trying to protect him," she said.

"He's not a little boy anymore, Highness. And he knows his father is dying. You can't shield him from this." Tyreal's pointed look met her snort. Gwen ignored that, too. She knew he was right, but she struggled to see Pippen as anything other than the baby she had cradled after their mother's death.

The feelings she had experienced then were akin to what she felt now. The grief from her mother's passing had been overwhelming, like a sea wave that could drag one under if not handled carefully. Pippen had been a tiny baby with dark curls and green eyes just like her own, and he needed her. Her mother had spent months impressing upon her the importance of being a big sister. Her father, consumed by his own sorrow, still had a country to govern. So, Gwen had taken on the role of a surrogate mother, shooing away the nannies with all the authority her eleven summers gone self could muster.

Tyreal's patience finally seemed to wear thin. "Akasha is surer-footed than nearly any other horse, Highness, but this path is too hilly to race across at such speed. What if you'd been thrown?"

Gwen pursed her lips, annoyed at the public chastisement. Yet it was familiar and no longer stung her pride as it once did. She knew he was right, so she settled for looking contrite. "You're right, Captain. I should have been more cautious. Especially now. I can't afford to think only of myself anymore, can I?"

"No, Highness," he agreed.

They approached the imposing stone wall that shielded Thorncliff from the outer world, a remnant of the continent of Valine's war-torn past. Between two guard towers stood a great gate crafted from interwoven iron bars, forming intricate patterns of vines and roses, echoing the Thorncrest seal. The metal bore the scars of countless battles, deep gouges and scratches a testament to its history of defense. How many had failed to notice or question these marks? The people of Tavia and Valine had long forgotten the wars and the magic behind them; for them, it was merely old fairy tales.

Gwen's heart raced as the gate loomed closer, its iron vines seeming to reach for her, seeking to trap her in a fate she couldn't escape. The gate was more than an entryway; it was the threshold between her past and her future, where she would become both an orphan and a queen.

To calm herself, she focused on the flags atop the wall: the crimson and gold of Tavia, the white flag with a golden rose for the Thorncrest family, and the emerald green with nine interlinked white circles, representing Valine's founding royal families. They glowed in the setting sun, their reflection making Gwen squint. She turned her face away, looking out over the cliffs behind the outer wall. Below, the soft crashing of waves helped to calm her.

Tyreal signaled for the gate to be opened, and Gwen continued to avoid looking at the castle ahead. For most of her life, it had reminded her of her father, steadfast as the setting sun. Passing through the outer gate, they entered the bustling village nestled between the inner and outer walls. They proceeded along the main street toward the wooden inner gate that led to the castle. The blacksmith's shop was open, the glowing embers of the forge visible through its wide doors. The smith, a burly man with soot-streaked arms, hammered away at a piece of red-hot metal. Nearby, the apothecary's shop displayed bundles of dried herbs hanging from the eaves, their pungent aroma mingling with the air.

Soon, small homes with whitewashed walls and dark wooden beams lined the cobbled roads. Thatched roofs and hand-painted window boxes full of blooming flowers added a quaint charm that Gwen adored. Mixed among them were market stalls usually bursting with colorful fabrics, fresh produce, and trinkets. Today, however, they appeared subdued. Vendors stood quietly behind their tables, their usual cheerful shouts absent.

As Gwen glanced around, the difference became apparent now that she wasn't speeding past. Normally, people greeted her with warm smiles and well wishes. Children played while their parents haggled. Today, however, people bowed low, their faces pinched with sadness. The news of her father's imminent passing must have spread quickly. A young girl, perhaps two summers gone, stood by the road, clutching her mother's skirts and crying. Her mother tried to comfort her, casting a sorrowful glance toward Gwen. The sight pierced Gwen's heart, even a babe picking up on the somber mood of those around them.

"Captain, wait, I want to stop for a moment," she said. She wasn't sure what she wanted to say, but her father had always emphasized her responsibility to be attuned to her people's emotions and offer what support she could in times of strife. Tyreal nodded and halted Braken ahead of her. The guards maintained their position behind her. Though Tyreal kept his hand on the hilt of his sword, his relaxed shoulders suggested he was not overly concerned in town. If he couldn't ensure her safety here, she wondered if she was safe anywhere.

Clearing her throat, Gwen addressed the crowd. "I know that news of King Lorne's illness has spread quickly." She tried to speak loudly and clearly, though the pain in her voice was evident. "The healers can no longer halt his illness, and it is believed he will succumb to the wasting disease before the morrow."

She closed her eyes, hearing murmurs of sympathy and a few more people crying as she composed herself. "Our king is beloved not just by me but by all of you. I will not mourn behind closed doors. If—when the king passes, we will hold a feast in his honor in the great hall. Every man, woman, and child of Thorncliff will join me to remember the great man who has led us for so many years. And when we send him out to sea on his funeral pyre, I want all of you and every citizen from all the districts to join me. Because we are Tavia! We are united in our grief, our joy, our lives!"

The crowd roared in response, and Gwen nodded to Tyreal. Her speech had brought a sense of calm. She felt ready to face her future. Tyreal had been right; she would not be alone.

"I know I likely made your job a thousand times harder, but it felt right," she said as they resumed their ride.

"You did. But they needed you. Spoken like a true queen, Highness."

CHAPTER THREE

As they passed through the large wooden gate into the castle courtyard, Gwen craned her neck, searching for Pip. The space was expansive, large enough to shelter most of the villagers in case of an attack that breached the outer walls—though such an event had never occurred in Thorncliff's history. Primarily, the courtyard served various functional purposes under King Lorne's orders. He had always been vocal about his disdain for any wasted space, particularly in decorative areas.

Once, when she had complained about the castle's courtyard in comparison to the opulent gardens of Vasar, her father had stated plainly, "The purpose of a castle is not to flaunt the royal family's wealth, Gwennie. While there should be enough beauty to inspire pride in its citizens, a ruler must remember that the castle is meant for protection and utility." As an adult, she understood his point, though she had sulked at not being surrounded by the vibrant colors and breathtaking beauty of the flowers that filled nearly every free space at Vasar Castle, home to her best friend, Anya Duges. Gwen smiled at the memory.

She glanced around Thorncliff's courtyard, comparing it to Vasar's gardens. There were statues and a sizable rose garden, painstakingly cultivated by her grandmother over the years. Nearby was an extensive herb garden beside the door to the great kitchen. Agnes, affectionately known as Cook, had insisted on this space when she couldn't procure her favored Cyundo spice and Toma leaves due to a harsh summer crop rotation. A sizable food larder nearby stored provisions for the cold season.

The stable, housing the royal family's and castle guard's horses, lay just past the larder. Gwen guided Akasha towards it, nodding to the men who bowed low as she passed. She stopped near the stable doors and dismounted carefully. Micah, a young stable boy, approached and bowed quickly. She smiled warmly at him.

"Please give Akasha a thorough rubdown and check her shoes for any rocks. I rode her harder than I should have. When you're finished, go tell Cook that I said you could have a sweet for your hard work fixing my mistake, alright?" she instructed. Micah nodded and returned her smile, though sadness lingered in his dark eyes. She gave him a fleeting embrace before straightening and looking around.

Gwen caught sight of Pippen's anxious face before he and his messy brown curls darted behind the stable door. She sighed and followed him inside. "Pippen, wait! I just want to talk with you."

"Leave me alone!" he shouted over his shoulder as he climbed to the ceiling rail above the horse stall, forcing Gwen to crane her neck to see him. She could make out his breeches, shoes, and a sliver of his face as he looked down from behind the upper beam. Gwen cursed under her breath, assessing her options and figuring out how he had gotten up there.

"Your Highness, I can see what you're thinking..." Tyreal began as Gwen grabbed her rumpled blue skirt and hiked it up to swing her leg onto the stall rail.

"Captain, my stubborn ass of a little brother won't come down on his own. We both know that. You can either stand there and lecture me or make yourself useful and position yourself to catch me if I fall." She climbed as she spoke, making a quick jump onto the upper rail where Pippen sat.

"Aye, Highness," Tyreal sighed and moved to the inside of the stall beneath her.

Gwen walked confidently along the beam, her poise and rigid posture a testament to her summers training with the Sisters of the Mist. She approached Pippen and plopped down beside him. His freckled face was dirty, with tear tracks down his cheeks. All her anger at his stubbornness melted away, and she nudged him lightly with her shoulder.

"Thought I'd be too afraid of Tyreal's lecture to follow you up here, didn't you?"

Pippen sniffed, rubbing his nose on his arm and looking away. After several moments of silence, he finally spoke. "No. Knew you wouldn't listen. You never do. Though he'll lecture you for a year for it."

"Mmm. He always finds something to lecture me about. His life would be void and empty of meaning if he ran out of topics." She heard Tyreal snort from below and couldn't help but smile. "I wanted to talk to you, Pip. Why did you run?"

"Figured you'd be mad at me for ruining your head start and telling on you." Pippen kicked his feet, still not fully facing her.

"No, Pip, I'm not mad! I'm sorry. I shouldn't have left like that. It was selfish and irresponsible." She took his hand and squeezed it. He finally looked at her, his eyes mirroring her own, filled with unshed tears.

"So why did you? They brought me to his room, and then you went tearing out of there like demons were chasing you."

Gwen breathed through her nose, struggling to explain her feelings. "I got scared. I'm still scared. I needed a moment to myself to process everything. It's sort of like you running up here because you were scared I'd be mad and because you're mad at me for running. You just needed a moment."

Pippen pursed his lips, considering her words before nodding. "You never give me time alone, though. You always follow me." He bumped her shoulder with his, and she smiled, knowing they were alright now.

"Aye, just as Captain Blackbane always follows me. Someone has to remind us when we're being silly or selfish."

Pippen giggled and then fell silent again. "Is he really going to die tonight?" he asked.

"Oh, Pip. It looks that way. If not tonight, then most likely tomorrow. We can be as unhappy about it as we want, but it's his time. He'll join Mama in the Everafter, and we should try to find comfort in that."

"But I don't want him to go. We'll be all alone." Pippen's voice broke into sobs as he laid his head on her shoulder. Gwen wrapped her arm around him as best she could in their current position, tears streaming down her face as his words pulled her deeper into her grief. *Can you run out of tears?* she wondered.

Heavy footsteps approached on the stone and straw floor of the stable, and Gwen glanced down to see Tyreal greeting the High Captain. Hedontas Wiffren, who had served her father long before he became king, would be replaced by someone she would name when her father passed. The thought of the responsibilities ahead, while battling her own grief, was overwhelming.

Hedontas looked up at her, heavy bags of exhaustion beneath his eyes. Deep frown lines showed around his mouth, as if he could barely recall what it was like to smile. "The king is asking for you both to rejoin him in his chambers. Klause believes his time is near."

Gwen nodded and glanced at Tyreal, who fetched a ladder for them. She laid her head against Pip's for a moment longer and squeezed his hand tightly. "It's time, Pip. We must be brave and help Papa into the Everafter. I love you, and I know you're brave and strong enough to help me with this, alright?"

Pippen nodded and took a deep, steadying breath. Gwen assisted him down onto the ladder before following. Tyreal helped Pippen off and then steadied Gwen as she descended the last of the thin wooden steps. She placed her shaking hand over his, and he rubbed his thumb against hers. "You can do this, Gwennie. I'm right here behind you, like always," he whispered, low enough for only her to hear. Gwen gave a sharp nod and straightened her shoulders, moving away from him. As she walked out of the stable holding Pippen's hand, she hoped she looked like a queen, despite the hay sticking to her skirts.

They entered the Great Hall and made their way towards the heavily guarded door leading to the royal wing. They passed several castle staff, many weeping—especially the younger maids—as word spread that Lorne had sent for his children. Normally Gwen would have stopped to console an upset staff member, but at that moment, it took all her strength to stay strong for herself and Pip.

Entering her father's chambers, they found Klause Hufique, their most skilled healer, waiting in the seating area. Klause, originally from the southern continent of Candova, was an older man with a serene presence. His skin was a rich, deep brown, and his face was etched with deep lines, high cheekbones, and a strong jawline softened only slightly by age. His short dark curls were streaked with gray and white, and his normally glorious smile was nowhere to be seen now.

"Princess Gwendolyn, I apologize if my earlier assessment of your father's condition seemed too blunt. Sometimes I fear my command of your language falters when delivering sad news. I didn't mean to upset you." Klause's accent was still thick, though he had been in Tavia for years, but his genuine concern resonated through his words. He reached for her hands, clasping them firmly between his large, warm, and soft ones.

"No, I should apologize. I shouldn't have run off like I did. It wasn't very mature or queen-like of me." She smiled as warmly as she could, trying to ease the worry lines around his dark eyes.

"Well, it's forgivable, as you're not yet a queen, no? And no one is completely mature when losing a parent." Klause returned her smile softly and handed her a handkerchief from a pocket on his long tunic. "Do try not to cry too much, dear. Your father is still here, even if his time is ending."

Gwen and Pippen followed Klause into the King's bedchamber. The large four-poster bed now stood in the center of the room, instead of against the wall where it had been for as long as Gwen could remember. Her father had been complaining of a chill even before they realized he was seriously ill. Despite the warmth from the roaring fire in the grate making the room uncomfortably hot, Lorne remained huddled under several layers of furs. Gwen and Pippen moved to either side of the bed, ready to sit beside him.

Her heart ached anew at the sight of her father, once so large and brave in her eyes, now shivering and frail beneath his blankets. His face appeared haggard, with prominent cheekbones and hollowed cheeks. His pale yellow curls, streaked with white and gray, hung limp and damp from the fever that had plagued him for over two moons.

Gwen picked up a cup of water from the near-by table. "Papa, I'm back. And Pippen is with me. Would you like a drink of water?"

Lorne opened his eyes and managed a weak smile. "There's my beautiful Gwendolyn. I wasn't sure where you had gone." His voice was hoarse as Gwen helped him take a sip.

"I just needed a moment to myself and to get Pip. But we're here now, to hold your hand while you try to get better."

Lorne's face twisted sadly. "We both know that won't happen, my darling. But try not to be too upset. I'll be reunited with your mother and our family soon. The Everafter is a place of warmth and love. I am far more concerned about you two than where I am going."

With gentle care, Pippen extended his hand towards Lorne's, treating him as though he were made of glass. "We're going to miss you so much. But Gwen and I will make sure every-thing stays okay here. We promise." His voice trembled, but he held his head up bravely.

Gwen smiled at Pip, feeling a swell of pride at his composure. "Pip's right, Papa. We're ready to do what we were born to do. It's our des-tiny, just like you always said. You don't have to worry about us. We'll be fine." Her words held more conviction than she felt, but she glanced away to bolster her confidence, meeting Tyre-al's eyes. They were dark with emotion, and he offered a sad, soft smile. Gwen let her lashes drop, nodding slightly at him before turning back to her father.

Lorne took a deep breath and squeezed their hands. "You two are the best things I ever did. I couldn't be prouder. Pippen, protect your sister and our land. Keep your blade steady and your heart pure. Hedontas and Tyreal will train you to be a fine warrior. Gwennie, I've taught you everything I know about ruling a kingdom. Take my knowledge and your mother's heart, and make Tavia better than I ever could."

He stopped speaking, his frail body wracked by deep coughs. Gwen helped him sit up, stroking his back. "Shhhh, Papa—"

Lorne raised a hand to silence her as his coughing eased. "This—this is important. I need to say it all. There is no question about your ability to rule. I'm only sorry it will be difficult for you to follow your heart. There's been no doubt about where your heart lies. It's the one thing I'd change about the path I've set you on if I could." He coughed again, and Gwen continued to soothe him, resisting the urge to glance at Tyreal once more.

"I know, Papa. I promise to do my best." She settled him back on the pillows, taking his hand once more. The skin felt thin and fragile, so cold that she stroked her thumb over it, trying to share her warmth. With her other hand, she brushed a lock of hair from his face.

They remained like that for some time. Pippen eventually climbed into the bed beside

Lorne, curling against his father's side. Gwen wasn't sure how long they sat there, busying herself with a cool rag on her father's forehead and helping him through his coughs. His head rolled to the side, his eyes glassy and unfocused. "The name... something with the name. Was so close. You must look—have to stop." He took another ragged breath, breaking into a fit of coughing before closing his eyes.

He struggled to even his breathing but never reopened his eyes. Gradually, his breaths grew slower, his chest sinking with each one. After a few moments, he gave one final deep gasp, and his body relaxed. Gwen bit her lip, holding his hand silently as Klause came over to check Lorne's neck. She saw Klause nod silently to Hedontas and Tyreal.

Gwen felt detached, as though observing from outside herself. She watched Hedontas move across the room, facing the wall and clenching his fists as he fought for control. Klause placed a hand on Hedontas's shoulder and spoke to him before they both exited the room. The other guards saluted Tyreal, a stark reminder of the promotion nobody wanted. Gwen couldn't bring herself to react or move until the sound of Pippen's sniffles broke her trance. She released Lorne's hand and gathered her little brother, holding him close as he broke down into sobs. Unable to hold back her own tears any longer, she joined him.

She sensed rather than saw Tyreal move closer to the bed. Reaching out a hand, he briefly held it before wrapping his arms around Gwen and Pippen, as if to shield them from their grief with his presence.

CHAPTER FOUR

"Your Majesty, it is time to wake up. We have much to do today." Cora's voice jolted Gwen from the warmth of her dream. She had been resting under the purple-leafed tree by the spring, the sun shining brightly down on her, a man's hand trailing down her arm. Gwen blinked at Cora, disoriented. Her head felt fuzzy, and she struggled to understand why Cora was waking her so early and addressing her as "Your Majesty" instead of "Highness". A sympathetic grimace tugged at the corners of Cora's mouth, darkening her usually cheerful round face.

Gwen remembered then. Her father had passed into the Everafter, and she was now queen.

"Ah. Yes, thank you, Cora. Do I have anything appropriate to wear? I didn't anticipate this day coming, so I never considered mourning attire. I was so overwhelmed last night that I didn't even change," she said, tossing her blankets aside and motioning to her dress. A stubborn piece of hay clung to it, and Gwen frowned down at it as she attempted to detangle her braids.

Cora tutted and gently moved Gwen's hands away. Her skilled fingers worked quickly, smoothing Gwen's hair into soft waves and curls around Gwen's shoulders before she grabbed the brush from the bedside table. "You have one black and one gray dress in the wardrobe. I had the seamstresses begin new mourning wardrobes for you and Prince Pippen yesterday," Cora explained, sprinkling water from a bowl over Gwen's hair until it was damp. Caring for Gwen's mass of curls was a job unto itself, and Cora had always been the one person who could truly master it.

"Thank you. I don't know how I could get through this without you." Gwen's voice was thick with gratitude, and tears threatened to spill from her swollen, sensitive eyes.

"It's my job, Your Majesty, but more than that, it's an honor to serve my friend. You've done so much for me over the years—things no one else probably would have," Cora said, her voice trembling as she gently squeezed Gwen's shoulder.

"Speaking of which, how does Tensha feel about your new promotion? She'll see you less."

Cora had fallen for Tensha the moment she laid eyes on the tall, dark warrior who had arrived on the same ship as Klause, the healer. Gwen had discovered them together and, despite Cora's fear, offered to help the pair.

Love between people of the same sex wasn't unheard of, but societal expectations of marriage and children still loomed large, even in Tavia. Gwen hoped to challenge these expectations when she took the throne. Her inner voice reminded her, *You already have the throne.* Gwen winced at the thought.

"Tensha appreciates my duties and the help you and Captain Blackbane have already given us. We're content," Cora said.

Gwen smiled softly. She liked Tensha, even if she could count on one hand the number of words Tensha had ever spoken to her. There was something comforting in Tensha's silence, and Gwen was pleased to see how happy Tensha made Cora. It took little introspection to understand why Gwen was eager to help secure positions in the castle for them, preventing expectations of a loveless marriage.

After Cora secured Gwen's hair with a simple twist and an onyx pin, Gwen stood and allowed her to undo the row of tiny buttons on her dress but shooed her away when it came time to change her undergarments. Cora rolled her eyes but was accustomed to Gwen's quirks. Gwen knew Cora thought it silly, but she simply didn't understand certain aspects of royal protocol. She could change her own shift.

Gwen tossed the rumpled discarded shift aside and slipped the new one over her head, careful not to disturb Cora's work on her hair. Cora pulled a dark gray dress from the wardrobe and presented it to her. "I thought it unlikely we'd receive visitors today, but possibly tomorrow. You can wear the black then. Do you agree, Your Majesty?"

Gwen nodded and lifted her arms for Cora to slip the dress over her. It wasn't an unattractive dress, but Gwen couldn't help but look sullenly at her reflection in the looking glass. She hated what it signified. She smoothed her hand over the bodice, feeling the intricately embroidered tiny black roses as Cora cinched the corset back.

"I know you're not in the mood to be prettied up, but you haven't been eating or sleeping well. With all the crying, you look like you might be ill. We don't want rumors of illness spreading right now. Allow me to at least do a little, Your Majesty?"

Gwen couldn't help but laugh. "Why, Cora, that's one of the nicer ways anyone's ever told me I look awful." Cora protested, but a knock at the door interrupted her. As she went to answer it, Gwen positioned herself at the vanity. Cora's logic was sound. She did look ill. Gwen frowned into the mirror, pressing at the bags under her eyes.

Cora re-entered, followed closely by Tyreal. Gwen looked up at him from her chair, his towering presence accentuated by her seated position. The black tunic he wore in mourning stretched tightly across his broad shoulders, and Gwen wondered if it was borrowed. Under different circumstances, the contrast between the tunic's color and his mahogany beard, along with his perpetually tousled hair, would have captivated her. But now, the dark circles under his stormy gray eyes and the gauntness of his face mirrored her own fatigue.

"The captain would like to speak with you, Your Majesty. I told him you weren't quite ready, but he's quite insistent." Cora gave Tyreal an exaggeratedly disappointed look and began preparing rouge from crushed rose petals.

"I asked if you were finished dressing, and she said that you were. I care about your reputation, despite what Lady Cora believes." Tyreal grinned at Cora—annoying her was one of his favorite pastimes. Cora rolled her eyes with a smile. His expression sobered as he turned back to Gwen. "Have you eaten?"

"Obviously not. I'm not presentable. Cora tells me I look ill and unappealing."

"That isn't—"

Gwen raised her hand. "I'm only teasing. I know what you meant, and you're right. We don't need people thinking I'm also succumbing to illness. I do look ill and unappealing."

Tyreal huffed in disagreement and walked out of the room, returning with a covered tray. "I spoke with Cook. She says you didn't eat at all yesterday and barely picked at food the day before. I can protect you from many dangers, but not from starvation. So, you leave me no choice but to sit here and watch you eat everything on this plate." He lifted the lid, revealing hard-boiled eggs, a sausage link, and a bowl of chopped berries.

"I'm not hungry, Captain," she said tersely. She knew she was being childish, but it felt wrong to eat while her father could no longer do so. How could she continue with normal activities when her entire world had been turned upside down?

"My Queen, forgive my frankness, but I really don't care. You need to eat, and you know it. Cook specifically chose some of your favorites that you can eat quickly." He set the tray on the vanity and crossed his arms, raising an eyebrow as he waited.

Anger welled up inside her, though she wasn't sure why. She knew he was doing his job, and he would do it regardless because he treated taking care of her like his need to breathe. Yet, the feeling simmered inside her like a cauldron of something foul. How could he stand there acting as if nothing had changed?

"Do not speak to me like a child, Tyreal Black-bane. I am a grown woman and the queen of this land. I am more than capable of taking care of myself." Her fists clenched as she struggled to control the surge of power within her. *Not now,* she thought. She shoved it back down but felt a strong urge to hit something to channel the darkness swirling inside her.

"Aye, you are. Yet here we are, and you've barely eaten in two days. Shall I allow Pippen to skip meals when he makes this same argument with me? He's barely eaten, and I'm heading to his room after this."

For the second time in as many days, Gwen felt detached from the situation. She grabbed a vase from the vanity and hurled it towards Tyreal, shouting, "DO NOT COMPARE ME TO A CHILD AGAIN!" The vase shattered, but Tyreal sidestepped it effortlessly, snapping Gwen back to reality. She gasped in shock, covering her mouth.

He crossed his arms and looked at her pointedly. "Are ye finished?"

Unable to speak for fear of what she might say, Gwen nodded. Fat tears spilled from her lashes, and Tyreal's face softened. He knelt in front of her. "Ah, Gwennie, don't cry. It's not me or breakfast you're angry with." If Cora was surprised by Tyreal using Gwen's personal name, she hid it well, and Gwen's tears flowed harder.

"I'm s-s-sorry. I can't believe I did that, spoke to you like that. I know you're right, but how can I go on as if nothing happened? He's dead, and I'm clearly not cut out for this. I've been queen for hours, and I'm throwing vases at the staff." She buried her face in her hands.

Tyreal pried her hands away, holding them gently in his larger, calloused ones. "You've been throwing things at me since you were a wee princess. Did you really think that would stop when you became a wee queen?"

Gwen laughed through her tears. "A wee queen? Really?"

Tyreal shrugged. "Aye. You're smaller than me. Not at all frightening. I knew you were about to throw that vase before you even moved. But you'll only get tinier if you don't eat. I know it feels wrong to keep moving forward, but imagine what your father would say if he could see you from the Everafter, watching you neglect yourself like this."

"He'd be furious with me. He'd want me to celebrate his reunion with Mama. Though, I imagine he wouldn't mind so much me throwing a vase at you." Gwen pushed lightly at his chest. He grinned and moved away. Gwen glanced over at Cora, who was finishing up cleaning the broken vase shards. "I'm so sorry. Thank you for helping me clean up my tantrum. I suppose I have some colors on my cheeks now, hmm?"

"Yes, but your nose is all blotchy, and your eyes are even more swollen than they were," Cora replied with a smile.

"Someone really needs to teach you two how to address your queen. This is borderline treason." Gwen reached for the plate and nibbled on her food.

Tyreal sat in a nearby chair, leaning forward with his elbows on his knees. "How long of a mourning period will you want before we have your coronation ceremony? I'll need to prepare the guard for the influx of visitors and would like to have a timeline."

Gwen closed her eyes, pushing her emotions aside for now. She didn't want to have this conversation, but it was unavoidable. "The timing is less than ideal. The people will need a moment of joy after this funeral and mourning period. However, the feast will impact our reserves for the cold season. I don't want to deplete our supplies further, so I'll speak to the council today about trades to boost our stock."

Tyreal nodded in agreement. "Aye, a solid plan. So, what are you thinking?"

She picked at her thumb with her other fingers, keeping her voice steady. "I think it's best to deviate from tradition. We'll have a simple coronation ceremony that coincides with the winter solstice festivities. However, the joust and games will be postponed until spring. I will—" She looked away, struggling to find the will to say the words. "I will combine the belated coronation games with the end of my official mourning period and begin screening candidates for King Consort."

The words brought a wave of nausea, and Gwen dimly wondered if eating had been a terrible idea after all. Tyreal went still in his chair, a muscle twitching in his cheek. When he spoke, his voice was clipped. "Aye, Your Majesty."

Gwen lifted her eyes from the spot on her skirt she had been staring at. She gnawed at her bottom lip, feeling an urge to explain. "Tyreal, I—"

He shook his head. "Your Majesty," he emphasized her title, "you need to finish your breakfast so you can meet with the council. I simply required a timeline to ensure that your guard is prepared."

"Of course. You're right. I'll finish my food, I promise. You don't need to watch over me. I'm sure you have much to do. We also need to perform your official oath as High Captain today. Assuming you wish to take on the position?" Her eyes conveyed more than her words, the unspoken question hanging in the air.

"What else would I do if not protecting you?" His eyes met hers for a moment before he glanced at Cora. "Make sure she finishes. I need to speak with my men and Hedontas. Are we placing Hedontas in charge of the prince's guard now, or would you prefer to choose a different captain?" He rose from his chair, his hand clenching around the hilt of his sword.

"If Hedontas wishes to accept the position, I believe he'd make an excellent Captain of the Heir's Guard. Though, I'm not certain he will want to. Either way, Pippen will hate the increased security that comes with being an heir.

Inform Hedontas and the other guards to remind Pip of all the times he laughed at my attempts to escape my guard whenever he complains about being watched constantly."

Tyreal nodded with a strained smile and exited the room after bowing to her. Gwen watched his retreating form until she heard the chamber door close behind him. She sighed and looked down at the food she had even less appetite for than before.

Cora resumed mixing the cosmetics. "Everyone dreams of being a princess and all the wonders it brings. But you're just as bound by society's rules as the rest of us, if not more so." Gwen didn't respond, and the silence stretched between them. Her heart felt heavier than ever, and it took all her strength not to cry again.

CHAPTER FIVE

Tyreal walked briskly away from Gwen's chambers, his stomach churning with the remnants of his breakfast. His hands trembled as he stepped outside and relieved himself of the soured contents into a bush, hoping any onlookers would attribute his distress to overindulgence in ale after the king's death. He knew he needed to speak with the prince, just as he had with Gwen, but he was in no shape just then.

For years, Tyreal had anticipated this day, but hearing Gwen's words—that she would begin screening for a Queen's Consort in the spring—felt like a knife twisting between his ribs and piercing his heart. It wasn't merely about possessing her, though that was part of it. The notion of anyone but him being with her seemed so foreign and wrong that it made him physically ill. How could a stranger ever understand or appreciate the complexities of Gwen, or ensure her safety? This man, whoever he might be, would likely pursue nothing more than her beauty in his bed and her fortune in his pocket. And why? Because of his last name?

With a final heave, Tyreal emptied his stomach of its last contents. He was now drained, both physically and emotionally, of the self-pity that served no purpose. His decision had been made long ago, during that day at the spring, long ago, when Gwen had offered herself to him, and he had turned her down. She had been too young then to fully grasp the implications, but he could never have bedded her and then given her up. Nor could he whisk her away to the mountains as he had once wished. Gwen was too vital to the future of the land he cherished; he could not steal her away for his own selfish desires. Instead, he would honor his love for her by being her steadfast protector until the end of his days, even if it meant standing by as she pledged herself to another.

He straightened his tunic and headed back inside, making his way to the prince's chambers. In the kitchen, Cook stood near the door. The room was empty of workers, likely because she had shooed them away when she heard him being sick in her bushes. She gave him a knowing look as she chopped vegetables, nodding towards a cup of water with mint. "To freshen your breath. Did she give you much trouble about eating?"

Tyreal gratefully accepted the cup and drank it down. "No more than expected. She'll finish it. Though something light for lunch would be appreciated—for both of them."

"Aye. It felt wrong to eat after my papa passed into the Everafter. We'll have a nice chicken soup for lunch, I think. It always soothes the soul." Cook glanced around to ensure no one else was in the kitchen. "We have a problem I need to discuss with you. I wanted to bring it up to you first so you can look into it before I bring it to her, given how worried and upset she already is."

Tyreal suppressed a groan, though it was a struggle. A new problem was the last thing he needed. "What is it?" he asked brusquely, knowing Cook understood his irritation was not directed at her.

"The larder is low. Very low. I don't think anyone else has noticed yet, as it's not obvious if you don't know what it should look like after the harvest. But I do. I hadn't been down there in a while, but when I went this morning to plan for the feast, I was shocked by the state of it."

"Low enough that we'll have issues come the cold season?" Tyreal asked, his frustration barely contained.

Cook nodded solemnly. "Yes."

Tyreal swore under his breath. "Take an inventory and see if you can find records from the last harvest to compare. I'll review the donation book and inquire with some farmers about the yields. For now, keep the key with you. No more leaving it hanging on the wall. If anyone questions it, blame my paranoia and my promotion to High Captain."

He ran a hand through his hair, a throbbing settling in his jaw. It'd be a miracle if he had any teeth left by the time this was all over, the way he'd been grinding them together from the stress. "We'll address this once we have more information," he added quietly. "For now, keep it between us. I'll need to discuss it with Gwen privately, she'll be furious if I keep it from her."

Cook took the heavy iron key from its hook and tucked it into her pocket. Tyreal washed his mint cup, set it to dry, and nodded to her before heading out.

Upon arriving at Pippen's chambers, Tyreal found Hedontas already there, trying to convince the prince to eat. Pippen, however, ignored him, staring sullenly out the window. Hedontas looked at Tyreal with exasperation, and Tyreal offered a sympathetic smile. Moving closer to Pippen, he sought the right words. "Your Highness, your sister has finally eaten her breakfast. Surely you don't want to be outdone by her. Though, if it helps, she did throw a vase at me before she agreed. So, if you haven't thrown anything yet, you might still win the most agreeable royal tournament."

Pippen didn't turn to look at him but stifled a laugh, and he knew he had his opportunity. "Eat, Highness. Your father wouldn't want this. Your sister has agreed, and now it's your turn. It's time."

Pippen turned, his face a stark reflection of his sister's—the embodiment of their mother, Queen Asya, with their dark curls and freckles. Like Gwen, the dark shadows of grief were etched beneath his eyes, painfully evident. Tyreal gave him an encouraging smile.

His guard duty had often included Pippen because Gwen had taken to mothering Pippen after Asya's death. As a young guard, he had watched Gwen chase a chubby Pippen around the great hall while the King observed silently before speaking to Tyreal. "I know she will be a great queen because she loves with all her heart. My Gwennie does nothing half-heartedly. All I must do is watch her with her baby brother to know that. I think this will make your job of protecting her more difficult."

Pippen's voice pulled Tyreal from the memory. "Did she really throw a vase at you?"

"Mmm, I'm too quick for her, though. She can't catch me. I'm as fast as one of Cook's mousers." Pip laughed, and Tyreal grinned. "Eat up. I have other tasks to attend to, but your sister will want you at the council meeting as heir. The guards will escort you shortly."

Tyreal turned and gestured for Hedontas to follow him outside. The older guard looked forlorn and weary. His eyes were bloodshot, and his tunic was rumpled. His once-pristine appearance now seemed unkempt and much older than it had a day prior. It was clear he hadn't slept, and it pained Tyreal to see him so. After his own father's death, Hedontas had been his only father figure.

"How did you get him to agree? I was almost ready to force-feed him," Hedontas asked.

"He's not quite a man, but he isn't completely a child either. It's a hard line to walk. I've found that if you can make them laugh first, they're more likely to see reason. I know it's tradition for you to step down to Captain of the Heir, but is it a position you truly want? The prince is not the same as King Lorne was."

Hedontas sighed and rubbed his hand down his face. It struck Tyreal how harsh the tradition was. Little thought was given to guards who outlived their charges. Hedontas had been protecting Lorne since he was younger than Pippen. They'd been close, almost like brothers. Watching Lorne die from something Hedontas couldn't prevent must have been excruciating. "There's no shame in retiring, you know. You saw our king to the end, just as you swore."

Hedontas bristled, his hands balling into fists at his sides. Tyreal remained calm, concern evident on his face. Hedontas must have seen that, as he seemed to fold inward before speaking. "I just don't know if I have it in me to do it again. I want to be here and help them. They're his children. But to put my entire life on the line for someone else again... I'm tired. So tired, Tyreal. I loved that man, and I don't even get a moment to mourn him."

Tyreal squeezed his shoulder. "Take your moment. Take as long as you need. I might have something brewing that I could use your help with, but that will be unofficial. If our queen agrees, and I think she will, you'll be officially retired. I'll find someone to head up the prince's guard."

Hedontas gave him a grateful look and placed his fist over his heart. Tyreal returned the gesture, and Hedontas left. Tyreal sighed and rubbed his temples. He had anticipated this. Hedontas had little patience for children. Now Tyreal needed to find someone he trusted to protect Tavia's heir and, more importantly, someone Gwen also trusted to guard her baby brother. It was no small task. Andais was a straightforward choice, but that would leave Tyreal searching for someone to protect Gwen in the evenings when he was off duty—a task even more challenging. Tyreal pinched his nose and closed his eyes. Sometimes he wondered why he felt compelled to bear this burden, but he couldn't imagine himself anywhere else.

He ducked back into Pippen's room and sat down across from the prince. "Hedontas will not take over as your captain. I'll need to name someone else. How do you feel about that?"

Pip shrugged. "Fine, I guess. Hedontas was sort of grumpy. Could you find me someone like you? Someone who's a friend, like you are with Gwen? Papa always said you two were thick as thieves and wished he could have changed things for both of you." Pippen's brow furrowed as he frowned slightly. "What did he mean by that? I asked him once, but he said he'd tell me when I was older. But now he can't." His shoulders slumped, and he looked down at the floor.

Tyreal exhaled slowly and flexed his right hand, trying to find the right words. "I think he was referring to the law from the Sisters of the Mist. It states that all royals must marry someone from one of the other founding royal families. It's one of the few laws the Sisters have made, and all the founding families have sworn to honor their decrees. Their word is final."

Pip nodded in understanding. "So, Papa meant that because Gwen is royal, she can't marry you. Because you aren't."

Tyreal opened his mouth to argue that he wasn't someone Gwen would want to marry, more out of reflex than anything. Pip's head was cocked slightly to the side, mirroring Gwen's look when she was too tired for courtly games and politics. Tyreal closed his mouth, a bitter-sweet smile flickering across his lips. "Aye."

Pip looked at him, lost in thought for a moment. "That's sad. I would have liked you as a brother. I hope I don't make the mistake of falling in love with anyone. Ever. It seems messy."

"You're not wrong, Highness. It is messy. But worth it, I think. You have a while yet before you need to worry about such things. If you're done eating, Jameson is out front and will walk with you to the council meeting."

After the prince and the guards had set off, Tyreal made a few more stops, checking on the horses at the stables. He assigned duties to the training guards for the day and met with other captains to outline basic plans for the upcoming funeral and relay the timeline Gwen had given him.

He waved at Micah as he left the stable and motioned toward Akasha and Braken. "Don't let those two eat too many sugar cubes today, you hear? They're spoiled." Micah's giggle made Tyreal smile. Even on the saddest days, there were still smiles to be found if you knew where to look. He spotted Tensha taking inventory of the training armory and made his way over. He didn't want to interrupt her count, so he leaned against the wall and waited for her to finish.

He had a deep respect for Tensha and was fond of her. She had an unmistakable aura of strength and confidence that Tyreal admired. She also had a hell of a right hook and was one of Tyreal's favorite sparring partners. To underestimate her because she was female was a deadly mistake.

Her skin, dark and cool like the night sky, bore the marks of every battle she had fought, and she displayed each one with pride. Her tight-coiled braids cascaded down her back like a waterfall. But it was her eyes that truly made Tensha stand out, and he guessed they were likely what drew Cora in. They were an incredibly rich brown with multiple shades and a whirlpool of gold around the center. She watched everything silently, and there was a depth to her gaze that could seem unsettling and intense to some.

"Cora is worried about her," Tensha said, cutting to the point as usual. Tyreal found her straightforwardness refreshing.

"We all are. But she's stronger than she knows. Are you alright with how busy Cora will be now? It's an important but demanding position."

Tensha shrugged. "We knew it would happen. Less time together means we cherish the moments we have even more. You also have more duties for me, no?" Her accent was noticeable as she spoke.

Tyreal nodded. "Hedontas won't be taking over for the prince. I need to find someone else for his captain. I'm going to have to shift guards more than I anticipated. I'd like to offer you a position as a guard in the prince's detail. You'd help with his training like we already discussed, but also take some guard shifts. I trust your skills."

Tensha raised an eyebrow. "I am a woman. You don't have women guards in Tavia."

"Our new ruler is a woman. And you can fight circles around half of these men. Are you interested or not?" Tyreal crossed his arms, waiting.

After a moment, Tensha gave a sharp nod. "Yes."

"Good. I'll discuss it with her after her meeting and let you know your additional duties. It will also give you a room in the castle, which might be beneficial—for reasons."

Tensha gave him a soft smile. "Yes, reasons. Thank you." Tyreal nodded and turned back toward the castle to check on his charge.

CHAPTER SIX

Tyreal moved through the castle, heading toward the library. He greeted the guards stationed by the door with a nod. "How is her first official council meeting going?"

"Our queen is putting old Skensy in his place," the younger guard chuckled. Jameson Randall, not much older than Gwen, had served in the guard since his youth. His swordsmanship was among the best Tyreal had seen, and he trusted him, despite Jameson's loose tongue. That trait had kept him from higher positions in Gwen's detail; her temper would incinerate him. Jameson might fit well with Pippen's detail, given Pippen's own tendency to speak out of turn. Tyreal noted it for a future discussion with Gwen.

Tyreal grinned at Jameson's remark. "Serves the pompous bastard right. What's he done to get on her bad side?"

Jameson shook his head. "Apparently, he's none too pleased with her plan to postpone her search for a consort until spring. He's pushing for a marriage with Prince Lovell from Adaltus. Lovell sent a proposal before King Lorne died. What an ass."

Tyreal's smile faded. He knew Lovell well enough from tournaments and banquets. The man resembled a greasy rat, with slicked-back hair and beady eyes. "He didn't think a proposal to a future queen warranted an in-person visit?" *So I could more easily slice his belly open with my blade.*

"Aye, she was mightily offended by the offer, and Skensy for even entertaining it. She tore into him like a fishwife on a drunken husband." Jameson chuckled but faltered under Tyreal's dark stare. "Er, not that she's like a fishwife. Just—"

Tyreal cut him off with a wave of his hand. "I know what you meant but mind your words or I'll have to remind you of your place. Not to mention what she'd do if she heard." He was relieved Jameson thought his dark look was about the fishwife joke rather than Gwen's marriage proposals.

Tyreal opened the door and slipped inside. Dressed in training attire instead of armor, he blended in more easily. Skensy, or Adolfus Skensington as he was formally known, sat glumly with his cup of wine. Gwen, at the head of the large table near the stained-glass window, looked every bit the queen she was becoming. Her dark gray dress contrasted sharply with her pale skin, and her silver circlet glinted in her curls from the sunlight filtering through the colored glass. The sight made Tyreal's heart tighten, reminding him of the sacrifices he'd made and would continue to make. She was destined to rule, and he could be nowhere else.

Gwen glanced up, her expression transitioning from annoyance to near fury. It might not be obvious to others, but Tyreal recognized her tells—the faint pink in her cheeks, the darkening of her eyes to a near whiskey hue, leaving barely any green. She was deeply offended by Lovell's proposal and Skensy's discussion of it. She nodded at Tyreal, acknowledging his presence as he took his place behind her, not interrupting her questions to Sir Jonah Manafort about trading cattle from Ravendell for Tavia's fish and salt.

"They aren't keen on trading beef so close to winter, Your Majesty. Given the funeral and other events, I believe our neighbors might be more agreeable, so it's worth asking," Manafort said, his plump face struggling to maintain seriousness as he spoke of the funeral. His disdain for Skensington was well-known, and Tyreal suspected he enjoyed seeing Gwen confront him.

"Good. See to it. If needed, I'll add some gold to sweeten the deal, but don't offer that unless the trade seems to falter. A large shipment of beef will aid the funeral feast and my coronation at solstice," Gwen instructed. Luca Fitzsimmon, the castle's keeper of the coin, made an unpleasant noise, and Gwen shot him a look. Though a small, nervous man, he overcame his nature when faced with spending money.

Tyreal glanced at Pippen, curious about his reaction to his first council meeting. Many his age might be bored, as Tyreal often was, but Pippen remained quiet and observant. His eyes tracked each speaker, occasionally narrowing in concentration or flashing disagreement. Tyreal felt a surge of pride. He'd known the boy since birth, and it was gratifying to see him embrace the serious responsibilities of an heir.

"Your Majesty, this is why I suggested the arrangement with Grigor Lovell. Adaltus has plenty of cattle," Skensington interjected. Tyreal's body tensed, his shoulders straightening as he narrowed his eyes. Why was Skensington pushing this issue so hard? Gwen had already given her answer, and she rarely changed her mind.

Gwen turned to face Skensington, her silence heavy before she spoke. "As I've already stated, Sir Skensington, I wouldn't consider a proposal sent upon hearing a rumor of my father's failing health, and not even delivered in person, more favorably than a proposal from a dog. I regard them the same." Skensington shifted uncomfortably, and Manafort barely contained a grin. Gwen continued, "This man has never properly introduced himself to me, and my father was not fond of him. Many places have cattle, but apparently, the ruling family of Adaltus lacks grace and propriety. Now, if you'd kindly explain why this is so important that you felt the need to bring it up again after I'd already given my answer, Captain Blackbane would love to hear the details."

Tyreal focused intently on Skensington, his posture tense. He was aware of his reputation. Tyreal was known for being fair, some might even call him good, but he would do *anything* necessary for Gwen's safety. This was a well-known fact. He'd killed before in service and had no qualms about doing it again. Skensington swallowed and began to stammer. "My lady—"

"I am not your lady, nor was I ever, Sir Skensington. I am your queen, and you will address me as such." Gwen's icy words were deliberate, chosen to make a point.

She turned to the council, her gaze unwavering. "Gentlemen, we have some matters to address now. I appreciate the advice and service you've provided to my father and Tavia over the years."

She paused to let her words settle. "My father was a great man," she continued, her tone softening as she spoke of him. "He taught me everything about being a good leader. However," her eyes narrowed, "I am not my father, and I am not feeling particularly well-advised."

Tyreal watched, intrigued by the direction of her speech. She had clearly made a decision. "If I find reason to doubt your ability to provide rational viewpoints, I will have you removed from this council. You serve at my leisure; it is not a birthright," she declared.

Her words hung in the air as the councilmen shifted uncomfortably. "Furthermore, we will be expanding this council. The fact that I only see faces of titled noblemen from within a small radius of Thorncliff tells me I lack perspectives from my entire kingdom."

She raised her voice to ensure clarity. "As such, I will reach out to lords and ladies from other districts and seek trusted non-noble council members." Her posture left no room for dissent.

Several men gasped, with Skensington protesting the loudest. "Your Majesty! Surely you don't mean to include commoners on the royal council! They... they can't be trusted!"

"We trust commoners every day with crucial aspects of our lives: our children, our food, even guarding our bodies. What I no longer trust is your place on this council. Thank you for your service, but it ends today."

"You stupid little girl! If you think—" Skensington's tirade was cut short by the tip of Tyreal's blade pressing against his throat, the steel digging into his skin until it made a pronounced cleft. Jameson and the other guard stood at attention but did not draw their weapons, making it clear who was in danger.

"Choose your next words carefully; they might be your last. You will not address our queen in such a manner, ever, not among your toady friends, and certainly not in my presence." Tyreal's gaze bore into Skensington's, daring him to continue. He almost wanted him to, just to slice out his insolent tongue.

Skensington carefully swallowed, raising his hands in surrender. He cast one last look at Gwen, his face icy and full of contempt, before shoving his chair back and storming toward the door. He slammed it open, the iron handle clanging against the wall, and muttered angrily as he exited. Tyreal gestured to Jameson to follow him.

Tyreal sheathed his sword with a decisive clink. The room fell into a tense silence as he returned to his place beside Gwen. The councilmen avoided eye contact, focusing intently on their papers or drinks. Tyreal almost laughed, but his anger kept it in check.

"I welcome any differing opinions on my decision, but they must be expressed respectfully. Does anyone else have anything to say?" Gwen addressed the room. Silence was her answer. "Good. Captain Blackbane has accepted his appointment as High Captain of the Tavian Guard, and Andais Kensington has accepted his position as Lower Captain. We will swear them in at a ceremony in the chapel after lunch. Most visitors are expected to arrive tomorrow, so we'll have a large dinner then. Captain Blackbane, did you speak with Captain Wiffren regarding his appointment?"

"Yes, Your Majesty. Captain Wiffren requests retirement from active duty to move into an advisory role for the guard. I have a candidate for replacement to discuss with you. Meanwhile, Prince Pippen's current guard detail will continue with an additional five guards I will select. The Lower Captain and I will handle over-watch duties until a Captain of the Heir is appointed."

Gwen nodded decisively. "I will grant Captain Wiffren his retirement and begin paying him the pension he has earned. Additionally, we will give him a five hundred silverling bonus as a token of our gratitude for his lifetime of service. He will need to vacate his room by the end of the day to allow you to move in. Until he finds new housing, he can stay in one of the guest rooms." She glanced at Luca, the keeper of the coin, raising an eyebrow, expecting him to object. Luca remained silent, clearly unwilling to provoke her or Tyreal's ire further.

Gwen scanned the councilmen around the table. "If there is no other business, the council is dismissed. I expect all of you in the chapel after lunch for the swearing-in ceremonies. Also, please have a list of potential candidates from the other districts ready for our next meeting."

The councilmen stood, bowed, and exited the room. Tyreal and Pip remained. Tyreal signaled the remaining guard to leave and stand by the door. Once the door was shut, Gwen slumped in her chair. "By the Gods, I hope this gets easier with time. Do you think asking for trades now might make us appear weak?"

She sipped her tea, her thoughts more aloud than directed at anyone. "Also, are we in agreement about Skensington?"

"Mmm. We'll investigate his ties to Adaltus and Lovell before the day ends. Personally, I don't think it will make us seem weak to approach trades now. During the king's illness, maybe, but now that you're in charge and with the large events approaching as the cold season sets in, it's necessary. Also, there's a potential issue with our food storage that we need to address. Cook just brought it to my attention," Tyreal said.

Gwen froze, her thumb coming up to her mouth to chew at the side, a nervous habit he thought she had outgrown. Tyreal's heart ached seeing her revert to it. "What sort of issue? If Cook is concerned, then I am very concerned."

Tyreal grimaced, reluctant to add to her stress but committed to honesty. "Cook reports that the food larder is much lower than expected for this time after the harvest. It's not obvious to anyone not familiar with the kitchen's demands over the cold seasons, but she's been here long enough to notice."

Gwen closed her eyes and rubbed her temples. "What have you instructed her to do?"

"I told her to take an inventory and compare it with records from previous harvests. Also, to keep the key on her person rather than hanging it on the kitchen wall. She can attribute it to my paranoia if questioned. We should keep this quiet until we have a clearer picture of the situation."

Gwen swore under her breath. "How? How in the bloody crows is it so low? I haven't heard anything about poor harvests, and I've been at nearly every council meeting for the past ten years."

"Perhaps someone is stealing from us," Pip suggested, sitting up straighter and twisting a piece of stray parchment between his fingers. With only Gwen and Tyreal in the room, the prince seemed comfortable enough to speak up. Tyreal felt another surge of pride—Pip had a sharp mind.

Gwen's eyes met Tyreal's, and she raised an eyebrow. Clearly, she agreed with Pip. He did too. "I'll look into it," he promised quietly.

Gwen stood and began to pace. "We need someone we trust to check the larders in other districts. Is it just Thorncliff? If it is, how can we quickly bolster supplies without causing panic while we figure this out? I don't want the upcoming dinners to make things worse."

Pip made a thoughtful noise. "Maybe you should offer villagers the chance to go hunting. We could invite them to participate in the great family feast. We can pay them, like our ancestors did when Tavia was new. Present it as a way to bring everyone together in honor of Papa."

Gwen's face brightened with a smile that transformed her entire demeanor. Tyreal loved how she looked when she smiled like that—well, he always loved how she looked, but especially when she smiled. "You are very smart for your age, Pip. You must have had a good tutor."

Pip rolled his eyes, but a smile tugged at the corners of his lips. He straightened his tunic and shifted in his seat, a hint of pink staining his freckled cheeks.

Gwen reached for a piece of parchment, scratching her pen across it. "That's a brilliant idea. I'll offer twenty-five shickles for a goat, thirty-five for a deer, and fifty for a boar. Any excess beyond what Cook needs for the feast can be salted and stored. It's not a perfect solution, but it's a start while we figure out what in the bloody crows is going on." She folded the parchment and affixed her seal. "Pip, please take this to the crier. He can spread the word."

"The guards will accompany you," Tyreal added.

Pip made a face about the guard but took the parchment and left. Gwen watched him go, her thumb coming up to her mouth again. "Less than a day, and my people might starve through the cold season. What a fine queen I'm proving to be," she murmured, her voice barely audible.

"It isn't as dire as it seems. We've caught it early, and the hunts will help. We'll uncover why the storage is low and correct it. You'll guide us through this," Tyreal reassured her. When she didn't respond immediately, he knew she wasn't fully hearing him.

"Gwen." He used her name deliberately. She lifted her eyes to his, worry swirling in their hazel depths. "You're brilliant. I won't tolerate treasonous words against my queen, not even from you. You care deeply for our people and will do whatever it takes. And I'm here to do what you need of me. Tell me you know that."

She turned her gaze away, staring out at the stained glass, her shoulders slumped. He reached out and gently pulled her hand away from her mouth, running his thumb over her roughened skin. "Stop hurting yourself. I don't allow anyone but me to do that."

His words pulled her out of her thoughts, and she gave him a faint smirk. "You haven't hurt me since you put that clothespin on my tongue for sassing you and Papa. He told you to come up with more creative punishments that suited my station." Tyreal grinned wickedly, and Gwen rolled her eyes but smiled, dismissing him with a wave. "Will you walk with me?"

"Always."

They walked in amicable silence until they reached her chambers. The door was open, and maids moved in and out, their arms laden with gowns and books. One of them attempted a curtsy but dropped two books she was carrying. Her cheeks flushed red as Tyreal stooped to help pick up the fallen items. The girl stammered a thanks and an apology before hurriedly retreating down the hall. Tyreal turned to Gwen, surprised she hadn't reassured the girl—it wasn't like her to be so uncharacteristically distant.

Gwen had a small frown on her face and a pinched look around her eyes. "I had forgotten this would be happening. I've been in this room my whole life." He understood then where her mind was.

"Ah, aye. It will take some getting used to. I don't know what I'll do with all the space in Hedontas' room." He ran a hand through his hair, struggling to think of something comforting to say. The presence of so many people around them limited his ability to speak freely. He hated these damn protocols and rules.

Her hands shook as she clasped them together tightly. She chewed at her bottom lip as another maid exited with more of her belongings, then took a deep breath. Straightening her shoulders, she forced a bright smile. "Well, at least you'll be right next door to lecture me whenever you want."

He played along with her attempt at normalcy. "Aye, and you'll have even more décor to toss at my head when I get on your nerves." He grinned at her.

She rolled her eyes. "Don't you have important work to do before you get ready for your ceremony?" She motioned for him to leave. He gave a low, exaggerated bow before walking away, needing to see if Andais was awake, and discuss Jameson and Tensha.

"Oh, Captain?" Gwen called after him. Tyreal turned to see her wide, teasing grin. "Please dress for the occasion. I'm sure your many female admirers will be in attendance."

He responded with another exaggerated bow. "As you wish, Your Majesty."

CHAPTER SEVEN

The long, white-sleeved undertunic looked striking against the gold chest armor. The Thorncrest sigil—a deep, golden rose—was stamped boldly onto the chest, and small lines of gold chain mail hung below, giving Tyreal a sense of satisfaction with the overall appearance. He slid his sword into the ornate dress sheath, its black metal adorned with intricate scrollwork, and fastened it at his waist with a tight cinch. King Lorne had commissioned the armor for him over a year ago.

The memory brought a sharp pang of grief. Lorne's death had unearthed many emotions from Tyreal's own father's passing. As his father's only child, they had been incredibly close, especially after Tyreal's mother had moved away from Thorncliff to the mountains. She had left when it became clear Tyreal would not abandon his plans to join Gwen's guard, though, truthfully, she had never felt at home at the castle, unlike Tommen and Tyreal. His parents had a unique relationship, never marrying—a scandalous choice in Tavia. Yet, his mother cherished her freedom, and despite the unconventional arrangement, they had loved each other in their own way.

Tyreal's father had passed seven summers ago while he was away on a training mission with the Tavian Army. The news, delivered by a crow, had felt as if the ground might swallow him whole. That memory still haunted him, and he understood what Gwen was going through, though he struggled to guide her through it. His way of coping had been to drown his sorrows in ale and the company of buxom barmaids—hardly the healthiest way to manage grief, he admitted.

With a heavy sigh, he shook off the melancholy that threatened to drag him down and turned his attention back to the looking glass. "She wants me to dress for the occasion. I'll do just that," he muttered to his reflection. His hands moved to a bottle of scented oil, a blend of cedar and sandalwood that Gwen had given him on his name day a couple of summers back. He rubbed it through his thick hair in a futile attempt to tame the unruly strands. The stubborn locks refused to stay flat, as always. The oil worked better on his beard, giving the dark hair a pleasant sheen and making it lie neatly along his jaw.

His gaze swept around his new quarters, taking in large bed that dominated the space, flanked by bookshelves currently holding his extra weapons instead of books. Next to the bedroom, a smaller chamber with a seating area awaited meetings with the other guards. The room felt strange, almost foreign. Hedontas had wasted no time moving his belongings out, but with most of Tyreal's time spent protecting Gwen, he had little to move in. He usually spent his free moments at the village pub or training with the guards.

He wondered how Gwen was adjusting to her new chambers. She had clearly struggled with the initial shock earlier in the hall, and he understood why. Custom decreed that a ruler's spirit might grow confused if its chambers were left empty and would linger rather than move on to the Everafter, so Gwen had been forced to move in immediately. He had never questioned it, but it was peculiar when you really thought about it.

Thoughts of the royal suite drew his attention to the large tapestry on his wall. Hedontas' face had been sympathetic, bordering on pity, when he had revealed the secret corridor the tapestry concealed. The one that led directly to the royal suite. "I certainly don't envy ye, kid.

I loved Lorne like a brother, so this was just something handy we used for Lorne to get completely sloshed on mountain spirits and make it back to his room, with no one being the wiser. I'd rather walk over hot coals than face the temptation you will with it," Hedontas had said, clapping Tyreal on the shoulder. The corridor was a fiercely guarded secret that no one in Tavia knew of except the High Captain and the ruler. Which meant he now had direct access to her that no one would ever know about until she took a husband.

Tyreal swallowed, sending a silent prayer to the gods for the fortitude he would need to resist that siren call. He exited his chamber and made his way towards the dining hall, cutting through the kitchen.

Cook was busy chopping vegetables and hollering at the kitchen staff. He flashed her a smile and snagged a carrot off the table. "Get out of my kitchen, Tyreal Blackbane, or I'll make you scrub all the pots, High Captain or no!" She wagged her knife at him as she yelled.

He snorted. "Think I'm afraid of scrubbing some soup pots? I've done my fair share of choring in here for you."

She made a hmph sound and shooed him off with her hands. He pushed through the heavy door separating the dining hall from the kitchen and glanced around. The servants were busy preparing for the impending visitors. The rich scent of beeswax and oil used to polish the wooden tables hung heavy in the air, and the small glass panes of the large windows on either side of the royal tapestries had been individually cleaned. Centered before them was a table with two ornate chairs, flanked by simpler ones for captains and high-ranking officials.

Gwen had not yet arrived, so he took his seat to the right of her chair. Until she married, Pip would occupy the seat on her left. The chairs had been given the same "company is coming" treatment as the tables, and he shifted uncomfortably on the crimson velvet cushion he sat on. Removing it, he carefully placed it on the chair beside him. Andais wouldn't be joining them for lunch, opting to squeeze in as much rest as he could before the ceremony. Working nights suited his friend, thankfully, because Tyreal had always hated how it disrupted his sleep. He'd never felt he could catch up.

Tyreal smiled at one of the servant girls as she poured him a mug of ale. He thought her name was Geneva, and she blushed prettily, her dark lashes brushing her cheeks. Tyreal didn't pursue the flirtation further. He had long ago decided that dalliances with the castle's girls were a poor idea for everyone involved. They'd see how he was around Gwen and only lead to heartache. Gods above knew Gwen had not been pleased regarding the last girl he'd openly flirted with in front of her. Instead, he stuck to girls at the tavern or those he met on his travels when called away from Thorncliff. Ladies who wanted no more than he did, but always dark-haired and curvy. He didn't need much reflection to understand why.

The doors behind him opened, and everyone in the dining room came to attention, prompting him to do the same. Gwen and Pippen entered together. Cora had styled Gwen's hair into an intricate cascade of curls and braids, with tiny gold beads shaped like roses woven into them. For the ceremony after lunch, she had added a black cape that draped over her arms and fastened to her shoulders with golden roses. No matter how often he saw her, she always took his breath away. The freckles across her dainty upturned nose, the sharp angle of her chin—it was all perfection to him.

Gwen's gaze fell on his new armor. A brief flash of shocked wonder crossed her face before her court mask slid back into place. It made Tyreal's heart sing, and he bowed low to her with a smirk. "Your Majesty, I believe you said to dress for the occasion," he said. He turned to Pip and asked, "Your Highness, do you like my dress armor?"

Pippen shrugged. "I saw it when Papa had it made. I thought it would look better with something other than our stupid flower sigil." He glanced down unhappily at his own gray tunic, with black roses embroidered along the shoulders to match Gwen's dress.

"Pippenach, mind your words!" Gwen admonished him.

The boy flushed from the use of his full name, which he hated, suddenly remembering they were in front of others. "Er, I just meant to say, I thought there were other things he could have gone with. But it looks very nice."

"You look... very dashing, Captain Blackbane." Gwen added. Her eyes roved over him again, and he just barely noticed her catch her bottom lip between her teeth for a moment before she glanced away. It was so brief, but it felt like fire coursing through his veins. What he wouldn't give to catch that plump lip between his own teeth, to devour her mouth as he'd dreamed of more times than he could count. He breathed deeply through his nose, calming himself. This was not the time or place for his desire for her to surface. He blamed that damned corridor.

Gwen sat, and everyone else followed. The servants busied themselves filling plates and glasses. "Just how long have you been holding onto that?" Gwen asked.

"Your father had it made for me a year ago. He assumed there was little question that you'd name me High Captain and I'd accept. He want-ed me to have something befitting the honor. It seemed very important to him."

Tears welled up in Gwen's eyes. "That—is so very like him." She blinked them back and cleared her throat to steady herself. She looked around the room, and Tyreal followed her gaze. The overall mood of the castle was still somber, though everyone seemed determined to con-

tinue with their routines. Black, swagged curtains hung at the tops of the large windows
as the castle prepared for the funeral. He saw
Gwen staring at them, and he dropped his hand
beneath the table to briefly squeeze her knee
in comfort. He didn't try to hide the action, just
gave her a look to let her know that he understood her struggle.

"I spoke with Andais briefly earlier," Tyreal
said, breaking the silence as he dipped a hunk
of bread into his chicken soup. "We both agree
that Jameson would be an excellent choice for
the new Captain of the Heir. What do you think
of that, Your Majesty?"

Gwen pursed her lips, stirring her spoon in
her bowl. Tyreal's pointed look reminded her of
their earlier conversation about food, and she
rolled her eyes before responding. "Jameson is a
fantastic guard, but didn't you say his temperament wasn't suited for promotion?"

"I said he wasn't ideal for your detail. He tends
to make jokes that might grate on your nerves.
However, his temperament aligns well with the
prince's," Tyreal explained, grinning at Pippen,
who returned the smile.

"Hmm... or he might encourage Pippen's bad
habit of speaking out of turn," Gwen mused.

"Hey, I only do that with you!" Pip protested,
twisting his napkin between his fingers. "I know
how to keep my mouth shut when I need to.
Besides, I like Jameson. He doesn't mind doing
fun stuff with me, sometimes, unlike Hedontas."

Gwen raised an eyebrow at Tyreal. "Do you trust him?" When Tyreal nodded, Gwen did too. "Very well then, we can appoint Jameson as Captain of the Heir."

Pip bounced slightly in his seat before frowning. "Wait. Do I really need a bunch of guards now?" he whined.

Gwen laughed. "Yes, you do. Mainly because you're now the heir, but also as payback for all the times you laughed at me. In fact, I might even triple the guards. It would serve you right."

Pip glanced around to ensure no one was watching and stuck his tongue out at Gwen. She flicked his knee in retaliation. "See? Bad habits," she said, looking at Tyreal.

Pip rubbed his knee and gave Gwen a dark look. "You won't triple my guard detail because Luca would never spend the coin. So there. Will my guard detail ease up when you have a baby? You know, when I'm no longer the heir?"

Gwen coughed, her eyes wide as she searched for the right response. Tyreal might have found it amusing if the topic had been less distasteful. "Um, well, you'll always have a security detail because you'll always be my brother and in line for the throne. But yes, once I'm married and have a child, your security detail will be less stringent."

"Well, I hope you find a consort and have a baby soon. It sounds awful to have this many guards. My horse isn't nearly as fast as Akasha. I'll never outrun them like you did. I barely know how to ride." Pip pushed his food around, pouting. The scraping sound of his spoon against the dish made Gwen wince.

Tyreal cleared his throat, eager to shift the topic. "Actually, I also wanted to discuss something else. I propose making Tensha an official member of the guard. She can handle guard duties here at the castle and assist with your riding training."

"A girl guard? Really? Well, if I must have one, Tensha is a good choice. She fights better than most of the guards we have. I bet she could teach me to use a sword even better than you, Tyreal—er, I mean, Captain Blackbane." Pippen's interest was obviously piqued by the idea.

"As I told Tensha earlier today, having a female ruler makes it seem less unusual. And yes, she's an excellent fighter, though you'll need to put on more muscle to match me, Highness. Her primary focus will be on your riding skills. And" he added with emphasis, "*not* so you can outrun your guards as your sister did. Hopefully, you'll be a bit more restrained."

Gwen sneered and stuck out the tip of her tongue. Tyreal squinted at her, recalling their earlier conversation about the clothespin on her tongue. As if reading his thoughts, Gwen pulled it back into her mouth. Tyreal chuckled darkly.

Desperate to regain the upper hand, Gwen smiled sweetly. "How are you finding your new room, Captain? Did Hedontas show you everything you needed to see?" Her words carried an unspoken challenge, and Tyreal inclined his head, pursing his lips.

"The room is much larger than I'm used to and very well appointed. There are areas I might never use," he replied.

"Oh, I don't know. I think everything can be used if you try. One must simply get their priorities straight and not be—too scared to try new things." She dabbed at her mouth with her napkin, the very picture of innocence.

Tyreal tightened his grip on his spoon, a multitude of retorts flashing through his mind, along with vivid images of how he might punish her for her beloved little word games—most involving her in his bed or bent over the table. "Perhaps you're right, Your Majesty. Maybe I just need to embrace new experiences. I had considered taking up woodworking. I saw a particularly fine paddle in the village recently. I bet I could find many uses for a big, thick paddle of my own making."

Gwen's cheeks flushed immediately, and she pouted, conceding that he had won this round of their playful banter. Tyreal grinned and resumed eating his lunch.

CHAPTER EIGHT

After the meal, the group headed to the chapel. Tyreal fell back behind Gwen and Pippen to walk beside Andais, who had finally joined them. The Lower Captain was dressed for the occasion in armor commissioned by King Lorne. Just as Tyreal's position was assumed, so was Andais'. There was no one Tyreal trusted more with Gwen's safety. The gold and white of Andais' armor contrasted with his burnished bronze skin, casting a warm glow that seemed to emanate from within. His meticulously neat tight row of braids along his scalp were oiled, catching the light with a subtle shimmer.

"Ready for this?" Tyreal asked him.

Andais shrugged. "Seems like a bit of unnecessary royal pomp to me. We've already accepted the positions. We have more pressing tasks, but I suppose publicly swearing an oath has its benefits."

"You're just cranky because we had to wake you up early." Tyreal grinned. "It's like her majesty's coronation ceremony—less significant, of course, but she's already queen. Putting a crown on her head and a scepter in her hand doesn't make her more of one. But words have power. Hearing them spoken aloud carries weight."

"Look at you, sounding like the castle poet. Getting rather superstitious in your old age?" Andais returned the ribbing with a smile, then grew serious as he looked at Gwen. "How is she? She cried out a few times last night. I had to check on her. Each time, she looked soundly asleep, but there were fresh tears on her face. I know she was feigning sleep."

Tyreal inhaled sharply, rubbing his thumb over his sword grip. "She's surviving. Cracks jokes now and then, but tears are always close by. I suppose that's all anyone can ask of her at this point."

The pair followed their charges into the chapel. Light streamed through the large stained-glass windows, casting colorful patterns on the polished white stone floor. Rich tapestries depicting the founding families being blessed by the gods before forming the nine kingdoms of Valine adorned the walls. Some showed magical creatures and events, reminding Tyreal of the stories told during children's worship. Those tales had sparked many debates among the village boys—were the creatures real? Had dragons once roamed the keep, and if so, where were their bones? Had magic truly existed? They never found answers, but the joy was in the questioning.

The thick tapestries muffled sound, and the colorful light made the chapel feel distinct from the rest of the castle. Tyreal often found Gwen there, seeking the quiet for introspection, usually seated in front of her favorite tapestry depicting her ancestor, Myaessa Thorncrest, riding a dragon into battle.

Gwen stepped onto the altar, where the Divine Arbiter, an old man named Malcolum, awaited. He smiled softly at her and bowed as best he could. Malcolum had been old when Gwen and Tyreal were children, and now he seemed downright ancient, with only a smattering of white hair over his ears and age spots on his bald head. Tyreal was fond of him, though they often clashed over philosophy and morals. Still, they both enjoyed their debates, even if they never changed each other's minds.

Malcolum cleared his throat to get everyone's attention and wrapped a gold and white robe around Gwen's shoulders, matching his own. Cora joined them on the altar, and Gwen knelt slightly so Cora could carefully remove the small silver circlet from her braided hair and replace it with a large crown that had belonged to Queen Asya and many queens before her. The crown was adorned with intertwined leaves and thorns, pearls, and small diamonds, with a large rose made of brilliantly cut rubies in the center.

Malcolum gathered Gwen's hands, despite his own trembling, and kissed them. They spoke in low, private voices, touching foreheads in thanks to the gods.

Gwen turned to the small crowd. "My good people, thank you for joining me today for the commitment ceremony of two fine men in the highest positions in Tavia. The High Captain and Lower Captain of the Tavian Guard are entrusted with overseeing our army, our lands, and preserving our way of life. The job leaves little time for family and is not always easy when dealing with stubborn royals." She allowed the audience to laugh. "It seems bittersweet that these important promotions only happen at mournful times, so I want to take a moment to acknowledge the accomplishments of the two men I regularly trust with my very life. Andais Kensington, please arise and join me at the altar."

Andais walked towards her, bowing low.

"Captain Kensington has served on my personal guard for as long as I can remember. His friendly demeanor might be mistaken for weakness, but few are as loyal to Tavia and me as he is. He has proven time and again that he will do whatever is necessary to protect me. I can think of no better choice for Lower Captain of the Royal Guard." She motioned for him to kneel.

"Do you solemnly swear in front of your queen and your fellow guardsmen at the altar of our gods that you will keep Tavia always in your heart and serve her and me until your final breath?"

"I do." Despite his earlier talk of the ceremony's pointlessness, Andais spoke somberly and held himself with dignity.

"Do you pledge your loyalty to the High Captain and recognize him as an extension of my hand?"

"I do."

"And will you oversee the Captain of the Armory, Captain of the Stables, and Captain of the heir with my best interest and the orders of your High Captain foremost in your mind?"

"I will, my queen." Andais swallowed, clenching his fists at his waist.

Gwen took a ruby and emerald-encrusted scepter from a pillow that Cora held and placed it briefly on each of Andais' shoulders. "Then I name thee Lower Captain of the Tavian Guard. Arise and receive your well-earned applause, Lower Captain."

Andais rose, bowed his head briefly to the crowd, and placed his fist over his heart in respect to Gwen before returning to his place.

Gwen nodded towards Tyreal. "Tyreal Black-bane, arise and join me at the altar."

Tyreal swallowed, suddenly overcome with an emotion he couldn't name. He walked towards her, the light from the windows framing her and her crown in an ethereal glow that tightened his chest. He reached the altar and knelt before her.

"Tyreal Blackbane has been a constant figure in my life since I was barely four summers gone. Though only four summers older than myself, he took to lecturing and guarding me as if it were his duty long before it officially became so. Serving first as a page and rising quickly to be the youngest person in Tavian history to be named Captain of the Heir, he is truly an extension of my hand and often knows my thoughts before I do. I trust him with my life. He will sacrifice everything," her voice trembled, and he wondered if she was recalling that day at the spring all those summers ago, "to uphold Tavia's laws and customs. He loves his land and the greater good more than himself. There is simply no other choice for High Captain."

She asked him the same questions she had asked Andais, and he affirmed his vows, dreading the last question.

Gwen kept her face neutral as she asked, "Do you, as High Captain, pledge your loyalty to me and my eventual Consort? To protect our bodies as if they were your own?"

"I do." The bubble of unnamed emotion burst in his chest. For the first time, Tyreal was an oath breaker. He had known what he would be asked and what he would be expected to say. Would he guard Gwen to his dying breath? Absolutely. That had never been in question since he was eight summers gone. But her consort? Tyreal felt he could step over that man's bleeding body without remorse, whoever he might be. A widowed queen had more leeway in choosing her lovers, especially if she had already produced an heir. And gods above help him, Tyreal knew that well.

"Then I name thee High Captain of the Tavian Guard, the highest position in our land. May you serve as an extension of my hand and protector of my body until one of us goes to the Everafter. Rise, please, to your well-earned applause."

The crowd clapped, but Malcolum raised his hand. "I'm afraid we aren't quite finished yet. I would like to say a few words, as we have not had a true queen in Tavia for some time. High Captain, please move to your queen's right side at the altar and stand facing me."

Tyreal rose and moved to Gwen's right side. Malcolum took Gwen's right hand and Tyreal's left, making them link fingers. "In our land, handfasting binds two souls in marriage through their left hands and the line to their hearts. As the High Captain is not of royal descent, our laws prevent him from truly marrying our ruler. Instead, he enters a marriage of duty, forsaking traditional marriage to devote his life to the ruler and Tavia. When a High Captain serves a king, their bond is one of brotherhood. When serving a queen, it is different—more like a marriage, but without physical delights or the raising of children."

The old man's gaze focused on Tyreal, who had come to him many times over the years to confess his feelings of confusion and anger regarding his feelings for the princess. Malcolum stared into Tyreal's eyes, urging him to listen closely. "Are you willing to enter this bond for the rest of your life? You will never take a wife. Tradition dictates that you should not take lovers. You will be akin to the Queen's husband without knowing her body. In fact, you will stand by her side when she weds her consort. Are you willing and able to undertake this duty?" Malcolum's voice was firm but not unkind, stressing the choice to Tyreal. "You aren't officially High Captain until I give my blessing."

Gwen began to untangle her fingers from his. "Tyreal—" her voice was a whisper meant only for him and Malcolum. Tyreal gripped her fingers tightly, preventing her from pulling away.

"I've known where I belong since I was eight summers gone. There is nothing else but serving her." Tyreal's calm tone surprised him as he spoke the words for everyone to hear. It didn't match the churn of emotions in his belly, but as he had told Andais, words had power.

Malcolum nodded, taking a golden wedding bracelet from his robe pocket and fastening it onto Tyreal's left wrist. "As you wish. What the gods have joined may no man tear apart. Tyreal Arden Blackbane, you are officially oath-bound to Gwendolyn Rosa Thorncrest, and I name thee the High Captain of the Tavian Guard with my blessing and the Gods'. For Tavia."

"For Tavia." The crowd responded. Tyreal gave Gwen's fingers one last reassuring squeeze before releasing her hand and moving back to his spot beside Andais. Gwen stood there for a moment, almost dazed, until Cora helped her out of the ceremonial crown and robes. Her eyes met his, and he couldn't face the emotions swirling in them. Not right now. He looked away, focusing on the altar.

"Well, that was unnecessarily brutal," Andais murmured. "As if any of us need reminding of what we give up for this job."

Tyreal nodded silently in agreement, unable to look away from the altar. Soon, he would watch her wed another in this very room. He had always known it, but there was no turning away from it now. He had sworn an oath to her, one he could never break.

Sometimes he wished his father had been content to live in the mountains with his mother and never sought to continue the Blackbane legacy of serving the Thorncrest family.

CHAPTER NINE

G wen sat in a chair near the fireplace in her chambers, struggling to see them as her own. These rooms had belonged to her father, and the weight of the past two days pressed heavily on her, making her shoulders slump and her body feel immobilized. Her nerves felt raw and exposed.

After the swearing-in ceremony, she had somehow managed to get through the day's remaining duties, greeting the few visitors who had arrived. Dinner had been skipped, and she had retreated to her chambers early. Tyreal's disapproval had been palpable, but she chose to ignore his pointed looks. The tray of food sent up by Cook had been tasteless and sat like rocks in her stomach. Her lack of appetite wasn't due to stubbornness; she simply had no desire to eat. She'd handle his lecture later.

Gwen wasn't sure how long she had been sitting there, staring blankly into the fire, when a soft knock at the door broke her trance. Blinking rapidly, she winced at the sight of the bloody mess she had made of her thumb from chewing on it. Cora entered, her face softening with concern. "Oh, Your Majesty, let me help you," she whispered.

Cora gently took Gwen's hand, tutting under her breath as she cleaned the thumb and wrapped it with a neat piece of linen, tying it into a delicate bow. Gwen remained silent as Cora removed her cape. She wanted to thank her or insist she could manage on her own, but the words felt lost amidst her overwhelmed numbness. She wasn't sure how to pull herself out of it.

"I know you're dealing with more than most of us can understand," Cora said, her voice soothing. "Andais and I spoke, and while it's not my place to discuss it—" Cora hesitated, taking a deep breath as if summoning the courage to continue. "But I think you should visit Captain Blackbane's chamber tonight. It pains me to see you like this, and I know he would be a great comfort to you. I can't imagine how it would feel to have to deal with all this and not be able to go to Tensha."

Gwen turned to glance over her shoulder at Cora, whose cheeks were flushed. "We all know it, Your Majesty," Cora continued. "It's not a well-kept secret that you and Captain Blackbane are in love. Andais and I can keep it secret if you choose to be with him. We'll both swear you didn't."

"I tried years ago, you know. I suggested we keep it a secret, that no one had to know. He turned me down, said I was too young and that it would hurt too much to see me marry someone else if we crossed that line." Gwen's smile was bittersweet as she looked at Cora, conveying her appreciation for the unexpected confession.

Cora shook her head. "Well, the age part makes sense. He's always been good about not taking advantage of younger women. But I don't understand the rest. It's going to be hard to watch you marry someone else, no matter what. I can't see how denying the truth beforehand would make it any easier." As she spoke, Cora undid Gwen's hair, letting it fall loose around her shoulders.

"That's how I see it, too, but sadly, he doesn't agree, and I respect his decision. Besides, that ridiculous old law says I must go to my marriage bed with my maidenhead, remember?" Gwen said, and both women rolled their eyes. Gwen managed a soft giggle. The weight on her shoulders felt slightly lighter, and she could breathe again. "Thank you. I'm sure the captain won't act on it, but I appreciate you and Andais being willing to cover for us. Your loyalty means everything."

Cora smiled warmly and helped Gwen change into her nightshift. "Do you need anything else, Your Majesty?" she asked.

"No, thank you. I just want to go to sleep." After Cora left, Gwen stood and paced the room. Her staff had done a commendable job making the chambers feel like her own while honoring her father's memory. A large painting of Lorne, a pregnant Asya, and Gwen adorned one wall, as did his favorite sword in its usual corner. Nearby, Gwen's books overflowed the shelves, a second wardrobe had been added for her dresses, and her drawing materials were neatly stacked on a small table by the window. The bed had been moved back against the wall, draped with white sheer material around its posts, and covered with her favorite blanket—a beautiful gold fabric with intricately hand-stitched roses and swirls.

She appreciated the changes and knew she would eventually come to see these chambers as her own, just as her father had eventually seen them as his after her grandfather's passing. At that moment, however, her gaze was fixed on the bed where her father had died.

Her eyes shifted to the painting that concealed the secret corridor, lost in thoughts of what Cora had said.

Tyreal unclasped the sheath of his sword and wrestled out of his golden armor. He could manage it alone, but he usually enlisted the help of a fellow guard. Tonight, however, he simply didn't want to deal with anyone else. Meetings with his men followed the ceremony, most of whom had been present and had given him heavy, sympathetic looks that grated on his nerves. He knew their concern was genuine, but it left him feeling as if he had run the length of the kingdom three times. After Gwen had left dinner, he considered heading to the tavern for some mead, but it felt wrong. The thought of the tavern girls throwing themselves at him while he was in such a foul mood made it seem even less appealing.

Ultimately, he decided to retire to his room early. Tomorrow would bring visitors, and the funeral pyre would follow shortly. It was going to be a heavy week, regardless of the day's events.

Tyreal glanced at the golden bracelet on his wrist, unsure whether to hurl it across the room or admire it in reverence. It represented his connection to Gwen, something he had desired for most of his life, yet he still couldn't have her. He couldn't help but wonder what atrocities he must have committed in a past life for the Gods to be teaching him whatever lesson they were trying to convey.

The tapestry covering the corridor seemed to mock him. Was it a lesson? Or a sign that he should reach out and claim what was laid before him? The Gods were notoriously cryptic. Standing in his breeches and sipping from a mug of ale, Tyreal stared at the tapestry, grappling with the mysteries of what the Gods wanted him to do. He was a simple man, not a philosopher. He enjoyed fucking and fighting, and all of this was giving him a headache.

A knock on the door interrupted his thoughts. Moving toward it, he grabbed one of his daggers from the small table. He opened the door a crack, holding the blade out of view. Andais stood patiently, waiting for Tyreal to let him in.

"What's wrong? Is she alright?" Tyreal's gaze flickered anxiously down the hall toward Gwen's door.

"Yes, I have someone at her door for a moment. I wanted to speak with you privately."

Tyreal nodded and opened the door wider. Andais looked uncomfortable yet determined, and Tyreal sensed the topic of their discussion. "What's on your mind, brother? Would you like a drink?"

"No. But I have something to say. Once I say it, that's the end of the discussion. I will never speak of it again," Andais began. Tyreal's raised eyebrow prompted him to continue. "I've seen amazing and terrible things in the guard. Never once have I doubted my decision to serve the crown. But I'm tired of watching two people I care about suffer because of an outdated law made by some old women in the mountains. I can't stay silent any longer."

Tyreal tensed, about to speak, but Andais raised a hand to stop him. "Don't. Don't insult my intelligence or my eyes by denying it. Your feelings for each other are the worst-kept secret in this kingdom. Continuing to pretend otherwise is not only a security risk but pointless."

Andais took a deep breath before continuing. "Cora and I agree that this doesn't make sense. You're not a sexless eunuch. What they're asking is too much. We want you to know that we will guard your secret and do whatever it takes to make this work. You're my brother, Tyreal. We've fought together, bled together, and killed together. She's my queen, and I'd lay down my life for her. I don't care about some pompous royal who has the right blood showing up here in the springtime. I care about you and her. So, know that. If you were to leave this room tonight, I'd swear you didn't."

Without waiting for a response, Andais turned and walked away to resume his post outside Gwen's door.

Tyreal stared at the door, unsure whether he felt anger at his friend's audacity or mortification that everyone knew his private feelings. Andais and Cora's willingness to go to such lengths for him and Gwen filled him with a swirl of emotions.

He turned his attention back to the wall of the hidden corridor, struggling to resist the allure of what the Gods were dangling before him. Since that day by the spring, he had convinced himself that keeping Gwen at arm's length was the best decision for both. It was his duty to protect her honor, though he did not agree with the sentiment behind that tradition. Selfishly, he worried he would find it just as difficult to let her go when it was time for her to marry someone else as he would to share her. The concern that he might actually kill the man was not unfounded.

Before he could decide anything further, the tapestry shifted aside. Gwen stood before him, barefoot, her hair loose around her shoulders. She nervously fidgeted with the hem of the golden silk robe draped over her shift.

They stared at each other in silence for a moment. Finally, Gwen took a deep, shaky breath. "I can't sleep in there. He—he died in that bed. It feels so wrong. Those are my father's chambers, not mine. I know I shouldn't ask, but you always say you're here to provide me with whatever I need. So, I just..."

"I think a part of me knew you'd end up here as soon as I learned this corridor existed. You can have my bed, Gwennie. You can have whatever you need, you know that." The urge to gather

her into his arms was overwhelming, and he had to open and close his fists by his side to keep from giving in. Her eyes held such hurt, and the linen Cora must have wrapped around her thumb to stop the bleeding, broke his heart. Her pain was his pain.

She chewed at her lip. "I—I want you to hold me. I know I'll likely regret it because it's going to make everything harder," she paused. "Right now, all I can think about is him dying in that damn bed and how everything is falling apart. I can't breathe." Unable to continue holding everything together, and finally away from prying eyes, her tears flowed freely down her cheeks. She gasped for air as she sobbed, pressing her hands to her chest.

He crossed the space between them in two strides, cupping her face with his large hands. "Shhhh, I've got you, Gwennie. Let it out, I'm here." He picked her up in his arms and cradled her bridal-style, sitting on the edge of his bed. Gwen clung to him, her overwhelming emotions pouring out in a torrent of tears. Tyreal pressed his lips to her temple, making gentle, soothing sounds against her skin.

After a while, the sobs subsided. She lifted her eyes to him, sniffling. "I'm so sorry. This isn't how I envisioned my first time in your bed."

"Gwennie, your father died. It's the only reason any of this is happening. Whatever this thing is between us, it's been there for years. It doesn't stop your grief. I've spent years yearning for any alone time with you. I am always here for whatever you need." He brushed a dark curl from her face, his desire to kiss her strong, but he refrained, wanting to comfort her more. Instead, he helped her lie down on the mattress, pulling the linens around her.

Gwen entwined her fingers with his and shyly rubbed his leg with her foot. "Are we finally acknowledging this thing between us? Apparently, it's common knowledge in the castle."

Tyreal sighed and rolled onto his back, propping his arm behind his head as he stared at the ceiling, contemplating what to say. "I guess Cora also talked to you? Andais left right before you came in."

She nodded, propping herself up on her elbow to look at him. "I'm not saying we must listen to them or give in to anything. I'm just tired of pretending it's not there."

"Do you need to hear me say it? Does it change anything?"

Gwen shrugged. "Maybe. Maybe not. Words have power. But I'd like to hear it, at least once."

He turned to face her, his eyes roved over her face, memorizing the finer details he normally couldn't see, since they were rarely this close. "I have never loved another, not in this life, nor any that may have come before. It has always been you, through every breath, every moment. It consumes me. I don't serve you because it's my duty. I chose to be your guard because the need to care for you is like the need to breathe.

Even if the world fell away, I would find my way to you."

He watched as she inhaled sharply, his heart pounding in his chest. Her eyes shimmered with unshed tears again as she swallowed, trying to hold back her emotions. She closed her eyes briefly, then met his gaze, sniffling and offering him a tender smile. "And you say you're no good with words," she whispered, her voice trembling. They both laughed softly, and she reached out to touch his chest, lightly twisting her fingers in the dark curls there. He noticed she was lost in thought, likely deciding what she wanted to say next, so he embraced the chance to savor her touch, even as he knew it was playing with fire.

"I tried to deny it, to hide it from everyone, myself included, after you turned me away at the spring," she whispered. "But every time you're near, every time your eyes meet mine or your hand brushes mine, it feels like I might burst into flame. You've always seen me, even when I couldn't see myself. I love the way you push me, believe in me—even when you argue with me. I don't want to hide it anymore. I love you, with everything I am."

"Bloody crows, Gwen." His voice was husky, and his throat felt tight. "What are we supposed to do now?" He pressed her hand against his chest, letting her feel his heart pounding beneath her palm.

She shook her head. "I don't know. We are a mess, I know that."

He leaned his forehead against hers, their noses brushing. The soft plumpness of her lips beckoned him, and he grumbled, "Do you have any idea how badly I want to kiss you right now?" His hand rested tentatively on her hip. He was glad he remained on top of the blankets and not underneath them with her.

Her voice was breathy as she arched closer to him, her lips grazed his, just enough that he thought he might have caught a taste. She was going to drive him mad. There was no other outcome to what they were doing. "Why don't you?" she asked.

Tyreal let out a growl and rolled onto his back beside her. "Gods, woman, you'll be the death of me. For one, you came here seeking comfort, not my cock. And two, I've spent the last seven summers denying myself to honor this outdated law about your maidenhead."

"You certainly won't get any arguments from me on that. Though it's rather presumptuous of you to assume mine is intact," she said.

He stilled, feeling as though someone had knocked the breath out of him. "I think you need to explain that statement, Gwendolyn." His voice was gravelly, dark emotions swirling inside him.

She pouted her lips and widened her eyes, giving him an innocent look. "Well, I simply meant that unlike certain other people I know,

I haven't made my preferences known to court gossip. Therefore, you don't know what I have or haven't done. Just because you turned me down doesn't mean others did."

Tyreal rolled their bodies so he was on top of her. "Tell me who didn't turn you down, and he'll find himself at the end of my blade." He was fairly sure he was jesting, but a current of possessive jealousy hovered in his senses, making his words feel less false than he'd hoped.

"Oh, so you can bury yourself in any barmaid with dark hair and large breasts, but I can't find solace in someone else's arms?" Gwen arched an eyebrow, challenging him with a fire in her eyes.

"Could I fairly say such a thing? Absolutely not. You have just as many rights as I do. But is there a part of me seething with jealousy over this thorn you've driven into my side? Absolutely." He traced a finger over her silky-smooth cheek and freckled nose. "I've wanted you for years, and I've denied myself to uphold this nonsensical law. So, there's some... feelings there."

"The law dictates I should not lie with any man other than my husband before my wedding night. The Sisters' text is explicit about that. I have never lain with a man, but that doesn't necessarily mean I still have my maidenhead. Riding a horse too roughly can also cause its loss," she explained.

"Aye, it can. But now you've piqued my curiosity. Have you lain with anyone?" Tyreal's confidence in knowing everything about Gwen was shaken. Finding something new was rare indeed.

"Yes, I have," she said, pausing as if searching for the right words. "Anya and I, well, let's just say those summer nights in the mountains with the Sisters of the Mist could get rather dull. So, we occupied ourselves." She shrugged and laughed. "We love each other, still do. In a different world, if we weren't royalty, things might have been different. I couldn't give her my heart, not truly, because it's always belonged to you." She gave him a sheepish smile, her cheeks flushed.

"She knew that, I think, even though I can't speak for her side of it. So, it never went as far as it might have. When we grew close with Max as well, it seemed unnecessarily messy for him to witness his future wife loving someone else while she saw me loving you. From then on, we chose to remain just friends."

Tyreal shifted, sitting up on the bed and crossing his legs. This was partly to hide the tent forming in his breeches and partly to create a bit more distance between their bodies. The thought of Gwen and the beautiful princess from Gagerland was certainly one that would fuel many fantasies in the future. He cleared his throat. "I know I should be just as jealous about you being with a woman instead of a man—"

"You realize you don't have much ground to stand on, given the number of dalliances I've heard about you," she said with a grin.

"Most of those rumors aren't true, you know. Well, a good number probably aren't. And since we're on the subject, are you ever going to tell me why you spent so many summers with the sisters? What were you training for?"

Gwen shifted uncomfortably, fidgeting with the bed linens. "Just training in protocols and traditions—boring royal matters." Her eyes darted away from him, a clear sign she was hiding something.

"Every summer for eight years? That's quite a lot of training." His gaze narrowed. He wanted to press further, but an enormous yawn escaped her lips, reminding him of why she had come to his room. "Arms up, Your Majesty."

She looked at him in confusion, and he gestured for her to lift her arms. Once she did, he carefully removed the robe she was wearing. "You need to get some rest. Andais told me you've not been sleeping well."

She pursed her lips. "Are we really going to rest?"

"Aye, we are. I can't promise that if you visit me again in my chambers, I'll have the same resolve, though. That corridor is for emergencies only—a fact we'll remember come morning. If we start down any other path, I won't be able to stop. Not until your belly swells with *my* child. Royal bloodlines be damned. I'm not that strong, Gwennie. I'm not."

"We confessed our love for each other, but nothing changes?"

He wrapped his arms around her, pulling her close while keeping himself above the linens and his breeches on. "For tonight, no. I don't know what the gods have planned for us. I just know you need to rest."

CHAPTER TEN

A beam of warm, golden sunlight streamed through Tyreal's window, casting a soft glow that stirred Gwen awake. She tossed her arms over her face, grumbling at the intrusion, until a soft chuckle from beside her made her pause. "If there's one thing in life I can rely on, it's your grumpy disposition in the morning," Tyreal said. Gwen cracked open an eye to glare at him, finding him propped against the pillows, fully dressed, and watching her with a smile.

"Were you watching me sleep? That's a bit much, even for you." She lowered her arm and reached out to brush a stray lock of hair from his forehead. Her fingers traced the lines of his cheek, savoring the soft yet scratchy feel of his beard. She knew she might not get many chances to touch him like this, especially with his insistence on keeping their distance.

"Well," he drawled, stretching the word, "I am technically tasked with keeping an eye on you. It isn't as sinister as it sounds. You're safe and quiet when you're asleep, not arguing with everything I say. It might be my favorite time of the day, actually. And it certainly doesn't hurt that the sunlight makes your shift a bit transparent. I'm just enjoying the view."

Gwen glanced down and confirmed his observation; the dusty rose outline of her nipple was visible in the sunlight. Her eyes met his, appreciating the desire that usually remained hidden from her. Perhaps *some* things have changed, she thought. "Oh, should I untie it then? Give you a better look?" She withdrew her hand from his face and toyed with the ribbon that held her shift at her shoulders. A dark, almost predatory glint flashed in his eyes, making her shiver and a heat tighten low in her belly.

Tyreal closed his eyes, inhaling sharply. She could see the internal struggle as he fought to suppress his desire. "I—I think that's an unwise choice for the reasons I stated last night. I can only resist so much, and I'm dangerously close to breaking."

"Dammit, I don't care about some old law about me being a virgin to be wed. No one expects the same from my future husband!" Gwen took a deep breath and pinched the bridge of her nose. "I'm sorry. I'm not angry with you. You're just trying to be honorable. It's just frustrating."

Tyreal moved off the bed and offered her a hand to help her up. "I understand. And I don't know why people don't hold men to the same standard. Well, I do. Men are supposedly less controlled, which is clearly nonsense. You're practically throwing yourself at me, yet I remain a pillar of steadfast willpower." He flashed her a broad grin, prompting her to pick up a pillow and throw it at him.

He helped her out of bed, his touch gentle and draped her robe over her shoulders. She tried to not feel the sting of rejection. He was probably right; this was the best course of action. She sighed softly, turning away from him to head through the corridor to her room.

"Fuck it," Tyreal growled.

In one swift motion, his hand shot out, catching her elbow and spinning her back to him. Her hair swirled around her shoulders, and she gasped, heart pounding at the sudden movement.

He kissed her with a fervor that made her toes curl, as if he were drowning and she was his only source of air. She moaned lightly against his lips, which he used to his advantage to deepen the kiss, his tongue tracing the edges of her lips before slipping inside. His other hand buried itself in her hair, gripping a handful of curls with a force that was both demanding and intimate. In that moment, he seemed to claim every inch of her being, and she melted against him.

Finally, when both were breathless and the air between them was thick with desire, he pulled away. "I'll never do that again. I just needed one chance to memorize the taste of you. I know when we leave this room, it's back to being the queen and the high captain, but gods above, Gwen, what I feel for you threatens to consume me." He rested his forehead against hers, giving them both a moment to collect themselves.

She wanted to respond, but her heart was pounding so loudly she feared he might hear it. She had spent years wondering what it would be like to kiss him, and now she knew. Suddenly she understood why Tyreal hesitated to cross that last line between them. She was already struggling to keep from begging for more.

They moved apart and stepped into the passageway between the rooms. The air was stale, and dusty cobwebs hung in the corners of the narrow stone corridor. Tyreal led the way, his broad shoulders barely fitting the space, and swept a practiced gaze over her chambers before allowing her to enter. Satisfied, he turned back, his eyes lingering on her with an intensity that made her stomach clench. He took in her disheveled hair, wild and tousled from his touch and her lips swollen from his kisses.

"By the gods, I can't get enough of you," he murmured, pulling her close. He leaned in, his lips hovering near hers when a gentle knock and Cora's voice interrupted them. "Fuck," he growled low in his throat, stepping away reluctantly and vanishing behind the painting into the corridor.

Gwen swallowed, frustration surging through her. She felt her control slip, and she lashed out, jumping as the embers in her hearth flared up, reigniting the flames. She closed her eyes and had to count backwards briefly in her head to bring herself back to where she needed to be. The last thing she needed right now was to reveal her powers. "Yes, Cora, you may enter."

Cora bustled in; arms laden with dresses. The sight of the black and dark gray fabrics felt like a cold bucket of water, washing away the lingering warmth of their moment in the corridor and reminding her of the grief and stress she faced. Cora's gaze flicked to the fireplace, frowning at the renewed flames that now crackled within. "Did one of the girls light your fire? Andais mentioned no one had been in yet."

Panic fluttered in Gwen's chest, but she managed a calm reply. "I can start a fire. I was chilly."

Cora nodded and placed the dresses in the wardrobe. "Do you want to wear this black silk with the gray underskirt and wide sleeves? The seamstress used two of your old dresses to make it."

A few minutes later, as Cora helped her dress, Tyreal knocked and entered. He met her eyes, and a soft smile curled the edge of his lips. "Ah, good, you're awake. We just received word that Princess Anya and Prince Maximillen are nearly here. They were already traveling through Tavia on their way home to Espera from their honeymoon when our crows arrived," he said.

"Oh, thank the gods. I've missed them desperately, and I couldn't attend their wedding because of Papa's illness." Gwen longed to match his playful tone, but darkness tugged at the edges of her thoughts, draining her energy. She sat at the dressing table, letting Cora tame her hair as she put on a simple necklace with a large obsidian stone at the base of her throat. "Do we know who else will arrive today?"

Cora and Tyreal exchanged a glance, and Gwen sighed, sensing they were picking up on the tone in her voice. Tyreal cleared his throat and answered, "I expect the heads of all the noble families from the districts to arrive today. I also received word that Princess Eliana from Obrye set sail yesterday. If the winds remain favorable, she should arrive in two days. This should also allow enough time for the royals from Egrax and Galeigh to get here."

Gwen nodded, her thoughts a tangled mess. The arrival of so many important figures meant it was time to officially assume the role of Tavia's queen—a burden she wasn't sure she was ready for. A headache threatened to bloom behind her eyes. "I think we should leave my hair down today, Cora. My head is already quite disagreeable, and putting it up will only make it worse."

She turned to look at Tyreal, who lounged casually in one of her chairs, his legs stretched out. "Have we heard anything about the other pressing concerns from yesterday?"

He straightened, his expression serious. "One of my spies followed Skensy after he left, and I expect to have answers about who he met with and what was discussed later today. I've also sent crows to my spies in Adaltus." Gwen nodded, rolling her neck a little to try to ease the tension building there as he continued. "As for the larder issue, Cook is right to be worried. I reviewed her inventory, and we're missing almost a third of what we should have compared to previous years."

Gwen frowned, her brows knitting together. "How do the donation books look? Has anyone spoken to Luca? Though I'm hesitant to involve him just yet."

"I reviewed the books yesterday after the ceremony," Tyreal replied. "They show low donations from all the farmers in our district. However, the farmers I contacted via crow reported an average harvest. Since Luca has the most access to the books, I'm wary of involving him for now. If he's involved, we need to proceed cautiously to keep this quiet."

Gwen sighed, wishing she could return to the warmth of Tyreal's bed. The thought of hiding under the blankets for a while, away from the demands of the day, was incredibly tempting.

CHAPTER ELEVEN

G wen's face throbbed with tension. Desperately, she longed to escape the throne room and retreat to her chambers, where she could contemplate the larder issue in peace, free from distractions. Yet, tradition dictated that she remain seated upon her throne, managing the delicate balance between appearing appropriately mournful at her father's passing and maintaining the composure expected of a leader. After all, an emotional woman could hardly be trusted to guide Tavia through such a tumultuous transition, despite having trained her entire life for this role. In truth, confidence eluded her. But no one else needed to know that.

Her temple pulsed painfully, even with her hair cascading loosely in a riot of dark curls down her back. The headache she had felt threatening earlier had now settled firmly in place.

Logically, she understood the significance of this moment. As the nobility streamed into the room, offering their hollow words of sympathy, it felt less like a unifying gathering and more like an exhibition where she and Pip were on display—gawked at like exotic animals. She struggled to focus on their faces and words, mostly captivated by the warm glow spilling through the massive stained-glass window behind her, which reached nearly from floor to ceiling, casting a kaleidoscope of colors across the polished stone floor.

Finally, a lull in visitors granted her a moment to breathe. She glanced back over her shoulder at Tyreal, who remained steadfast behind her. "Could you please have someone ask Klause to brew something for my headache? Perhaps a tea?" she murmured quietly. He nodded, stepping away to find a servant.

Gwen tapped her fingers on the armrests of her throne, intricately carved with dragon heads, their deep crimson rubies eyes glistening in the light. She glanced at Pip, who had seized their moment of solitude, slumping into his own throne—a mirrored image of hers, though adorned with crows. The chairs were not particularly comfortable, even with their plush velvet cushions. "I hope we only have Anya and Max left to greet," she whispered to him. He perked up immediately, straightening his shoulders with newfound energy. He practically hero-worshipped Max, always following him around with an endless barrage of questions. Gwen couldn't help but smile.

Just as Tyreal returned, the doors swung open, and the crier announced loudly, "Prince Maximillen and Princess Anya Hellerus of Espera, Your Majesty!" A wave of relief washed over Gwen. As her friends entered, she admired the handsome couple they had become; marriage seemed to suit them well. Max was striking, with sun-kissed olive skin that gleamed against the gold damask print jacket over his silken green tunic. Taller than Tyreal and leaner yet well-muscled, he carried an aura of warmth in his friendly eyes, framed by soft waves of dark hair.

Anya stood beside him with her usual effortless grace. Her golden hair, long and perfectly styled, cascaded down her back without a single strand out of place, as if travel hadn't touched her at all. She gathered her pale pink skirts and curtsied low while Max bowed, his guard, Alric, following suit. Alric was a massive and intimidating man, so his bow nearly made Gwen giggle. His broad face had a large scar running down one cheek, a remnant of a battle that nearly cost him his eye. Gwen knew his loyalty to Max mirrored Tyreal's commitment to her, so despite his size, she simply couldn't be frightened of him.

"Your Majesty, Your Highness, we are so sorry to hear of King Lorne's passing. We came as soon as we received the message from the crow." Max's voice was formally diplomatic yet imbued with genuine sympathy. Gwen offered him a sad smile. He always clung to protocol, as if waiting for someone else to break it first, a habit she both admired and found quietly frustrating.

Anya, however, wasted no time with pretense. She broke away from Max and approached Gwen with arms wide open. Gwen rose from her throne and stepped off the dais, practically throwing herself into her friend's embrace.

"Oh, dearest, I am so, so sorry. When you wrote that he was too ill to attend the wedding, I feared this might happen, but by the gods, I didn't expect it so soon," Anya crooned, her soothing voice wrapping around Gwen like a warm blanket. Anya rubbed a comforting hand down Gwen's back, and Gwen melted into the hug, taking a deep, shaky breath. Tears spilled over her lashes, and she sniffed, desperately trying to hold them back. Anya pressed her lips to Gwen's temple. "It's okay, Gwennie. We're here now."

"It's not okay. It's not," Gwen replied, her voice trembling. "Everything is a mess. We're low on food because someone is stealing from us, most likely to make me look inept and weak. I *feel* inept and weak. Papa would have known how to handle this." The words tumbled out in a rush, her feelings of helplessness laid bare. Somehow, saying them only made her feel worse. Wasn't that the opposite of what was supposed to happen?

Tyreal cleared his throat, and Gwen pulled away from Anya to see a servant entering the throne room with a tray. The girl curtsied as best she could while balancing it. "From Klause, Your Majesty."

After Gwen thanked and dismissed the girl, Max regarded Gwen and Pip with a serious frown, concern etched across his features. "Someone is stealing food?"

Tyreal glanced at Gwen, and she nodded, granting him permission to explain. "Cook informed us yesterday that the food larder serving Thorncliff castle and supporting many villagers in the Exester District during the cold season is dangerously low." As he spoke, he poured the tea from Klause, raising an eyebrow pointedly at Gwen until she drank it.

Max hummed thoughtfully, pursing his lips. "I assume you're investigating the records?"

Tyreal nodded. "Aye. When we reviewed the books, they indicated low amounts collected from all the Exester farms, but the farmers report no such low yields."

"So someone has been forging the records *and* stealing? No wonder you feel overwhelmed." Anya rubbed Gwen's back again, her touch an anchor point that Gwen clung to as she let the soothing warmth of the tea wash over her.

"Do you know how long this may have been happening? It must have been in small amounts for no one to have noticed until recently," Max asked.

Gwen shook her head. "No. I planned to investigate myself after greeting guests. We have some time before dinner. Would you join us? More eyes are always helpful."

Max nodded and moved closer, enveloping her in a hug. "Of course. While I haven't experienced this yet, as an heir, I can imagine the pressure you must feel. It's an odd system that demands we be our strongest when we're emotionally weakest from losing a parent." She smiled gratefully, squeezing his arms before stepping back.

Linking her arm with Anya's, they exited the throne room together. The men followed behind a ways, granting them the privacy to speak.

"How are you, truly? Can I help in any way?" Anya asked softly.

Gwen shook her head. "No, I wish there were something you could do. It's been a struggle. I've nearly lost control several times—set the hearth ablaze right before Cora walked in." She grimaced at the memory.

Anya mirrored her expression. "I was worried about that. Remember when you caught the tapestry on fire after your argument with

Tyreal about us sneaking out to ride the horses at night? We had to concoct a story to explain it to your father."

Gwen snorted. "I don't think he ever bought that one." Clearing her throat, she sought to shift the topic before thoughts of her father summoned tears again. "How are you finding married life? I know you both had concerns. I'm truly sorry I couldn't be there with you on your wedding day."

Anya's smile softened. "I completely understood, sweets. Besides, it was an overwhelming day, and I was mostly in a foul mood. You didn't miss out on good company; Mother was beside herself. You'd have thought it was her wedding, not mine! Especially ridiculous since I'm not even her first daughter to marry. She wanted my hair styled as tall as a birdcage with tiny jeweled birds clipped in. Can you imagine?" Anya rolled her eyes dramatically. "The dress was beautiful, though. I'll concede that."

Gwen laughed, easily picturing the tiny queen of Gagerland with her love of over-the-top fashion designing extravagant bird clips with Anya's hair in mind. "Still, I wish I could have been there to distract her and keep your mood from souring. And what about you and Max? Is everything good?" She raised an eyebrow, giving her friend a questioning look.

"Yes. We've found an arrangement that works for us. I'll tell you all about it later, preferably over a platter of sweets while we pretend we're just simple girls again. And what of you and your captain? Has his promotion changed anything?" Anya returned the raised eyebrow and waggled it with a flourish.

Gwen rolled her eyes. "Yes and no. Another story for later over sweets. Although," she leaned in closer, "he did finally kiss me. Thoroughly, in fact. Nothing more, though."

"Well, I definitely need to hear all about *that!*" Anya whispered, then squealed in delight as they turned a corner into the kitchen and spotted Cook. She rushed to embrace the older woman tightly.

Cook laughed, backing away from the exuberant princess with a grin. "I heard you were approaching the castle, so I whipped up a batch of your favorite thumb-print jam cookies." She gestured to a platter resting on a counter.

"Oh, thank the gods for you, dearest Cook. I've had nothing decent to eat in days," Anya lamented, quickly snatching a cookie and nibbling eagerly.

"My wife jests. We had plenty of good food on our travels through Tavia. It's just she believes she's starving if dessert is absent," Max interjected smoothly. With older siblings ahead of her for the throne, Anya had never truly been in line for it, giving her more freedom to cultivate a wilder public persona than Gwen could afford.

It was this very personality that had drawn Gwen to the bubbly princess during their training in the mountains. Though many people dismissed her because of it, beneath Anya's playful demeanor lay an astute mind. She certainly possessed more patience for their training than Gwen had ever shown, resulting in far better control over her emotions and powers.

Cook nodded knowingly. "Oh, I'm well aware of the princess's sweet tooth. I chased the two of them out of the kitchen nightly during her visits." Despite her words, she smiled indulgently at Anya. Gwen noted that Cook conveniently omitted how the kitchens were always stocked with extra desserts whenever the princess visited.

"We're all taking a walk to discuss the upcoming feast. I thought I'd show them the larder. Prince Maximilien is considering renovating his based on ideas he gathered in Obrye, and I want to see if they can be implemented here," Gwen said just loud enough for any nearby staff to overhear.

"Yes, Your Majesty. I've kept the key as the captain instructed. Should you need it, just send someone to find me." Cook produced the key from a small leather pouch tied to her skirts, giving Gwen a pointed look.

"Of course. I appreciate your thoughtfulness. I'll have the captain return it to you when we finish. Now, we'll leave you be. I know you have much to prepare before the meal this evening," Gwen said, taking the key.

"Aye, I do. Asking everyone to take part in the hunt has kept us busy preparing the meats rolling in. It was a wonderful idea."

"That one was actually Prince Pippen." Gwen watched as Pip puffed with pride, seemingly growing a few inches taller.

They moved from the kitchen and out into the courtyard toward the larder. Tyreal unlocked the door, ducking inside to ensure the space was secure before allowing them entry. He spoke quietly with Alric, who agreed to remain outside as a guard.

Gwen resisted the urge to roll her eyes; investigating a locked space seemed excessive. Yet, she also knew to trust Tyreal's instincts, particularly when it came to her and Pip. He reemerged, giving a small nod, and they followed him down the stone steps into the larder.

Thorncliff's larder was a sprawling chamber carved deep underground, its ancient stone walls illuminated by flickering torches. Tyreal lit a few more, so the group could see better, and shadows danced along the walls. The air was rich with the scent of dried herbs and spices, mingling with the earthy aroma of aging cheese and the sweet tang of cured meats.

Rows of sturdy wooden shelves lined the walls, each groaning under the weight of boxes stacked with provisions. Over the tops of the boxes, wheels of cheese wrapped in muslin cloth and sacks of grain peeked through. Along one wall stood rows of wooden barrels, their rough-hewn surfaces stained with age and use. They were all meticulously labeled with Cook's bold scrawl, marking their contents.

Amidst the abundance, obvious signs of scarcity emerged for those who knew what to look for—empty spaces where fall squashes should have been, gaps among the barrels. Gwen surveyed the room, biting her bottom lip as concern twisted in her stomach. "I believed Cook, of course, but this *is* troubling. Why would someone do this?"

Max responded quietly as he walked around the room, studying the shelves. "A lack of food is a sure way to turn people against a ruler. I doubt it would reach starvation levels; unless the other districts are also short. Tavia's allies would intervene before it got to that point. But sowing seeds of discontent and questioning your decisions? That's a different matter."

"I'm less concerned about why and more curious about how. How does one steal food from a larder under one of the best-guarded castles in the kingdom?" Anya replied, shifting a sack of grain only to squeal loudly when a mouse scurried out. Tyreal and Max instinctively reached for their swords.

"It's just a mouse, gentlemen. Calm down," Gwen admonished, her attention fixed on a stack of crates that troubled her. Some crates contained items, while others remained empty, though they should have been grouped with the rest of the discarded ones. She approached the stack, noticing that the crates with food held only a few items, making them easy to move. As she unstacked them, a small tunnel was revealed. "Bloody crows," she whispered.

Tyreal was at her side in an instant, taking her elbow to guide her away from the opening. "Where does it lead?" she asked, her mind racing with possibilities. She attempted to maneuver around Tyreal so she could move inside, only to be met with a fierce growl.

"If you think I'm letting my queen enter some damned tunnel without knowing where it leads or who might be waiting on the other side, I need to stop being High Captain right now because you don't know me at all."

"But—"

"No buts. None. You're the *queen*. If something happens, Pip will have to face all of this alone. Do you want that?" His fierce gaze locked onto hers, making her look away.

Frustration bubbled within her, but she relented. "What will you do, then?"

"At this moment? Nothing. We'll restack these crates and return to the castle. Tonight, when I know you and the prince are safely in your chambers with guards at your door, I'll come back with Hedontas and Andais to explore the tunnel and see where it leads. I want to ensure that anyone behind this doesn't suspect we're onto them."

CHAPTER TWELVE

Andais, Hedontas, and Tyreal descended the steps of the larder in silence, the gravity of their task weighing on them. Tyreal had briefed them on the situation, and they were eager to assist after ensuring Gwen and Pip were settled for the night. Gwen, with her usual tenacity, had insisted he share his findings the moment he returned. But with the pinched look of pain and exhaustion darkening her face, and the way she winced at even the torchlight, he doubted she would still be awake. Before leaving, he'd ordered another tea from Klause for her headache, with luck, she was already asleep.

Clad in their fighting leathers, the trio melted into the shadows cast by Hedontas' flickering torchlight. Years of relentless training under Hedontas' watchful gaze had prepared them for situations just like this, navigating through treacherous terrain in low light. Tyreal had loathed those grueling sessions and Hedontas more than a little, but he had to admit, the skill came in handy more than it did not.

He gestured toward a stack of crates that concealed the tunnel's entrance. Andais moved them aside, groaning as he spotted the narrow opening. The tunnel was low and cramped, forcing the men to stoop uncomfortably as they entered.

As they stepped inside, a chill crept into Tyreal's bones, the air thick with the scent of damp earth. The uneven walls bore jagged marks of hasty excavation, while rough-hewn timber logs jammed into the soil at irregular intervals, their surfaces splintered and uneven, barely held back the weight of the earth above. "We'll be lucky if this damned thing doesn't collapse on us," Hedotas muttered from behind.

Roots hung from the low ceiling like skeletal fingers, their twisted knots casting eerie shadows in the dim light and tickling the faces of the men as they walked along. Each step was deliberate, careful to avoid loose stones and clumps of dirt that threatened to betray their presence.

Time blurred as they pressed forward through the stifling tunnel. The weight of the earth above seemed to press down on Tyreal's shoulders, and the constant threat of collapse gnawed at his nerves. His thoughts raced. Who could be behind this? Whoever it was must believe fiercely in their cause to risk such measures for stolen food. While dissenters existed, as they always did in every kingdom, Tyreal had never encountered anyone in Tavia with grievances severe enough against the Thorncrests to warrant such drastic actions. No, this felt orchestrated by someone from beyond their borders.

As they ventured deeper, the packed earth gradually gave way to a wider expanse. The air shifted, cooler and infused with the scent of damp stone rather than earth. Hedontas extinguished the torch, and an ethereal blue light illuminated their path. The tunnel expanded into a cave, revealing the source of the glow.

Softly glowing algae lined parts of the cave walls like a shimmering curtain. The trio halted, kneeling in silence to assess their surroundings for signs of danger. Though concealed in shadow, they were aware of how exposed they would be upon emerging. The air was cool, and they could faintly hear the echo of the distant sea waves.

In the cave's heart lay a pool of water nestled amidst the rocky terrain, its surface reflecting the gentle glow of the algae. The light refracted off the water, casting intricate patterns of light and shadow that danced with each ripple. They crept from the tunnel, fanning out to take in the cave's full scope. Stalactites hung like jagged teeth from the ceiling, their pointed tips glistening with moisture, while the ground sloped downward toward the pool.

Ahead, a large cart held sacks of grain and various food items, its shadowed curve blending with the cave wall beside it. They moved behind the cart, peering cautiously around the corner of a new corridor.

Tyreal strained to listen, catching the sound of hushed voices ahead. He signaled to Andais and Hedontas, slipping into the focused calm he relied upon when violence loomed. Anticipation tingled in his muscles as they edged closer. Soon, a group of five men came into view, but it was the one in the center, with his back to them, who ignited a bloodthirsty rage within Tyreal. Clad in the uniform of a Tavian castle guard—one of Tyreal's own—a traitor whose betrayal had sealed his fate, a rapid approach to the end of his life.

He knew Andais and Hedontas shared his fury, though their years of training kept them silent and stealthy as they pressed against the corridor wall to listen.

"I'm telling you; they've caught on. Tyreal had the larder locked and ordered us to increase the guards in the courtyard. I barely slipped away to reach this cave unnoticed. We need to get the rest of this out and shift our focus to the rumors," the Tavian guard warned his companions.

A brutish man beside him, with a tangle of greasy hair over an equally grimy brow and a thick beard, spat on the floor. He wore a stained tunic that may have been white at some point in its life, but now looked mostly yellow and brown. "You think I give a shit about Tyreal Blackbane? We all know that bitch has had his balls in her pocket since she was a lass."

Two others snickered at the brute's jest, but the Tavian guard shook his head. "You're a damned fool if you underestimate him. He's obsessed with her, and that makes him dangerous. I'm already a dead man if he even catches wind that I'm helping you. Let's just get out of here."

"*Oh, that you certainly are,*" Tyreal thought, a wicked grin spreading across his face as he stroked his thumb over his dagger's hilt.

"Relax; they're all too busy with the funeral and the nobles to look too hard into anything for a couple of days," the brute said, moving closer to the guard and clapping him on the shoulder. "Besides, we're ready to part ways." Before the guard could respond, the brute sliced his throat, quick as a snake.

The man fell, gasping and clutching to the floor, grasping at his throat as if he could stop the fountain of crimson blood spilling out of it. The brute looked down at him with a twisted smile. "Think of it this way, Mendias: this is more merciful than what Tyreal would have done to you. Because while I may not be afraid of him, you were right to be. No one likes a traitor in their midst."

Tyreal, Andais, and Hedontas exchanged glances. With the guard dead, further eavesdropping seemed futile. With a silent nod, they emerged from the shadows, swords drawn but lowered, seeking to de-escalate the situation.

"That was rude," Tyreal drawled. "I had my own plans for killing him, and you just went and ruined it. So honestly, you owe it to me to make this easy and just surrender."

The brute turned, surprise flickering across his face before a wicked grin spread across his face. "Well, well, if it isn't Tyreal Blackbane himself. What a pleasant surprise."

"Pleasant?" Hedontas chuckled darkly. "You have a strange definition of pleasant, my friend. Now, why don't we all play nice and lay down your weapons?"

"Play nice?" One man laughed, a high-pitched, nervous sound. "We've heard stories about you lot. No thanks."

"Stories, is it?" Andais smirked. "You should know not to believe everything you hear. Though," he added with a wink, "in this case, they might be right."

The brute's grin faltered slightly. "Do you really think we're just going to roll over and surrender? We outnumber you."

"Outnumbered, maybe," Tyreal replied casually. "Outmatched? Absolutely not."

The brute spat, eyes narrowing. "Big talk for a man who hides in shadows."

"Big words for a man about to be bested," Tyreal retorted, his grip tightening on his sword hilt. "Last chance: surrender, and perhaps I'll let you live to see another day."

"Or," Hedontas added with a lazy smile, "we can skip to the part where we wipe the floor with you."

The air crackled with tension, a taut string ready to snap. The men shifted, hands twitching toward their weapons. "Well then," Tyreal said, a dangerous glint in his eyes. "I guess we're doing this the hard way."

With practiced precision, Hedontas moved, his sword flashing in the ethereal light as he parried blow after blow from the two men closest to him. It was almost effortless, and the old man looked renewed with life for the first time since Lorne had fallen ill. With each strike, he pushed them back. In one swift motion, he sank his blade into one's belly and spun to sever the sword hand of the other. The man fell, screaming, clutching the bleeding stump.

Andais faced off with the other man beside the brute, whom Tyreal had silently claimed, two gleaming daggers ready. Taller than his opponent, Andais nonetheless faced a skilled swordsman. They circled each other, movements cautious. Andais grinned wickedly, inviting the smaller man to strike. He lunged with a swift diagonal cut, aiming for Andais' flank.

Andais deflected the blow and countered with a flurry of strikes, his daggers a blur.

The clang of metal echoed through the chamber as their blades met, the force vibrating through them. The smaller man stumbled, off-balance, as Andais pressed forward. Andais' movements were precise as he unleashed a flurry of strikes with the daggers, which the smaller man tried to block with his sword. But he was no match for Andais' relentless speed. With a final thrust, Andais' dagger found its mark, slicing past the man's guard and forcing him to drop his sword, quickly subduing him.

Meanwhile, Tyreal and the brute circled, sizing each other up. "So the lapdog thinks he can best me? Cute. I meant what I said: that cunt has had your balls for as long as anyone can remember. I'm going to enjoy crushing you like a bug."

"By the gods, you talk too fucking much," Tyreal spat.

The brute's face twisted with rage, and he charged, fists swinging. "I'll kill your whore of a queen right after I kill you, you spineless cuck!"

"More skilled than you have failed, on both counts," Tyreal hissed, his voice dripping with menace. He dropped low, spinning his leg to sweep the man's feet from under him. As the man crashed to the ground, Tyreal thrust his sword upward, slicing from navel to throat. Blood and entrails spilled over Tyreal, and he relished in the heat of it, the sheer visceral carnage the only thing that soothed the rage inside him.

Tyreal stalked toward the man Andais had subdued. "Is anyone else in this cave?" he demanded, pressing the bloody tip of his sword against the man's throat. The man's eyes widened in terror as he gazed up at Tyreal, who must have appeared as a blood-soaked demon rising from the depths of Ganderly's nightmares. "Start talking, or I'll force every bit of his guts down your throat until you beg for death. Why are you stealing food, and who are you working for?"

"I swear, I don't know who!" the man screamed, panic rising as Tyreal lifted his sword once more. "Henry is the one who organized this... that's the big man you just killed. He only got instructions from a crow. Said he didn't know who it was, but I think that was a lie! He mentioned it was from another country!" The small man raised his hands in a plea, desperation etched across his features.

"What country?" Tyreal growled, his instincts prickling. He had a suspicion but needed confirmation before reporting back to Gwen.

"I don't know! Henry wouldn't tell us anything. All he said was they didn't want some," he hesitated, fear twisting his face, "a woman on the throne. Said she was too weak, and we needed to prove it. The quickest way to do that was to target the food supply, spread rumors that she was going to steal from the other districts, that people were already starving, and the castle was covering it up. I'm so sorry," he sobbed. "I just wanted to make some gold. I've got nothing against the queen, I swear. Please don't kill me!"

"No promises," Tyreal replied coldly, though a flicker of pity crossed his mind. "But you won't die today. Let's take these two," he nodded toward the man at Hedontas' feet, who had passed out from the pain of losing his hand, "back to the castle. We'll tend to their wounds and see what more they can tell us. Well, when that one wakes up, anyway."

They approached the cart filled with stolen supplies, rearranging it to restrain their two prisoners inside. Hedontas grinned, "I believe I'll let the young bucks pull this heavy cart. I'm but an old man, after all."

Tyreal rolled his eyes, cleaning his sword, hands, and face in the pool of water nearby. "An old man who just took down two men while barely breaking a sweat, but sure, we'll pull the cart. Wouldn't want to get a reputation. I'm nothing if not respectful to my elders."

CHAPTER THIRTEEN

Gwen barely slept in the days following the discovery of the tunnel, and she had little time to speak with Tyreal alone, except for reports regarding what they had discovered and the prisoners now residing in the dungeon. But now, after completing all the preparations and gathering the visiting royals, it was time for her father's funeral pyre.

As Gwen approached Pip's chambers, she acknowledged Jameson with a nod. Standing just outside the door, he placed a fist over his heart and bowed respectfully. Gwen had appointed him Captain of the Heir, and she was relieved to see that he and Pip were getting along well. His quick wit often drew laughter from the other guards, which was a large part of why Pip favored him. Though close to Gwen's age, Jameson's tousled yellow curls and boyish charm made him seem much younger. Tyreal had assured her though, that Jameson's skills were nearly as sharp as his own, and that Pip was in capable hands. Gwen tapped softly on the door. "Pip, it's time."

Pip turned from the window to face her, and her heart ached at the sight. Where she usually found a playful smile and a spark of mischief in his eyes, today they were somber and drawn. She offered him a sad smile. The court seamstress had delivered their funeral attire the night before. His doublet was a deep onyx, intricately stitched with crimson and gold roses on the shoulders. Tailored to his slender frame, it made him look older than she was accustomed to. The leather covering his breeches and boots matched the somber shade. "You look dashing in black. I wish it were for a happier occasion," she said.

He straightened his doublet, shrugging. Though he resembled her and their mother in coloring and eyes, the way he carried himself was every bit Lorne Thorncrest, amplifying her grief. He seemed so mature, much like she had when their mother died, yet he was still so young. Each moment felt like daggers in Gwen's ribs. "Aye, perhaps I'll wear black forever. It feels like we'll be mourning forever," he whispered.

Gwen shook her head. "No, we won't. It feels like it now, but eventually, every day will lighten. He and Mama are watching from the Everafter. They are with us still."

He eyed her doubtfully, finally speaking, "Your dress looks heavy. How can you walk in that thing?"

She glanced down at her stunning gown, crafted from ebony velvet and layered over black satin. The long flowing sleeves trimmed with delicate lace, and a gemstone-encrusted waist-cincher gathered the fabric to her curves. She hated it, no matter how beautiful it was, and he was right—it was dreadfully heavy. "With years of practice. Come on, let's see Papa off. We'll get through this together."

Fussing with his hair, she straightened his diadem before they departed. He shot her an annoyed look, and she raised her hands in surrender. They made their way out of the chambers, with Jameson falling in step behind them.

Despite Gwen's brave words to Pip, each step felt heavier than the last, as if she were trudging through the deep, sucking mud that existed near the spring. Panic bubbled in her chest. This was her first true appearance as queen before the general populace, and without Lorne, she felt completely lost. How had he managed this? Was he never worried? Did he ever feel so choked with fear that breathing became a struggle? If he did, he had certainly never shown it. She glanced at Pip, trying to calm herself with the thought that she needed to be strong for him. Yet her heart pounded as if it might burst from her chest.

As they entered the garden annex, all the guards came to attention. She scanned the group for Tyreal, longing for his reassuring presence. Finally, she spotted him making his way toward them. Clad in attire befitting the occasion, he looked as dashing as ever, though she hated his outfit, too. *Maybe I'll ban black from now on. I can do that kind of thing now. I can do whatever I want—except hide from this or marry the man I love.*

The thought was absurd, nearly making her laugh, but she quelled it—such a reaction would surely lead people to question her sanity. Her cheeks flushed, and despite her efforts to appear composed, she felt the weight of her anxiety. When her eyes met Tyreal's, she wondered if they showed the panic swirling within her.

His brow furrowed as he approached. "Men, please go out front and instruct the perimeter guards to mobilize the mourners for the family. I need to speak to Her Majesty and His Highness privately."

As the guards shuffled away, Gwen's façade of bravery crumbled. She took deep, gasping breaths. "I... can't... breathe."

Pip looked alarmed, moving to help her, but Tyreal stopped him with a hand on his shoulder. He stepped closer to Gwen, taking her hand

and forcing her to meet his gaze. "I'll help you. Breathe with me. In... then blow it out."

Her eyes darted around like a startled animal, but he gently took her chin, moving his face nearer until he filled her line of vision. "Breathe with me, Gwendolyn. Now." His voice was rich with emotion and commanding. She tried to listen, but her lungs refused to cooperate.

"He's supposed...to...be...here," she gasped, desperately struggling to mimic his calm, deep breaths.

Tyreal shook his head. "No. He's not. His time is done. He taught you and Pip well. That's how life works—it keeps moving on, whether you want it to or not. Keep breathing. I'm here." They stood there for a moment, just breathing, while Pip moved closer, looping his hand through the crook of her elbow.

"I'm scared. A queen shouldn't be scared." Tears filled her eyes, spilling down her cheeks. Tyreal brushed them away, his hand lingering against her skin. She leaned into his touch, closing her eyes and focusing on calming herself.

"Nonsense. A good leader should always have a healthy amount of fear; it keeps them sharp," he said fiercely. "But there's nothing to fear here. I'm right behind you, as I always will be. Your friends are up ahead, and Pip is beside you. Your father is where he belongs, and now it's time for you to go where you belong. He needs you one last time, sweet girl, and your people need you too."

Pip squeezed her elbow until she opened her eyes and looked at him. "Gwennie, you were right. Papa is with us. And it's time. You can do this. We can do this." He squared his small shoulders, and a wave of pride mixed with shame washed over Gwen. Her little brother was handling this better than she was. Surely, that was some sign from the Gods about her ineptitude. Despite her feelings, she let him lead her away from Tyreal and toward the gate. She swallowed hard, lowering the black lace of her mourning veil over her eyes, grateful for its concealment.

Cora stood waiting ahead with Tensha, their hands nearly brushing as they stood side by side. As Gwen approached, Cora stepped forward with practiced grace, adjusting the crown atop her head. She moved around her, fluffing and smoothing the veil trailing down Gwen's back while Tensha stood protectively nearby, her posture mirroring Tyreal's. "You're ready, Your Majesty," Cora said softly, squeezing Gwen's hand gently.

Tensha stepped forward, bowing low. "He was a good man. You are going to make a fine queen, even if you don't feel it now. Tavia is lucky to have you."

"Thank you, Tensha," Gwen replied thickly, appreciating the guard's words all the more for their rarity.

Tensha nodded, her eyes softening briefly before she returned to her position beside Cora.

The two women exchanged a fleeting look, a silent conversation that Gwen could guess the subject of. They were worried about her, everyone was. Further proof she wasn't cut out for this. She turned to Tyreal, giving a nod over her shoulder as he commanded the guards to open the gate wide.

Trumpets blasted, heralding the entrance of the queen and the prince. The gathered crowd along the walkway fell silent, their conversations ceasing as they turned to watch.

It was silent—no, not quite. The men continued to blow into the trumpets, cheeks puffed with effort. The ocean waves crashed against the shore, shifting the sand beneath their relentless assault before pulling it back out to sea. Gwen was still breathing, her heart still beating, but she heard nothing. Pip's lips moved beside her, and she blinked, frowning. He repeated himself when she did not reply. "This was a good idea. You did a good job."

The sounds of the world returned as she surveyed the scene before her. It had taken meticulous planning and compromise to ensure everyone could gather for the funeral while adhering to Tyreal's strict safety rules, especially after the recent treason among her guard. They finally agreed to allow castle staff and trusted townspeople to line the walkway to the beach, with a high guard presence interspersed among them and archers stationed along the castle walls, vigilant for any sign of danger.

The crowd on the beach was immense, a sea of faces stretching nearly as far as she could see, yet they were held back at a safe distance. The sight of so many gathered to honor King Lorne took her breath away.

Somber clouds loomed overhead, the perfect accompaniment to the day, the air thick with the weight of collective grief. Gwen and Pip continued down the path, silent except for the occasional sobs and wails from the mourners. She sucked in her breath as they finally reached the beach and spotted the pyre. She felt Pip do the same, and he tightened his grip on her hand.

Towers of wood and kindling rose high, carefully chosen logs hewn from trees across Tavia. The aroma of the wood mingled with the salty sea breeze, heavy in the air. Atop the pyre, tightly wrapped in fine white muslin, lay her father's body.

Malcolum stood waiting beside the pyre, dressed in dark ceremonial gowns that billowed around his legs in the breeze. He offered her a soft smile as she approached, bowing his head to her and Pip. Turning to face the gathered royals and dignitaries closer to them, he projected his voice to the masses somewhat farther off. The criers would take notes to help spread the word of what was said.

Gwen knew, dimly, that Malcolum was beginning. His voice resonated with solemnity, but the actual words were lost to her as she bowed her head in prayer at the appropriate moments. All she could hear was the crashing of sea waves. She thought of her last memories of her father and puzzled over the meaning of his last words. What name was important? Had that truly meant something, or was it just feverish delirium?

Malcolum finished speaking and looked at her expectantly. Gwen nodded, taking a deep breath as she carefully lifted the veil from her face, staring out into the crowd and the faces of everyone she cared about. With Tyreal and Pip near her, she found the strength to speak.

"Dearest friends and beloved people of Tavia, today we gather to bid farewell to my father, our beloved King Lorne. I stand before you with a heart heavy with grief yet brimming with gratitude. For I was lucky enough to know my father as an amazing man who shaped the very essence of who I am." She paused, the grief threatening to pull her under again. She glanced out into the crowd and saw Anya, who gave her an encouraging, sad smile. "From the moment I was born, especially after my mother's death, he devoted himself to nurturing and guiding me, instilling in me the values of compassion, integrity, and wisdom that define his legacy. He stressed to Prince Pippen and me the importance of always leading with empathy and humility." She turned to look at Pip, who was trying very hard not to cry, but wasn't succeeding. She reached for him and squeezed his hand as she continued, not caring if people thought it improper.

"It was not just in grand speeches or royal decrees that my father taught me the art of leadership, but in quiet moments that often went unnoticed. He led by example—sharing a meal with the castle staff after a long day, stopping to speak with farmers about their crops during his morning rides, or sending our best healer to the bedside of an ailing child, offering comfort without any courtly display. These simple acts of kindness were just as vital as any public decision. Each one reflected his unwavering commitment to our people and kingdom. Though his reign has ended, his legacy will endure, passed from me to my children, as Pippen will to his, and down through every Thorncrest line. Let us not mourn the loss of a king, but celebrate the life of a man who touched the hearts of all who knew him. To King Lorne! To Tavia!"

The crowd echoed her cry, and she turned to face Tyreal, seeking reassurance in his gaze. He nodded, his eyes shimmering with tears. Malcolum handed her and Pip the first torches, and together they turned to set them amongst the pyre, still clasping each other's hands. Slowly, flames ignited the kindling among the logs. She heard Pip whisper, "Goodbye, Papa."

Gwen swallowed hard, her eyes drifting to the sky. Tendrils of smoke rose, and she followed them with her gaze. "I promise to make you and Mama proud. Rest now, Papa," she whispered. Murmurs from the crowd mingled with the crackling of the fire and the call of seabirds echoing near the cliffs. Tyreal laid a hand on her shoulder and guided them away from the pyre, allowing other mourners to approach and set their torches down until the flames reached their zenith. They passed by in a procession, bowing and curtseying, offering words of sympathy. She kept her face passive and her breath steady, though she felt numb despite the tears streaking down her cheeks.

Finally, after what felt like an eternity, the last of the mourners retreated into the castle for the feast. Pip and Jameson walked back toward the castle with Cora and Tensha. Tyreal, Anya, and Max remained beside her. She stared into the fire silently, and her friends gave her space to gather her thoughts. Anya moved closer, laying her head on Gwen's shoulder and holding her hand.

"I didn't hear a word he said. I just kept thinking about Papa's last words. It may have just been the fever, but I can't shake them," Gwen confessed, her voice surprising herself.

"What were they?" Anya asked, unfazed. She always met Gwen where she was.

"He said something about a name. That he was so close to figuring it out, but he couldn't crack it. I don't know what he meant. What name?"

Anya shrugged. "The sisters always said that death brings clarity along for its solemn ride. Whatever it was, even if you don't understand it, it was important to him. Maybe you should ask them about it. If Lorne was researching a name, he would have reached out to them first, since they house all the records."

Gwen hummed thoughtfully. "I need to speak to them soon, anyway. I suppose we should head up to the feast now. This will burn all night, and we'll gather the ashes tomorrow to spread at sea." Anya nodded and moved back to Max's side. They walked ahead, leaving Gwen and Tyreal on the beach.

He moved close to her side. "You did wonderfully, Gwennie. Are you ready to go inside? If not, they'll wait until you are. They can wait all damn night if necessary."

She smiled gratefully at him. "I'm ready. Thank you. You were exactly what I needed, as always." Pressing her fingers to her lips, she blew a kiss toward the pyre one last time. "Goodbye, Papa. I love you."

CHAPTER FOURTEEN

They entered the dining hall, a vibrant sea of faces so abundant that makeshift tables had been arranged outside in the courtyard to accommodate the overflow. Flickering candlelight danced off the grand chandeliers suspended from the sturdy wooden beams on the ceiling, casting a warm glow over everyone inside. A large painting of King Lorne and Queen Asya, captured on his coronation day, loomed above the grand fireplace, tugging at Gwen's heart. The ache of missing them both was sharp and bittersweet.

The town crier announced their entrance, and everyone rose in acknowledgment of Gwen. She lifted her hand in gratitude, encouraging them to return to their conversations. Spotting Anya, she navigated through the crowd toward her friend. Anya stood with her arm linked with Princess Eliana of Obrye, a striking figure with her tall, slender frame clad in a flowing, deep purple gown. The garment draped elegantly over her, cinched at the waist with a delicate golden girdle in the style of Obrye. Long, billowy sleeves tapered into cuffs intricately detailed with golden thread, and a circlet of golden leaves adorned her shiny ebony hair, artfully braided and twisted into a low bun at the nape, embellished with small golden clips.

As Gwen approached, Eliana curtsied, which forced Anya to do the same. Gwen stifled a smile, aware of the eyes upon her.

"Princess Eliana, I'm so grateful you could make the journey to honor my father. You look stunning. How long has it been since our last summer with the sisters?" Gwen inquired warmly.

"It's been at least five summers, Your Majesty," Eliana replied, her deep voice quavering slightly. "King Lorne's friendship and support of my family were treasures, as is yours. It's an honor to stand with you and Tavia to remember him. My parents would have attended, but my sister is due any day now, and they didn't want to miss the birth of their first grandchild." A blush crept across her cheeks as she glanced nervously around, clearly uneasy among so many unfamiliar faces.

Once the Prince of Obrye, Eliana had embraced her true self when her magic manifested. Her mother, who had trained under the Sisters, recognized the signs and guided her through the transition, despite the scandal it ignited in Obrye. Gradually, the people accepted their new princess, but acceptance beyond her island home remained elusive.

Gwen reached out, squeezing Eliana's hand affectionately, ensuring those watching from her court noted the gesture. Although she couldn't fix everything with her position—especially her own tumultuous love life—she was determined to ease her friend's burdens. "You will always be welcome here in Tavia, Princess Eliana, and you are counted among our dearest friends," she proclaimed, her voice loud enough for all to hear.

Eliana offered a grateful smile and a small nod of appreciation.

Anya smoothly shifted the conversation, her tone bright and inviting. "You must tell me everything about this stunning gown you're wearing! That fabric looks so much more comfortable than all these pleats and ruffles I'm drowning in." She gestured to her dove-gray dress, its tightly cinched corset and layered skirts epitomizing Gagerland's formal fashion. Though undeniably elegant, it seemed even more restrictive and cumbersome than Gwen's.

As Anya and Eliana moved away, chatting amiably about their dresses, Gwen felt a sense of relief. Anya had a remarkable ability to make others feel at ease—her bright and pleasant demeanor was a balm in any company.

A low, deliberate clearing of the throat cut through the air, drawing Gwen's attention. She turned to see King Korian Drakon of Galeigh, his commanding presence impossible to ignore. Tyreal shifted closer to her, his hand settling on the hilt of his sword—a subtle but unmistakable statement.

King Korian's sharp, penetrating blue eyes scanned the room, absorbing every detail with an almost predatory awareness, yet revealing nothing of his thoughts. They felt cold and calculating, making Gwen shiver as if he could see right through her.

His once-rich copper hair, now streaked with gray, framed a sharp, angular face locked in a perpetual scowl. Everything about him was severe or excessive, from his harsh demeanor to his ostentatious love for jewels—an ironic display for a kingdom that constantly bemoaned its lack of resources. He wore more gems than Gwen and Anya combined: tiny diamonds studded the collar and cuffs of his doublet, while a sapphire as large as a robin's egg gleamed at his shoulder, fastening his cloak. Each of his fingers bore a ring, each one a gaudy testament to his wealth. She didn't like him—and she never would.

Gwen curtsied as he bowed in return, a customary acknowledgment between monarchs. "Your Majesty, thank you for coming to Tavia to honor my father. I hope your journey from Galeigh was pleasant. Did you travel by boat or by horse?" she asked, forcing a smile despite her discomfort in his presence.

"I was close to the Tavia border when I received my crow, so I could come by carriage. I arrived last night, though neither you nor your brother greeted me," he replied, irritation lacing his tone.

Gwen felt Tyreal's barely contained fury at Drakon's impertinence.

"I apologize for that. We had not received word on your arrival, and I'm told you came after both the prince and I had retired for the evening. With everything happening, I'm sure you understand. I hope my staff greeted you properly and provided accommodations befitting your station?"

Drakon frowned, muttering, "They did," as if annoyed he couldn't voice a complaint. Gwen noted his failure to address her as Your Majesty, an oversight that ignited her desire to confront him, yet she knew this was neither the time nor the place. Tyreal shifted, sensing her agitation; she knew if she signaled him, he would act without hesitation.

"Wonderful. Please excuse me, I need to signal for the feast to begin. I hope you enjoy your meal." She purposefully omitted his title, observing as he gritted his teeth in response. Tyreal muttered something under his breath as they moved toward the royal table, and she didn't need a seer to guess that it wasn't kind.

Pip had already taken his seat at the table, flanked by Jameson and Hedontas at his left. Gwen stood behind her chair, waiting for Tyreal to pull it out for her. Before sitting, she raised her glass, clearing her throat as all eyes turned toward her, awaiting her blessing to eat. "I, on behalf of Tavia, would like to thank you all for joining us to honor my father. As we partake in this meal, let us remember King Lorne. May his soul find peace in the Everafter, and may we draw strength from one another's company."

A murmur of agreement rippled through the crowd, and Gwen nodded to the serving staff to begin. Tyreal leaned close, his voice a low murmur above the clamor of the dining hall. "Are you okay? The feast will continue, even if you aren't here. Also, can I stab him?"

A reluctant smile crept onto her lips. "No, let's not start a war tonight, thank you. But I'm alright to stay for dinner. The worst of it is behind us now." Turning to Pip, who gazed silently over the crowd, she added, "How are you doing, Pip? I feel a bit better now that we've said our good-byes." He nodded, but remained quiet, lost in thought. He often needed moments of silence to process his feelings. "Later, if you want to talk, come find me, okay? I don't care about the hour—whenever you're ready."

The rich aroma of roast meat filled the room, mingling with the earthy scent of freshly baked bread and the subtle sweetness of root vegetables. As the first course was served—golden-brown savory pies—steam curled from the flaky crusts, filled to the brim with venison from the community hunts that Cook had marinated in spiced wine and herbs. The pies were perfectly browned, crisp to the touch. Gwen broke hers open, revealing the tender, glistening meat within, releasing an irresistible aroma that made her stomach rumble in anticipation.

"I'm surprised I'm actually hungry," she murmured to Tyreal, relief evident in her voice.

"Well, that's one less thing for me to worry about. You haven't been eating enough," he replied, nodding in thanks as a servant filled his mug with frothy ale.

As they ate, the room hummed with conversation, silverware clinking against plates, and the occasional crackle of the fire. Gwen tore off a hunk of bread, squeezing the warm softness between her fingers before dipping it into the savory juices on her plate. The food warmed her, easing the tension in her shoulders as she savored the feast prepared with such care by Cook and her staff.

Finding food supplies in the caves, along with the bounty from the community hunts and secured trade, had eased some of their worries about the approaching cold season. Yet, many questions lingered, particularly whether anyone had stolen from other parts of Tavia. So far, it seemed not, but the mystery of who sought to undermine her rule remained unsolved.

As the meal reached its conclusion, a group of musicians in the corner began to play. The harpist sat gracefully in her dark gown, fingers dancing over the strings, producing a cascade of delicate notes. Beside her, the flutist added depth to the melody, while two fiddle players wove their bows effortlessly across their instruments, harmonizing beautifully.

The music began with a soft, mournful tune, each note dripping with sadness, but as it progressed, the melody brightened, infusing the air with hope. It washed over her, reminding her of sitting near a window and watching a ray of sunshine breaking through a cloud bank on a stormy day. It may not remain sunny, but there was always the reminder that the sun was still *there*. It couldn't rain all the time. Gwen smiled broadly, applause bursting forth as the piece concluded, her spirits lifted.

Gradually, as the wine and ale flowed, guests began sharing fond and funny memories of the king. Some stories brought tears to her eyes, while others prompted laughter from her and Pip, as if her father's presence lingered among them. People sang along with the musicians, and the atmosphere transformed, mirroring the evolution of the music itself.

A jester stepped forward, dressed in vibrant robes decorated with patterns in deep, jewel tones that shifted with each movement. Merriflair's face was a canvas of dramatic make-up—crimson and gold highlighted his eyes, likely crafted from crushed berries and ochre mixed with beeswax. His lips were painted a deep wine hue from a paste of mulberries and oil, a technique he had once shown Gwen. The makeup gave him a striking theatrical and captivating appearance. Gwen's father had been quite fond of him, and seeing Merriflair brought a warm smile to her lips. He responded with a low, exaggerated bow, his robes sweeping the floor.

"If it pleases the queen, and is not deemed inappropriate, I would be delighted to continue lifting the spirits of everyone here, as your father often encouraged me to do," he announced.

Gwen nodded in approval, and he turned to address the room. With a gleam in his eye, he launched into a series of anecdotes filled with courtly drama and mischief. He recounted a tale about Lady Beatrice, a young widow renowned for her beauty and the vast estate she managed after her husband's untimely demise. Rumors of her search for a new partner had swirled through the court.

"Lady Beatrice, ever the heart's conqueror, set her trio of admirers on a quest to explore the world," Merriflair began, a grin spreading across his face as he gestured dramatically. "One ventured to distant Adaltus, another amassed wealth in Obrye, while the last remained within Tavia's borders. When she asked him why he hadn't gone out like the others, he answered with his heart in his hands." The room hushed, anticipation hanging thick in the air. "He said, 'You are my world; I need not look anywhere else.'" A chorus of 'aaws' erupted from the guests, and Lady Beatrice rolled her eyes indulgently.

"And who did she choose?" Merriflair paused for dramatic effect, letting the suspense build. "Why, the wealthy suitor from Obrye, of course! Lady Beatrice is many things, but a fool? Never!" Laughter erupted as Merriflair danced around, bowing theatrically.

He wasn't finished. Turning to Tyreal, his eyes sparkled with mischief. "And what of our valiant High Captain? Rumor has it he's not just our fiercest warrior, but a hopeless romantic—smitten with any dark, curly-haired barmaid!" He seized the hand of a nearby dark-haired lady, pulling her into an exaggerated dance. She pushed him away lightly, and he fell back dramatically, hands over his face.

Laughter filled the hall, and everyone clapped and whistled loudly. Gwen flushed, covering her mouth in an attempt to hide her smile. She glanced at Tyreal, who seemed torn between laughter and the urge to strangle Merriflair. The jester continued, "Tell me, Captain, do you have any coins left after your visits to Rosegate?"

"Move along to a new victim, you old buzzard!" Tyreal shouted, though no real heat underlined his words. Merriflair giggled, bowing low in response. He then turned to Luca Fitzsimmon and began another tale about how Luca had squeezed two coins until they screamed for mercy. Someone approached Tyreal, whispering something in his ear. Concern creased Tyreal's brow as he whispered back, and the man nodded before exiting with Andais in tow. Gwen noted the tension in Tyreal's right hand, flexing into a fist, a telltale sign of his unease.

"What is it?" she asked quietly, leaning in closer.

Tyreal's voice was low, meant only for her ears. "Our two prisoners were found murdered in the dungeons. There are signs someone may have attempted to enter the royal suites. Keep smiling and laughing as if nothing is wrong," he instructed.

Gwen forced a laugh, joining the crowd's merriment, though a knot of anxiety twisted in her stomach. "Are we safe here?" she murmured through clenched teeth, maintaining her smile.

"Aye, I don't believe anyone would be brazen enough to act in such a crowd. They likely hoped the festivities would distract our guards, which it seems to have done. But if you and Pip are with me, you're safe. Andais will sweep your rooms," Tyreal assured her, nodding toward Jameson and Hedontas. He gestured discreetly, catching their attention, prompting Jameson to casually adjust himself so that his arm was closer to Pippen's chair. Hedontas straightened in his seat but made no other adjustments to his body language.

Gwen willed herself to keep up the facade of enjoyment as Merriflair entertained the crowd. A flicker of worry gnawed at her thoughts—who could be behind these continued attacks? Disputes over land borders occasionally flared, particularly between King Drakon and the royals from Egrax due to Galeigh's peculiar borders which looped around the other country, but overall, the continent had known peace since the great war. There had been no clear attempts to undermine the ruling families; their intermingled lineages through marriage created a fragile web of alliances. Could it be a foreign threat from across the sea?

She scanned the room, observing the attendees. Andais returned, appearing slightly unsteady, clapping backs and shoulders while loudly thanking everyone for attending the banquet. He resembled someone who had indulged in too much ale, but anyone who truly knew Andais would recognize his demeanor as a performance, not reality. He would never shirk his duties like that.

He settled back into his chair beside Tyreal, a wide grin on his face as he leaned in closer to whisper to them both. "The suites are clear, and only trusted guards stand at their entrance.

We should get you both to your rooms sooner rather than later to ensure no further threats."

Gwen discreetly tapped Pip's leg four times beneath the table, a silent code taught by their father for moments of danger. Two taps meant to leave immediately, three to stay alert, and four to cause a distraction for a hasty exit. Pip inhaled sharply before yawning exaggeratedly. "Can we go soon? I'm bored and tired!" he whined, sounding every inch the spoiled child.

Gwen smiled indulgently. "But Merriflair isn't done yet! Are you sure you don't want to stay a little longer?"

"No! I'm tired and just want to go to bed!" Pip insisted, his voice rising in impatience. Gwen leaned down, kissing the side of his head gently.

"Aye, it has been a hard, long day." She stood, prompting everyone else to rise with her. Raising her hand to calm them, she declared, "Everyone, it seems our Prince has had his fill of this long day. I will also admit to being more than a little exhausted from the events. Thank you, Merriflair, for your wonderful performance. Please continue the revelry in honor of my father, but we are retiring for the night."

The crowd raised their cups. "To Queen Gwendolyn!"

Gwen smiled, bowing her head as she linked her arm with Pip's. She caught Anya's questioning look, and simply smiled back, knowing her friend's curiosity would drive her to find out why they left early. Turning to Tyreal, she raised an eyebrow, and he, along with the other guards, began clearing a path for their departure.

As soon as they exited the hall and distanced themselves from the crowd, Pip opened his mouth to question her, but she quickly shook her head. He fell silent, continuing to walk calmly beside her down the hallway toward their rooms.

Upon reaching the royal suites, where four guards now stood watch near the entrance, they stepped into Gwen's chambers. Once inside, she finally exhaled, tension unwinding from her shoulders. "What's going on?" Pip asked, his voice tinged with anxiety.

"The two prisoners we had for interrogation were found murdered," she explained.

"Apparently, the guard assigned to them excused himself for food, and when he returned, they were dead. I'll deal with him personally for abandoning his post," Andais added, fury tight in his words.

"Are we safe?" Pip echoed Gwen's earlier question, and she wrapped her arm around his shoulders, pulling him closer.

Tyreal answered swiftly, "Yes. Andais conducted a thorough search of the suites and found no one. The guards are searching every closet and hiding spot nearby. You're safe, but we need to separate the two of you."

Gwen's eyes widened in shock. "Absolutely not! Pip stays with me. If there's a threat, I want him here." She looked to Tyreal, hoping for support, but the expression on his face told her she would find none.

"Tyreal, please. I can't risk something happening to Pip, not so soon after Papa."

Hedontas stepped into her line of sight. "We all feel the same way, Your Majesty. But you know protocol. There are only the two of you now, and we cannot risk losing both of you and wiping out the Thorncrest line. Jameson, myself, and the other guards will keep him safe, just as you know that Andais and Tyreal will for you. Think of what your father would have done," he said.

Gwen gritted her teeth, breathing deeply. Logically, she understood he was right, but the thought of Pip being in danger away from her sent panic racing through her. She finally nodded sharply. "But if anything happens to the prince, I will personally see all of you on the gallows, mark my words." She shot a dark look at Tyreal, hating the feeling of being out of control once again. "That especially includes you, Tyreal Blackbane."

"Aye, Your Majesty, I harbored no doubts about that."

CHAPTER FIFTEEN

Hedontas and Jameson guided Pippen away from Gwen's room, while Andais took up his post outside her door. Gwen slumped into a chair, her hand covering her face for a moment before she reached up to remove her veil and crown. She laid them carefully on the table, enveloped in silence.

Tyreal observed her with concern, recognizing her struggle to process the chaos of recent events. He knew she was wrestling with her emotions—particularly her rage due to his decision to send Pip away. He could relate; rage simmered within him too—fueled by the thought of her in danger and the unsettling possibility of another traitor among them. Beneath that anger, though, his worry for her overshadowed everything else.

She had lost her father, and now enemies gathered around her, growing bold enough to strike with violence. His chest tightened at the thought of all she carried alone. And yet, he was forced to keep his distance, to offer only what comfort was allowed. If only things were different... He clenched his jaw, shaking the thought away. It served neither of them—never had.

"I need to get out of this dress. It's too heavy, and I can't fight in it." Her voice was quiet but firm, the resolute edge in her tone bringing him a measure of relief. She was strong—stronger than anyone gave her credit for. As long as she wasn't giving up, he knew she could endure whatever came next.

"You won't be doing any fighting on my watch. Not with me here to guard you."

She rose from the chair, turning her back as her fingers struggled with the cords of her waist-cincher. Tyreal stepped in silently, his hands brushing hers aside with practiced ease. As he worked the black ties loose, his jaw tightened. He hated the damn law that kept him from truly being hers. He didn't just want to ease her burden in fleeting moments like this—he wanted to fight for her, stand with her, always.

The cincher dropped into his hands, and he folded it carefully. Gwen exhaled deeply, her shoulders easing as the weight lifted. "Bloody crows, you aren't lying. This thing is heavy. Is it worth a small fortune? Are these real gemstones?" he questioned.

He tried to divert his focus away from her as she unbuttoned the small black buttons of her velvet gown, instead examining the craftsmanship of the cincher he held. Gold roses with tiny red rubies nestled among their petals outlined its edges, while black lace veiled the golden silk beneath that contained the hard boning of the corset.

"Aye. It's only brought out from under lock and key for royal funerals. I suppose it could be worn at a wedding since it's quite beautiful. But people are so superstitious about black at weddings." She shrugged off the heavy black velvet overdress and draped it over a chair. "I'm going to change. Then we should meet with Andais to discuss a plan on how to handle this."

She moved away from him, disappearing behind her dressing screen. Tyreal stepped over to the table laid out with her drawing supplies. "I can plan with Andais, Gwennie. You should really try to get some rest. Today, of all days, let me handle things."

He heard her soft sound of disagreement followed by silence, and the corner of his mouth tipped upward, amused by her likely upcoming argument against his care. It was a strange mix of endearing and incredibly frustrating, but he wouldn't change her if he could.

His fingers traced over the large parchment, pushing aside scattered charcoal stubs and pigment sticks to reveal the drawing beneath. His breath caught at the raw emotion captured in Gwen's work. A figure, unmistakably Gwen, stood at the center, her back to the viewer. Her form was etched in deep, velvety strokes, distinct from the surrounding scene. The skirts of her gown, touched with vibrant colors, grew muted and sad as they rose toward her heart. She held her crown aloft, its bright gold cloaked in flames. Shadows swirled around her, creeping toward the light, threatening to consume her entirely.

"Oh, Gwennie," he whispered to himself, his heart aching. He longed to sweep her up, to escape to the mountains, where they could pretend to be anyone but themselves, raise beautiful dark-haired babies near his mother's home. He knew that was a fantasy, but for a fleeting moment, the vision was clearer than the picture before him.

A sound snapped him from his reverie, and he hoped she wouldn't notice the sheen of tears threatening to spill from his eyes. He turned to face her, about to ask if she would let him care for things while she rested for once in her damn life, but the words faded.

Gwen stood before him, nude, with Skensington's blade pressed to her throat, a tiny drop of crimson pooling around the tip. Behind them, the large painting that concealed the corridor between him and Gwen's chambers stood open. Instinctively, he reached for his own blade, but

Skensington pressed harder. "Ah, ah, Captain. I wouldn't do that if I were you. I'll have her pretty throat split before you can even draw it. And yes, you'll surely kill me afterward, but it won't bring her back. Will you leave Tavia with a child king?"

"You're already a dead man, Skensy. It's just a matter of how much I make you beg for the end before it happens." Tyreal's body had gone completely still, his eyes locked on that tiny drop of crimson rolling down her pale throat.

Skensington let out a sharp, bitter laugh. "Perhaps. Likely even. Not from you, though. Maybe not at all if I can still deliver our queen here to Lovell as promised." He squeezed one of Gwen's breasts painfully, pressing his lips to her hair, inhaling sharply. "I wonder if he would still want you if you weren't intact. Though I suppose I could sample the goods and blame it on the captain here. Everyone has suspected you two of fucking for quite some time."

Tyreal had to fight the urge to lunge at him, forcing himself to remain locked in place. He looked into Gwen's eyes and found her gaze steady, unafraid. The blade was pressed too tightly against her skin for her to risk speaking, but she glanced toward the fireplace and the glowing embers smoldering within. The fire had yet to be stoked, and she shivered dramatically, widening her eyes at him as if trying to signal something. His mind raced, trying to decipher her intent. Clearly, she wanted him to tend to the fire, but why? Surely it wasn't merely because she was cold.

He forced himself to relax, choosing to trust her plan and see how it unfolded. If nothing else, he could keep Skensington talking and try to alert Andais. "She's still intact, thanks to you. I've been trying to get into her bed for years, and I think I could have pulled it off just now." He shot Skensington an annoyed look. "I wondered when you'd show up again. My spies say Lovell's unhappy you didn't convince the queen to accept his proposal—he blames you for not explaining how she'd react to his absence. Bit unfair, if you ask me."

"It is unfair! I tried to tell him he needed to come in person, but he thought Lorne had already told her he's been proposing for years. Lorne is the only reason they aren't already married, and I'm left to deal with all of this!" Skensington whined, but then seemed to remember his precarious situation. He tugged Gwen backward a step, keeping the blade tight against her skin.

Tyreal moved toward the fireplace, keeping his steps slow and deliberate. "Lovell's men made me the same offer—to bring her to him. We don't have to be enemies here. With me backing you, we could leave this castle together, claim it's a diplomatic visit. Say you convinced her to make peace with Adaltus."

He turned his back, forcing himself to appear calm despite the tension knotting his shoulders. Reaching for the fire poker, he jabbed at the embers, letting the crackle of the fire fill the silence. Skensington needed to believe he wasn't a threat—and that Gwen's safety wasn't his primary concern.

"Why would you do that?" Skensington scoffed. "Everyone knows you're obsessed with her. Hell, you just threatened me the other day for speaking out of line to her. And what are you doing by that fireplace? I mean it, Blackbane. I'll kill her if you try anything."

"What else would I be doing at the fireplace? Trying to escape? She's shivering, and I've been trained since childhood to pay attention to such things." He continued to stoke the fire, hoping he appeared convincing and that Gwen had some sort of plan. "As for being obsessed with her, I'm obsessed with her body. I've been trying to lie with her for years. At every turn, she refused me because I don't have the right blood or enough coin. All I wanted to know was if royal cunt tasted better. But apparently, I won't get the chance. You need my help to get out of here. I want to be a rich man who can get whatever kind of pleasure I want. I see no reason we can't both get what we want." He grabbed a handful of kindling from the woodbin and tossed it onto the stoked embers, watching them catch flame.

Tyreal turned from the flickering warmth of the fire and poured himself a glass of wine. "Would you like some?" he asked, his tone calm, almost casual. He let his gaze flick to

Gwen's nude form, lingering just long enough for Skensington to notice. "She is beautiful, isn't she? If you plan to indulge, I'll have to join in—especially if I'm the one who takes the blame. It's only fair." He sipped the wine, his eyes dropping briefly to the streak of blood on her throat, his rage held tightly in check.

"Hmph. We can't indulge without her spilling the truth to Lovell once they're wed. So, no—I can't. But you might be right about needing your help to escape. No one would believe you'd let her leave without you." Skensington frowned, his gaze distant as he weighed his options. Tyreal's eyes flicked to the blade pressed to Gwen's throat. Skensington's arm drooped slightly, fatigue creeping into his grip. He wasn't a trained killer. If Tyreal could move the blade even a fraction, the advantage would be his.

"That's the problem," Skensington continued, his voice bitter. "I had a plan, but the guards returned too soon. Only fate led me to that hidden corridor in your room—proof that the gods favor me. Tavia shouldn't be ruled by a woman."

Skensington fidgeted, biting his lip as he thought aloud. "Yes, you will help me. Obviously, it's a plan I would've devised myself if only I had time to think. Lovell will be thrilled. He'll likely triple what he intended to pay me, and I suppose I can share some with you. This has all worked out rather nicely. The gods truly are on my side." He beamed, inching the blade away from Gwen's throat.

Gwen extended her hand toward the fireplace, and time seemed to blur for Tyreal. She conjured a ball of flames that hovered toward her, settling over Skensington's hand. The flames danced without touching her skin, a mesmerizing display. Fear constricted Tyreal's heart as he struggled to comprehend what was happening. Skensington screamed, swatting at the flames and losing his grip on the blade. In that moment of shock, Gwen raced to Tyreal, and his training surged back to the forefront. He drew his blade and unclipped his cloak, tossing it over her.

As he moved toward the burning man, Andais burst into the room, weapon drawn. Taking in the chaotic scene, he shot Tyreal a wild look, eyebrows shooting up. "It seems we've located our intruder," Tyreal remarked dryly.

"I see that. Care to explain how this happened? I checked this room thoroughly. Ah—" Andais halted mid-sentence, noticing the askew painting and the darkened corridor behind it. "That would have been helpful to know about. Were you aware of it?"

"Aye. Only the High Captain and the ruler know of its existence." Tyreal seized a pitcher of water and doused Skensington's flaming flesh, who was still howling in agony.

"And neither of you thought to investigate before relaxing your guard? You both fucking know better than that," Andais snapped, frustration lacing his words. Tyreal winced at the reprimand, and Andais, clearly deciding to drop the subject for now, added, "I suppose you handled the situation. She's safe, and that's what matters. How did he end up on fire all the way over there?"

"Tyreal used the ash shovel to toss a hot ember at him after I ducked out of the way," Gwen said, emerging from behind Tyreal, his cloak enveloping her small frame.

"She's a damned liar and a witch! She conjured the fire from thin air and threw it at me!" Skensington shouted, desperation coating his voice.

"Clearly, he's delusional from pain. None of that is important, though. What *is* important is that he broke into my room, held a blade to my throat, and groped my naked body—all because Lovell and Adaltus are determined to wed us by any means necessary. I want this piece of garbage interrogated until he spills every bit of information he has about their intentions. Then, just as High Captain Blackbane promised, he will beg for the end of his life." Gwen's voice was ice, her hands clenched as fury radiated from her.

Andais glanced at the clean ash shovel still propped against the fireplace and then back at Tyreal, raising an eyebrow. Tyreal kept his face neutral, and finally Andais shrugged, clearly deciding he didn't care about the lie. "Yes, my queen. I believe we can manage that. Do we still want to keep the corridor a secret?"

Tyreal nodded. "Aye, we'll tell everyone we suspected he was hiding here and laid a trap for him."

Andais seized Skensington, pinning his arm painfully behind his back. "I'll take him down to the dungeons to await your orders. Might want to dirty up that shovel before anyone else enters, though. I'll send for Cora to assist Her Majesty."

CHAPTER SIXTEEN

Gwen watched Tyreal as she removed his cloak, and pulled her shift back on over her head. A heavy silence had settled between them since Andais and Skensington had left. He searched her room and the corridor relentlessly, as if other attackers might still lurk in the shadows. Cora would arrive soon, and if they were going to speak openly about what had happened, it had to be now.

"Are you going to tell me what you're thinking, or should I arrange for someone to put you in a cell next to Skensington and torture it out of you?" The poor joke fell flat, and she winced, wringing her hands together. The urge to pick at her thumb was nearly overwhelming as she waited for him to respond—anything would do. She had just revealed the most significant secret she possessed, one she had sworn a blood oath never to disclose, and yet all she faced was silence.

"Was that what I think it was?" he asked quietly, his gaze fixed blankly on the fire.

She fidgeted, pacing around the room, struggling to formulate her response. "If what you think it was, was magic, then yes, it was."

He turned to her, his expression dark and unreadable, flexing his hand on the hilt of his sword. "Explain." The word emerged harshly, like a command he might give to one of his men who had acted out of line. She swallowed hard, suppressing the urge to respond defensively. She had just dropped a world-altering revelation in his lap; the least she could do was allow him the time to process it.

Gwen took a deep breath, trying to steady herself. She twirled the curls of her hair around her fingers, letting each ringlet straighten before springing back into place as she pondered how to begin. "How much do you remember from our history lessons about the founding families?" she finally asked.

Tyreal's dark look softened into confusion. "The gods blessed the nine royal families and granted them the nine kingdoms that make up Valine."

"Partially true," Gwen replied. "There were ten. When they first arrived, the land was rich with fertile farmland and lush forests. For a time, there was peace. But soon, the powerful men in each family believed they should rule over all the land. And as powerful men are always prone to do—they fought."

Gwen watched him closely, wishing she could climb inside his head and see what he was thinking. She had heard this story so many times growing up that she could recite it from memory, but to him, it was all new. How many times had she longed to tell him? Yet, she never pictured it happening quite like this.

"They didn't fight like you would. They wielded powerful magic that could shape and bend matter—magic we know little about today. For over a generation, they battled. The land was scarred by relentless magical onslaughts. Fields yielded blighted crops, and the settlers lived in fear and starvation. You can still see remnants of that time if you look closely. The marks on Thorncliff's gates are just one example. Something had to change. The gods had turned away from us."

Tyreal ran a hand through his hair, clearly mulling over her words. "So, what changed? It's been a long time if no one knows magic exists—or at least, *most* people believe it doesn't." A hint of anger laced his voice, mixed with something deeper that eluded her grasp.

Gwen sighed. "A group of women came together and declared enough was enough." Tyreal shot her a disbelieving look, his eyebrows furrowing. She shrugged, her hands raised. "I'm serious. My ancestor, Myaessa Thorncrest, sent secret messages with the crows to the women of the other families, summoning them to the Misty Mountains. Women from nine of the families answered the call. They understood they had to set aside their differences and end the war to protect their children and future generations. Thus, the Sisters of the Mist were born."

"What about the tenth family?" he asked.

"According to our records, there were no women left in the tenth family. They were the most violent and had orchestrated the attack that killed Myaessa's husband and child. She might not have even reached out to them. We simply don't know." Gwen made herself sit in a chair and motioned for him to join her, but he shook his head, remaining standing. Something about his refusal unsettled her, though she couldn't pinpoint why. "What we know is that they pooled their magic and created a spell unlike anything the world or the gods had ever seen. A spell to eradicate magic once and for all—mostly. But it required a major sacrifice. Myaessa volunteered. She had already abdicated her throne and lost her family. It was noble, but also tragic."

"I've known soldiers who laid down their lives for similar reasons, though on a far less grand scale," Tyreal said, his tone softening slightly. He finally sat across from her, though he perched on the edge of his seat, still unready to relax. "Clearly, the spell worked, but what happened?"

"Chaos," Gwen replied simply. "The spell rippled across the land, erasing most magic but leaving behind small embers among the women of the ruling families. This residual magic was weaker and less understood than before, and it remained only in a few of them. They hid this, knowing the repercussions if men discovered that magic still existed, even in diminished form.

"We never learned what happened to the tenth family. The sisters feared that if any embers of magic remained within them, they might one day return to Valine with dangerous intentions. Eventually, the nine families had to come together to navigate this new magic-less world. They divided Valine into the kingdoms we know today and formally established the Sisters of the Mist.

"The Sisters were tasked with preserving history and creating laws to maintain peace. Unofficially, they became a sanctuary where royal women with traces of magic could train and learn to control their powers."

His eyes met hers, and a muscle twitched along his jaw. "So that's where you went every summer. I presume this magic stuff is also the reason for the law about royals not marrying commoners—to keep the magical bloodlines pure." She winced but nodded, acknowledging the uncomfortable truth. She wanted to refute him, but how could she? That *was* indeed the reasoning behind the Sisters' law. "That's what I thought. I guess all I really need to know is why you didn't tell me and how many others have hidden this from me?" His tone dripped with bitterness, and Gwen felt the sting of his words.

"I couldn't. We took a blood oath not to reveal it. I don't even think my father knew. I've wanted to tell you so many times. No one else in this castle knows—well, except Anya and Eliana. They have magic as well. The whole point of our training was to ensure that if the tenth family ever returned, we could use our magic to defend ourselves and our lands."

"This affects your security; I should have been informed." He stood up and began pacing again. "As if it wasn't enough that I nearly got you killed tonight. Now I find out you've been keeping secrets from me." His voice trailed off, and he looked away, as if he hadn't meant to speak that part aloud.

"Tyreal, you didn't almost get me killed. It was a mistake. Nobody but me, you, and Hedontas were supposed to know about that corridor. We couldn't have guessed he would stumble upon it by chance." She approached him and placed her hand on his arm, but he jerked away, making her recoil inwardly.

"No. I should have guessed. It's my duty to anticipate every danger lurking around every corner. It's the only good I am to you!" Tyreal's voice trembled with suppressed fury. "Instead,

I was thinking with my heart, focusing on caring for the woman I love like a husband would, rather than how a guard should think about his charge. My common blood might not be worth much to your magical royal womb—" he hissed, his temper flaring.

Gwen gasped, her eyes widening, but he pressed on. "But I'm usually good at my job. I failed today because I was too caught up in this little make-believe bubble we created, pretending to be something we'll never be. That mistake won't happen again. From here on out, I am your High Captain, and nothing more. Good night, *Your Majesty.*" He spat the words and hurried out, seemingly desperate to escape her presence.

Gwen stood there, staring at the closed door, then instinctively flung herself onto the bed, muffling her scream into a pillow to prevent the guards from bursting in. How had everything gone so wrong so quickly? Her father was dead, her country under attack, and now the man she loved—the only one who truly understood her—was turning away from her. She had never felt more alone.

The panic she had felt that morning on her way to the beach surged back, tightening her chest like a vise. She sat up, gasping for breath, but her thoughts screamed inside her head like a chorus: *Useless. You're useless and alone. You'll never be as good a ruler as your parents were.* Gwen sobbed silently, struggling to fill her lungs as she dimly sensed Cora's entrance. She could hear her trying to speak in a panicked voice, but it felt distant—like she was underwater, and Cora was above.

A little later—it could have been moments or hours—Gwen felt a firm grip on her chin, forcing her to look up into Anya's sapphire-blue eyes. She heard Anya say something to Cora, followed by the soft click of the closing door. Anya's fingers gripped her shoulders with an intensity that would have been painful had Gwen not felt so numb. Abruptly, Anya's magic surged forward, crashing against Gwen's mental defenses. In her youth, Gwen had imagined Anya's magic as storm-driven waves crashing against the cliffs on which Thorncliff castle was built. Now, as an adult, it felt more like a tidal wave.

The sensation was immediate and overwhelming. A fiery burn scorched Gwen's consciousness while an icy chill settled over her body. The dual assault on her senses made her head spin, and she gasped. Sharp pain radiated through her psychic barriers, threatening to shatter them unless she countered Anya's relentless magic. Amidst the pain, the panic that had choked her thoughts began to dissipate, evaporating like morning fog. Anya's eyes met hers, and her friend smiled wickedly. "That's right, Gwennie. Get out of your head and fight me."

Anya moved off the bed and pulled a fireball from the flames in the fireplace, just as Gwen had done with Skensington, hurling it toward her. Gwen rolled instinctively, twitching her hand to force the fireball back into the fireplace. Anya didn't attack again; she simply stood there, eyebrow raised. "Are you done?"

Gwen nodded, her lip trembling as she sobbed. Anya's face softened, and she climbed onto the bed, gathering Gwen into her arms and pressing her against her small frame. "Tell me everything, sweets, so we can figure out what to do."

So she did.

Tyreal dropped into a chair at the alehouse, exhaustion weighing him down. He had finally gotten Skensington to divulge details about Lovell, then rounded up the two guards involved in the murder of the prisoners, locking them in the dungeon to await his attention tomorrow. When he had gone to Gwen's room to share what he had learned, it was Anya who met him at the door.

"She's asleep. Finally. No thanks to you and your *complete* mishandling of this entire situation." Her voice was even icier than Gwen's when she was angry. Tyreal opened his mouth to defend himself, but she shot him a sharp look, and he snapped it shut. His own well of self-loathing ran deep enough at that moment that he had no defense to offer. She shifted slightly, allowing him a glimpse of Gwen, who, indeed, lay asleep. "Whatever you need to tell her can wait until morning. I'll stay here tonight with her. I've already informed my husband. Goodnight, *High Captain.*" With that, she slammed the door in his face.

Unwilling to return to his room and be alone with his thoughts—haunted by the image of that crimson drop of blood running down Gwen's neck—he did what he usually did when everything felt overwhelming. He cleaned up and made his way to Rosegate.

"Captain Blackbane. A pleasure, as always, to see you, though unexpected on such a somber day. What can I get you? Just an ale, or do you perhaps have other appetites that need fulfilling?" Tyreal looked up to see Tish regarding him with a curious and suggestive gaze.

Tish, the bar's owner and his friend, might have been a good match for him in another life. But she had no desire to be his—or anyone's wife. Widowed young, she had inherited the bar and raised her boy alone, content without another man in her life. It was just as well; Tyreal's heart wasn't available.

"Haven't you heard, Tish? I'm practically a married man now." He waved his wrist, where the gold band sat—a curse that would damn him for the rest of his mortal life, and likely into the Everafter. His words tasted bitter, like his mood.

"I had. Though you aren't *actually* married, so it doesn't change my question." She raised an eyebrow and placed her hand on top of his. He took a deep breath, considering her offer. They had enjoyed each other's company more than a few times, with no expectations of one another, and it had always helped take the edge off lonely nights. Plus, Tish was gorgeous—long dark hair piled high upon her head, with her corset cinched tight enough that her full breasts nearly spilled out.

He almost said yes. He should have said yes. He would not darken Gwen's door as anything more than her captain ever again. Gold band or not. But he flashed back to that damned crimson droplet and the hurt on Gwen's face when he had lashed out at her, and his stomach soured. He shook his head. "No, Tish. Thank you. Just the ale tonight. My mood is foul, and I'm not fit for anyone's company. I just want to get drunk."

She nodded, unaffected by his rejection. She grabbed a mug and poured it full of ale. "Aye, well, I can certainly help you with that, High Captain."

CHAPTER SEVENTEEN

Tyreal stirred, caught in the liminal space between wakefulness and dreams. He felt an urgent need to go to her, though he couldn't recall who *her* was. The door creaked open, and instinctively, he reached for his blade. The dim room was suffused with the faint pre-dawn light that barely penetrated the heavy curtains. His heart raced as he blinked through bleary eyes, struggling to focus.

As his vision sharpened, he recognized Andais' familiar silhouette. Tyreal let out a weary sigh, loosening his grip on the blade as he sank back onto the pillow. "Go away. Has the sun even risen yet, you insufferable man?" he groaned.

Andais simply walked over and yanked the curtain open, flooding the room with bright morning sunshine. Tyreal cursed, pulling the pillow over his head, while Andais laughed, dropping into a chair. "Got a bit drunk, did ya, you lazy bastard? A little torture and murder not enough to take the edge off?" He propped his feet up on Tyreal's table and began cleaning under his fingernails with a small blade, utterly unconcerned. "Did you do anything else fun to dull the pain besides indulge in ale?"

"Leave me alone," Tyreal muttered, his voice muffled by the pillow.

"Tempting, but no. One of my jobs as Lower Captain is to call you out when you're being an ass—"

"Not part of your duties."

"Is now," Andais countered. "Cora told me this morning that our queen had a hell of a panic fit after you stormed out of her room."

Tyreal bolted upright, concern flashing in his eyes as he looked at Andais, desperate to understand. Andais silenced him with a glare, his playful demeanor vanished.

"After," Andais added, "she was attacked and held at knifepoint. On the day we burned her father. So tell me, will I need to prepare for the queen to be even more upset when a rumor circulates that you were fucking a barmaid while she lay in bed sobbing?" He leaned forward, and despite his calm demeanor, the same darkness

Tyreal sometimes saw in his own eyes mirrored back at him.

Tyreal sat up, swallowing hard. His head protested the movement, the room tilting unnaturally. Bloody crows. It had been a colossal mistake to drink so much. But then again, he'd been making plenty of those of late. What was one more? "No. I just got drunk, which I deeply regret now."

"Good. Now you need to tell me what the fuck is going on. I thought we agreed that you two would handle your mess while Cora and I dealt with the aftermath." Andais leaned back in his chair, resuming his nail cleaning.

"I never agreed to that plan. You just informed me it was an option. But..." Tyreal trailed off with a sigh. "We came close, not physically exactly. More emotionally, I suppose? That's why I forgot about the corridor. That's why Skensington had his filthy hands on her. And why I haven't noticed that *three* of our guards have turned traitor. It has to stop."

Andais snorted. "That's bullshit. But I can tell I won't sway you from this stubborn ass decision—not yet. So best get up and clean yourself up. Cora and Princess Anya have already risen, and she'll be waiting for you to report what we learned from Skensington."

Tyreal groaned again. "I think it would be better if you reported what was said. I need to gather my wits. Plus, I want to deal with the traitors."

Andais laughed. "Oh no, that's a solidly High Captain duty. I didn't piss anybody off, so I'm not getting stuck in a room with the two of them. Princess Anya seems the type to be sweet until she's not. No, I believe I will take care of our traitors downstairs." He rose, face suddenly serious. "All jokes aside, what we learned last night, you need to handle. If she wants us to go to war over this, it'll be you who readies the army."

Tyreal shook his head. "She'll do anything to avoid war. We've had peace on this continent for centuries. Gwen—" He grimaced, catching himself. "Her Majesty will not want to be the one to break it, no matter what Lovell is doing. If it were up to me, I'd ride to Adaltus myself and handle it. Or at least send an assassin. But I know she'll likely refuse that idea."

Andais nodded. "Likely so. It would be so much simpler if she didn't, though. Come find me afterward, and we can figure out our next steps."

Freshly bathed and dressed, Tyreal stumbled into the library, still suffering from a pounding headache and bloodshot eyes. He pushed open the door, wincing as sunlight streamed through the tall stained-glass windows, casting vibrant patterns on the polished wooden floor. He squinted against the brightness, scanning the room filled with towering bookshelves for Gwen.

He spotted Alric first, the hulking man hard to miss, standing nearby with a knowing grin. Gwen, Anya, and Max were seated at a small table near a window, instead of the larger one she used for council meetings. Gwen's radiant smile lit up the room as she laughed easily with her friends. Cora had tied a black ribbon around her throat to conceal the mark from Skensington's blade, but it complemented the crimson silk gown edged in black lace that she wore. Custom dictated that she return to some color now that the pyre was behind them, but she would keep black on her person for six moons.

Tyreal's heart tightened at the sight of her smile, a stark contrast to the look she wore before he left her room the previous night. The memory of their fight lingered, guilt gnawing at him. Seeing her happy with her friends made him acutely aware of the chasm that had opened between them, yet he still believed he was doing the right thing. When she saw him, her smile faded, and her court face slipped into place. A painful pang hit him in the gut, and his confidence in his plan wavered.

"High Captain Blackbane, nice of you to join us. Were your efforts in the dungeon fruitful?" she asked, setting her teacup down on its saucer, her gaze fixed on him as if he were a stranger.

"Yes, Your Majesty. I gathered the information we sought. It's up to you if I share it now in front of your guests or if you prefer it alone. It's quite serious." Tyreal kept his posture straight, avoiding her eyes. She glanced at Max, and all three of them frowned.

The prince leaned forward, brow furrowed. "Could this potentially affect my kingdom?"

"Or my parents?" Anya added.

Tyreal remained silent, waiting for Gwen to decide how she wanted him to proceed. He liked both the prince and princess, but his loyalty lay with Tavia and Gwen. She nodded softly, granting him permission. "At the moment, from what I've gathered, no. But there is a potential down the road if it isn't dealt with."

Max exchanged glances with Alric, who had perked up at Tyreal's words. Everyone turned to Gwen, awaiting her decision. She chewed on her lip, deep in thought. Finally, she spoke. "I trust everyone in this room implicitly. They're already aware of the attack on the food larders. If this new information could impact any of us, we should discuss it openly. My father always said that secrets breed more secrets."

Tyreal wanted to give her a pointed look, to jab at her magical secret, but decided this wasn't the time or place. Instead, he nodded and began to speak. "Skensington gave us the names of two guards he bribed yesterday to kill the prisoners in the dungeons. He believed one of them was also working for Lovell. When we searched their rooms, we found evidence to support that. They're currently in the dungeon with the Lower Captain. We will root out the treason corrupting the guard *today*. We have an all-guard meeting tonight where we'll talk with everyone at once. For safety reasons, it will require you and Prince Pippen to attend, but I won't lie—it won't be pleasant."

Gwen grimaced and shook her head. "I do not think Pip should be subjected to that unpleasantness at his young age."

Max and Tyreal exchanged a look. Max turned back to Gwen. "Your Majesty, I was younger than Prince Pippen when I first began attending my father's punishments. It's not pleasant, but neither is the truth I'm about to give you. There has already been one attempt on your life. If someone succeeds, Pippen will be king. The time to hide him behind your skirts has passed," he said firmly, though not unkindly.

She glowered at her friend. "Hiding behind my skirts? Really? You make me sound like an overbearing mother." When no one disagreed, she sighed. "I suppose you're right. I trained for years to become queen, and I'm still finding it overwhelming. Pippen will need all the preparation we can give him in case something happens to me."

"Nothing is going to happen to you." Tyreal's voice was gruff and forceful. "We were ill-prepared last night. It won't happen again. Also, I don't believe there's a threat to your life—not based on what Skensington told us and what I've gathered from my spies' crows. He didn't plan on killing you. Lovell wants you very much alive. Adaltus seeks to control Tavia—not by outright invasion, but through subterfuge. He knows he could never best our armies, and the cliff protects Thorncliff too well."

"So if he won't invade, how does he plan to control us? Does he really think that if I marry him, I'll just roll over and play the dutiful wife, giving him control of my kingdom?" Gwen's cheeks flushed with anger as she paced around the table.

"I believe part of him thinks that's a possibility. From what I gather, Adaltus holds very regressive views on what women are capable of, especially since Lovell's father became king. But based on what I've learned..." He hesitated, knowing her reaction would be explosive. "I believe there will be attempts on Prince Pippen."

Gwen went deathly still. "What did you say?" He nodded softly, and he saw her fists clench at her sides. "They seek to kill my brother to control me?" Her voice trembled with barely contained rage. Anya moved closer to Gwen, but she raised a hand to signal that she needed space.

"I believe they mean to at least threaten him. Likely stage a kidnapping. It's your one vulnerability. Everyone knows that you've raised him and dote on him," Tyreal said. The urge to comfort her was overwhelming, but he fought it, determined to maintain his distance.

She raised her chin, her face dark as she spoke firmly, "This is an act of war." Her voice barely quivered, sending a chill down Tyreal's spine. He was accustomed to his own darkness, but Gwen rarely displayed any hints of it. He heard Anya and Max's sharp intakes of breath, but he kept his eyes locked on her. The seriousness of the situation overshadowed his desire to look away.

"It could be thought of as such, yes. All you must do is give the order, and it will be so. The Tavian army is yours to command." His voice matched the icy determination in hers. If she sought to become Tavia's dark queen, he would make it happen. He would unleash the full force of the Tavian army, transforming her will into reality, no matter the cost.

As he stood before her, a part of him recognized the lengths he was willing to go—for her and her alone. But in that moment, he didn't care. The world could burn if that's what she desired, and he would be the one to light the match. The thought settled in his mind with disturbing clarity. No matter what was happening between them, that fact hadn't changed.

"Gwen—" Max stood, prompting Tyreal to move closer to her. He trusted the prince, but given the gravity of the situation, he couldn't allow anyone else near her. Max raised his hands in apology and shook his head toward Alric, who had moved in for the same reason. Max returned to his seat. "There has been peace for centuries. You know Espera and Gagerland will support you, but please carefully consider your next step."

"I *know*," Gwen hissed. "Do you think I want to be the queen that finally breaks it? It was my ancestor who ended the last great war." Max furrowed his brow in confusion, while Anya shot her a look that Gwen waved off. "Never mind. I don't want to be the person who brings war to Valine. But what do I do? Adaltus has stolen from us, sought to undermine my ascension to the throne, and now plots to force me into marriage and possibly kidnap the crown prince? Am I to turn away from that?"

Tyreal cleared his throat. "That's not all, Your Majesty. They're not working alone. I don't have all the details yet, but there's someone else involved. My guess would be Galeigh. King Drakon has been acting strangely, and he was extremely close to our border when Lorne passed. There are rumors he's amping up a plan to invade Egrax. I could easily see Galeigh and Adaltus striking a deal to support each other's ambitions."

The three royals winced. Everyone knew Galeigh and Egrax had been battling over their borders for years, but it had never escalated beyond tensions and unnecessary tariffs. "So, war may come to Valine no matter what I do," Gwen slumped back into her chair.

"We need to consult the sisters," Anya suggested softly. "If war is on the horizon, we need to talk to them, especially the High Sister. She will know what to do. We should leave at once."

Gwen took a deep breath and nodded. "You're right, we do. But I need to assist Captain Blackbane with this guard problem and ensure Pippen is safe before I make any travel arrangements. Captain, do you believe we could leave for the Misty Mountains within the next couple of days while ensuring the Crown Prince remains *safely* here?"

"If Your Majesty wills it so, I can make it happen." His hangover headache throbbed even worse at the prospect, but he kept his expression neutral.

"Good, do so. For now, we'll act as if we don't have this information. We'll figure out our next steps after consulting with the sisters. We'll tell everyone that I wish to visit the other districts to bolster my council and see my people. Hedontas can act as Counsellor of the State, assisting the Crown Prince while I'm away."

"Aye, Your Majesty. It seems Princess Anya will accompany us. Will that extend to Prince Maximillen as well?" Tyreal began mentally preparing for the journey.

"Well, I'm certainly not letting my wife travel through a foreign country without me," Max said dryly. "Alric and I will be joining. We'll simply say we are extending our honeymoon because we cut it short to attend the funeral."

Tyreal nodded curtly. "With your leave, then, I'll begin speaking with Andais and Hedontas."

Gwen nodded, her expression impassive once more. "Of course. You're dismissed, High Captain."

He refrained from wincing. This distance was what he wanted. He just hoped it wouldn't hurt forever.

CHAPTER EIGHTEEN

Cook emerged from the kitchen's out-er door, cradling an assortment of cloth-wrapped bundles, each tied meticulously with twine. Gwen approached her with a bright smile, eager to relieve her of some of the heavy load. However, the older woman tightened her grip, a playful tut escaping her lips as her eyes crinkled with barely restrained amusement.

"No, no, Your Majesty. None of that," Cook chided, her voice light yet firm. She nodded toward the courtyard with her chin, urging Gwen to lead the way. The cool morning air brushed against Gwen's face, a refreshing contrast to the humid warmth of the kitchen.

As they walked, Cook continued, "Your Majesty, you'll forgive an old woman for being forward and speaking her mind, won't ya? I've known you since you were just a babe."

Gwen nodded, intrigued by where this conversation was heading. Cook was known for her candidness, whether welcomed or not.

The older woman's expression shifted, her brow furrowing slightly as the lines on her kind face deepened. "While I'm prouder than you can imagine about your efforts to bring more common folk onto the council, I can't shake my worry about the chilliness between you and the captain these past few days. This is not the time for quarrels. Your trip—on horseback without a carriage—is unheard of for a queen, especially given the dangers lurking around you lately. You'll need to work together."

Gwen sighed, discomfort washing over her. It was awkward knowing that her and Tyreal's issues were so evident. They had clearly failed at keeping their struggles hidden. "The High Captain and I had a… disagreement after Skensington's attack attempt. But we will sort it out. We're both grown and can act accordingly."

Cook let out a hearty laugh, her round frame straightening as she drew in a breath, eyes sparkling with mischief. "Should I box his ears for ya? He's the one in the wrong, of course. I have no doubts about that."

Gwen couldn't help but chuckle at the thought of the stout, good-natured Cook taking on Tyreal. Despite his foul mood since the attack, Gwen had no doubts Cook would emerge victorious in that battle. "No, Cook, that won't be necessary. We're just both being stubborn. It'll pass." *I hope*, she thought, a lingering worry twinging at her heart.

Cook snorted, still smiling but with concern lingering in her gaze. "You both have a healthy dose of stubbornness in you, I'll grant you that. Still, I worry."

Gwen shook her head, a soft smile gracing her lips as they continued through the courtyard. The early morning light cast long shadows across the cobblestones, and the distant sound of horses whinnied from the stables. "I've traveled to the Misty Mountains often enough," she said, glancing at the familiar castle walls, "and while this is a different route, I'm not afraid."

They passed under the archway leading to the stables, the rich scent of hay and leather enveloping them. "I firmly believe that Skensington and the few guards swayed by coins are not the norm for Tavia," she continued. As they approached the stables, Gwen paused, pondering. "Even though the High Captain and I might be at odds right now, I know he wouldn't let any harm come to me. I respect his experience in keeping us safe on the road."

With a resolute nod, they reached the stable doors. "So, I will listen to his advice without complaint," she stated, reminding herself as much as reassuring Cook.

As she spoke, Gwen spotted Tyreal busy near the stables with Braken and Akasha, finishing up loading their saddlebags with supplies. He had the sleeves of his tunic pushed up around his elbows, and the sunlight caught in the dark hair on his forearms, revealing hints of gold and red. The sight tugged at her belly, the familiar ache of want settling in. Yet, she could also still hear the sharp click of the door closing behind him, feel the rising panic that clawed at her chest and left her gasping for air as the walls closed in. Crossing this "chilly" divide between them felt impossible, especially when Tyreal seemed intent on treating her as nothing more than a royal he was duty-bound to guard. Should she even try?

Cook's expression softened, the lines of worry easing. "I suppose that's as good an answer as you can give right now. I hope you find your way back to each other. It feels strange around here with things like they are, and we've had enough sadness for a while. Just promise me you'll be careful, Your Majesty. You mean a great deal to us all, and not just because you're the queen." She shifted the bundles in her arms, nodding toward one with her chin. "I've packed some sweets for Princess Anya, who's already bemoaning going back on the road. She'll have to make them last—worse than Prince Pippen with her sweets."

Gwen sighed, frowning as her thoughts turned to Pip. "I'm so very worried about leaving him behind." She glanced back toward the castle, knowing he would come to bid them farewell, but understanding his reluctance to be left behind. The thought of his safety conjured a thousand scenarios of potential harm. Part of her felt she should be equally concerned for her own safety, yet she had been truthful with Cook—she truly wasn't afraid if Tyreal was by her side. Even now.

"Hogwash! It'll be good for him to take on some responsibility. The prince is perfectly safe here. Hedontas, Jameson, and Andais themselves are watching over him around the clock. I'll make more rounds to check in on him, too."

Gwen giggled. "Well then, I shall lay my mind to rest. I know no one will dare risk your wrath." As they entered the stable stall, Cook handed Tyreal the bundles of food to stow in the saddlebags. Gwen felt her smile fade, replaced by coolness as she regarded him. "Good morning, High Captain."

He cinched one of the bags shut, avoiding her gaze. His refusal to meet her eyes had become the most frustrating part of their recent interactions since that day in her room. It stung, even though she knew it shouldn't. She understood, to an extent; he had made a mistake, and her safety had been compromised—something he struggled with at the best of times. But that didn't justify treating her like a stranger.

"Good morning, Your Majesty. Prince Maximillen and Princess Anya should join us shortly, and then we'll be on the road. I'd like to reach Bernsend before nightfall tomorrow. There's a small but decent inn where we can rest for the night and a stable for the horses." His voice was clipped, as if eager to end the conversation.

Gwen nodded, unable to find words. Instead, she pressed her face into Akasha's mane, fingering the silky strands as she murmured a hello to the horse. She heard Cook clear her throat and lead Tyreal away, a small warmth blooming in her chest knowing that he was getting a dose of Cook's "opinions," likely more scathing than she had. There were indeed perks to being the ruler.

Voices echoed from the courtyard, and Gwen turned to see Anya, Max, Alric, Pip, and Hedontas approaching the stables. They looked so relaxed and carefree that it deepened the ache in her heart. Her country teetered on the brink of war; her father was gone, and Tyreal had turned away from her. Did he truly fear that their relationship would compromise her safety? Or was he afraid of her now because of her magic?

A sigh escaped her. Perhaps it wouldn't be so bad when she finally wed her consort. She knew she wouldn't love him, but at least marrying another royal would lighten some of this burden. They might understand how lonely it felt to have an entire nation depending on her. Tears threatened to well in her eyes, but she shook her head slightly to dispel them and straightened her posture as her mama had taught her.

As the group entered the stable, she smiled and embraced Pippen. "I'm going to miss you terribly, brat. Please try to keep my castle running smoothly in my absence, won't you?"

He rolled his eyes, hugging her back. She could sense his unease mirrored her own about their separation. "I don't think I could get in trouble if I tried. Andais and Jameson watch my every move. Even Tensha is barely letting me do anything. Since you put Hedontas in charge, I don't even get to do any kingly stuff."

Pip pouted slightly, though it was half-hearted. She had seen the look of relief on his face when she had explained what a Counsellor of State did.

"Kingly stuff, hmm? What kind of stuff would you have liked to enact? I haven't made any new rules besides this council business. Perhaps I'm missing out. You'll have to give me pointers when I return." She ruffled his hair, smiling.

"You are going to return, right? Swear on Mama and Papa's souls that you will. Or on Tyreal's life. Well... maybe not his life since you're mad at him. But you have to swear it on something." Pip's eyes glistened with unshed tears, much like her own had moments before. She squatted to meet his gaze, despite the pang of realization that she'd have to do so less often soon, as he would soon surpass her height. She extended her pinky.

"I'll do better than any of that. You can't break a pinky promise in Tavia. Remember when Prince Pippen forced King Lorne to make it a law?" Their father had orchestrated a grand event, crafting a formal scroll and signing it with a flourish before the council. The scroll had been proudly displayed in the dining hall for weeks, when Pip was just four summers gone. Pip had recently declared pinky promises were for babies, but she was certain he would make an exception this time.

Sure enough, he extended his own pinky, linking it with hers. "I remember. And you're right; you can't break it. If you do, I'll be king. I'll make your soul come back from the Everafter to stand trial."

Gwen nodded solemnly. "As you should for breaking such a sacred Tavian law. You must also promise me you'll stay safe. Be better than I am—listen to your guards and don't argue. They'll keep you safe. It's important, Pip." He nodded in agreement, and they shook pinkies once more. Satisfied, she hugged him tightly before stepping back.

Hearing Cora's voice from outside the stables, Gwen stepped out to greet her. Cora sat on the wagon bench as Tensha conducted a final check on the horses. They had decided that Cora and Tensha would inspect the larders in the nearest districts to see if Thorncliff had been the only affected area. Bearing documents with Gwen's official seal, Cora could dispel any rumors about the queen's actions and communicate with them via crows during their travels.

Gwen walked out to finalize last-minute plans with Cora. Out of the corner of her eye, she noticed Tyreal returning from his discussion with Cook, his cheeks flushed and one ear bright red. She forced herself to suppress a smile, recalling a rare occasion when she had been naughty enough to get Cook to break protocol and grab her by the ear for a scolding. It seemed Tyreal had not outgrown the receiving end of such reprimands.

Clearing his throat, Tyreal said, "If everyone is ready, we need to hit the road." He glanced at Max, Anya, and Alric, who all nodded in response before looking directly at Gwen. She wondered what Cook had said to him. His expression still held a cloud of misery, indicating that nothing had magically changed between them. "Are you ready, Your Majesty?"

With a slight dip of her chin, she donned her riding gloves, her hand delicately grasping the pommel of Akasha's saddle as she swung her leg over it with practiced ease. Dressed in her favorite black riding breeches and a long-tailed waistcoat, she settled comfortably onto the sheep fur lining atop the saddle. While she could ride in a dress, breeches were far more practical for the long journey ahead. At *the very least,* she mused, *my legacy will be that I made riding in pants fashionable for women in Tavia.* Ease and comfort had also driven her decision to ask Cora to braid her hair away from her face, preventing it from whipping around in the wind, and she could go for a few days without washing it while they were on the road.

Beside her, Max, Anya, and Alric mounted their horses. Tyreal approached her to check the girth under Akasha's belly, ensuring her saddle was secure. "I assure you, I can check my own saddle, High Captain," she snapped, but as she caught sight of Cook and recalled Pip's words about being mad at Tyreal, she sighed. "But—thank you for your diligence," she added, forcing the words from her lips.

"I know you're capable, Your Majesty. I never meant to suggest otherwise. I just—I can't bear the thought of a world without you in it, especially if it were due to my negligence. Don't you understand that?" His voice lowered to a near whisper, meant for her ears alone. But before she could respond, he moved away to mount Braken, leaving her with a whirlwind of unresolved emotions.

As they rode out from the stables and into the courtyard, she frowned, wondering if that was as close as she would get to an apology from him. Even if it was, did it change anything? They were playing a fool's game by toying with temptation, and the reality remained: she would have to marry a royal to preserve the magical bloodlines, and Tyreal wasn't one.

Determined to shake off that train of thought, which led to nowhere, she turned and waved to everyone as they trotted out, especially Pip, whom she blew a kiss. He blushed, holding up his pinky in response, a reminder of their promise. She raised hers in response and took her position next to Anya, with Max slightly ahead of them. Alric and Tyreal took their respective positions, fanned out slightly from the trio of royals.

"He'll be okay, Gwennie," Anya reassured her. "They won't let anything happen to him. And once we reach the mountains, the High Sister will provide all the guidance you need on how to proceed. With everything." Anya nodded toward Tyreal.

Gwen sighed, hoping Anya was right. But something massive loomed on the horizon, and she couldn't discern if it was a threat or an opportunity. Hopefully, the High Sister would know.

CHAPTER NINETEEN

As they approached Bernsend, Tyreal felt the ache in his lower back and thighs intensify, an unmistakable sign that the royals were likely reaching a breaking point as well. He had anticipated Gwen's response to the ride; she would pout about sleeping outdoors, but she was an experienced rider and hunter, accustomed to the rigors of the wilderness. His greater concern had been Max and Anya, but to his relief, they had managed well thus far without complaint.

The previous day's ride had brought a slight thaw in his relationship with Gwen. He hoped she had understood his "apology" for what it was. Cook's lecture about his coldness toward her still echoed in his ears, and his left ear still stung from her admonishments. He knew Cook was right—he had been an ass. Even after his half-hearted attempt at reconciliation, Gwen remained distant, and the coolness between them gnawed at him.

Throughout the ride, he had caught her glancing at him, her expression a mix of confusion and hurt. He would look away quickly, pretending not to notice, but each avoidance only heightened the silence between them. Tyreal still believed that putting distance between them was the right choice; he needed to protect her, even if it meant protecting her from himself. Yet the memory of the hurt on her face haunted him.

His thoughts drifted back to the attack that had set them on this path. With hindsight and a few days of clarity, he recognized that his outburst had been driven by fear. It wasn't Gwen and her power he feared, though he suspected she worried he did. What terrified him was his inadequacy in protecting her. In a world steeped in magic, what good was he to her without any of his own? It was painful enough to feel unworthy of her love; the thought of being unable to safeguard her—his life's duty—was a dagger to his heart.

As they neared Bernsend, he stole a glance at Gwen. She sat tall in her saddle, eyes fixed ahead, projecting strength. Yet, the tension around her mouth betrayed her. He yearned to reach out, to express everything he felt, but the words caught in his throat.

Cook's stern voice echoed in his mind. "You're a fool, Tyreal Blackbane. She needs you now more than ever, and you've shut her out. Fix it before it's too late, or you'll regret it." He had promised to try, but he didn't know how to bridge the gap while maintaining the distance he believed necessary.

They halted at a small stable beside the inn where they would spend the night. "With me, Your Majesty. We'll secure rooms and pay for the stables while Alric settles the horses." He offered his hand to help her down from the saddle. After a moment's hesitation, she accepted it, wincing as her feet hit the ground. "Are you alright?"

She managed a thin-lipped smile. "I'm fine. How should we present ourselves tonight? Am I Queen Gwendolyn, alerting the town to my presence, or just another dark-haired beauty accompanying Captain Blackbane on a mission?" He couldn't decipher whether she was teasing or taking a dig at him.

"I don't take women on missions. I just... happen to find them along the way," he replied defensively. Why did he feel the need to defend himself? Wasn't this what he wanted? "Given our proximity to Thorncliff, honesty seems best. There's a chance someone could've heard we were preparing to leave. The more eyes on us, the easier it is to keep you guarded—for now."

Gwen retrieved the crimson waistcoat she had rolled up earlier when the day turned warm, shaking off the dust before slipping it on. Forgoing her hood, she reached into her saddlebag for a delicate gold diadem, pinning it atop her braid with practiced grace. He dampened a rag with water from a water skin hanging on the side of his saddle and handed it to her. The surprised look in her eyes at this simple act of kindness struck him. Had he really been that awful? Apparently, he had.

After a moment, his queen stood before him—poised and regal—where before had been Gwen, the freckled beauty he knew he could never have. He must have worn an odd expression because she asked, "Do I look alright? Will they recognize me?" Her voice trembled with uncertainty.

He cleared his throat. "Yes, you look as beautiful as ever. They'll recognize you just fine." He gestured for her to lead the way toward the building. As they approached the rustic wooden door, it creaked softly, worn and weathered from countless travelers. Above them swung a sign, the faded and chipping paint proclaiming it to be "The Wandering Mare."

Bernsend marked the first significant stop on their journey away from Thorncliff, leading into Tavia. Despite its small size, the town thrived on the traffic of travelers, especially in the wake of King Lorne's funeral. This business had also pushed Tyreal to reveal Gwen's identity—he wasn't sure they could secure lodging otherwise. The royals deserved a proper bed tonight, for it would be several days before they could rest as comfortably again.

Stepping inside, they were enveloped in a warm, inviting atmosphere. The scent of freshly baked bread mingled with the hoppy aroma of ale, while the hum of conversation and clinking tankards filled the air. As soon as Gwen entered, the room fell silent; men bowed low, and women dropped into curtseys.

The innkeeper, an old man with several missing teeth and a shock of white hair, bustled over quickly, bowing low. "Your Majesty! We had no notice you'd be visiting! To what do we owe this fine pleasure?"

Gwen smiled warmly at him and the patrons. "Please, don't stop enjoying your dinner on my account. I'm here to visit the Tavian districts in my efforts to expand the royal advisory council. As Thorncliff's nearest neighbor, Bernsend is, of course, our first stop. And if my father's stories hold any truth, you serve the finest rabbit stew in all the land. Would you be able to help my party procure some of that?"

The old man nearly crowed with delight, and it tugged a smile even from Tyreal, though he remained alert, observing the reactions around the room. It wasn't surprising to see that the response was overwhelmingly positive. Gwen had always possessed a natural charm. "Of course! King Lorne was always kind when he stopped here. We are all sorry for his loss. I could not attend the funeral, but my daughter Amaya said you gave him a beautiful send-off to the Everafter. Opening that to the masses certainly wasn't bad for my business, so I thank you."

He led them to a large table in the corner. "I'm Gideon Oakheart, by the way. The Wandering Mare has been in my family for well over a hundred summers. Whatever you need, my daughters and I will provide. I assume you'll be needing lodging for your party. Is it just you and the High Captain?"

Gwen shook her head. "No, Prince Maximillen and Princess Anya from Espera are accompanying me. They shortened their honeymoon to attend the pyre, and I wanted to show them some of our beautiful country before they return home. Their guard, Sir Alric, is traveling with them as well."

Tyreal could see the old man doing calculations, trying to come up with rooms for them. The dining area was crowded, so he guessed it would take some maneuvering. "We can manage with just two rooms, Mr. Oakheart. Sir Alric and I will take guard shifts and rest in the hall. We know you're busy after the pyre, and we also have five horses in need of care."

The old man waved his hand. "Just Gideon, please, no need for 'Mr. Oakheart.' Aye, we can do two rooms. I'll have them ready before you finish dinner. Just fifteen shickles for the horses. Lodging and dinner are on the house in King Lorne's memory."

Gwen began to protest, but Tyreal gave her a sharp shake of his head as he retrieved coins from the pouch on his belt. He recognized Gideon as a proud man who valued hospitality; Gwen's insistence on paying would offend him. With the efforts to undermine her rule, she couldn't afford any additional bad blood. Gwen's mouth closed, and she smiled warmly at Gideon. "Thank you. That means the world to me. My lady and her companion will arrive tomorrow in a wagon meant for Riverdon. I'm sure they'll stop here as well, which means even more business for you."

Tyreal handed the coins to Gideon, who hurried to the kitchen, calling for his daughters. "Look alive, girls! We have *three* royals, including our glorious queen in the house, and we'll show them how we do things at The Wandering Mare!"

Gwen chuckled softly, her eyes scanning the room as they made their way to their table. The buzz of conversation returned, but it was clearly about them. Ladies whispered behind their hands, and everyone craned their necks to get a better look at the queen. Though accustomed to attention, Tyreal knew it still made her uneasy, particularly away from the safety of Thorncliff. After Asya's death, Lorne had been reluctant to let Gwen and Pip wander too far from home, save for her trips to the Misty Mountains. He noticed her nervously picking at her right thumbnail with her other fingers, and he knew she was resisting the urge to chew on the skin there.

"You'll make your finger bleed. And it'll sting inside your glove while you're riding." He kept his voice low and gentle, offering his observation rather than criticism. She spread her fingers wide and said nothing, visibly relaxing when Anya, Max, and Alric entered the room. At least she wasn't the center of attention anymore.

The crowd struggled between staring at their new queen and Anya, who turned heads wherever she went. Anya was far more comfortable with the attention than Gwen was. While Gwen could charm people easily in smaller settings, she had to put a lot of energy into doing so with crowds. Anya had an ability to work a crowd that seemed to come naturally. She grinned and waved, toying with her hair, which was braided in such a way that it wrapped around the curve of her head and then bounced down over her shoulder in a singular long yellow curl. Her mint-colored riding habit hugged her form, complementing her pale complexion. She wasn't Tyreal's usual type, yet he couldn't help but wonder what she and Gwen must have looked like together in bed, because she was gorgeous.

"Wherever you go, you attract attention, wife. Lucky for you, I'm not a jealous man," Max teased, pulling a chair out for Anya near Gwen. She scrunched her nose at him in response, and he pressed a kiss to her forehead before sitting beside her, motioning for Alric to join them. Alric, like Tyreal, remained vigilant, his hand near the pommel of his sword, scanning for any lurking dangers. Finally, he relented, sitting with his back to the wall, facing the room.

Tyreal leaned forward, addressing Alric. "I spoke with the innkeeper. They're packed tonight, and I believe they'll have to shuffle a few guests to accommodate us. I suggested we only need two rooms, and you and I can rotate guard duty. Does that work for you?"

Alric shrugged, but Anya tilted her head. "It seems foolish for neither of you to get a full night's rest when we have so many more days of riding and sleeping on the ground ahead. You'd be better off refreshed and alert to keep a watchful eye." Her tone was sweet, but her eyes glinted with mischievous malice, aware of Tyreal's reluctance to share a room with Gwen and that Alric would not let her or Max out of his sight.

Not that he feared anything happening between them. He knew Gwen was still upset with him, and nothing had changed. But he wasn't a glutton for punishment. He would get little rest with her sleeping just a few feet away. No amount of soft bedding would prevent that exhaustion. As one of Gideon's daughters delivered several bowls of stew and a freshly baked loaf of crusty bread to their table, Tyreal yanked his bowl closer and broke off a hunk of bread, inhaling deeply.

"I agree. Alric is a bear when he hasn't slept, and I'm in no mood to deal with him when we get back on the road. This place seems exceptionally Thorncrest friendly, and we are being watched so closely, I doubt someone could sneak into either of our rooms." Max tore a piece of bread from the loaf, adding his thoughts once they were alone.

Alric shot Max a dirty look at the jab. "This is Captain Blackbane's territory. He knows the dangers better than I do, so we'll defer to his judgment. But I'd prefer to protect my charges from the comfort of my bedroll rather than sit exhausted in the hallway." Alric's eyes sparkled as he took a swig of ale, glancing at Tyreal.

Tyreal exhaled through his nose, trying not to let his frustration show. He tapped his spoon against his bowl before finally agreeing. "I seem to be outnumbered on this. I admit I don't sense any imminent danger. With our bedrolls placed on the floor in front of the doors, no one could sneak in. A full night's rest it is."

He caught a glance between Gwen and Anya, noting the princess smiling to herself as she lifted her spoon daintily to her lips. He turned to Gwen to see what he had missed, but she was pointedly focused on her meal, avoiding his gaze. He groaned inwardly. A full night's rest indeed.

CHAPTER TWENTY

Gwen shook out her riding breeches, gave them a quick sniff, and deemed them good for another day or two. They smelled decent enough—the only scent being the musty warmth of Akasha—so she hung them carefully on a peg along with her waistcoat to air out. The aged floorboards creaked beneath her as she moved around the room. She was blissfully alone for a few moments, determined to enjoy the peace while she could. Tyreal had muttered something about checking on the horses when they had come up to their rooms, leaving her to freshen up while Alric stood guard in the hallway.

Gideon had assured her he was providing her with the finest room in the inn. She wasn't entirely convinced it wasn't his own room he had offered, but she accepted it graciously. She longed to find a way to give him some extra coins for the trouble they had caused during such a busy time, but Tyreal insisted that pushing the issue would wound the man's pride. Men and their damn pride.

Gwen glanced around the space, taking in the walls adorned with heavy wooden panels intricately carved with vines, flowers, and roses. A row of flickering candles along the mantle of the small stone hearth in the corner cast gentle shadows, enveloping the room in a cozy glow she found comforting. She sank into the sturdy four-poster bed, the soft feather mattress and thick quilts easing her tired, achy muscles. Gideon had mentioned that her parents had visited the inn, and since this was the finest room, it was likely they had stayed here. She craved a connection to them, a spark of something to help ease the loneliness she felt as she navigated the chaos of her ascension to the throne. But all she felt were the lines of stitching on the quilts beneath her fingers.

How had she never stayed here before? They had made the trip to the Misty Mountains often enough, but they always took a different route, a slower one. With time not on their side, Tyreal had pointed out that they could shave off three days by using the more populated roads, even if he didn't love the idea. Was it a safety concern? Something her father insisted upon to protect the heir? Or a dictate from the sisters with their cryptic rules and protocols? She made a mental note to add that to her list of questions for their journey.

With a groan, she forced herself off the bed and made her way to the heavy wooden dresser across the room. Gideon had offered to draw a bath for her, but she'd seen how busy they were. It felt wrong to have someone take the time to heat and carry a tub of water up the stairs. Instead, a ceramic vase and bowl sat atop the dresser, along with hand towels and soap for her to freshen up.

Reaching around to untie the strings of the riding stays she wore over her chemise for support, Gwen felt a pang of envy for Anya's smaller breasts. Anya didn't have to worry about such things, because she could ride all day without feeling like her back would lock up at any moment from the weight. She tossed the stays aside and peeled off her chemise, left only in the simple sleeveless undergarment she'd helped the seamstresses create when she first started riding seriously and insisted on breeches. Made from the softest cotton they could find, it fell just under her bottom, keeping her comfortable during long rides and absorbing sweat while remaining easy to wash by hand.

But washing it now would leave her completely nude. Chewing her lip thoughtfully, she decided that was Tyreal Blackbane's problem, not hers. She wanted her clothing fresh for the morning, so she removed the undergarment. Quickly washing her body, she then rinsed out the garment in the bowl, wringing it dry and searching for a place by the hearth to hang it. Just then, Tyreal knocked at the door—two slow taps followed by three rapid ones. She considered telling him to wait but heard herself say, "Enter," before she could think better of it.

He inhaled sharply upon entering, the door closing quickly behind him. She glanced over her shoulder, half-expecting him to bolt. To her surprise, he remained, trying hard to focus on the floor near her feet. She noticed his right hand flexing near his sword hilt—his tell for high emotions—and a smirk tugged at her lips. Anya had suggested using nudity and proximity as a form of revenge, but Gwen hadn't honestly planned on it.

"Why do you torture me like this? Put some clothes on," he rasped, his voice rough and igniting heat in her cheeks, a tingling sensation coursing through her. She ignored it, determined *not* to give in to her desires. She was here to remind him of what he was denying himself, though she couldn't quite remember the endgame of this little game.

"I shall not. I want my clothing items clean and dry for our ride tomorrow. My royal womb will be under thick quilts soon enough, and you won't have to concern yourself with my unwanted nudity," she snapped, surprised by her own venom. She thought Tyreal's not-quite-an-apology earlier had eased her wounds, but clearly it had not.

"Unwanted? You know better than that. Don't pretend for a moment that you think I turned from you because I don't want you. We talked about this," he said.

"Talked? We didn't talk about anything," she hissed, her voice low to avoid being overheard. She turned to face him, no longer caring about her nudity, and jabbed her finger into his chest. "*You* ranted a bunch of nonsense and insults after I revealed my deepest secret, then walked out, leaving me to deal with the worst panic fit I've ever had—after being attacked and held at fucking knifepoint on the day we burned my father's body. *Forgive* me if I don't consider that a conversation."

"I apologized! What more do you want from me? Please just get under the quilts or put something on," he pleaded, backing his body as far away as he could, edging back into the doorway. The dull thud of metal within his leather cuirass against wood resounded as he retreated. She followed, pressing her body against his, leaning up as if to kiss him, close enough to smell his male musk, leather, and a hint of soap. He must have cleaned up before coming upstairs.

"No," she whispered into his ear, pulling back and trailing her fingers down his chest, teasing her nails along the leather. "And if you call that an apology, you need a serious remediation session with the Divine Arbiter about asking for forgiveness, because you're terrible at it."

He looked down at her face, his eyes impossibly dark and dangerous. She should have been concerned, pushing him like this, but her anger burned hotly, desperate for an outlet—not just at him but at the entire situation. At her father for leaving her in this mess, at Skensington and Adaltus, and at the sisters with their damned rules. Those rules were all that kept her from claiming this man and being claimed once and for all.

"You're playing with fire, Gwendolyn." He pressed his hand to her throat, forcing her to step back so he could exit the doorway. "You're right; I didn't give you a proper apology. I was wrong to leave you alone like that. But this little tantrum isn't the right way to have this conversation. I'm just a man. A needy, grumpy one at that. I have my limits, and you're pushing me to the edge."

This only stoked her anger further. Even now, he couldn't offer a simple apology. A tantrum? Really? She covered his hand with hers, pressing it harder against her throat, staring defiantly into his eyes. "I can control fire, and I'm not afraid of you. You swore you'd never touch me again, and I wouldn't let you if you *begged* me at this point." The last part was a lie, but her fury was consuming.

He squeezed lightly, just enough to constrict her airway, but not hurt. To her shock, the reaction sent heat coursing through her. "Little liar," he growled. "If I slid my fingers between your thighs right now, would I not find you wet for me?"

She shoved his hand away, and he let her, though his hand flexed as if he wanted to grab it again. Defiantly, she moved to the bed, leaning back on her elbows and parting her thighs—not fully, but enough to make her point. "I suppose you can look if you want, but you most definitely do not get to touch. You said never again, and I can't have a liar as my high captain."

Tyreal swore, taking a step towards her but stopping himself. "Alright then, little minx. You want to play games to punish me? We can do that. Spread your legs. Let me see what I'm missing. Or will you suddenly get shy and remember you're out of your depth, little girl?" His words were a challenge, and they both knew it. She felt out of her depth, but she wouldn't, *couldn't*, back down now.

Kicking her leg out, she balanced one foot on the edge of the feather mattress, allowing it to fall open. Exposed like this, she wondered if he *could* see the sheen of wetness glistening on her skin. A low sound—almost a growl—slipped from Tyreal's chest as he took her in. "Can you see alright, High Captain? Getting a good long look?"

"Aye, I see your sweet little cunt practically weeping for me. Tell me more about how you wouldn't let me touch you if I begged. I do love hearing lies fall from the mouth of my queen." He stepped forward but clenched his fists, forcing himself to stop with a deep breath.

Her cheeks flamed with embarrassment at his words. She couldn't recall ever hearing him say "cunt" in front of her, nor had she encountered such filthy talk from anyone before. Instinctively, she started to close her thighs, but the urge to back down evaporated. Winning this battle of wills suddenly felt vital, though she couldn't quite articulate why if pressed.

She tipped her chin up, locking eyes with him. Yet, he wasn't looking at her face—his gaze was fixed on her core, as if it were water and he was a man dying of thirst. The thought emboldened her. With a deliberate motion, she slipped one hand down, fingers gliding between her folds, exposing herself further to his hungry gaze. "I wouldn't let you touch me if you were the last man on this continent."

"You lie so pretty for me, sweet girl. But that's fine. Show me how you touch yourself, Gwennie. I want to see. Or perhaps, since you're intent on putting on a show tonight, I could invite a few others to join us. I'm sure Anya wouldn't mind." He unfastened the belt holding his sword and daggers, placing it at his feet within reach, positioning himself between her and the door. Somewhere beneath the anger and lust, she felt

a flicker of appreciation that he was still thinking of her safety.

"Now who's lying? You aren't the type to
share, and you certainly wouldn't let anyone
else watch." Her voice was nearly breathless,
but she complied with his command. She wondered how far he would let this go before he
broke. Because she wasn't going to—she'd sooner give up her crown than beg him to touch her.
Tonight, at least. Her fingers teased along her
clit, the delicate strokes igniting a fire within.
With her other hand, she cupped a breast, tugging lightly at her nipple.

"No, I don't share. You're right there. I'll gut
anyone who dares to see you like this again,
and therein lies our problem, doesn't it? Harder,
Gwennie."

She shook her head. "You said to show you
how I touch myself. You don't get to dictate how
I do it. And I can't yet. If I rush, it hurts." She exhaled a slow, breathy sigh as pleasure began to
build from her touch. "But once I'm there—well,
that's a different story. Anya used to count how
many times she could make me fall apart in one
evening. She probably still knows her record."
Tyreal cursed again, a half-groan of frustration. She continued her teasing strokes, shifting from performance to pursuit of her own
release, seeking to ease the coiled tension in
her belly.

Through heavy, half-lidded eyes, she watched
him palm himself through his breeches, the

sight enough to coax a soft whimper from her throat. She slipped her middle finger inside herself, gathering her wetness and then bringing it back up to stroke lightly over her hardened clit. As her eyes fluttered closed, she imagined him closing the distance between them, replacing her hand with his own. How different would his calloused fingers feel? How tightly could he stretch her around his thicker digits?

The tension coiled tighter within her as her fingers danced toward release. Cracking her eyes open, she saw Tyreal closer now, but not quite at the bed. He had pulled himself out, stroking his length, his face dark with yearning hunger. Having never seen a man nude before, the sight of his cock—hard, thick, and angled slightly upward—was enough to send her spiraling over the edge. She bit down on her lip to contain a cry, but a soft keening noise escaped her, prompting Tyreal to take another step toward the bed.

"Gods, Gwennie. I've spent years imagining what you'd look and sound like coming undone. Nothing I pictured came close to the real thing." He pulled his tunic over his head, revealing his own nakedness. "Now I want—no, *need*—to spend the rest of my days making you sound just like that, over and over." He approached slowly, as if wary of her response. "I need you. I yield. I can't resist any longer. Tell me what I must do to earn your forgiveness."

"I don't want your apology just because you now wish to fuck me." She rose onto her elbows so she could look into his eyes. "Nothing has truly changed since the other night."

Tyreal shook his head, his voice trembling as he knelt before her. "Everything has changed," he whispered, his eyes tracing her face with a mixture of desperation and reverence. He reached out, hesitating, knowing he hadn't yet earned the right to touch her. Instead, he placed his hands on the mattress beside her thighs. "To see you spread before me like that, to hear the sounds you made... I'm done for."

He looked down, shoulders slumping. "The gods might banish me from the Everafter for my sins," he said, voice thick with emotion, "but to die without having made you mine in whatever way I can? *That* would be torture."

His hands clenched into fists. "I can't bear it any longer," he confessed in a harsh whisper. "I'm sorry for panicking and leaving you alone. I should have been stronger."

Tyreal's gaze met hers again, pleading. "You need me to be stronger," he murmured. "And even if you don't let me touch you now, I'm still sorry."

He bowed his head, breath uneven. "I can't face the challenges ahead without you by my side," he finished, his voice breaking on the last word.

"I needed you. You're the only one I can rely on right now, and you turned away from me. I don't care if we never touch, but you pushed me away and left me alone." Her voice trembled, each word bubbling from a deep-seated pain, cooling her anger into something softer.

"I know, sweet girl. I'm so sorry. I should have talked to you. Really talked to you. But when I saw that knife at your throat, and the drop of blood, then the magic... I panicked. I was terrified and felt like such a failure. Please forgive me." He gripped the quilts tightly, remorse etched across his features. Even though he deserved it, seeing him hurt ached in her heart.

She tilted his chin up, forcing him to meet her gaze. "I forgive you. Just promise never to push me away again. We'll talk through everything from now on." Tyreal nodded solemnly, leaning so his cheek filled her palm. "Good, so now that we've sorted that, I think I will let you touch me."

His eyes darkened with a predatory gleam. "You think? Oh, sweet girl, I need more than that. I need to hear you're sure. I'm not a man who takes anything not freely given."

She swallowed, feeling both exhilarated and apprehensive. "I very much want you to touch me, and I want to hear what sounds you can draw from me."

CHAPTER TWENTY-ONE

Tyreal's hands slid down to grasp behind her knees, yanking her legs toward him with a swift motion. The sudden pull forced her bottom to the edge of the bed, leaving her flat on her back. A surprised gasp escaped her lips, but he didn't allow her time to react any further. He pushed her knees up toward her chest, settling his shoulders beneath them, and pressed his face against her mound, inhaling deeply. "Oh, Gwennie, the things I'm going to do to you."

He dragged his tongue slowly up her slit, gathering her wetness on the tip, letting out a delighted groan against her skin. She tasted better than anything he had ever experienced in this life. He felt certain he could spend a lifetime right here, blissfully lost. She made a delicious little sound, squirming beneath him. Apparently, the statement about her being very sensitive was true; she was quite the responsive little thing. He hadn't even begun to touch her yet.

Flattening his tongue, he pressed it forcefully against her pretty little clit, nestled within its cloak. The thought of tying her up and teasing it out with his teeth crossed his mind, but this being her first time made it feel too advanced. Still, it was a tantalizing idea for later if they ever got more chances. As *if I'll ever let her go now*, he mused. Gwen tried to wriggle away, but his large hands held her firmly in place.

He pulled her against his mouth with fervor, feasting on her. His tongue alternated between hard, flat strokes and dipping into her tight little hole. Suddenly, he sucked her clit between his lips, flicking rapidly over the tip. Gwen's hands flew up to cover her mouth as her juices coated his tongue and beard, her body tensing as she came undone. He coaxed her through it gently before removing his mouth and climbing above her.

Her skin was flushed, and she panted softly. The dusky pink nipples on her heavy breasts were tight and pebbled, and he couldn't resist twirling them between his fingers. She bucked gently beneath him as another small wave of pleasure crested within her. He grinned. "Two," he murmured against her lips, kissing her deeply, forcing her to taste herself on his mouth.

She sucked his lips between her own, unashamed of her flavor, sending a throb through his already aching cock. Perfect. She was fucking perfect. He was never letting her go.

"Mmm—technically, I gave the first one to myself. So, I think you're still at just one," she teased, a giggle escaping her as she leaned in for another kiss. In response, he pinched one nipple playfully, causing her to gasp, and they both laughed together. He rolled them so they lay stretched out on the bed, side by side.

"I believe you're correct. I'll have to adjust my count," he said, nipping at her shoulder as his hand slipped back between her thighs. He cupped her mound gently, holding her, wanting to savor every moment of their time together. "I wonder how many it will take before I think you're ready for me. I want this to feel so good for you," he whispered against the silky soft skin along her collarbone.

Gwen reached out, tracing her fingers over the taut lines of his stomach muscles. She propped herself up on her elbow to watch herself play with him, brushing her fingertips over the dark trail of hair leading down from his navel. He sucked in his breath, rolling onto his back to give her space to explore. He wasn't sure how long he could hold back before his control snapped, but he would grant her as much time as he could.

Sliding further down, she gripped his cock in her small hand. If she felt any shyness about the newness of the experience, she didn't show it. If there was one thing Gwen was good at, it was barreling headfirst into new experiences, and he appreciated that quirk more than ever. He groaned, the sensation like tiny sparks racing along his skin, reminiscent of being outside in a lightning storm.

"I've never seen a grown man nude before. I've seen some drawings, but they don't do it justice. I certainly didn't expect it to be so... thick. Does that make me sound terribly naïve?" she asked, her voice a mix of innocence and burgeoning desire as she stroked him slowly, letting the extra skin near the head glide up and down.

Tyreal clenched his fists, pleasure surging through him with each movement. Every part of him screamed to roll her onto her back and sink as deep as he could inside her. "Not naïve, sweet girl. Just inexperienced. And that's not a bad thing. Everyone was at some point," he answered through gritted teeth.

Her eyes darted up to his. "Am I doing it wrong or hurting you?" She started to pull her hand away, but he quickly reached down, stopping her and holding it in place.

"No. You're perfect. It's just taking everything I have to let you explore and make this first time as memorable as you deserve." He guided her hand, slowly moving it to the top, tightening her grip slightly. She was a quick learner, and soon he was fisting the quilts, counting backwards in his mind to keep from losing all control. She traced her thumb over the tip, collecting a drop of moisture that had beaded there.

"May I put my mouth on you how you did to me?" Her voice was shy yet husky with desire. She slowed her movements, looking up at him expectantly. He didn't trust his voice to respond without squeaking like a young boy, so he simply nodded. Gwen moved down, positioning herself between his spread thighs, gazing up at him. The sight nearly drove him to madness—curls escaping her braids, lips plump and well-kissed, and holding his cock was better than any fantasy he had ever imagined.

Gwen flattened her tongue like he had done to her, stroking it up the underside of his shaft, coaxing a needy growl from Tyreal that made her smile. She relished seeing him like this, vulnerable and desperate. They had much to figure out about their future, but for now, this moment was more than enough. She wrapped her hand around the base of his cock and slid him between her lips. After a few moments, she worked her way to take almost all of him comfortably.

It didn't take long for the combination of stroking and sucking to make Tyreal lift her from him and flip her onto her back. "Enough," he growled, a note of desperation in his voice. "I'm going to spill before I even get a chance to get inside you. We can't have that." His lips found hers again, kissing her deeply while his fingers slid between her thighs to check her readiness. He eased two fingers inside her, curling them gently as his thumb rubbed her clit. She keened softly against his mouth, squirming beneath him. "I'm going to make you come undone again, Gwennie, and then I'm going to fill this greedy little pussy with my cock. Do you want that?"

She nodded eagerly, breathless, unable to form words as his fingers worked their magic inside her. Her body responded, the tension building to an almost unbearable peak as her muscles tightened. Finally, the wave crested, and she reached up to cover her mouth, muffling her cry to ensure the entire inn couldn't hear her.

Tyreal didn't allow her a moment to relax. He gripped her thighs, lifting them around his hips so he could notch the head of his cock against her. Still overwhelmed by her previous sensations, she barely noticed the discomfort as he slid past her maidenhead. There was a slight pressure that straddled the line between pain and pleasure, but the sound he made ignited the flames of her desire, tipping it wholly into ecstasy.

"Bloody crows, you're so fucking tight. Absolutely perfect. Am I hurting you?" His voice was strained, clearly holding back. He hadn't fully seated himself inside her yet, taking his time to ensure she was comfortable. He stroked his fingers along the outside of her thigh, peppering kisses on any skin he could reach while waiting for her response.

"No, it's good. Tight. But good. Please don't stop," she moaned, turning her head to capture his lips with her own, lifting her hips to encourage him to move. The shift caused him to slide further inside, and they both groaned. He slid his hand under her knee, lifting it higher so he could sink completely into her. Unable to hold back any longer, he moved, reaching one arm up to palm the wall behind the bed for leverage, thrusting as deeply as possible. To her, he was the embodiment of lust, muscles in his arms taut and powerful, making her feel small and cherished in a way she didn't fully understand.

"You're mine, Gwennie. From this moment on. I don't know how we will manage it, but no one will ever touch you like this but me. Do you understand?" His voice was low and harsh, each word sending shivers through her. She felt the tension building again, and she nodded helplessly. "Say it. I need to hear you say it," he growled.

"I'm yours. And you are mine," Gwen gasped, gripping Tyreal's back as he drove into her, their bodies entwined in a primal dance. Years of longing and denial surged between them, overwhelming her senses. Her nails scratched at his skin, a fleeting echo of pain and pleasure as she reached her peak once more. The intensity of the moment, heightened by their connection, left her breathless. But suddenly, the weight of him on top of her felt almost suffocating, each wave of pleasure crashing over her, making it difficult to draw a deep breath.

As if sensing her need—something he had always attuned to—Tyreal rolled them over, positioning her above him while he continued his relentless thrusts. His hands gripped her hips, and she gasped at the new angle, trying to process the new sensations. "Ride me, sweet girl. I've dreamt of you like this so many times."

Gwen rocked her hips, searching for the rhythm that would send them both spiraling. She felt a twinge of discomfort from her sore thigh and back, remnants of a long day of riding, but she brushed it aside. Placing her hands on his chest, she began to move, his eyes wide with a mix of awe and desire as he watched her. She reached up, grasping one of her heavy breasts and teasing her nipple, seeking one more release. Tyreal slid his hand down his stomach, nestling his thumb between them until he found her pearl and applying just the right amount of pressure as she rode him.

The friction sent her spiraling, and Gwen bit her lip hard, fighting back a scream as pleasure consumed her once more. She tightened around him, and in that moment, Tyreal followed her, his cock throbbing as he released himself inside her, moaning her name.

She collapsed onto his chest, and he ran his hand soothingly down her back. "That was so fucking perfect, sweet girl. You're perfect. I'm never letting you go," he whispered into her hair. They lingered in the aftermath, hearts and breaths gradually settling until he softened enough to slip from her. Reluctantly, he rolled away, grinning at her small sound of protest. "Just going to get you something to clean up with. I'll be right back." He moved to the dresser, dampening a cloth with water from the pitcher.

When he returned, he lay beside her, gently cleaning her with the cool cloth. "Are you terribly sore? I'll admit, I've never lain with a maid before. I wasn't exactly sure what I was doing, other than trying to ensure you were ready for me."

Gwen shook her head, smiling. "Not terribly. I think I'm more sore from a day of riding than what we just did. There's a little pain, but it's the good kind—the kind that reminds me of everything when I move just right."

Tyreal groaned playfully. "Don't talk like that, you minx. It'll be hard enough to keep my hands off you tomorrow, knowing you're remembering me inside you every time you move." He leaned in to kiss her softly.

"I know we didn't discuss it, and it's a bit late now, but you do take barrenflour root, right? I obviously don't, and it would be... complicated to be with child right now," she murmured, tracing her fingers over his arm.

"I do. Have for years. No worries about little Blackbane bastards running around. I'll keep taking it until you tell me to stop, but I won't lie with anyone else. I meant what I said—you're mine now. I don't know how, but everything in me says it's right. That the Gods are on our side in this."

Gwen yawned, curling closer to him. "I hope you're right. Now that I've had a taste, I'll want this all the time. And since you've said you'll gut anyone else, I suppose I'm stuck with you to get my fill." She grinned wickedly, and he swatted her backside, making her gasp.

"No one here to give me lashes for spanking you this time, my queen. So, I'd watch that wicked little mouth of yours," he warned, a playful glint in his eyes.

Gwen giggled. "Wanna know a secret?"

Tyreal pulled the blankets up around them both. "Always. I want to know everything about you, you know that."

"I think I liked it when you spanked me. I didn't realize it until years later when I looked back on that day. The part about you getting dragged off and punished was awful, but the actual spanking? I've thought about it several times over the years."

"Bloody crows, woman, maybe you are a siren. That was a dangerous and foolish thing to admit. I swore to myself I wouldn't take you again tonight, so go to sleep before I break another oath." He kissed her, pressing his growing desire against her, and she laughed, heart racing with anticipation.

CHAPTER TWENTY-TWO

"**I** love you, and I love my country, but I do not want a war. Do you think if I say it often enough, my muscles will ache less and a plate of delicious food will magically appear?" Anya whined as she tied her horse next to Akasha, where they could access a small stream and some fresh grass. "I'm going to send a crow for Cora and Tensha to come pick me up in the carriage. I swear it."

Gwen laughed, offering her an indulgent smile. "I promise to have Cook make you all the thumbprint jam cookies you can eat when we return to Thorncliff. Tyreal says we have about five more days before we reach the mountains. Just think of how good the hot springs will feel after this." She untied a blanket from her saddle and spread it on the ground for them to rest on. They had stopped for lunch upon spotting the stream. Nearby, the men gathered kindling for a small fire. The air grew chillier as they approached the mountains.

"I'm going to soak in the springs for an entire day as soon as we finish talking with the sisters. You and Tyreal can find some other way to ease your aching muscles." Anya teased, drawing out the last word as she flashed a mischievous grin. She plopped down on the blanket, moaning as her muscles relaxed into a flat position.

Gwen's cheeks heated, and she shot a dirty look at her sunshine-haired friend. Anya had her eyes closed and didn't see it, but it still made Gwen feel better. She hadn't told Anya about her and Tyreal finally giving in to their feelings. Anya had seemed to know—maybe because the pair had been finding every excuse to be alone together over the past several days since leaving Bernsend. Or perhaps it was because Tyreal was in a better mood than Gwen could remember him being.

"I'm sure I don't know what you mean."

Anya cracked an eye open and laughed. "It's just the two of us here. I don't know why you keep pretending. You two are terrible at sneaking around. Plus, you looked like a cat that found a saucer of milk after you checked on the horses in the stable before we left the village this morning."

Gwen playfully huffed, her dark curls bouncing as she feigned indignation. "I've changed my mind. Cook will never make you cookies again because you're horrifically mean to me," she declared. She laid down on the blanket beside her friend, her curvy figure sinking into the soft grass beneath. With a scooting motion, she curled closer to Anya's petite form, enveloping them both in the voluminous folds of her thick cloak.

"Also, you'd better be nice, or I won't share my cloak and warmth with you," Gwen added, tightening the cloak around them with an exaggerated tug. The fabric draped over them, soft and heavy, creating a cozy barrier against the crisp air. Anya chuckled and stretched, and they lay in silence for a moment, letting their bodies relax from riding as they listened to the birds chirping in the surrounding trees.

"Is it everything you hoped it would be?" Anya asked.

"Yes. And more. I don't know what we'll do when we return home, but for now, it's dreamy—other than the looming war." Gwen grimaced. "I want this for you, too, you know. We never really talked about how things are between you and Max. I see you two getting along, but what about the rest of it?"

Anya shrugged. "Our love differs from what you and Tyreal share, but we are happy in our marriage. We've agreed that taking lovers is acceptable as long as we remain discreet. As for producing an heir..." She sighed. "That's something we haven't quite figured out yet. Fortunately, being newlyweds means no one is pressuring us about it—for now."

"Ah yes, the lovely joys of being the bearer of the royal womb." Gwen rolled her eyes. "That's the only reason the sisters outlawed any chance I have of marrying Tyreal. They're so worried about diluting the bloodline. I also don't know what I'll do about an heir when the time comes. We've both sworn not to be with anyone else. In fact, I've been told Tyreal will gut anyone who tries." Gwen laughed, her tone light, though a part of her wondered if he was serious. "Do you have any ideas on how to produce these required royal heirs, given our ridiculous circumstances?"

"You know damn well he's not kidding," Anya said with a chuckle. "My current plan is for Max and me to drink copious amounts of ale and wine and bring another girl into bed with us. If I'm thoroughly distracted between her thighs, I don't think I'll notice what he's doing, if he can be quick about it. Max is less keen on that plan. He says he has no desire to take me when I don't want him. He mentioned something about using a hollow horn and his seed, but that sounds... messy. I think my plan is better."

Gwen snorted. "I know we're limited in our knowledge of men and activities in the bedroom. But if Tyreal is a good example of what most men are like, you will notice what he's doing. It's distracting enough when you want it; I doubt it would be less so if you didn't."

"Ah ha! She finally admits it!" Anya shifted to face Gwen, propping her head up on her hand. "Tell me everything. Well, maybe not everything, but I want to hear most of it."

"Are you sure? I was worried it might upset you. Considering we ended that part of our relationship because of my feelings for him." Gwen mimicked Anya's position so they could face one another while still sharing the cloak.

Anya wrinkled her nose. "I'm sure. That was years ago, and we were practically children. We were friends first—other than that brief time when we hated each other when we first went to the sisters." They both giggled at the memory. "I think we're better as friends than we would have been as anything else. So, tell me."

"Well, it started with an argument," Gwen began. Anya feigned gasping, and Gwen shot her another dirty look. "Yes, shocking, I know. I sort of listened to your suggestion and was nude when he entered. Then we started arguing because I was so angry with him. It just spiraled from there, and then we both broke."

"Pretty much exactly how I expected it to finally happen. Did he break my record?" Anya wiggled her eyebrows suggestively, and they both burst into laughter.

Gwen sobered, sitting up to scan the area with a frown. "Why aren't they back yet? They were just supposed to gather kindling. Tyreal would never leave me unattended for long."

Anya sat up as well, frowning. "True. Alric wouldn't either. Do you think something happened?"

Gwen narrowed her eyes, considering. "I'm not sure, but I intend to find out." With sudden decisiveness, she stood, the warmth draining from her expression as the cloak dropped to the ground. "Do you want to stay here with the horses, or come with me?" Anya nodded towards her, and Gwen crept up the hill, motioning for Anya to follow.

Gwen carefully placed her feet with each step, avoiding piles of crunchy leaves and dodging low-hanging brittle branches that could betray them. Her father, an avid hunter, had insisted on taking her and Pippen out with him since they were small. While hunting had never truly appealed to her—despite her exceptional skill with a bow—she adored tracking. After seeing how much she loved it, Tyreal made it a point to add tracking to her defense training over the years.

Gwen halted abruptly, raising a fist to signal Anya to stop. Anya peered around her and quickly covered her mouth to stifle a gasp, trying not to reveal their presence. In the clearing ahead, Max knelt with his hands raised in surrender, while a man stood behind him, a sword pressed to his throat.

Red ringlets peeked out from under the man's battered hat at odd angles. His clothes were filthy, a layer of road dust and grime covering him from his ragged top to the tips of his boots. His four companions stood near Tyreal and Alric with weapons drawn.

Tyreal and Alric's weapons lay on the ground, a clear sign of what had occurred. Max had strayed from their side, and when they caught up to him, they had to put their weapons down for fear of the prince's life. Gwen bit her lip, weighing the best course of action to prevent injury to Max. She knew that Tyreal and Alric were doing the same.

"You're welcome to take whatever you want from us and the horses," Tyreal stated to the men surrounding them, trying to calm everyone. "We don't want any trouble. Just let us go our own way."

"Bullshit. You think we can't tell just by looking at you that you love trouble? That one's the size of a damn mountain, and he didn't get that scar down his face by avoiding it." The man behind Max nodded toward Alric as he spoke. "No, you're playing too nice. I think this might be the party we heard about—the one with the two beautiful women along for the ride."

Gwen watched Tyreal give the man a passive, almost bored look. His casual indifference sharply contrasted with Alric's intensity. Alric was silent, his eyes fixed on the red-haired man standing behind Max, his gaze sharp and menacing, as if envisioning the man's head atop his sword.

Tyreal's voice broke the tense silence, his tone cool and detached. "We aren't traveling with any women. We've just been hired to protect this noble," he nodded toward Max. "We like fighting well enough, but we barely know this man. I'm not in the mood to risk getting run through for the sake of a few gold coins." His words hung in the air, a clear dismissal of any deeper loyalty to their temporary charge.

"Is the stream near enough for your magic to reach? You always did better with water than I did," Gwen whispered to Anya, so low that only she could hear. Anya shook her head, and Gwen silently cursed their limited powers. What good were these embers of magic if a threat from the Tenth Family ever truly came?

One man poked at a saddlebag on Braken, who neighed nervously, his ears pinned back. Tyreal flicked his eyes to him, a frown crossing his face.

"Hey boss, these bags have the royal crest stamped into 'em. Bet we could get a nice sum for 'em." He rummaged inside and shouted, "Bloody crows! Look at this!" He held up Gwen's thin gold diadem, which she had stashed in Tyreal's bag that morning instead of her own in her hurry to get re-situated after their romp.

"Shit," Gwen hissed through clenched teeth. Having the marauders discover her presence would certainly complicate matters. She glanced at Anya, who made a swirling motion with her finger. Gwen nodded and turned to face the men. She took a deep breath, grasping Anya's hand, settling into the place within herself she accessed when using her magic. Air was notoriously hard to manipulate. Neither girl had ever fully mastered it, in fact, the High Sister was the only one who seemed to control it fully. But if they combined their powers, they might create enough of a distraction.

Tyreal shrugged, adopting a nonchalant demeanor. His gaze swept lazily over the assembled group, settling firmly on the leader. "So, I did a little light robbery at the castle during King Lorne's pyre. Surely fine gentlemen like yourselves can't fault me for that, can you?" He smiled, but his tone dripped with thinly veiled sarcasm.

The man with the sword to Max's throat shook his head, his lips curving into an unamused frown. "Nah, I don't buy it. You'd have sold it or melted it down quicker than shit. Not traveled this far north with it." As he spoke, his grip on the sword tightened, knuckles whitening around the hilt. With a deliberate motion, he pressed the blade deeper against Max's skin. The sharp steel kissed it just enough to underscore his words, causing a small indent that didn't yet draw blood but was enough to make Max's breath hitch. The lump in Max's throat bobbed, perilously close to the blade, his face paling under the threat. "What's your name, fine nobleman? It wouldn't be Prince Maximillen, would it?"

The air around them stilled, tension palpable. Tyreal's façade of indifference cracked, a flicker of concern flashing across his face. Max remained impressively composed under the blade, though his eyes communicated a silent alarm. "Do I win a prize if I say yes?" he asked, flashing his best charming smile.

The man was about to answer when a gust of wind swept through the clearing, dead leaves swirling in a funnel shape around them. It howled, a ghostly sound that sent a chill down Gwen's spine. Dust and debris danced in the whirlwind, limiting visibility. The man with Gwen's diadem let out a frightened cry, and the horses panicked. Braken lifted his head and flared his nostrils, pawing at the ground. Alric's massive chestnut draught horse stood on its hind legs, snapping the rope that tethered it to the tree before bolting.

The next moments unfolded so quickly that Gwen and Anya barely had time to drop their hands and release the air. Tyreal and Alric seized the opportunity the distraction had bought them, both spinning in nearly synchronous movements. A small blade emerged from Tyreal's leather gauntlets, springing outward from a hidden mechanism. He slashed it across the throat of the man closest to him, letting the body fall as he reached for his sword on the ground.

Tyreal gave three sharp rapid whistles as he turned toward the man who had been holding him and Alric at sword-point. Hearing the whistles, Braken calmed from his panic, neighing loudly in response. The large horse turned its shoulder, lining himself up to kick the man with the diadem square in the center. The man landed with a harsh thud several feet away, gurgling wetly.

Alric seized the man behind him so suddenly that the man had no time to react before being lifted off the ground by Alric's giant arm. With a sickening crack, Alric snapped the man's neck before turning to let out a primal roar, grabbing his sword from the ground and charging toward Max and the red-haired man.

Alric was such a hulking figure that witnessing him run in a fit of rage with his sword drawn must have been terrifying. The red-haired man took a step back, dropping his sword from Max's throat.

Gwen and Anya ran into the clearing. Alric led the way toward Max, while Gwen focused on Tyreal, who was locked in a fierce sword fight with the last man near him. The man charged at Tyreal, who slid sideways, narrowly avoiding the attack.

Tyreal spotted Gwen running toward him and shook his head sharply, silently urging her to stay back. The man, noticing Tyreal's distraction, swung his sword again. Tyreal dodged just enough to avoid a direct hit, but the blade still grazed his thigh, leaving a minor flesh wound. He stumbled, letting out a shout of pain, but quickly regained his balance.

Gwen froze, her heart pounding as she watched the exchange. Tyreal gritted his teeth, parrying the next blow and retaliating with a swift strike. His sword clashed with the man's, ringing out in the tense air.

The man turned to see what had distracted Tyreal, giving Tyreal a brief opening. With a swift, low swing, Tyreal's blade found the back of the man's knee. The man screamed, collapsing forward, leaving the bottom half of his leg still standing. Tyreal quickly ended his misery rather than letting him bleed out, his movements slowed by his injuries.

As the man's body hit the ground, Tyreal took a moment to catch his breath, blood running from his thigh. Gwen finally reached him, eyes wide with concern. "Tyreal, you're hurt!" she exclaimed, reaching for him.

"I'm fine. Get behind me!" he commanded, grasping her arm and pulling her back.

The red-haired man's eyes darted frantically from face to face, breaths quickening as he registered the absence of his friends—all now dead. Alone and cornered, his shoulders tensed, and Gwen could see the realization setting in: he was losing the battle. Max glanced over his shoulder at his captor, and the man struck. His sword pierced through Max's middle, the tip emerging coated in blood so dark it was nearly black. Anya let out an anguished scream of "No!" as Max looked down at the sword protruding from him in shock before the man pulled it out and fled, leaving Max's body to crumble slowly to the ground.

CHAPTER TWENTY-THREE

Anya chased the red-haired man through the trees, her heart pounding. Alric had sprinted straight to Max, and she couldn't bear the thought of watching her husband die, so she had kept running. The man fled as if his life depended on it, which it did, until he looked back and realized Alric was no longer pursuing him—only Anya. He slowed but continued weaving through the foliage, clearly underestimating her. *That's a mistake*, she thought.

The man darted left toward the stream and down the hill where Akasha and Anya's horse were tied. As he neared, he turned to face her, a nasty grin twisting his lips. "Sorry to ruin your honeymoon, Princess. But hey, if you need a bedwarmer to take your grief out on, I'm sure I can oblige. You're a pretty thing."

Anya slowed, inching closer to the stream, her breath coming in heavy gasps. The chill in the air mixed with the turmoil inside her, leaving her skin flushed and splotchy. Tears blurred her vision, the bitter warmth of them warming her cheeks.

Anguish and anger tore through her chest like a dagger, creating a gaping void that threatened to swallow her whole. Max had been a constant in her life, betrothed to her since birth. Though she may not have desired him physically, it did not make her love for him any less.

She could not fathom how to exist in a world without him. He had been her anchor. And she knew there was no way he could survive a gut wound like that—not with the sisters still so far away. Even if they intervened, it was unlikely he would live. And for what? Because this man wanted some gold? She had heard Tyreal offer him to take what he desired.

She stared as the man, clearly uneasy under her silent scrutiny, moved to untie Akasha. He slung himself onto her saddle, and Akasha snorted, tossing her head in protest.

"Why? Why would you kill him when you could have just taken the gold? You all could have walked away. But now your friends and my husband are dead, and all you have to show for it is a stolen horse," she asked quietly, raising her chin to meet his gaze. "Why?"

"To slow down that mountain of a man headed my way. It worked, obviously. And now I get to live another day. Sometimes that's just how the world works, your highness." He sneered at the title, as if it disgusted him.

"That's where you're wrong." Her voice remained quiet, but the rage in her heart was icy, threatening to consume her soul. Max had been good and kind, accepting her for who she was and who she loved. They had been determined to make their unconventional marriage work. There was no justice in this world if this man walked away unscathed.

He gave her a confused look, his brow furrowing at her words. Anya raised her hand, pulling a rope of cold water from the stream and lashing it at him. The water wrapped around his waist like a lasso, pulling him off Akasha and tossing him onto the ground.

"What the fuck? What are you? A fucking witch?" he screamed, scrambling away, but the water held him in place.

Another tear streaked down her face. "I suppose I'm a widow. Thanks to you." She clenched her fist, and the water flattened, covering his body and face. It forced downward, into his mouth and nose. The man struggled against it, scratching his face as if to scoop the water out, panic filling his eyes. Anya watched him, tears rolling down her cheeks.

She thought she should feel something—horror, perhaps, at what she was doing. The sisters had warned them to use their magic only in self-defense and as a last resort. But what choice did she have? The world could not continue with this man alive and Max dead. It would tip the balance of good and evil, for Max had been undeniably good. Wasn't everything in this world about balance? Hadn't that been drilled into them for years?

He stopped struggling, and Anya stood silently, staring at his corpse but seeing instead the dark, bloody sword sticking out of Max's middle, and the shock that had covered his face. What had been the last words she said to him? The memory escaped her now. She sat back on the blanket she and Gwen had shared just a short while ago, laughing while the red-haired man and his friends captured Max. Guilt flickered within her, but all that remained was a numbing cold. So, she wrapped Gwen's abandoned cloak around her and waited.

As Max collapsed, Anya took chase, while Gwen and Tyreal rushed to him. Gwen's breath caught as she saw Alric on his knees, his thick, curly light-brown beard brushing against his chest as he leaned over Max. His large hands, despite their strength, were helpless against the dark blood oozing from Max's wound, pooling and staining the ground beneath them.

Gwen's eyes widened, her heart racing. Alric's shaggy hair fell into his face, partly obscuring his expression, but she could still see the fear marring his features. His hands trembled as he pressed down on the wound, desperation flickering in his eyes.

Tyreal, limping slightly from his own injuries, placed his hands over Alric's and shouted, "Go. Go find Anya! She's your charge too, and she's alone with that man!"

For a moment, Alric stared at him, blinking in disbelief. Gwen could see the shock in his eyes—a look so uncharacteristic of the normally steadfast man. It was as if the chaos and blood had momentarily paralyzed him.

But then, slowly, the words registered. Alric's expression shifted; the dazed look cleared. He pulled his hands away, blood smearing his fingers, and let Tyreal take over. He stood, his movements sluggish, as if moving through water.

Gwen watched as Alric straightened, squaring his shoulders as he forced himself to shake off the daze. He glanced down at Max one last time, lips pressed into a thin line of determination. Then, with a nod to Tyreal, he turned and took off in Anya's direction.

She dropped to her knees beside Max, cradling his head in her lap, a sob escaping her lips. How had everything gone so wrong so quickly? Was she about to lose someone else she cared for so soon after losing her father? Anxiety and terror clawed at her, but she struggled to push them back, focusing on comforting her friend.

"He—he stabbed me. I can't believe the bastard stabbed me." Max's voice was strained, his eyes wide and glassy.

"Shh... you're going to be okay. We'll get you some help. Tyreal, you have to help him!" She looked up at Tyreal, her eyes pleading. She knew deep down there was nothing he could do, but logic eluded her now.

Tyreal looked back at her, a hollow expression in his eyes, a mixture of profound sadness and weary resignation. "Gwennie, I wish I could. By the gods, I wish there was something I could do. I'm so sorry, sweet girl."

As he spoke, a warm golden glow formed around his hands, spilling outward. Max groaned, and Tyreal's eyes widened in fear. He began to pull his hands away, but Gwen reached forward, stopping him, holding them in place. The light faded.

"What were you thinking just then?" she demanded.

"I don't even know what the fuck that was!" Tyreal snapped.

"I know that. But I need you to listen to me right now. Answer my question. What were you thinking, Tyreal? It's important." She poured queenly command into her words, hoping his training would override his fear.

"I guess I thought I wished I could do something—anything—for your friend. But he's going to die. There's nothing we can—" He tugged against her hands, and she knew he wanted desperately to back away from this thing he didn't understand.

"Shh! Hold on to that thought. Wish there was something you could do. Just... hold on to that thought and focus on his body beneath your hands. For me. Do it," she ordered, squeezing his hands.

He gave her an incredulous look but finally closed his eyes. Gwen stared at his hands, desperate to see the golden light again. She knew she had seen it; it had been real, and she needed it to be real again, because Max's breaths were slowing. Finally, the glow formed stronger this time as Tyreal didn't pull away.

Max let out a pained sound, writhing beneath Tyreal's hands. Gwen gently shushed him, moving one hand from Tyreal's to stroke Max's hair. Her eyes remained fixed on the soft glow radiating from Tyreal's hands, willing it to stay. Later, she would need to understand how Tyreal was performing magic—because that's exactly what it was. Healing magic hadn't existed in Tavia or anywhere in Valine since Myaessa's spell, and no man had wielded any magic since. As the light gradually faded, Max's breathing evened out, and he settled. Hope made Gwen's heart race.

"Open your eyes, Tyreal. If I'm right, I think you can move your hands," she whispered, praying to every god that would listen that she *was* right.

Tyreal slowly opened his eyes and moved his hands away, revealing a raw, puckered scar where the wound had been. The hole was closed; Max was no longer bleeding. He was still dangerously pale and unconscious, but he was alive. Gwen pressed her fingers to his throat and found a steady pulse beneath her fingertips.

Tyreal scrambled backward, away from Max. He looked down at his own leg, which was also no longer bleeding or showing signs of injury. "What in the bloody crows was that? How is he not dead? Why the fuck am I not bleeding anymore?"

Gwen gently eased Max's head off her lap and onto the grass. She stood slowly, approaching Tyreal with her hands in front of her in a placating gesture. "I don't know how, but I know what. That was magic. You performed healing magic. Maybe the sisters will help us understand why you could do so, but for now, let's just be grateful that Max is okay." She cupped his cheek, raising his chin to meet his stormy eyes. "You're okay. I am okay. We're all okay. So just—take a deep breath for me." She pressed her lips to his gently, kissing him sweetly until she felt some of the tension ease out of him.

They both heard the dry shuffling of leaves and turned to see Alric guiding Anya back, his large hand resting on the small of her back. Her arms were wrapped tightly around herself, her gaze hollow and vacant as she stared straight ahead, refusing to look at Max's body. Gwen hurried over to her. "He's alive. He's well," she said.

"Bullshit," Alric snapped. "No one survives a gut wound like that."

Gwen gestured toward Max with her hand. "See for yourself. I can't explain it, but look and see. He's well." She tried to make Anya meet her gaze, but it was as if her words weren't reaching her. "Anya, look at me."

Alric knelt beside Max, his hand resting on Max's rising and falling chest, tears spilling down his cheeks. Gwen looked back at Anya, who was still staring blankly. Sighing, she knew what she needed to do, much like Anya had done for her that awful night of her father's funeral.

She placed her hands on Anya's shoulders and pressed against the shields surrounding her mind. In Gwen's mind, Anya's shields resembled a web of silver gossamer, interwoven with flowers. Beautifully intricate yet deceptively strong, they resisted any push, revealing a core fortified with steel and thorns.

After a few attempts, she felt Anya respond, shoving back. Anya then physically pushed her away forcefully, causing Tyreal to step closer. Gwen held a hand out to stop him, locking eyes with her friend, who now stared back, fury twisting her pretty features. "He is alive, Anya. LOOK."

Anya turned to Max and tentatively moved beside Alric. "Max?" Her voice was a scared whisper as she brushed a dark wave from his forehead. He stirred, not fully waking, but responding to her voice. Anya inhaled sharply, a choked sob caught in her throat.

Alric stood and coughed, as if to cover his lingering tears. "I, er, need to find my horse. Can you look after them for a moment?" he asked Tyreal. Tyreal nodded, and the larger guard walked away.

"How did you do this? The sisters said healing magic doesn't exist anymore, and you've never been able to do anything like this." Anya brushed her fingers over Max's pink scar tissue, delicately, as if it might reopen at any moment.

"It wasn't me," Gwen said simply, folding a blanket that Tyreal had retrieved from Braken's saddlebag and placing it gently beneath Max's head.

Anya's mouth opened, confusion furrowing her brow. "I don't understand."

"It was Tyreal. He had his hands over the wound, and he said that he was thinking about how much he wished he could help. Then a golden light glowed around his hands, and the wound closed." Gwen watched Tyreal's face as she explained, wondering what he was thinking. She wasn't sure what she was feeling, and she at least had years of knowing her magic to fall back on. Tyreal had only known of its existence for less than a moon cycle, and he certainly never thought he'd wield it.

Anya shook her head, opening her mouth as if to ask a question. "I know," Gwen said, holding up her hand. "I don't have an explanation either. All we can do is talk to the sisters and thank the gods that Max is okay."

Anya bit her lip, her expression suddenly shifting. Her face paled again. "I—I killed that man. With magic. I thought—well, I thought he had killed Max. I couldn't understand a world where someone as good and kind as Max could die while that man lived. So, I used my magic against him. Oh, Gwennie, I broke my oath for no reason." She covered her mouth with her hands, tears welling in her eyes.

Tyreal squatted beside them. "Highness, I know a thing or two about killing men. I've killed many—hells, today alone I've killed two, well, three if you count the one I had Braken do. They weren't good men. They intended to rob and kill us, and that doesn't even account for what they might have tried to do to you and Gwen. The one you killed stabbed the prince for no reason. Who knows how many others he has killed without cause? You can mourn a life lost, but don't tear yourself apart over that man's death. You've saved lives by ending his."

"The sisters said we must never use our magic against another except in self-defense, and even then, we shouldn't kill with it." Anya's voice was small, tears streaming down her cheeks.

"The sisters also said healing magic doesn't exist anymore, and that non-royals and men can't wield it. But here we are." Gwen took her hand. "I am not sorry you killed him. He made his choice when he refused the chance to walk away that Tyreal offered him."

CHAPTER TWENTY-FOUR

Gwen watched Tyreal, bent over his collection of rolled out maps, making the most of the fading sunlight. He occasionally squinted up at the sky, glancing at the compass in his hand before marking something on the map. The small, magnetized needle floating in its bed of water had never made much sense to Gwen, much to her frustration. While tracking beasts or foes through the foliage came naturally to her, determining her direction was another story entirely. She sat down beside him, resting her hand on his thigh.

They lingered in silence for a while. A soft breeze rustled the amber and russet leaves overhead, causing them to tremble and dance.

If she strained a little, Gwen could hear the gentle bubbling of the stream that had drawn them to this spot. The nearly setting sun cast dappled patterns of golden light onto the forest floor surrounding their clearing. If not for the tumultuous events of the day, she would have felt completely at peace, able to relax in her lover's arms.

"We're close to my mother's cabin—just a half-day ride from here. I think it would be wise for her to check on the prince. If he feels up to sitting astride his horse, I want to leave at daybreak." The undercurrent of tension in his voice was unmistakable.

"That sounds like a good plan. Marie is a skilled healer. Though, it seems he's on the mend; his color has improved, and he managed to keep down some water earlier." She traced a soothing circle with her thumb on his leg, gathering her courage to voice her question. "Are you going to ask her about what happened?"

"How can I? You said no one outside the sisters and female royalty even knows magic exists. We're fortunate Alric hasn't pressed for answers, and I don't know *what* to say to the prince when he wakes up," he snapped.

"Don't snap at me. I'm not the one you're angry with. I understand your fear, but what happened was a gift from the gods. I refuse to see it as anything less." She pulled her hand from his leg, twisting it into the folds of her cloak.

Tyreal ran a hand through his hair, stood, and began to pace. "Of course I'm scared. I'm not ashamed to admit it. I've held in plenty of men's guts over the years without being able to save them. Why him? Why now? I don't understand, and without understanding, I can't plan. And how can I protect you if I can't make plans?"

"Tyreal, you can't plan for every danger that exists. You keep me as safe as possible. Perhaps the gods merely used you as their conduit, and this may never happen again. Maybe Max has a fate he needed to be alive for." She stepped closer, grasping his hands in hers and looking into his eyes. Her heart ached from the worry pinched around the edges of his expression. She glanced over her shoulder to check on the rest of their group.

After tracking down his horse, Alric had helped Tyreal clear away the remains of the marauders who had attacked them. They'd built a makeshift shelter for everyone to rest under. Max and Anya were now inside, and the nearby fire crackled, casting a soft orange glow over the scene. Alric tended to it, roasting a rabbit he'd caught. He caught Gwen's eye and nodded, signaling that everything was under control.

Gwen turned back to Tyreal, her gaze softening. "I know this isn't simple. Whatever happened, whatever that magic was, it chose you. That means something. We'll figure out what it is. And we do that the way we do everything—together."

He squeezed her hand gently, searching her eyes for a moment before he nodded, the lines of worry easing slightly. "Together," he echoed, and there was a newfound strength in his tone.

"We should rest," Gwen suggested. "I know you'll want us to leave at an ungodly hour if Max feels up to it. And you woke me far too early this morning for that romp in the barn."

Tyreal snorted. "Didn't hear you complaining about the hour when your thighs were around my hips."

"Well—no, I worried about someone finding us." She blushed, the memory of her excitement at the thought of being discovered and the mind-blowing release that followed making her stomach tighten. Clearing her throat, she tried to summon a more regal tone to mask her embarrassment. "But I am complaining now. And since you're grimy from the fight, my thighs will be nowhere near you until you've bathed."

"There's a spring right beside us, Your Majesty. I already planned to clean up before bedding down for the night." His tone dropped, and he rubbed his thumb across her bottom lip. "Besides, as greedy as you've been since I bedded you, I'd wager you wouldn't turn me away, no matter how I looked. Particularly if I promised to do that thing with my fingers you like."

Her mouth fell open to protest, and he lightly pinched her lip between his thumb and forefinger. "Oh yes, let some pretty lies spill from those sweet lips. You know I love punishing you for it."

She clicked her mouth shut, stepping back and giving him a dirty look. Her cheeks were aflame, but so was the rest of her. He was not exaggerating her greed, but he didn't have to voice it.

Tyreal chuckled but let her retreat, following her back to where Max and Anya rested. Max slept soundly with Anya curled protectively around him, a blanket draped over them. Anya's eyes were closed, but she kept soothing her hand over his arm as if to reassure herself that he was there and all right.

Tyreal spoke softly with Alric, laying out plans for their morning ride before stepping outside their makeshift camp to clean up in the stream. The large man sat quietly against a log, sword at hand, clearly not letting his guard down after the day's events. He watched Gwen with a questioning look, but didn't voice his concerns immediately.

"You want to know how he's still alive," Gwen stated.

"I do. But I also don't. I think I know the answer, and it scares the hell out of me. Excuse my language, Your Majesty." His cheeks flushed as if he suddenly remembered their roles.

She waved her hand dismissively. "Don't. I hate titles among friends. I've told you that. And given how much you care for Max, I certainly count you as one now. You can speak freely around me."

"You and the prince are very much alike," Alric said, glancing up through the tree canopy at the stars dimly emerging in the twilight. "It's rare, from what I've seen, to have royals as kind as you three. It gives me hope. My king, and your father were good men. But they held themselves somewhat apart. They didn't challenge how things have always been. But you three do, and I think that's a good thing."

Gwen had never heard him speak so many words at once in all the years she had known him. It shocked and touched her simultaneously. "Thank you, Alric. I hope we can make a difference for everyone in our countries, leave the world a better place than we found it."

He grunted. "Well, hopefully we can prevent a war. That'll be a good start."

Tyreal returned, hanging his freshly washed clothes on nearby branches to dry. His chest was bare, only a pair of breeches slung low on his hips. Gwen eyed the expanse of skin and the light dusting of dark curls across it hungrily. Tyreal caught her gaze and smirked, reminding her of his earlier words about her greed. She looked away, pointedly ignoring him as she went through her nighttime rituals—cleaning her teeth and doing what she could with her clothes.

Trying to make herself comfortable on the makeshift pallet, she wondered if she would have any luck finding sleep. Tossing restlessly, she fidgeted with her cloak, which served as a blanket since they had given the others to Max. Tyreal laid beside her, pulling her against his chest. He shrugged at her look of surprise, clearly no longer hiding their relationship from their companions. "Sleep, Gwennie. Alric and I are taking shifts to keep watch. You're safe. We all are."

She closed her eyes, letting the sounds of the forest wash over her—the soft crackle and occasional pop of the fire, the distant call of night birds, and the croaking of frogs by the stream. Eventually, the sounds and the warmth of Tyreal's chest against her cheek lulled Gwen to sleep, her worries about his magic and what it might mean for their future drifting away.

Morning came with a gentle light filtering through the leaves. Gwen opened her eyes, blinking a few times to reorient herself. She sat up, noticing Tyreal was no longer beside her; he was readying the horses while Alric prepared breakfast. With the fire extinguished, they had a simple meal of hard cheese and dried fruits.

Anya approached, somehow looking impeccable despite the trauma of the previous day and sleeping in the wild. Sometimes, Gwen hated her friend. "Your hair is a mess. You don't want to be seen by your lover's mother in such a state. Let me fix it." Her voice was subdued, different from usual, but Gwen took it as a positive sign that she was concerned about appearances.

"How is he?" Gwen asked as Anya began untangling the remains of her braids. Max leaned against the log that Alric had used the night before, quietly conversing with him. Though his color had improved, it was still too pale for Gwen's liking.

"He says his body feels heavy and just wants to sleep. He's confused about what happened but isn't ready to face the answers. So, he hasn't asked any questions yet." Anya dampened a brush with water from a small canteen, working it through Gwen's curls as best she could.

Gwen grimaced as her friend roughly tamed her hair. She missed Cora desperately. Anya could make her hair look good, but she was not nearly as gentle. "Alric was much the same. OW! You know that's attached to my head, right?"

"Hush." Anya quickly gathered and plaited Gwen's hair, pinning the braids to her head with a few long bodkins.

"I'm a queen. You can't speak to me like that. I outrank you, Princess." Gwen ducked away before Anya could retaliate for her words on her poor head.

"You aren't *my* queen. And I'm sorry you're such a baby that you cry whenever I have to tame the bird's nest on your head." Anya swatted at her with the brush, and Gwen barely sidestepped in time.

"If this little royal squabble is over, I'd like to get on the road soon. The prince says he feels up to riding," Tyreal interrupted, handing Gwen her portion of breakfast. She stuck her tongue out at Anya, who returned the gesture before walking back to Max.

The sun was high in the sky as they navigated through the tree line surrounding Tyreal's mother's cabin. Tyreal spotted her first, bent over a grove of wild mushrooms next to a downed tree. Her once raven-black hair was now streaked with white, always kept in a practical bun at her nape. A small basket lay beside her, filled with ingredients she had gathered in the woods.

She looked up at the sound of approaching horses, squinting against the sun to see who was coming. Her skin bore the inevitable marks of time, yet it radiated a healthy glow from a life spent eating well and immersing herself in nature. Her expression shifted rapidly from weary to surprised, then to joy as she recognized Tyreal.

Standing, she wiped her hands on the apron tied over her skirt, which already showed signs of a long day's work. Morning dew still clung to the hem, and she shook it out as they approached, giving Tyreal a once-over, inspecting him from head to toe. "You're thinner. Good thing I felt like making a big pot of venison stew today. Plenty for you and your friends." He smiled at her brusque tone.

"Aye, Mama. I love you too, and I'd be glad for a bowl of stew." He dismounted, wrapping her in a warm hug. She smelled of woodsy earth, her clothes warm from the sun despite the morning chill. Being around her always soothed his soul, easing the tension he had carried since the attack.

She patted his cheek before stepping back, her attention shifting to Gwen. She dropped into a curtsy. "Your Majesty, I'm sorry to hear of your father's passing. He was a good king and a good man to my son."

Gwen smiled fondly at her. "Thank you, Marie. He was fond of you too. We were all sad when you chose to move away from court."

"Psh, court was never for me. I only stayed long enough to get this one to some semblance of adulthood, since he was determined to serve in the guard like his papa." She waved her hand dismissively. Her gaze then lingered on Max, who looked especially pale and like he was struggling to stay in his saddle. "You look like you need some help, sir. I'm afraid I don't recognize you, so forgive me if I'm being impolite and missing a title."

"My name is Maximillen Hellerus. I am the Crown Prince of Espera, but if you can help me feel even a little better, you can call me whatever you wish, fine lady. This is my wife, Princess Anya Duges, and my guard, Sir Alric," he motioned toward both, swaying slightly in his saddle. His voice remained smooth and cultured, but the exhaustion beneath it was undeniable.

Marie considered him for a moment before nodding with a thoughtful hum to Tyreal. "He needs off that horse. I imagine you'll need to fill me in on what happened and why you've come here unannounced. Nothing good, I suspect."

CHAPTER TWENTY-FIVE

They walked the rest of the way to the cottage, and Marie showed Alric where he could put the horses for the night. The cottage, built from sturdy timber, had weathered to a soft gray, blending almost seamlessly with the earth. Moss and climbing ivy clung to the exterior walls, enhancing its camouflaged appearance amid the dense forest backdrop. A small, welcoming porch overflowed with scattered pots of herbs and wildflowers, its heavy wooden door standing ajar.

A large orange tabby cat slept peacefully on the front step until Marie shooed him away. He cracked open one eye, swishing his tail in annoyance, before reluctantly relinquishing his spot, as if it had been his idea all along. Gwen stifled a giggle, glancing at the cottage where Tyreal had grown up after Marie left court. He made it a point to visit her at least once or twice a year, and Gwen could easily picture a younger version of him sharing the porch step with the tabby, a book in hand.

Inside, the cottage was a blend of functional but cozy living and working spaces. The main room served as both a sitting area and Marie's workspace. A large, rugged table dominated the space, cluttered with jars, dried herbs, mortars and pestles, and stacks of weathered books and scrolls. Next to it sat an oversized chair, which Marie indicated Tyreal should help Max into. The fireplace cast a warm glow across the room, highlighting rows of shelves filled with meticulously labeled bottles of herbs and ingredients.

"Now then, Your Highness, show me where you're hurting," Marie's tone was gentle yet firm. Max carefully eased himself into the chair. She knelt beside him, her keen eyes scanning his face for signs of pain.

"The problem is, I don't exactly hurt, though I most certainly should." Max lifted his tunic, revealing the pink and puckered scar. "I found myself on the wrong end of a sword."

"Yes, it certainly appears you did." She ran her thumb along the healed skin. "This should have killed you. It almost certainly pierced your liver, not to mention other important bits. So, what happened?"

She stood and moved to the shelves, pulling down a small vial of murky liquid and gathering various herbs. Everyone turned to look at her, and Gwen bit her lip, wondering how much Tyreal could—or should—share with his mother. Ultimately, she decided that the truth, or at least a version of it, was best. "We don't know exactly what happened. Tyreal was applying pressure to the wound while I begged him to help my friend. Then his hands glowed, and the wound repaired itself."

Marie paused in the middle of crushing dandelion heads with her pestle. It was a brief but noticeable moment. She resumed grinding and nodded. "Alright. The biggest issue the prince is facing is blood loss. Even though the wound is healed and he is no longer on death's door, he still needs to replenish his blood to feel better."

Gwen cocked her head, her mouth slightly agape in surprise at Marie's acceptance of the situation. She looked at Tyreal, noticing his shoulders had relaxed for the first time since their attack. A pang of jealousy surged within her. What she wouldn't give to know the feeling of a parent's acceptance and reassurance again. She shifted her gaze to Anya, hoping her emotions didn't show on her face.

Anya offered a small, understanding smile before placing her hand on Max's shoulder. He looked up at her fondly, placing his hand atop hers and giving it a gentle squeeze.

"It doesn't matter what it was. All that matters is that he isn't dead," Alric spoke from the open door. Marie gave the large man a long, considering look before returning to her grinding.

"While I mostly agree, the world and nature hold many mysteries we do not and will never fully understand. It matters if it means that people will come for my son," she replied.

"No one will come for me, Mama. No one in this cottage will speak on it. I trust them. And the man who inflicted the wound is dead." At Tyreal's words, Anya shifted uncomfortably, and Gwen tried to offer her a reassuring look.

Marie regarded them all with a skeptical look, before shrugging. "If you trust them, I will as well. Tyreal, go fetch me some fresh water from the barrel outside and fill this kettle. Sir Alric, please make yourself useful and dip out a bowl of stew for the prince." Her commanding tone was so reminiscent of Tyreal with his men that it shook Gwen from her lingering bitterness.

Gwen watched Tyreal comply with his mother's orders, moving with an ease that spoke of the familiarity that comes from growing up in a space. He caught her looking and grinned, winking. She playfully rolled her eyes, but then noticed Marie watching and felt her cheeks flush. Clearing her throat, she shifted. "I'd like to help. Is there anything I can do, Marie?"

"You can set that kettle on the hearth to boil when Tyreal returns with it. Then we'll brew his highness some dandelion tea, to which I'll add a stinging nettle tincture. It may not be the best tasting, but a bit o' honey will help it go down." She turned to Max. "This will help build your blood back up. You need to drink it two to three times a day until the full moon. I have plenty of tincture, but I'll need help grinding the dandelion heads to send with you."

Anya perked up at the opportunity to help. "I can do that," she said. Marie smiled and motioned for her to take over the mortar. Anya carefully took the stone pestle, beginning to grind.

Alric handed an earthen bowl filled with steaming root vegetables and savory chunks of meat to Max. Max offered him a weak smile in thanks. Tyreal returned, and Gwen settled the kettle on the hook above the hearth, letting the water come to a boil.

"Tyreal, Gwen, would you both walk with me out to the garden? We can gather more dandelions while their highnesses are busy." Marie said, using her apron to wipe away the golden dust that had settled on her fingers from the flower heads.

She led them through the small kitchen adjacent to the main room, out the back door into a small, well-tended garden. There, Marie had cultivated a vast array of medicinal plants and herbs. People from the surrounding area frequently visited, seeking help for all sorts of ailments.

Gwen surveyed the neat beds of plants and the narrow path winding between them, leading down to a clear, tranquil pond. The water reflected the sky and trees, and in the distance, she could just make out the faint outline of the Misty Mountains. "It's beautiful out here," she breathed. The whole place exuded a sense of peace she had only ever found by her purple fig-leaf tree by the spring near Thorncliff.

"Aye, that's why I chose this spot for the cottage. But I think we have much to discuss while we gather these flowers for your friend. What are you not telling me?" Marie's gaze was directed at Tyreal, a stern maternal look that made him fidget uncomfortably, despite his age. He glanced at Gwen, silently seeking her guidance.

"We haven't lied to you, Marie. I swear it. We truly don't know what happened or why," Gwen said, her voice sincere but cautious. "The magic that saved Max—it was spontaneous. Nothing Tyreal has ever done before. We're still trying to understand it ourselves."

Marie nodded slowly, her shrewd eyes assessing them both. "Magic, spontaneous or not, has its roots and reasons, just like every other natural thing. It doesn't simply appear out of thin air. It's a gift or a curse, depending on how it's used. I find it interesting that neither of you seems shocked that magic exists. You're more focused on stressing that it's odd Tyreal could do it." She plucked a dandelion from the ground with practiced ease, her gaze now mostly on Gwen, presenting an unspoken challenge.

Gwen pursed her lips, weighing her response carefully. "It doesn't seem that you're particularly shocked about it, either."

Marie chuckled. "You know, I thought I would never miss the twisted games of court, but there's a certain beauty in watching someone sidestep a question without revealing their hand. But alright, I'll concede. You're my queen, and my son has loved you for almost his entire life. So, I'll trust you. No, I'm not overly shocked. Healing is a kind of magic that women in our family have been able to wield for centuries. We don't know why, but it comes naturally to us. I am, however, as confused as you are about why Tyreal could do it. He's certainly shown no signs of feeling like he is a woman, and he would have likely shown me some sign of power much earlier, even if he did."

Gwen felt herself gaping as Marie's words settled in. "Wait—did you just say that only women in your family could do this healing magic?" She saw Tyreal look up sharply out of the corner of her eye, but she kept her focus on Marie.

Marie put her hands on her hips, her narrowed gaze shifting between them. "Aye, only women. But not all of them—just some. Which clearly means something to you both. Tyreal, I've told you since you were little that keeping secrets, even well-intentioned ones, can cast dangerous shadows."

"Seems hypocritical to throw that at me right now when you're telling me we've had magic in our family for generations, Mama." Tyreal crossed his arms, his voice cracking higher than usual. A crease formed between his brows, and he shifted his weight from one foot to the other.

Marie frowned with concern, placing a hand on her son's arm and looking at Gwen. "Mayhap it is hypocritical. But I still think you should fill me in if it's something this concerning to both of you."

Gwen shook her head. "I can't. We can't. At least, not yet. What I'm thinking makes little sense in my mind right now, and I need to sort it out. The Blackbanes have always been in Tavia."

"Well, yes. But I am not a Blackbane. I am an Ardienne. And it is my line that are healers, not Tommen's. We came to Tavia around a hundred summers or so ago. Before that, we were across the Orlesian Sea in Candova."

Gwen's breath caught in her throat as Marie mentioned coming from Candova, the words hanging in the air like a dense fog. For a moment, the world tilted, the ground beneath her feeling decidedly less steady. Instinctively, she looked to Tyreal, seeking something familiar. As much as she didn't want to confront it, only one answer could explain the women in Marie's line having healing magic and what Tyreal had done for Max: the Ardiennes were the tenth ruling family.

"I... need to speak with Anya. Tyreal, can you please go get her for me?" He nodded and ducked back into the cottage. Gwen turned to face Marie, taking her hands. "Marie, I promise we will eventually fill you in on what this means. But I need to wrap my head around everything first, and we must speak to the Sisters of the Mist."

"Is my son in danger?" Marie's voice turned cold, and when Gwen looked at her face, she saw the same calculating predator that sometimes showed on Tyreal's. This was a woman who would do anything to protect her child, even if he was a skilled warrior.

Gwen shook her head. "Not at this moment, no. And I do not believe he will be. I will let nothing happen to him. I—"

"You love him. I know. I can tell. Always have done. But will that be enough to truly keep him safe if people find out he's a man so close to the throne with some kind of magic? For that matter, will you be safe?" Marie shook her head and sighed. "I knew you lot weren't bringing anything good."

CHAPTER TWENTY-SIX

G wen watched as Anya hesitated at the threshold of the cottage, her full lips drawn downward into a frown. A cool breeze swept through the garden, carrying the scent of damp earth and wildflowers, tugging at a few stray wisps from Anya's normally immaculate braids. Anya's gaze roamed over the beds of plants until it landed on Gwen, and she hurried to her friend, her boots crunching on the gravel path.

"What's going on? Tyreal said you wanted to see me—he looked stressed," Anya asked, her voice thick with concern.

Marie gently tucked the dandelions they had gathered into her apron pocket. "I'll leave you two alone. But remember your promise, Your Majesty," she said firmly, wiping her hands free of soil. With a nod, she brushed past Anya, her skirts swishing softly as she disappeared into the cottage.

Gwen turned her gaze toward the still pond, feeling lost in thought, the earlier tranquility shattered. Anya reached out, resting a hand on Gwen's arm. "Gwennie, talk to me. What is it?"

"They're the tenth family. Tyreal and his mother," Gwen confessed, her voice barely a whisper, nearly drowned by the gentle rustling of leaves and plants around them. Speaking the truth made it feel all the more real, and a heavy weight settled in her chest. She searched Anya's eyes for understanding, but her friend's brows knit together in confusion.

"What do you mean?"

"Marie revealed that some women in her family have possessed healing powers for generations. They only settled in Valine a hundred summers ago. Before that, they were in Candova."

Anya exhaled sharply. "And our royal families haven't seen such powers since magic fell."

Gwen nodded solemnly, her gaze drifting toward the mist-cloaked mountains. "There are still so many questions about how any of this happened. Tyreal is still a man. How did he heal Max? I want to ask the Sisters about it, but how can I ensure his safety while sharing this knowledge?" Marie's words echoed in her mind, making her stomach churn. How *could* she ensure his safety?

Anya stepped in front of Gwen, locking eyes with her. "Don't you see what this means?" she urged. "You two can marry now. The law of the Sisters is explicit: only a member of the founding royal families is eligible. And he *is*. That's how you'll keep him safe. He will be King Consort."

Gwen shook her head, voice trembling as anxiety swirled within her. "A founding royal family that is virtually unknown. Almost everyone believes there were only nine founding families. They certainly don't know magic exists, so how would I explain how we figured it out? How can I present this to my people? Will the Sisters even sanction a marriage to the tenth family, or will they condemn him and his family instead?" She began to pace, the myriad of questions racing through her mind. "The last we knew of his family, they had committed war crimes. Our training specifically prepared us in case his family kept their power and intended to wage war again."

"But they haven't! They have lived right here in Tavia for over a hundred summers, doing nothing more than healing people with the small ember of magic they retained, just like the rest of us. And presumably, before that, they did the same in Candova; we've heard nothing to the contrary," Anya countered. She took Gwen's hands, halting her restless pacing. "How could you possibly wage war with healing magic? The Sisters aren't unreasonable, Gwen. They'll see that. You're scared because everything you've ever wanted might finally be within reach, and you don't know what to do with it."

Gwen opened her mouth to respond, but the scuffling of feet on the path behind them interrupted. They turned to see Tyreal, his expression uncertain. "Is that the truth of it? Or is it that you don't want to marry me?" His voice was quiet, but when he looked up at her, his eyes were full of vulnerability and fear.

"No, Tyreal, of course not. You know better than that." She dropped Anya's hands and moved toward him, heart racing. "I've only ever wanted you. But you also know I'm right to be concerned. This will shake the very foundation of everything our people believe if we reveal it. I'm terrified of not keeping you and my people safe. If I can do that and be your wife, I will be the happiest woman alive. But if I can't have both, I'll choose yours and Tavia's safety every time."

Tyreal closed the gap between them, pulling her into his arms. "As long as you want me by your side, I will be. Possibly even if you didn't want me there. But it's I who should be worrying about keeping us safe. It's my whole job." He tilted her chin up, pressing his forehead to hers. "As for the Sisters, I still don't care what a bunch of people I've never met say about my worthiness to be with you. I figured out long ago that I'm not worthy. But I love you. With every fiber of my being." He kissed her then, his lips moving reverently against hers.

Gwen closed her eyes, trying to relax in the feel of his arms, the kiss, and the certainty of his words. Yet panic still raked at the edges of her mind. Was Anya right—was she simply scared at the idea that she could have what she'd always wanted? Or was her fear justified?

"Let's go back inside and discuss this with Max. I think we're past the time to fill him in on everything, anyway. He'll be a good gauge of how people will respond to all of this since he was unconscious when Tyreal healed him," Anya suggested.

Gwen gaped at her. "Are you, of all people, suggesting we go against a direct order from the Sisters?" Anya had always followed their orders to the letter during training. If she hadn't already been betrothed to Max, Anya would likely have become a Sister herself.

Anya met her gaze, cheeks pink. "Hush. The Sisters are usually right, and I don't really consider this going against them. Max already knows magic exists now. I'm just filling in the gaps."

"I'm just teasing. I agree. Go ahead inside. I want to talk with Tyreal a bit more. If you want to fill him in without us, you can. Or we can do it together." Gwen gestured toward the house. Anya nodded and headed in.

Turning back to Tyreal, Gwen sighed. "I'm scared. The word of the Sisters is final. Our continent's foundation is built on that principle. All the countries agreed to it when they were formed after the war. I came on this trip wanting their advice about Adaltus and Galeigh, but now I—"

Tyreal kissed her forehead and took her hand, leading her away from the garden. "Walk with me. There's something I want you to see." They strolled along the path, fingers intertwined. Both fell silent, and Gwen wondered if all the revelations of the past two days weighed as heavily on him as they did on her.

The path widened, bordered by delicate ferns and creeping ivy, transforming from gravel to dirt as it wrapped around the pond she'd glimpsed from the garden. He motioned toward a secluded opening nestled among the roots of a giant tree, trailing vines partially obscuring the entrance. As he moved them aside to usher her inside, Gwen felt a flutter of anticipation.

Inside, her gaze drifted upward. High above, the cave's ceiling revealed a handful of sleeping bats and several cracks and holes, through which slender beams of sunlight filtered in, casting a romantic glow over the interior. The space was small, with a flat ledge just wide enough for the two of them, dropping off over a natural cenote. The beams of sunlight danced across the azure water, making it shimmer with an otherworldly glow.

"This is gorgeous," Gwen breathed in awe.

"I've wanted to show this to you since I first discovered it as a boy." He tugged his tunic off, dropping it onto the small ledge.

"What are you doing?" she asked, playfully feigning weariness.

"A hot spring feeds this pool. There's nothing in this world that will relax you quite like the feel of its waters. And I've longed to have you in it for almost as long as I've wanted to show it to you. So, sweet girl, take off your clothes." He untied his breeches and removed his shoes.

"But—"

"No buts. Max and Anya are safe with my mother. He needs to rest and eat before we can get back on the road. We can't deal with anything related to the Sisters, magic, or anything else right now. And I can see you getting lost in that head of yours with all the what-ifs." Now nude, he closed the distance between them, tugging her top from her waistband. "So, we're going to get into that water. Maybe we just lay there and let the heat ease our aching muscles from all the riding. Or maybe the gods will smile upon me and grant me the fortune of distracting you in ways I much prefer. But either way, you're taking off your clothes and getting in. Even if I must throw you in."

"You wouldn't dare."

"Gwennie, you've known me almost your entire life. You know damn good and well that I would dare, and that a part of me hopes you push me to it." His fingers grazed over the skin of her breast, and she could feel it break out in chill bumps as her nipple hardened. She bit her lip, looking up into his eyes, which darkened with desire.

"Sounds like I don't have much of a choice. Whatever shall an innocent girl like myself do in such a predicament with a dastardly rogue of a man?"

Tyreal smirked. "I think 'innocent' went out the window when you teased me until I broke. But aside from that, you probably shouldn't wander into secluded caves with dastardly rogues, Your Majesty." He elongated her title with a hint of mockery, making her flush. He helped her remove the rest of her clothing, pressing hot, light kisses along the revealed skin as he did so.

Determined not to let him throw her in for the fun of it, she seized the moment of his distraction, darting away from his kisses and leaping into the pool. She heard him laugh as he followed her. The water enveloped her, silky with minerals—almost uncomfortably hot, yet just the right temperature for her body to melt into bliss.

Gwen resurfaced, groaning in delight. Tyreal's arms snaked around her, pulling her roughly against him. "Naughty little minx, you ruined my fun," he growled into her ear. His mouth pressed against her throat while his hand slid down her front, nestling his fingers between her thighs. Gwen groaned for an entirely new reason.

"This is the first place I've been able to have you without worrying about keeping you quiet. So, I fully intend to make you scream my name," he growled, his breath hot against her skin. She shivered, need flooding her senses and making her toes curl.

"And how do you intend to do that? You seem extremely confident." She rolled her head back, granting him better access to her throat. Her eyes fluttered shut as his fingers teased her.

"I know it's only been a little while, love, but I'm a quick learner—particularly on my favorite subject: all things Gwen. You're more beautiful than anything I've ever seen in my travels, even the sun rising over a field of lilabrock flowers. And the sound you make when you come un-done with me inside you?" He inhaled deeply, as if savoring a fine wine. "There's no sound in this world that rivals its perfection. So, yes, I've already learned several ways to recreate that sound, and I intend to keep finding them."

As he spoke, his fingers continued to stroke and tease until she squirmed restlessly against him. She reached back to grasp him, to tease him in return, but he captured her wrist with his free hand, holding it tightly. "You don't get to move. You're going to take everything I give you like a good girl." His words ignited a flood of heat across her body, and she gasped.

It was as if the warmth of the water and his actions placed her in a trance. Minutes melted away, sensations overwhelming her as she finally allowed herself to feel.

"That's right, sweet girl, let go." His voice was hot against her skin, fingers moving just right, and she came undone, a soft cry escaping her lips. "No, no. We can do better than that."

Tyreal spun her to face him, gripping her bottom cheeks and spreading her thighs, lining her up just right. He pressed the length of his cock into her, and when he was fully inside, Gwen thought she could die content, ready to enter the Everafter.

His lips met hers as he maneuvered them toward the back of the cenote, directly beneath the ledge she had jumped from. He kept her afloat, wrapping her legs around his hips so he could remain inside her as he pressed her back against the smooth rock wall, lifting her slightly out of the water.

Tyreal took his time, alternating his pace and movements until she felt her mind sink into a blissful quiet where nothing existed but his body inside hers. By the time he finished, she screamed his name so loudly that she startled the bats overhead.

CHAPTER TWENTY-SEVEN

A crow landed on the small wooden table beside Gwen, carrying a neatly rolled piece of parchment in a leather carrier strapped to its leg. Setting aside the bundle of herbs she was tying, Gwen wiped her hands on her borrowed work apron and gave a distinct whistle—the unique pattern that signaled her identity to the crow. It responded with three sharp caws, stomping its claw three times until the carrier popped open, and the parchment slid free.

"Thank you, my feathered friend," Gwen murmured, gently stroking the crow's sleek head. It blinked at her, and she gestured toward the flower and herb beds. "Help yourself, but be quick about it—Marie will chase you from her garden if you linger."

As the crow hopped away, Gwen unfurled the parchment, her expression darkening. Previous updates from Pip and Hedontas had been promising, detailing successful trades and a well-stocked larder while they awaited Max's recovery at the cabin. This message, however, was different; it was from Andais and addressed to both her and Tyreal:

L en route to Tavia. Journey expected to take another moon. If HM not returned, need orders on how to greet him.

Tucking the parchment into her apron pocket, Gwen made her way through the garden to the lean-to where they were sheltering the horses. Inside, Tyreal was mucking out the stalls. She watched him handle the pitchfork with practiced ease, lifting soiled straw into the wheelbarrow. The sun glinted off his skin, highlighting the effortless way he moved despite the hard labor. He seemed so peaceful here in his mother's home; she regretted the impending return to court politics and talks of potential war.

"You're thinking so loudly I can hear you from here, Gwennie," Tyreal said, not pausing in his chore.

"We received a message from Andais. Lovell rides for Tavia. He's asking if we'll return within a moon and if not, how he should proceed," Gwen relayed.

Tyreal paused, planting the pitchfork in the ground and leaning on it. "That's not really a 'we' question, is it? How do you want him to proceed?"

"It is a 'we' question. You're the High Captain, and the defense of Tavia falls under your command. Plus, if the sisters agree, you'll be King Consort." She raised the side of her thumb to her mouth in thought, but Tyreal's expression had her lowering her hand.

"All of which still requires me to follow your orders. If it were up to me, I'd send an assassin and be done with it. Politics isn't my strength; that's always been your area. What's your take? Ideally, we will be back before Lovell arrives, but if not, Andais needs guidance."

Gwen sighed, weighing her options and their potential outcomes. "I'll tell Andais to entertain Lovell and keep him monitored until I decide otherwise. They must tighten Pip's security—that's crucial."

"Obviously," Tyreal nodded. "I'm sure Hedontas and Andais already have that covered."

"We must leave today, even if Max isn't fully recovered. We can send a crow to Cora and Tensha and have them come get him if necessary, but we need to reach the sisters and get these questions answered so we can return home where we belong. Or, at least to where I belong. You seem quite peaceful here..." She let her words drift off, surveying the charming little farm.

"Taking a holiday is always peaceful for a while. But I have a home, and it is by your side. You can't get rid of me that easily. The horses are well-rested. I'll talk with my mother and Alric about what we need to do for the prince and princess. If we hurry, we can still make good time before sundown."

Marie and Max had both agreed that he was strong enough to ride, as long as he continued his tincture. This worked out well since Anya was reluctant to ride without him but eager to see the High Sister. For the next few days, they traversed the rugged mountain trails, the time blurring under the relentless pace. By nightfall, their bodies succumbed to a bone-deep weariness only hard travel could produce. The comfort of inns and warm hearths lay behind them, replaced by makeshift camps under a vast night sky.

As they ascended further north, the air turned sharply cold, carrying the crisp promise of impending snow. Each inhaled breath felt borderline painful, icy, though not a single snowflake had yet fallen. The famous mists, from which the mountains took their name, thickened around them, shrouding the path in an eerie, ghost-like embrace.

Gwen pulled her cloak tighter against the chill. She recalled her summer visits to the sisters when the paths were adorned with wildflowers instead of frosted fallen leaves. "This is why," she muttered to herself, gazing into the thickening gray, "travel this far north is only for the warmth of summer."

Eventually, the dense fog parted enough for them to glimpse the massive iron-bound gate, forged from the dark minerals of the mountain. Nestled among the towering cliffs, Mist Castle loomed beyond—a formidable silhouette against the dimming light.

"It looks deserted," Tyreal murmured beside her, his face unreadable as he beheld the castle for the first time.

"The sisters retreat to their rituals early, especially now that nights are growing longer," Gwen explained softly, dismounting from Akasha. "In this fog and dark, a guard would be useless. The gate is impenetrable, so they don't waste the labor."

Max groaned. "Then how are we to get inside? I, for one, would prefer not to sleep on the ground again tonight if I can help it. I fear I'm rapidly reaching my limits as a spoiled prince."

Gwen and Anya exchanged smiles. "We have our ways," Gwen said, approaching what appeared to be decorative stone boxes flanking the gate. With practiced ease, she struck flint to kindling, the sparks catching despite the misty, damp air. Anya poured water from her flask into the receptacle opposite Gwen's. Together, they summoned their elemental magic—fire and water mingling, glowing—a soft illumination against the darkening sky. As their powers swelled, filling the carved confines of the stone, the gate responded, groaning loudly as ancient metal yielded, slowly creaking open.

Max watched them with his mouth agape, eyes wide with disbelief. He shook his head, a mix of awe and unease in his expression. "You all explained this to me, but seeing it in action... that's something else entirely," he admitted, forcing a strained smile at Anya. While he had taken the revelation about magic in stride, it clearly unsettled him more than he cared to admit.

Anya returned his smile, taking her horse's reins and walking through the gates. "You get used to it eventually."

Tyreal continued to stare at the gate in wonder. "That's incredible. Could you do something like that to Thorncliff's gate?"

Gwen shook her head, a sad smile crossing her face. "No, I'm afraid that's beyond our magical abilities now. Myaessa crafted this gate and the entire castle herself, before she called all the women here to gather."

The courtyard was slick with mist, cobblestones glistening underfoot. Gwen and Anya led their horses with sure steps to the stables, familiar with every inch of the path. As the heavy sound of the closing gate reverberated through the foggy twilight, they were almost finished helping the men secure the horses when a sudden movement caught their attention. A young girl, barely past her fourteenth summer, emerged from the shadows of the stable. Her gray robe, trimmed in blue to mark her as a novice, was slightly askew, as if she had hastily thrown it on. Her wide, alarmed eyes flicked between Gwen, Anya, and the men.

"Your Highnesses, you brought men here?" she hissed, her voice trembling with both fear and a hint of betrayal that made Gwen wince. "Inside the gates without the sisters knowing?"

Gwen stepped forward, hands raised. "Sister, these are serious circumstances, and these men are trusted. Prince Maximillen is married to Princess Anya now. As I am now Queen of Tavia, this is my High Captain, Tyreal Blackbane. We wouldn't have made the journey if it weren't of vital importance." She kept her voice calm, despite the tension knotting in her stomach. How did the girl not know that Gwen was queen now? Something felt off.

The girl bit her lip but dropped into a quick curtsey. "Forgive me, Your Majesty. I was unaware of the change in your station. But how did you open the gates? Surely you didn't—" Her voice trailed off as her gaze fixed on Tyreal and Max, who were trying to appear non-threatening. Alric made no such attempt; his size rendered him imposing, so he merely stood, stroking his horse's mane as he waited for them to proceed.

Anya stepped closer to Gwen. "Yes, we used our powers to open the gate. They know the truth." The girl's expression shifted to alarm, and her mouth opened as she pressed a hand to her chest. "Rest assured," Anya continued, "this is part of the serious matter we mentioned. Please run inside and inform the High Sister we are here. We will explain everything once we've gotten inside and warmed up."

Still hesitant, the girl nodded slowly. "Yes, Your Highness. I'll announce your arrival, but please, wait here." She turned and dashed toward the castle.

Gwen sighed. "That could have gone better."

Tyreal watched the young girl disappear inside the castle, his expression serious. He flexed his hand, glancing around warily. Moving closer to Gwen, he asked, "Are you certain we did the right thing by coming here?"

"Yes—" Anya started.

"I hope so," Gwen interjected. "For all our sakes, I hope so. But I'll admit, I'm uncertain." She met Anya's gaze; her friend looked disappointed, her pretty features pinched in a frown. Gwen shrugged, unwilling to hide her doubts.

Minutes passed before the novice girl returned, silently motioning for them to follow her inside. She led them through winding paths that cut through the meticulously maintained gardens, now cloaked in mist and darkness. The gardens had always been a favorite retreat for Gwen during her brief breaks from training and chores. She would snag a book from the massive library and curl up in a shaded spot, reading until it was time to resume her duties. A fond smile curled her lips at the memory, easing her anxiety some. She *knew* this place and the people inside.

The girl turned to them, her expression unreadable as she grasped the latch of the giant doors to the main keep. Gwen felt Tyreal shift uneasily, his hand moving toward his sword hilt, though he refrained from touching it. Just as quickly as it had left, Gwen's anxiety returned.

As the heavy door closed behind them, they entered the vast entry hall of Mist Castle. It looked as it always had to Gwen: a cavernous space with high arched ceilings that vanished into shadows. Tapestries lined the walls, mingling with statues of previous High Sisters. Flickering torches mounted in wrought iron sconces cast dim, dancing light, throwing their long shadows along the cold stone floor. Each step echoed loudly, magnified by the silence that enveloped the castle.

The air inside the great hall was even cooler, carrying the scent of pine resin and old stone, but thankfully marginally warmer than outside. Gwen longed for a roaring fire in a hearth; the chill and damp had seeped into her clothing, and she had not bathed since leaving Marie's cottage. She sincerely hoped this initial meeting would go smoothly, allowing them to retire to their chambers quickly.

"The High Sister awaits you in the Chamber of Councils. Do you remember the way?" The girl twisted her robes nervously. She tried to keep her gaze on Gwen, but her eyes flicked toward the men, a blush staining her freckled cheeks.

"Yes, sister. Thank you," Gwen said, offering a reassuring smile.

Anya marched ahead, leading them through various hallways and up a large spiral staircase. They finally reached the door to the Chamber of Councils, flanked by a large statue of Myaessa Thorncrest—Gwen's ancestor, who had sacrificed everything to end the war by eliminating magic. Gwen placed her fingers on the statue, casting a silent prayer for guidance. *Help me figure this out and keep everyone safe, please. Don't let me be the one who ends the peace you gave everything for.*

Anya knocked softly on the door, and the High Sister's voice bid them enter. The chamber was small and intimate, centered around a large round table surrounded by high-backed chairs. Heavy velvet curtains covered the wall of windows, muffling the howling mountain winds outside. A roaring fire crackled in the fireplace, and Gwen silently thanked the gods for it.

The High Sister stood as they entered, her presence as striking now as it had been when Gwen was a child. Tall and regal, her silver hair flowed down around her shoulders, and she wore the traditional deep blue and silver-trimmed robes that signified her rank. Age lightly lined her face, but in truth, Gwen didn't know how old she was. She had been High Sister when Gwen first arrived and appeared no older now than then. Her pale blue eyes were sharp and discerning, surveying each of them before finally resting on Gwen and Anya. Despite the small, almost wistful smile she gave them, she only bowed slightly in acknowledgement of their ranks—something that made Gwen acutely uncomfortable.

"Welcome back to Mist Castle, Gwendolyn. It has been too long since you visited," she stated, her voice warmer than Gwen had expected.

Gwen smiled in response, but the lack of her title bugged her. "Thank you, High Sister. It's good to be back. Though I wish it was under better circumstances."

The High Sister's attention shifted to the men behind them, her expression unreadable. "Yes, your companions are most unexpected, but I trust you have your reasons."

Anya stepped forward. "We do, High Sister. We originally began our journey to seek your guidance. After King Lorne's passing, when Gwen ascended to the throne, other countries sought to move against her in what could be considered acts of war."

The High Sister's gaze remained fixed on Gwen as she made a thoughtful sound. "Well, that is certainly a very important reason for the journey, though it doesn't explain your company, nor why you felt it was necessary to expose our greatest secret."

The tension in the room became palpable, and Gwen's heart thumped uncomfortably in her chest. She forced herself to give a small nod with a mildly contrite smile. "There's a good reason for that High Sister—one that was unavoidable. But I would appreciate the chance to warm up, eat, and clean ourselves before delving into that particularly lengthy tale." Her tone was cool and respectful but also unbothered; she was the queen here.

The High Sister's eyes narrowed into a look Gwen couldn't decipher, but her smile seemed friendly enough. "Of course, forgive me. The sisters pride ourselves on our hospitality. You and Anya may retire to your usual rooms, and your guests will be provided accommodations."

Gwen caught Anya's confused expression out of the corner of her eye but stayed focused on the High Sister. "We appreciate your gracious hospitality, given the uniqueness of our visit." The High Sister stilled, waiting for Gwen to continue, which Gwen did, somehow resisting the urge to pick at her finger and hold strong. "However, as visiting royals seeking your guidance and not as your trainees, we must insist on appropriate accommodations. Princess Anya and Prince Maximillen are married, and Alric prefers to stay close to the Crown Prince as part of his oath. My High Captain goes where I go."

"Very well," the High Sister replied in a low voice, a hint of disapproval lacing her words. "Wearing the crown is such a heavy burden. I do hope that your time among us has prepared you for it."

Gwen hesitated, the words catching in her throat. There was no outright accusation in the High Sister's tone, but something about the way she spoke felt... pointed. "I hope so," Gwen replied evenly, meeting her gaze. "It was your guidance that shaped much of who I am."

The High Sister's smile softened, the lines around her eyes crinkling. "As it should. The Sisterhood exists to shape women into the leaders this world needs." Her eyes flicked over towards Tyreal and Max again. "And yet, there is always more to learn. You have grown, Gwendolyn, but growth often comes with missteps. I trust you will tread carefully as you navigate the path before you."

Anya cleared her throat, clearly uncomfortable with the shift in conversation. "As young royals, we are grateful for everything we learned here and will be glad to make sense of recent events with your help."

It did not escape Gwen's notice that, though the High Sister smiled and inclined her head in agreement, she never once looked at Anya, let alone acknowledged her. The slight stiffening of Anya's shoulders and the flicker of hurt that passed over her face confirmed that she had noticed the omission as well. Gwen forced her lips into a warm smile, determined to mask the unease gnawing at her. As she turned to follow the servant from the room, she glanced at Tyreal. His expression was impassive, a mask of practiced neutrality, but his eyes betrayed him—angry and full of questions. She wasn't imagining it. This entire encounter felt wrong. But why?

CHAPTER TWENTY-EIGHT

Marta, a servant close to Gwen and Anya in age, guided them through the dimly lit corridors of the castle, leading them toward a secluded wing Gwen had only glimpsed during her visits the previous summer. The heavy doors creaked open, revealing a suite of rooms opposite one another. Anya, Max, and Alric claimed one room, while Gwen and Tyreal stepped into the adjacent one.

Inside, a large, ornate bed dominated the chamber, its headboard intricately carved with moons and stars. Velvet curtains, faded with time, hung around it, casting the room in a muted glow. Beside the bed, under a stone archway, sat a modest single bed nestled in a smaller alcove. Its simple frame stood in stark contrast to the grandeur of the larger one.

A cold, unused fireplace seemed to beg for a flame, and nearby, a large wooden tub stood, awaiting water. Gwen almost wept at the sight of it—the road had offered no such comforts. She turned to Marta, who nervously moved about the room, dusting off furniture with the apron of her dress.

"Someone will come shortly to light the fire and bring water for your bath, Your Majesty. We have garments for you and Her Highness to change into..." Marta's gaze flicked to Tyreal, unease creeping across her face as her words trailed off. "However, we have nothing for your... guests."

Gwen stiffened. "That can't be true. There should be clothing from when Princess Eliana was here. It would fit Prince Maximillen—he's about the same size."

Marta flushed, her gaze dropping to the floor. "I'm sorry, Your Majesty."

Tyreal, ever calm, gestured toward the saddlebags he had brought in from the stables. "It's fine. We have our own clothes, though they need laundering. If your staff can assist, we'll manage. In the meantime, a few large, clean shifts will do for us 'strange male creatures.'" He flashed a charming smile, hoping to lighten the mood.

"Of course, High Captain," Marta replied, quickly scooping up the saddlebags before practically fleeing from the room.

Tyreal sat on a bench near the smaller bed, rubbing his hands over his face. "This feels like the beginning of a very long night," he muttered, pulling off his tunic and grimacing at the smell.

Gwen nodded, watching the servants bustle in and out with steaming water and firewood. When Marta returned, she handed Tyreal a bundle of shifts, her eyes widening at the sight of him shirtless. Gwen stifled a giggle at the flustered reaction.

"Captain Blackbane," Gwen teased, "please try not to distract the staff." She motioned to the screen. "Ladies, can we set this up for some privacy?"

With the bathing area arranged and Tyreal stationed at the door to maintain the illusion of her virtue for the servants, Gwen finally sank into the hot water. The heat enveloped her, easing the exhaustion from her bones. Bundles of lavender floated atop the water, a thoughtful gift from one of the girls. She smiled and plucked one from the surface, inspecting it. *Perhaps not everyone in the castle resents me for bringing men.*

"Are you joining me now that they've gone?" Gwen called, her voice echoing in the chamber as she sunk deeper into the tub.

Tyreal peered around the screen. "As much as I'd love to, sweet girl, I must decline. This place puts me on edge, and I won't risk being caught off guard lounging in a bath with you." Despite his words, he moved closer, pulling a chair near the tub and gently scrubbing her shoulders with a cloth, forming suds with the bar of soap. "The High Sister is certainly different than I expected. Is she always so... friendly?"

"She's always been intimidating," Gwen admitted. "But there's a sharpness to her now that I didn't feel before. I'm not sure if I simply didn't notice it when I was younger, or if something has changed. Anya trusts her implicitly, though—"

"But you don't," Tyreal finished.

Gwen shook her head. "Not like I used to. Things feel off. I'm not convinced telling them about what happened with Max is the right move. But I don't know how else to explain why Anya would've told him. With you, I can explain Skensy, but him and Alric... they're a different story." She sighed. "And I can't get permission for us to wed without revealing who you are. I wish I had more time to think, but we're running out."

She took the cloth from him, and he pressed a kiss to her forehead before returning to his post at the door. Gwen appreciated how he always seemed to know when she needed space. After finishing her bath and drying off, her mind swirled with questions about their next move. A soft knock on the door broke her reverie, and she heard Tyreal and Anya speaking outside.

Quickly, Gwen donned a simple shift and dress Marta had left behind the screen. She towel-dried her hair, letting it fall in damp ringlets down her back. When she emerged, she found Anya standing with her arms tightly crossed over her chest, unbathed and unchanged, which told Gwen that something was wrong.

"I don't understand why the High Sister was so cold," Anya began, her voice tight with frustration. "Why did she treat us like we were still just trainees? Why put us in our old childhood chambers? I've always been given a room befitting my station when I've visited, and she wouldn't even look at me."

"It's a power play to punish us for breaking our oaths," Gwen explained, her tone gentle. She hated seeing Anya so upset. "She sees our breach as a serious offense. I don't think she'll accept our reasoning."

"They can't seriously think we're the first women in centuries to tell our husbands the truth. That's absurd. We had a good reason, and we didn't lie about it," Anya paced in tight circles, her frustration palpable. "We're some of the highest-ranking royals on this continent, and we're sisters. Why would they question whether our reason was justified? Surely, they understand we wouldn't break our oath unless we had no choice."

Gwen walked to the window, gazing out into the misty darkness. "It's not about understanding. It's about control. The sisterhood has ruled with almost unchecked power since magic fell. We've never questioned it, because they trained us. They stand apart from royal customs and bow to no one—even though they live in my country. They don't pay taxes, while our nations do. Anything—or anyone—that threatens that balance is seen as a threat."

Anya scoffed. "What are you saying? That the sisters are some evil force we need to dismantle? Having a neutral party is useful. Shouldn't we trust them to guide us?"

"No," Gwen said firmly, turning to face her. "I respect them, but we need to tread carefully. We're not little girls anymore, blindly following our training. We're playing a political game now. I'm the queen, and you will be soon enough. Something doesn't feel right, and we can't blindly worship the sisters. We need to see this from every angle."

Anya chewed on her bottom lip, considering Gwen's words. "Normally, I'd think you're being dramatic, but the High Sister was different. Maybe it's naïve of me to dismiss your concerns." She sighed heavily. "I'm going to bathe. And pray there's something sweet and delicious to eat afterward."

Gwen watched her friend leave, her mind churning with possibilities. Tyreal's voice startled her, making her blink. "What?"

"I asked how many of the actual sisters have magic," he repeated, his voice tense. "I assume at least some are commoners; there aren't that many royals."

Gwen pursed her lips, thinking. "I'm not sure of the exact number, but Mama always said it's about a third of royal women who present with magic. Most of those don't stay in the sisterhood because they're heirs or betrothed, like Anya. If I had to guess, about eight or nine have magic, not counting Anya or me."

"Not terrible numbers, considering they've got magic and are trained to use it offensively," Tyreal said, more to himself than to her. He seemed lost in thought, his mind calculating. "All of them must have a source with them, like you and Anya?"

Gwen nodded, her stomach churning at the thought of Tyreal needing to fight against the women who had shaped so much of her childhood. "They all carry sources."

He raised an eyebrow. "You never thought to do that for yourself? They didn't train you to carry a source?"

Gwen frowned, irritated by his tone, though she had to admit he had a point. "I tend to ignore your lectures." She shrugged. "But I'll admit, it's a good question. Tyreal, I don't think it'll come to that. I don't want violence."

He scoffed. "Obviously, Gwen. I'd rather not be fighting a bunch of women—or, more accurately, getting my ass handed to me by their magic. But we need to know what we're up against, especially if things go sideways. We have two magic users, and they have eight or nine."

Gwen walked over to him, wrapping her arms around his waist, resting her head against his chest. "It won't go sideways. I won't let it. Now go clean up. I want us all at our best when we go downstairs to eat."

He nodded, leaning down to kiss her, but a knock interrupted them. Tyreal grumbled, moving to check the door. He returned with Marta, who was carrying a tray with steaming tea and cups.

"Forgive me, Your Majesty," Marta said, "There were scones, but Princess Anya took them all and said you wouldn't want any."

Gwen laughed. "That's fine, Marta. I know her sweet tooth well. She's just in a mood from the travel." She refrained from mentioning the High Sister's chilly reception.

Marta set the tray down and turned to Tyreal, sheepish. "I owe you an apology, High Captain. Seeing you menfolk startled me, but I shouldn't have hesitated to offer warmth, clean clothes, and food. You still needed it, and I should've remembered my mama's rules."

Gwen smiled at Marta. "You were right to remind me of Princess Eliana. She struggled with her adjustment here, too, because of the High Sister."

Gwen exchanged a silent glance with Tyreal, then gestured for him to clean up behind the screen. Her gaze flicked toward the fire, a quiet reassurance that she was safe and more than capable of defending herself. He nodded faintly and excused himself.

"I didn't know Eliana well at first," Gwen said, pouring tea into two cups. "But by the time we grew close, she was too focused on finally becoming her true self to dwell on past troubles." She handed one of the cups to Marta with a small, knowing smile. "Captain Blackbane, of course, would scoff at tea. He's more of an ale or spirits man. But for now, let's savor this quiet moment, shall we?"

Marta hesitated, her gaze flickering between Gwen and the cup, but the warmth in Gwen's smile softened her expression, and she accepted the tea. They settled into seats near the crackling fire, and Gwen sighed in contentment at the familiar warmth.

"Thank you, Your Majesty," Marta said, her voice soft. "You've always been kind. I apologize for my earlier coldness. Tensions in the castle have been high, and your arrival only seemed to stir them more."

Gwen nodded, taking a sip of tea to steady herself. "Tensions seem to be everywhere these days. But tell me, Marta—was it difficult for Princess Eliana when she trained here? It saddens me to think she might have faced hardship, and I never knew."

Marta's fingers traced the grain of the wooden table, her eyes distant as she considered Gwen's words. "The High Sister holds firm views—on tradition and what's proper. Her methods... aren't always kind. I don't think she ever truly accepted the Princess for who she was. There were whispers, of course, but few were brave enough to speak out. It was hard for the Princess, at least in the beginning."

Gwen's brow furrowed in concern. "Hard enough to cause harm?"

Marta lowered her voice, her eyes darting toward the door. "Hard enough to make some question it," she said carefully. "There are sisters here who believe compassion should guide us more than rigid rules. They might speak out, under the right circumstances."

Gwen leaned forward, her interest piqued despite the caution that tugged at her. "Might? Or would they act, if it meant bringing about real change?"

Marta glanced nervously toward the door, her unease clear. "I couldn't say for certain. I shouldn't have said anything."

Gwen reached out, briefly covering Marta's hand. "I'm not stirring trouble. But I need to know if others are concerned. I'm queen of Tavia, and I care for all of you. Can you quietly arrange a meeting?"

After a long pause, Marta gave a small nod. "I'll try. For the Princess."

"Thank you," Gwen said softly, letting her gratitude show. "This stays between us for now."

As Marta left, Gwen sank back into her chair, the warmth of the tea grounding her. Tyreal's hand slid into hers, gently pulling it away from her mouth, where she'd been absentmindedly picking at her skin.

"Did you hear any of that?" she asked, surprised.

"Most of it," he replied. "I just hope we can gather our potential allies before we really need them."

CHAPTER TWENTY-NINE

Tyreal walked beside Gwen, their footsteps echoing softly through the dimly lit hallways as they made their way toward the dining hall. Max, Anya, and Alric followed, an unspoken tension thick in the air. They moved in silence, each of them no doubt contemplating the many ways this dinner could unfold.

He stole a glance at Gwen. Her curls were wild and untamed from her bath, and in the plain, borrowed dress, she almost looked like any common girl he might encounter in a village. Under different circumstances, he would have relished the idea of pretending to be just two ordinary souls, imagining the trouble they could stir. But instead, they were here to curry favor with people he didn't know—people who could easily end his life. Not nearly as fun.

Gwen paused beside a tapestry, its edges worn and faded, yet the golden rose of her family crest still glimmered proudly at its center. She stared at it for a moment, her fingers brushing the edge of the fabric, her expression distant. Tyreal remembered her stories of the ancestor who had built this castle, and for a brief moment, he wished he could read her thoughts. Then, with a small shift in posture, her shoulders squared, and she moved forward, reclaiming her place in the history that surrounded her. She wasn't just a guest or a former student—she was the queen of this land.

Tyreal felt a swell of admiration. Yet beneath it, a gnawing unease churned in his gut. Walking into this dining hall and explaining everything that had transpired felt like painting a target on their backs. The danger was undeniable, no matter what Gwen and Anya might want to believe. He hadn't even begun to come to terms with his newfound magic—or the startling truth of his royal bloodline. Now, he was expected to bare it all before a council of women who could decide his fate with a word.

As they approached the massive, intricately carved doors of the dining hall, servant girls pulled them open. The sight before him took his breath away: the room glowed with hundreds of candles, casting a soft, golden light over the vast space. The tables were arranged as they were at Thorncliff Castle, save for one long table elevated above the rest, where the High Sister and four other women sat, looking down upon the novices and sisters.

Something about the scene irked Tyreal, though he couldn't pinpoint why. That none of the women rose to acknowledge Gwen certainly didn't help. The other sisters glanced nervously at the High Sister, waiting for a cue. When none came, their discomfort was palpable.

The High Sister gestured toward a row of seats, her smile not quite reaching her eyes. "Please, be seated. Sisters and guests, we gather tonight to share in the bounty of our land and the strength of our fellowship," she began, her voice resonating in the high-ceilinged room as she led them in a prayer to the gods.

Tyreal could feel the tension radiating off Gwen, sharp and unrelenting. Her earlier conversation with Anya echoed in his mind—the tithes every country paid to the Sisterhood, the unquestioned authority it wielded. Was this truly the legacy their ancestors had intended? From his vantage point, the High Sister didn't just act like a leader; she carried herself like a queen—or worse, as though she stood above them all.

As the meal began, he couldn't ignore the whispers that rippled through the sisters, their furtive glances flickering in their direction. He forced his posture to remain calm and unthreatening, but his instincts prickled with unease. Something was brewing here—something he couldn't quite name. For a fleeting moment, the reckless urge to stand, hoist Gwen over his shoulder, and flee this place surged through him. It felt like the most sensible option of all.

Beside him, Gwen picked at her food, her tension palpable. Perhaps no one else noticed, but he knew her better than he knew himself. She set her fork down with deliberate care, her shoulders stiffening before she rose to her feet. The soft murmur of voices around the room stilled instantly, replaced by a charged silence. Every pair of eyes turned toward her.

"It's strange," Gwen said lightly, almost conversationally, as though she were commenting on the weather. "I distinctly remember visiting Mist Castle as a child with my mother. At the time, I recall everyone here rising to acknowledge her as queen. Has this practice changed, or am I mistaken?"

The sisters shifted in their seats, exchanging hesitant glances. Slowly, more than half the room rose and curtsied, their faces carefully composed, while the others remained seated, their eyes flickering nervously toward the head table. The High Sister remained still, her head tilting slightly as she regarded Gwen with a cool, inscrutable gaze. Tyreal's breath caught, his hand instinctively brushing the hilt of his sword. Gwen's bold move had caught him off guard—not because she acted, but because she acted so decisively. She was staking her claim, making it clear that she wasn't just a guest here; she was their queen. His gaze darted to Alric, whose subtle nod mirrored his unease.

The High Sister's voice broke the silence, calm but laced with an edge. "Customs evolve, Your Majesty, though respect for the crown has never wavered among these walls." Her words were gentle, but the weight behind them was unmistakable, and Tyreal couldn't help but sense an unspoken reprimand. "Perhaps those gathered here were simply unsure how to act, given the unusual nature of your visit."

Gwen's lips curved into a smile that didn't quite reach her eyes. "Unusual, yes. But even uncertainty can be overcome when one recalls the traditions we all hold dear."

"Of course," the High Sister said smoothly, inclining her head slightly. "And we are all eager to hear of the journey that has brought you back to Mist Castle. It is no small matter, I'm sure."

Gwen didn't sit. Her hands rested lightly on the table as she met the High Sister's gaze. "You're right—it isn't. Magic revealed itself to our companions without any action on my part or Princess Anya's during our journey here. Investigating this phenomenon forced us to reveal the information." Gwen chose not to mention Skensington's attack, and Tyreal approved of her decision.

"I don't quite understand how that would be possible without one of you revealing yourself," the High Sister mused thoughtfully, her fingers steepled before her. "The oaths we take bind us to protect something far greater than ourselves. To break such vows, no matter the reason, is not a decision to be taken lightly. Perhaps you might elaborate, so we can better understand the situation?"

Gwen's expression tightened, but before she could respond, Max rose from his seat beside her. He flashed an easy smile, his charm defusing some of the tension. "I think I can help explain," he said. "Because I was dying, and Captain Blackbane laid his hands on my wound and healed me. An event that surprised us all—especially me."

A wave of whispers rippled through the room. The sisters at the high table exchanged astonished and concerned glances. All eyes turned to Tyreal. He stiffened under their collective gaze, his jaw tightening. The High Sister's expression remained unreadable, but a flicker of interest passed through her pale eyes. He also stood, positioning himself protectively beside Gwen, hand still resting on his sword—a silent declaration of his readiness to defend his queen.

"That is a bold claim," the High Sister said, her voice calm, though a sharp edge lingered beneath the surface. "And not one to be taken lightly within these sacred halls. Such an assertion, if untrue, would dishonor the traditions we have all sworn to uphold."

Her tone was sharp, and she leaned forward, her hands clasped on the table as her jaw tightened.

Anya's hand slipped into Max's, her chin lifting defiantly. "How dare you question our truthfulness! Gwen and I trained here for years—devoted ourselves to the traditions of this order. You've always told us that our lineage as descendants of the founding families was the foundation of our worth. Does that mean nothing now?"

A murmur rippled through the room as the sisters exchanged uneasy glances. Sister Seraphine, calm but firm, stood. "Perhaps we should all take a moment to center ourselves," she said, her voice soothing. "Her Highness is right. We are all sisters here, and there is no reason to assume deceit. Let us listen before passing judgment."

The High Sister's gaze flicked to Seraphine, her lips pressing into a thin line. For a moment, it seemed she might object, but she exhaled softly and leaned back in her chair. "Of course," she said, her tone returning to its composed state. "Sister Seraphine is right. While your story is... unusual, your words as royals carry weight. Please, explain further what transpired."

Her words were polite, but her eyes remained cold, calculating, as they moved from Gwen and finally settled on Anya. A flicker of disdain crossed her features but was gone too quickly for Tyreal to be sure. He was certain, though, that she intended to dissect every detail of their explanation.

"Well, I will defer to my wife and the Queen, as I was mostly unconscious for the largest part of it. But—" Max lifted his tunic to reveal the twisted scar tissue beneath. "I can assure you this wound should have killed me."

Whispers broke out anew as the women regarded the handsome prince and his scarred belly.

"The prince suffered a mortal wound when marauders attacked us on the road. Captain Blackbane laid his hands on him and expressed his desire to help. I witnessed his hands glow as the flesh repaired itself." Gwen spoke clearly and confidently, her voice steady. Gods, how he loved this woman.

"High Sister, there may be an explanation," a soft voice piped up from the back of the hall. Heads turned as a petite figure emerged from the shadows. Her steps were tentative, her hands trembling as she clasped them tightly in front of her, but she held her head high. Her hazel eyes, so like Gwen's, caught the light, and her dark curls framed her face in the same way. Tyreal studied her, noting the resemblance with quiet curiosity—could this be a relative from Asya's line?

"Sister Lila. Please enlighten us," the High Sister said dismissively, raising Tyreal's hackles.

He barely knew this woman, yet he was quickly beginning to dislike her.

Lila swallowed hard, her eyes darting briefly to Gwen, who offered her an encouraging nod. Gathering herself, she turned back to the High Sister. "If Captain Blackbane is of royal lineage, there is precedent. Myaessa's original spell included provisions allowing men of royal bloodlines to wield healing magic when aiding another royal family. There are... records of this."

A ripple of astonished gasps swept through the hall, quickly silenced by the High Sister's raised hand. Though her displeasure was palpable, she seemed to relax at this revelation. "An intriguing possibility. We always suspected that royal bastards might exist among the common folk, given the appetites of men. Though older records are often incomplete or misinterpreted by less skilled scribes."

Lila flinched under her words, retreating slightly, her courage visibly wavering.

Gwen cleared her throat, the small sound slicing through the tension. "High Sister, this revelation aligns with what I have come to understand. Captain Blackbane's lineage is undeniable. That is why, in addition to seeking your counsel regarding the political maneuverings from Adaltus to undermine my rule, I am here to formally announce my intention to marry him—thereby making him King Consort of Tavia, in accordance with the laws of the Sisterhood."

The High Sister laughed, her mirth dark and derisive. "We will not grant permission for a high-born royal to wed a bastard," she sneered, slamming her hand on the table, causing Lila to flinch and scurry back to her seat. Tyreal could see red flush Gwen's pale skin as her temper flared. The situation was spiraling.

Gwen stepped closer to Tyreal, placing a hand on his arm. She lifted her chin defiantly. "First, I am not *asking* permission. I am the queen. As you know, the law requires only that a consort be of royal blood to preserve the magical bloodlines. Tyreal has already demonstrated his abilities, which should suffice. Second, your accusation is baseless—Tyreal is not a bastard."

A hush fell over the hall, the weight of Gwen's words pulling the room into stillness. The High Sister's expression didn't waver, but the faintest flicker of surprise crossed her pale eyes. Tyreal stood motionless, his heart pounding.

"We stopped at Tyreal's mother's cabin on our way here, after the prince's close call," Gwen said, her tone steady but firm. "In our lands, she is known as a gifted healer. Many of you may have heard of her—Marie Ardienne."

Sister Seraphine inclined her head, her voice soft as she looked between Gwen and the High Sister. "We know of Marie. Her skill with herbal and natural remedies is widely respected."

Gwen nodded, her gaze sweeping the room before landing briefly on the High Sister. "Marie shared something with us after we explained how the prince survived his injuries. Her family possesses innate healing powers. Before returning to Tavia nearly a hundred summers ago, they resided in Candova, where her ancestor settled after leaving Tavia with nothing but the clothes on his back, five hundred summers ago."

Tyreal laid his hand over Gwen's, the warmth of her skin grounding him. When he spoke, his voice carried across the room with quiet authority. "This is my life too," he said, locking eyes with the High Sister. "And I won't stand by as a silent observer."

He straightened, his tone firm but not combative. "The evidence is clear. The Ardiennes are the tenth family. My ancestors. My bloodline. That makes me as royal as anyone else here, like it or not."

CHAPTER THIRTY

The silence that followed was oppressive, as if the very air had thickened with unspoken weight. The High Sister's expression remained unchanged, but there was something in her eyes—a glint, cold and sharp, unreadable. Slowly, she leaned forward, her hands folding with deliberate precision on the table.

"Royal blood," she said at last, her voice smooth, almost disarming. "An intriguing claim. And yet, one that warrants scrutiny. You understand, Captain, that the Sisterhood's purpose is not to elevate individuals, but to preserve peace and uphold our traditions. We cannot simply bend the rules at our convenience—"

Gwen shifted, stepping forward to interrupt. Tyreal reached for her arm, but she shrugged him off, her gaze fixed on the High Sister. Her tone was clipped, each word sharp with the fury beneath her calm exterior. "What traditions?" Gwen demanded, her voice cold. "Our traditions were meant to prepare for the day the tenth family seeks to reclaim power and prevent war. Yet while we've focused on threats long dead, real enemies have been working in the shadows."

The High Sister's head tilted, just enough to signal her interest. "Explain yourself, Your Majesty."

Gwen stepped forward, chin lifted in defiance. "Since I ascended the throne, Grigor Lovell, Prince of Adaltus, has conspired with Galeigh to undermine my rule. He's bribed my guards, stolen from Thorncliff's larders to spread rumors that I would let my people starve, and even threatened my brother Pip to force me into a marriage alliance. He seeks to destabilize the crown of Tavia for his own gain."

The High Sister's mask of composure remained unbroken, but her hands clenched tighter, her knuckles whitening. "These are grave accusations. I hope you have proof to support them," she said, her voice a quiet threat.

Gwen didn't flinch. "I do. Letters intercepted by my guards, confessions from those who once served Grigor and were caught in their treachery." Her voice dropped, low and unyielding.

"This is no baseless accusation, High Sister. He seeks to undermine my rule and control Tavia. And while the journey here revealed Tyreal's lineage and our magic, I will not ignore the very real threat of war at our borders."

The High Sister's lips parted as if to respond, but the tension in the room seemed to still her words. Her mouth snapped shut, teeth clicking as she inhaled sharply. "If this is true," she said after a pause, "it is indeed troubling. But as for the Ardiennes being the tenth family, we must conduct research before we act on such a theory. Sister Lila, collaborate with the other scribes and review the archives to determine if there is any evidence to support the queen's claims."

Lila hesitated, her hands trembling as she rose, clearly unnerved by the High Sister's tone. "Of course, High Sister," she murmured, bowing her head before retreating.

Gwen's fingers curled into fists, her nails biting into her palms as she fought to maintain her composure. She took a deep, steadying breath, her chest rising and falling with the effort to keep her voice even. "The Ardiennes' legacy is undeniable, whether your records acknowledge it or not. But I will not allow bureaucracy and tradition to overshadow the genuine threats we face."

Before she could continue, Sister Seraphina stepped forward, her voice low and calming. "What the High Sister means, Your Majesty, is that further research will help us understand the implications of this situation for the Sisterhood and how we can assist Captain Blackbane in controlling his magic. We are equally concerned by the activities you've described. Preventing war is the very purpose of our order."

She glanced around, seeking silent consensus from the assembled sisters. "I believe tempers are high, and we are all weary after a long day. Let us retreat to our rooms, offer ourselves to the gods in prayer, and seek their guidance. We can revisit this tomorrow."

Despite Seraphina's attempt to soothe the tension, Gwen's anger simmered beneath the surface. Her jaw clenched as she prepared to unleash her thoughts on the High Sister, but before she could speak, Max's voice cut through the charged air. "That sounds like an excellent idea," he said, flashing a broad, disarming smile as he rose to his feet. "I'm still recovering, and we've all had a long journey. A night of rest will do us all good."

As he surveyed the room, his sincerity was obvious, and Gwen felt the subtle shift in the air. Shoulders relaxed, and murmurs of agreement rippled through the sisters. Max had a way of softening even the most hostile rooms without breaking a sweat. Sometimes, she thought he wielded diplomacy better than any sword. "It's always easier to discuss matters of state with a clear head and a full belly," he continued, linking his arm with hers in a gentle yet firm grip that helped pull her back from the brink of anger.

Gwen caught the slight nod Max exchanged with Seraphina, who gracefully gestured for the sisters to leave. The council filed out of the dining hall, whispers lingering in the air, and Seraphina subtly steered the High Sister away, her touch light but insistent. As Max guided Gwen toward the door, her eyes locked with the High Sister's. There was no warmth towards her within them. This battle was far from over.

Tyreal, Anya, and Alric quietly fell in step behind them as they made their way back to their rooms. "Thank you," she whispered to Max.

Max smiled with a shrug. "Sometimes, the most powerful weapon a leader has is knowing when to retreat."

Gwen gave a small nod. It was a skill neither she nor Anya had quite mastered.

Once in the safety of the hallway, Alric broke the silence. "We should combine rooms," he suggested, his tone brokering no argument. "We'll rotate guard shifts through the night."

"Agreed," Tyreal said immediately, stepping ahead to inspect Gwen's room before allowing anyone inside.

As Alric and Tyreal rearranged furniture, fortifying the space into a makeshift stronghold, Max stretched out to rest. It was evident that he was still recovering. His skin had a sickly pallor that she didn't like. Gwen moved closer to Anya, noticing the defeated slump in her shoulders. "Are you alright?" she asked, knowing Anya had hoped for a better outcome this evening.

"Yes. Maybe? I don't know." Anya's voice faltered, a hint of bitterness creeping in. "She seemed so different from what I remembered," she confessed, her gaze shifting from the flickering flames in the hearth to meet Gwen's eyes. "Oh, come here," she suddenly changed the subject, a small smile flickering across her lips. "We must do something about this nest on your head, or it will be utterly unmanageable by morning."

Gwen grimaced but dutifully turned and seated herself in a nearby chair. She knew Anya often needed to occupy her hands to sort her thoughts. Anya dipped her fingers into a basin, scooping up water and working it through Gwen's tangled curls, which had dried into a chaotic mass after her hurried bath.

As Anya detangled the knots, she spoke softly. "I've always thought being a sister meant something important. Once I got over missing Mama that first summer, I was excited to be a part of it. Back home, I was just the forgotten princess—fourth in line to the throne, not even the only girl. But I had magic. Something rare, something that mattered. And the Sisterhood... it felt like family, a purpose. We stood for peace, goodwill, even protecting the realm when needed. I think I worshipped them, in a way."

Gwen listened intently as Anya's fingers lightly threaded through her hair. "Tonight, it felt as though the High Sister was more concerned with upholding traditions for tradition's sake than actually listening to us. Like she wanted to punish us for breaking the oath, not help us." Anya sighed deeply, a weariness that seemed to settle in her bones. "I think—I think I feel a bit betrayed. Not just by her, but by myself. Was I blind to this all along? I never even considered what you mentioned about the countries sending the sisters tithes until tonight. What kind of queen will I be if I don't see those things?" Her voice trembled.

Gwen reached up, resting a hand lightly on Anya's arm. "You believed in what the sisters should stand for, in what they could be. That doesn't make you blind or a bad future queen—it makes you hopeful. And hope is never a bad thing."

Anya smiled faintly, her eyes glistening. Gwen leaned back, brushing a stray curl from Anya's forehead. "Besides," she added with a smirk, "we don't know that all the sisters are like her. The High Sister may be drunk on power, but we haven't seen the same in Seraphina or the others. Hold on to that hope. We're going to need it."

Anya chuckled softly. "Your hair looks less awful. But I think only Cora can save you now. You're doomed until we get back to Thorncliff."

They both turned as a knock sounded at the door, and Marta was allowed to enter by Alric. Her fiery red hair escaped the confines of her bun as she quickly scanned the room, assessing the new furniture arrangement and the fact that they were all gathered in one place. She gave a quick curtsey.

"Your Majesty, Your Highnesses, and, um... Captain Blackbane." She stumbled over his title, unsure what to call him after the revelations in the dining hall. "I came to check on you again before I retire for the evening. Your Majesty, about what we spoke earlier... A few friends wish to meet with you in the library at midnight. They wanted you to come alone, but I told them I didn't believe the captain would agree to that plan."

"He would not," Tyreal quipped.

Marta's expression softened slightly as she smiled, her eyes flicking to Tyreal before settling back on Gwen. "They understand the concern but are worried—frightened, even. They think it's best to keep the gathering small, to attract less attention."

Gwen nodded. "I understand. I know they're risking the High Sister's wrath by secretly meeting with me. Tell them I'll come, but Captain Blackbane accompanies me. No negotiations on that," she stated firmly. Marta gave a small nod, the lines of worry easing from her freckled face.

She looked toward Max, who had propped himself up on his elbows on the bed, and Anya as Marta left. "I trust you three can stay safe while we're at this little clandestine meeting?"

Anya snorted. "My magic is just as good as yours, Gwendolyn, if not better. And we have Alric."

"What she means is that we'll be fine," Max interjected. "Just make sure you both come back to us in one piece. I'm already tiring of Mist Castle and desperately want to return to Espera soon." He smiled softly, though exhaustion was creeping back onto his face.

Gwen turned back to Tyreal, her brow furrowed. "I don't like this, but I trust Marta's friends. They wouldn't risk this if it wasn't important."

Tyreal nodded, his gaze still fixed on the door Marta had just exited. "They may have valuable information, but we can't afford to rely on others to hand us everything. We're playing catch-up here, Gwen. I need to investigate the castle—find out if the High Sister is hiding something, and that's why she's acting off."

Gwen straightened, a flicker of defiance in her eyes. "Then I'm coming with you."

"No," Tyreal said firmly, his voice low but resolute. "Not for this." He reached out, brushing a stray curl from her face, his touch lingering on her cheek. Her lips parted to protest, but he placed a finger over them. "This isn't about doubting your skills. You're the queen, Gwen. Your presence is too easily noticed. I'll be fine."

Her fingers curled around his wrist, holding his hand in place. "You don't know that. She has magic, Tyreal. You don't. That puts you at a disadvantage, no matter how skilled you are."

"And yet, I've managed to survive worse odds," he replied calmly but firmly. "You're thinking too much again, sweet girl. This is what I'm trained for, Gwen. I know how to move unseen, how to find answers without raising suspicion."

Her eyes softened, though her jaw remained tight. "You think I'll just sit here and wait? While you're out there alone, risking your life?"

He chuckled low and grinned at her. "No, I think you'll pace the room until Alric threatens to tie you to a chair, then glare at anyone who dares suggest you calm down. But I need to do this alone. If I'm caught, I'm just a guard overstepping his boundaries. If you're caught, it's an act of treason against the Sisterhood. We can't risk that."

Gwen hesitated, torn between reason and the fierce instinct to protect him. Her grip tightened briefly on his wrist before she let go, exhaling a sharp breath. "I hate when you're right."

Tyreal smiled, though his eyes remained serious. "I'll come back, Gwen. I promise."

She pressed her lips to his. "You'd better," she whispered. "Or I'll never forgive you."

"I wouldn't dare disappoint you," he murmured, deepening the kiss until Anya made gagging sounds. He stepped back reluctantly, his fingers trailing along hers until the space between them grew.

"Be careful," she called softly as he moved toward the door.

"Always," he replied, disappearing into the shadows.

Tyreal moved silently through the dim corridors of Mist Castle, his steps light and measured. Though this was his first time within these walls, their design felt strangely familiar. Mist Castle mirrored Thorncliff in structure, with subtle variations he had noticed immediately. The same winding halls, the same hidden alcoves for servants to slip by unnoticed, the same strategically placed vantage points woven into the architecture. Myaessa had recreated her home, but tonight, it served a more urgent purpose—it was a map for him to follow.

He paused at the threshold of a doorway, pressing himself against the cold stone as faint voices drifted down from above. He waited, counting the seconds, until the sounds dissolved into silence.

This was not his first time working in hostile terrain. As a soldier, he had learned to adapt quickly—reading people, recognizing patterns, seeking out weaknesses. Here, he couldn't afford even a single misstep. Mist Castle might have been a haven for Gwen and Anya, but it was clear not everyone within these walls shared their values. The High Sister's icy gaze from earlier still burned in his mind. She was hiding something—of that, he was certain. The question was, what?

It made sense that if the High Sister ruled this castle, and if the castle mirrored Thorncliff, then her chambers would lie in the same wing as Gwen's at home. As he ascended the staircase to the eastern wing, his mind raced. He couldn't risk approaching the High Sister's door directly. If she was inside, or worse, if someone caught him tampering with it, the consequences would be swift and severe. But Thorncliff hid many secrets, including a concealed passageway between Gwen's suite and his own. Perhaps Mist Castle had one as well.

He reached the door that separated the suites from the rest of the castle, eyes narrowing as he focused on the heavy wooden door he assumed led to the High Sister's quarters. A little farther down, a second door stood—its frame plainer, less ornate. Tyreal moved toward it, chewing his lip as he debated. No light seeped from beneath the door, a good sign. It suggested the room wasn't in active use, but appearances could be deceiving. His hand brushed the handle, and it turned easily—unlocked.

He cracked the door, straining his ears for any sounds inside or approaching down the hallway, but heard nothing. He cautiously pushed the door open wider, slipping inside. The room beyond was dimly lit and frigid, clearly used for storage rather than as someone's chambers.

His gaze swept over the walls, searching for any sign of a hidden passage—seams in the stone, worn flooring, anything. At home, a hidden passage ran behind a large tapestry near the fireplace, but there was no such adornment here. Moving toward the hearth, he ran his hands along the stone edges. His fingers brushed a subtle groove—barely perceptible but unmistakable. His pulse quickened as he pressed it, feeling for resistance. A soft click echoed, and the stone panel shifted inward.

The air smelled faintly of smoke, a scent that set his instincts on edge. He peered into the opening, only to feel his heart drop. The passage was blocked.

A thick slab of stone had been wedged into the narrow gap, likely with magic. Its edges were sealed with mortar, the work rough but effective—a hasty barrier meant to deter any would-be intruder. Tyreal searched for a weakness, but found none.

Clever, he thought grimly. The High Sister hadn't simply locked her doors—she had anticipated that someone might try to access her chambers through hidden means. He stepped back, frustration knotting in his chest. The blocked passage revealed two things: the High Sister was hiding something, and she was willing to take extreme measures to protect it.

Reluctantly, he slid the panel back into place, restoring the room to its unremarkable state. If he couldn't access the High Sister's chambers directly, he would have to find another way to gather information. His thoughts turned to the servants' quarters. At Thorncliff, the staff often knew more about the castle's secrets than the nobles—overhearing conversations or witnessing things they shouldn't.

As he moved down the hall, he overheard a low murmur—a pair of servants conversing in hushed tones.

"...a fire? What do you mean?" one voice asked, sharp with concern.

"Just what I said. She burned something... and now she's acting paranoid. The queen's incident at dinner made her worse than usual," came the reply. "Had us clean out her hearth and carry the waste to the west storage chamber after she was done. Said the ashes didn't belong in her quarters. Whatever that means."

"Strange."

Strange was an understatement. Tyreal's mind raced. The west storage chamber. That could be his lead.

Once the servants moved on, he darted through the kitchens and down the hall to the west wing, descending to the lower levels where the storage rooms were located.

The room was small and cluttered with broken shelving, discarded furniture, and crates piled haphazardly. In the center, a brazier sat on a low metal stand, its edges blackened with soot. Tyreal crouched beside it, scanning the ashes. Among the remnants were faint scraps of parchment, some too charred to read. One piece, however, stood out. Its edges were singed, but its center remained intact.

Carefully, Tyreal picked it up, his heart thumping as he read the inked words: "*Lovell line... right the wrong... in agreement.*"

Lovell. His grip tightened around the fragment. His suspicions were starting to solidify. Was the High Sister involved in Lovell's plot?

The faint sound of footsteps broke his concentration, and Tyreal swiftly tucked the fragment into his pocket, moving into the shadows just as the door creaked open. A novice entered, eyes scanning the room with suspicion. Tyreal held his breath, fingers brushing his sword's hilt, ready to act if needed. But the novice didn't linger. Muttering something too low to catch, she left, shutting the door behind her.

Tyreal waited a few beats before slipping out, retracing his steps toward the guest quarters. His mind churned over the implications of what he had discovered. The evidence wasn't enough to implicate the High Sister, but it was a start. A piece of the puzzle he had to share with Gwen as soon as possible.

CHAPTER THIRTY-ONE

Tyreal slipped into the guest quarters as quietly as he had left. Gwen sat near the fire, her posture tense but composed as she spoke softly with Anya. Alric leaned against the doorframe, arms crossed, while Max lay on the bed, his face pale yet alert, nursing a steaming cup of tea.

Gwen's gaze shot to Tyreal as he entered, her expression softening with relief. She crossed the room quickly, throwing herself into his arms. "You were gone too long," she murmured against his chest. "What did you find?"

He pressed a kiss to her forehead before stepping back to look at her. "Enough to raise more questions," he replied, his tone grave. He pulled a charred scrap of parchment from his pocket and handed it to her. "This was in a brazier hidden in the west storage chamber. It's not much, but look at the words."

Gwen unfolded the fragment, her brow furrowing as she read aloud, "Lovell line... right the wrong... in agreement."

Her lips pressed into a tight line as she exchanged a glance with Anya. "Adaltus and Lovell again," she murmured, her voice laced with anger. "Quite a coincidence."

"Indeed," Tyreal agreed, settling into the chair opposite her. "The brazier was buried in a storage chamber far from her usual spaces. She didn't just burn this; she tried to hide it. She's working hard to cover her tracks."

Alric pushed off the doorframe, stepping closer. "The High Sister? Working with Grigor Lovell? What's the connection?"

"I'm not sure yet," Tyreal admitted. "But that 'right the wrong' line has me concerned."

Anya's hands fidgeted in her lap, her knuckles white against the fabric of her gown. Her voice trembled, barely above a whisper. "Right what wrong?" She looked pale, as if she might be sick. Tyreal's chest tightened at the sight. It couldn't be easy for her—the image of someone she had once idolized beginning to crumble.

"That's the question," Tyreal said. "Whatever it is, it's big enough for her to take serious precautions. The passageway between her suite and the room next door is sealed off, and she's hiding burned evidence where it's unlikely to be noticed."

Gwen stared at the fragment in her hand. "If the High Sister is working with Lovell, she's not just betraying the Sisterhood. She's putting the entire realm at risk."

She placed the parchment carefully on the table, her fingers curling into fists. "We need more than this fragment. We need proof—proof that can't be denied or explained away."

Tyreal leaned forward, his voice low but resolute. "We'll find it. But for now, this gives us a direction. Do you still want to meet with Marta's friends?"

Gwen nodded, her expression firm. She turned to Tyreal. "It might be a trap," she said, her voice steady. "But I don't think it is, and it's a risk we need to take. Allies like this could make all the difference."

He nodded, though his expression remained grim. "Aye. But I dislike you being involved. Just want that noted for the record."

They slipped out of the room, Gwen leading the way with Tyreal close behind. The hallways were dimly lit, the torches reduced to embers to conserve resources during the night. They moved quickly but cautiously, alert to every shadow and sound.

As they neared the library, Tyreal paused by the door, his eyes darting around, listening for anything amiss. Satisfied, he nodded to Gwen, and together they stepped inside, the door closing with a soft, ominous click behind them.

Tyreal drew Gwen closer, his gaze sweeping the vast library. Towering bookshelves lined the walls, stretching into the shadows that swallowed the farthest corners of the room. The air was thick with the scent of parchment, leather-bound tomes, and the faint trace of moss that clung to the castle's ancient stones.

Gwen moved ahead, her footsteps light across the worn stone floor, weaving through the labyrinth of bookshelves toward the meeting place Marta had described. A faint noise pricked at Tyreal's ears—a voice, low but sharp, cutting through the quiet like a blade. Tyreal's hand shot out, catching her arm. She froze, her gaze meeting his.

With a finger to his lips, he signaled for silence. He crouched low, urging her to follow. He slipped from one shadow to the next, his training guiding him closer to the source. Cautiously peeking around the corner, Tyreal's heart sank.

The High Sister stood in the center of a small group of women. He recognized one of them, Lila, the young woman who had explained his healing abilities. She bit her lip, her eyes downcast as she fidgeted with her fingers. Behind him, Gwen let out a soft hiss of air, barely audible.

The High Sister's voice dripped with bitterness. "Chasing shadows is futile. The bastard theory is more plausible. The queen wants us to believe him royal for her own ends. Focus on your duties—documenting decrees and prayers. Nothing more."

Tyreal's gaze moved to another sister in the group. She stood out, her deep brown skin catching the faint light, her dark, tightly coiled hair haloing her face like a cloud. Her strong, graceful features were taut with fear, yet a spark of defiance lit her eyes as she found the courage to speak. "But Sister Seraphina—"

"Sister Seraphina is not High Sister. I am." The High Sister's voice cracked like a whip, her lips curling into a sneer. "Would you like a reminder of that? I demand obedience and faith, not questions. Is that understood?"

The women nodded and replied in unison, "Yes, High Sister."

The High Sister extended her hand for the large tome Lila clutched. Lila quickly surrendered it, retreating with her gaze fixed firmly on the floor. The High Sister turned sharply, her robes swirling around her ankles as she strode away, only to slow as she neared the stack where Gwen and Tyreal hid. She paused, her head tilting as if catching their scent. Tyreal tightened his grip on his weapon, every muscle coiled and ready to strike. His eyes darted around the room, searching for any source of magic she might draw upon.

Running a finger along a nearby shelf, she hissed, "These stacks have far too much dust. Inform the servants to clean them by morning, or they will have me to answer to." With that, she turned and exited the library, the door clicking shut behind her.

Gwen exhaled slowly, and he could feel her shaking with suppressed rage behind him. Tyreal waited a few moments to ensure it was safe, then signaled for her to stand. Lila spotted them and approached nervously, her voice a whisper. "Your Majesty, is that you?"

Gwen lowered her hood and embraced her. "Lila, are you alright?" Pulling back, she gestured to Tyreal. "Captain Blackbane, this is my cousin, Lila."

Tyreal nodded, his eyes scanning their surroundings even as he offered a reassuring smile. "I suspected as much. Your eyes mirror hers, Your Majesty."

Lila returned his smile timidly, ducking her head. "Marta said you might want to speak with those sympathetic to your situation. But that was too close for comfort. Perhaps this isn't a good idea. We're just scribes."

"I seek only information and allies," Gwen replied firmly. "As I told Marta, I have no intention of causing trouble. I came to announce my plans to wed and seek advice. But the High Sister seems far different from when I was last here."

Lila exchanged a glance with the other women. Tyreal watched with keen interest; it was clear they were not fond of the High Sister, but fear kept them from speaking out. The sister with the coiled hair spoke first, her voice trembling. "Each year, she grows worse. She imposes new rules under the guise of strengthening our commitment to the order. We aren't even allowed to communicate with our families without her direct permission."

Lila nodded, her expression grave. "Kelra is right. Things have become increasingly unsettling. I didn't even know Uncle Lorne had died until you arrived and announced you were queen at dinner." Her voice broke, and tears welled in her eyes. Tyreal's fists clenched, a dark rage curling in his gut. He briefly contemplated whether Gwen would allow him to kill the High Sister. *Maybe I could stage it as an accident—oh, how awful, she fell from the castle's highest tower...*

Gwen reached for Lila's hand, squeezing it tightly. "Oh, Lila, I'm so sorry. We sent a crow, but I never imagined she would intercept it."

"It isn't just the isolation," Kelra added. "She insists on regular confessions, demanding to know our every thought. It feels more like an interrogation than spiritual guidance. She barely allows us to practice magic. I dread what will happen if we get new trainees next summer."

Gwen's expression hardened. "This is far worse than I imagined. How did it deteriorate so quickly? It hasn't been that long since Anya or I visited. Her control over everyone here is completely unchecked."

Tyreal tried to focus on details rather than his anger. "And how does she enforce these rules? Does she use threats, or is there more?" he asked, suspicion lacing his tone.

An older sister spoke up. "There are punishments for those who disobey or question her. Nothing severe, but enough to humiliate or frighten us into compliance. She makes a spectacle of it, ensuring everyone understands the consequences."

Gwen clenched her fists, her eyes blazing. "And what of the council? Does no one intervene? She rules through fear."

"Sister Seraphina tries," Lila answered quietly. "She's the only one who can temper the High Sister when she's truly angry. But she can't be everywhere at once, and our orders are clear: a High Sister serves until death."

Tyreal shot Gwen a dark look. "Your Majesty, it's clear we're dealing with someone who doesn't lead but dominates. This isn't about maintaining order—it's about absolute control. She won't change."

Kelra sighed, the defiance in her posture giving way to exhaustion. "That's my fear too. Most are too afraid to speak up; they've seen what happens to those who do. We need help, but we don't know where to find it. The High Sister oversees the sisterhood, and no one oversees her."

Gwen closed the distance between them, her shoulders squared and her eyes locked with an intensity that left no room for doubt. "I promise you, as the Queen of Tavia and a sister myself, I will find a way to help."

"She is afraid of you," Lila whispered, her eyes darting toward the door as if the High Sister might appear at any moment. "Of what you and the High Captain represent. If there's no threat from the tenth family, what purpose do the sisters serve? Beyond preserving historical texts and training royals to control their magic? That's why she doesn't want us investigating."

"We heard her tell you to stop investigating," Tyreal growled. "I don't care about my ancestry, except for what it means for marrying the woman I love. But if I can help bring an end to all of this, I'll scour every text in this place myself."

An older woman spoke up again. "I think we were close. There's something about the name—Ardienne—that's been bothering me. The book she took has records from before magic fell, detailing name changes over the centuries."

"Something about the name..." Gwen repeated, trailing off with a strange look on her face. Tyreal frowned at her, trying to decipher her thoughts, but she merely shook her head. "We need that book."

"She'll have taken it to her office or her room," Kelra said with a resigned sigh. "Both are locked with a key she keeps on her person."

Tyreal snorted. "I'd wager she doesn't clean those rooms herself, am I right?"

Kelra made a thoughtful face. "Well... no. She's obsessive about cleanliness, but she won't do it herself."

"Then someone has access," Tyreal said. "We just need to befriend the right servant. Or I could bust the door down, but I assume my queen would prefer a more subtle approach."

Gwen rolled her eyes but offered a small smile. "Yes, Captain, I think subtlety would serve us best—for now. We need that book, and if we can gain access without raising alarms, we'll have a better chance of undermining her without endangering anyone further."

Lila's face lit with cautious hope. "I might know someone. Sara cleans in that wing. She's close with Marta and unhappy with the High Sister's behavior. If Marta speaks to her, she might help us get the keys."

"Perfect," Gwen replied, her tone decisive. "We'll speak with Marta in the morning. I need to return to Thorncliff soon. The situation with Adaltus is also pressing."

Lila hesitated, glancing nervously at Kelra. "The High Sister is from Adaltus," she said finally. "She had me scrubbing stones in the aviary a moon ago, and I saw her receiving crows from Prince Lovell. I looked into it—she's his aunt. I was furious that she could communicate with her family while we can't."

Gwen's expression darkened. "I knew she was originally from Adaltus, but I didn't realize she was so closely related. It's highly unusual for a High Sister to maintain family connections after taking her vows."

Tyreal met Gwen's eyes, his jaw clenching as tension coiled through him. He could sense the darkening expression on his face, causing the women, except Gwen, to take nervous steps back. "Could be a coincidence, but my father always said there's no such thing," he hissed quietly

"Mine too," Gwen murmured. "But one problem at a time. First, we need that book, and I need to speak with Sister Seraphina in private. Thank you, all of you. Keep your heads down, and we'll find a way through this mess."

They nodded, and Tyreal followed Gwen back through the library and out the doors. They traced their way up toward the room, the silence of Mist Castle at night feeling entirely different from the peaceful quiet he had grown accustomed to at Thorncliff.

When they reached their quarters, Tyreal rapped lightly on the door in a pattern he and Alric had established. Alric opened it for them, relief and exhaustion showing on his face. Inside, Max and Anya were already asleep in the large bed.

"We'll discuss everything in the morning," Tyreal said quietly. "Get some rest, Alric. I'll take over."

Alric nodded and moved toward the smaller guard bed. Tyreal turned to Gwen, catching the protest forming on her lips before she could speak. "No," he said firmly. "Climb in beside Anya and get what sleep you can. You'll need to be rested for whatever the High Sister throws at you tomorrow."

For a moment, Gwen looked ready to argue, but something in his expression softened her resolve. She nodded, stepping closer until she stood just before him. Rising on tiptoe, she lifted her chin, silently asking for what they both needed.

Tyreal couldn't resist her. He bent down, his hand cradling the back of her head with a tenderness at odds with the strength of his grip. Their lips met, the kiss gentle at first but quickly deepening, carrying the unspoken emotions between them. Fear, anxiety, need—it all poured into that moment. He kissed her as if trying to reassure them both, grounding himself in her presence even as he tried to give her comfort.

When Gwen's breath hitched, he forced himself to pull back, resting his forehead against hers. His voice was a low murmur, meant only for her. "Get settled, sweet girl. I'll keep you safe, and we'll face everything tomorrow."

She nodded softly, her fingers trailing across his chest as she stepped away. Tyreal's heart clenched at the loss of her touch, but he watched as she moved to the bed, settling quietly beside Anya. Only when she was tucked in did he exhale, turning toward the door with a resolute sigh. Standing watch was something

he could control, and he would do so with unwavering focus. Whatever tomorrow brought,
he would be ready.

CHAPTER THIRTY-TWO

As the first blush of dawn painted the sky in soft hues of orange and pink, the light roused Gwen from her slumber. For a moment, she struggled to recall where she was, especially with Anya's slender arm draped across her middle and soft snores tickling her ear. Gwen stretched, careful not to disturb her, and quietly slipped from beneath Anya's embrace. Alric, sprawled across a chair that blocked the door, gave her a silent nod. She smiled at him before glancing toward Tyreal's bed.

He lay on his stomach, one arm shoved under his head, the other resting just within reach of his sword, propped against the bedframe. A rumpled curl of brown hair fell across his forehead, and the sight brought a soft smile to Gwen's lips. He looked so peaceful, so content, that she almost wished she could crawl beside him, pressing gentle kisses to his face until he awoke. But she knew better than to rouse him abruptly; his heightened senses made such awakenings dangerous.

"Good morning, Captain Blackbane," she whispered, perching at the edge of the bed.

He cracked open one eye and, without a word, pulled her into his side. "I know we have spying and thievery to attend to, but for just a moment—let's pretend we're a normal couple, starting the day together," he grumbled. Gwen giggled and nestled closer, savoring the hard warmth of him pressed against her thigh.

A soft knock at the door shattered their moment. Tyreal threw his head back with a dramatic groan. Reluctantly, Gwen pulled away as Alric checked the visitor. A moment later, he let Marta in, her arms laden with freshly laundered men's clothing.

"Did your meeting go well last night?" Marta asked.

Gwen nodded. "We had a close call—almost ran into the High Sister—but we managed to meet. I wish I'd known how dire things had become here."

Marta's smile didn't reach her eyes. "It's been difficult, though I think it's worse for the novices and scribes. She always overlooks those of us who are common-born and lack magic."

"No surprise there," Alric grumbled. "Lots of nobles ignore the common folk until they need something."

Gwen's heart ached as she searched for the right words. Alric was right—she'd seen it herself in her own council at Thorncliff. Her idea to expand the council felt more urgent than ever. "I'm sorry you've both been treated this way. Once we've dealt with these crises, we'll work on changing that mindset."

Tyreal took the bundle of clothing from Marta's arms. "Thank you. It'll be nice to wear something other than this ill-fitting shift today. Do you know a servant named Sara?"

"Aye. A sweet girl. Why?" Marta narrowed her eyes, protective instincts flaring.

"Lila suggested we speak to her. We need to retrieve a book the High Sister took from the library last night. It's almost certainly in her room or office," Gwen explained.

Marta nodded, understanding dawning. "Ah, and you're hoping she'll help you get the key. But how will you ensure her safety?"

Gwen met her gaze steadily, feeling the weight of her crown and the responsibility that came with it. "We can't promise complete safety," she admitted softly, "but we'll do everything we can to minimize the risks, just as we will for ourselves. Sara's role is crucial, but ultimately, it's her choice. I'll understand if she doesn't want to."

Marta's lips pressed into a thin line, her brow furrowing as her gaze lingered with unease. "Sara is brave, but she's young. She knows nothing of political games."

"I know," Gwen replied, her voice firm despite the knot in her stomach. "But we believe the book she took will help prove the captain's lineage—something the High Sister seems determined to conceal. I also suspect her correspondence with the Prince of Adaltus is part of a larger scheme. If I'm right, revealing these truths could shift the balance of power and provide the leverage I need to gain support from the other royal families in removing her as High Sister."

Tyreal, now fully dressed, emerged from behind the privacy screen, his tone serious as he joined the conversation. "We're not asking Sara to confront the High Sister directly. We just need her help accessing the book safely."

"If she gets me the key, I'll do it myself." Anya's voice surprised them, and they turned to find her sitting up in bed, arms wrapped around her knees.

Max sat up beside her, brow furrowed. "Anya—"

"No," she interrupted firmly. "I need to do this. I've spent time in her office; I used to help her with chores there. I know the layout, and I'll be careful. I need to do this—for me." She looked at Gwen for support, and after a moment, Gwen nodded in agreement.

Marta's expression softened as she looked between Gwen and Anya. "Alright. I'll talk to her. She trusts me and likes both of you."

Gwen smiled, grateful for Marta's loyalty. "Thank you, Marta. Please come find us after you've spoken with her."

As Marta left to find Sara, Gwen turned to Alric and Tyreal. "Once we have the book, we'll need to figure out how to get the information out quickly. I also want to meet with Sister Seraphina as soon as we can. I need to see where her true alliances lie and why she hasn't fully put a stop to the High Sister's tyranny."

Alric's expression darkened. "We'll need to plan carefully. From what Tyreal told me, the High Sister is ruthless. If she suspects you're doing more than just trying to get married, she won't hesitate to strike."

A chill ran down Gwen's spine at his words. She knew they were right, but a part of her still hoped diplomacy could prevail. As a sister, she didn't want to undermine the order from within. But the injustice rotting it from the inside—and the conspiracy threatening to control Tavia—couldn't be ignored.

The castle corridor was eerily quiet, save for the rustle of cloaks brushing against cold stone floors as Tyreal, Anya, and Gwen made their way toward the servants' wing. This part of the castle was less ornate, its bare stone walls stark in comparison to the grandeur of the main halls. Long, slanted beams of light streamed through the windows, illuminating dust motes dancing in the cool air. Sparse, unlit torches dotted the spaces between them.

Growing up, Gwen had always imagined this wing resembling what Myaessa had first pulled from the mountain. She loved to run through these halls, pretending to be her ancestor, making grand, sweeping motions in the air to mimic the magic. As she matured, she came to understand the agony Myaessa must have endured to devise her plan to end magic, yet the castle's creation remained impressive in her eyes.

They reached a heavy wooden door, and Gwen knocked softly. Tyreal tensed beside her until the door opened, revealing a young maid with pale skin and wide, nervous eyes. She glanced around before stepping aside to let them in. Dropping into a curtsey, she spoke quickly. "Your Majesty, Your Highness. Marta told me what you need."

Gwen pressed her hands to the girl's trembling ones. "Yes, we need your help. But only if you're certain. We understand it's a risk."

Sara bit her lip, then nodded. "I have the key," she whispered, barely audible, as she handed a small, ornate key to Anya. "She keeps all her personal records in her office—documents no one else may touch."

Anya accepted the key, her expression serious. "I'll start there. Be careful, all of you. If what we suspect is true, there's no telling how far the High Sister will go to protect her secrets."

Gwen squeezed Anya's shoulder reassuringly. "We'll be vigilant. Find what you can, and meet us back in the room."

After Anya slipped away, Gwen turned her attention back to Sara. "Thank you. This is very brave of you."

Sara nodded, swallowing hard. "I need to get back before I'm missed. I have kitchen duty now, and I'm scheduled to clean her office after lunch. I'll need the key back before then."

Tyreal stepped aside, giving her room to pass. "You'll have it in plenty of time. I'll find you in the kitchen and make a big fuss about being starving. I can slip it to you then."

"Go quickly, and act normal," Gwen urged, her voice soft but firm. As Sara slipped out, Gwen lingered by the door, waiting a few moments to ensure the young woman had a head start. She glanced back at Tyreal. "I hate putting others at risk for me."

Tyreal's expression softened as he stepped closer, brushing his lips against her forehead. "It's not just for you, Gwennie. This is for all of us."

Gwen opened the door and stepped out. "Let's find Sister Seraphina," she whispered, glancing back at Tyreal. "It's time we understood exactly what game the High Sister is playing."

They found Sister Seraphina in her usual spot by the chapel's garden. Gwen remembered often bringing her tea when she was a novice, watching as the older woman lost herself in devotions beneath the sunlight for hours. The older woman sat alone, eyes closed, her face serene—yet her posture betrayed a lingering tension.

Sister Seraphina was stout, her round face framed by wisps of gray hair that had escaped her long, coiled braid. Despite her soft, motherly appearance, there was an undeniable sturdiness about her, making it clear she was no easy target.

"Sister Seraphina," Gwen called softly, not wanting to startle her.

The older woman opened her eyes, her expression unreadable. "Your Majesty, Captain Blackbane," she greeted, her voice steady. "What brings you to the garden on this chilly morning?"

"I feel unsettled about the events at dinner last night," Gwen said quietly, hoping she sounded mildly regretful. "I may have spoken too bluntly, but the High Sister seemed far different from how I remember her." She chose her words carefully, hoping to build trust.

Sister Seraphina's gaze flickered, a shadow passing over her features. "You are not wrong," she murmured. "I barely recognize some things around here anymore." She looked around at the gardens and the grand chapel, its stained-glass windows casting a dim glow. "I first came to Mist Castle when I was seven summers gone. We had a completely different High

Sister then—Helena. I worshipped her as only a child can. She was kind and just. Once I completed my novice training, I chose to stay here, believing in everything the sisterhood could be."

She let out a heavy sigh, her hands twisting together in her lap. "I've stayed near the High Sister, not out of loyalty, but because I had to. She wasn't always like this. Something shifted a few summers ago, and since then, I've done what I could to limit the harm."

Gwen sat beside her, her voice quiet but steady. "Was that around the time Princess Eliana arrived?"

Sister Seraphina nodded, her hands still wringing in her lap. "Yes. That's when everything began to change. She grew distant, retreating into the library for hours on end, pouring over old scrolls and sending letters to her birth family. That alone was unusual. A High Sister is supposed to see us as her only family, to dedicate herself fully to the role. But it was more than that." She hesitated, her voice dropping. "She couldn't accept Eliana. She saw her as a crime against nature, an affront to the traditions she held sacred. It unsettled her deeply, and from there, she became... different. Her actions, her decisions—they've only grown stranger since."

"You mean the Lovells from Adaltus?" Gwen's stomach tightened at the name.

"Yes," Seraphina confirmed, her eyes narrowing. "I've been concerned about that correspondence for a while, especially when she continued it but forbade everyone else from contacting their families. But when you arrived and said Adaltus was plotting against you..." She trailed off, fear flashing in her eyes. "Now I fear her ambitions are disastrous, but I don't know what they are."

Gwen's fingers traced the lines of a rose carved into the bench, her mind racing. "I don't have all the pieces yet either," she admitted. "But I know Grigor Lovell seeks to weaken my claim, destabilize Tavia, and open the gates for Adaltus. If she's working with him, I can only assume she hopes to position herself—and the sisterhood—in an even greater position of power by his side."

Sister Seraphina stood abruptly, shoulders squared, her voice resolute. "If that's true, and we can find proof, I will stand against her. The majority of the council will listen to reason. But there are five sisters who serve her blindly—her inner circle. Nothing you or anyone else says will sway them. She rules them completely."

Tyreal crossed his arms, his gaze hardening. "Every tyrant has lackeys," he said grimly. "We'll find proof if that's what you need. But don't underestimate her—or them."

Seraphina's lips pressed into a thin line, her voice soft but steady. "I don't. And neither should you."

CHAPTER THIRTY-THREE

Tyreal stayed close behind Gwen as they returned to their room. The meeting with Sister Seraphina had offered valuable insight into the High Sister's shifting behavior, but something about the incomplete picture gnawed at him. The burned letter fragment and Seraphina's veiled concerns hinted at something bigger—something dangerous—but the pieces refused to fit together. His spy had mentioned a potential collusion between Adaltus and Galeigh to undermine Gwen's rule, but the evidence was thin. Was Galeigh truly involved, or was it merely easy to suspect because King Korian was so universally disliked?

When they stepped inside, Tyreal's relief at seeing Anya safe was brief. She stood by the table, her arms crossed and her expression grim. The surface was covered with scattered parchment and scrolls, some rolled, others flattened as if hastily examined. As Tyreal shut the door behind them, Anya's gaze flicked between the table and the two of them, tension etched in every line of her posture.

"What happened?" Gwen asked, rushing to Anya's side. "Did you find the book?"

"No." Anya's voice was sharp, frustration clear. "It wasn't there. But I found these in her office." She gestured toward the table. "It's bad, Gwen. Really bad."

Tyreal stepped closer as Gwen picked up a letter. Bold, fresh ink smeared at the edges, the paper stained as if hastily discarded. A cold dread twisted in his chest. He remembered his warning to Gwen about Lovell's intentions—a war was no longer just possible; it felt inevitable. The urge to shout, *Don't read that, put it down*, gripped him, but he pressed his lips together, forcing the words back.

Gwen's eyes narrowed as she read aloud: "The gods have provided what I need for the project. Its success will alter the course of the world, as we discussed. Those unworthy will fall into line or be handled."

"This was in her office?" she asked, her voice tight with disbelief.

Anya nodded. "It wasn't addressed, but given everything else, we can assume it was meant for Lovell or someone close to him. I found these too." She gestured to the scrolls and other parchments. "She's been hoarding items from the restricted archives—pieces about Myaessa's spell, ancient blood magic, and how the fall impacted the royal families."

Gwen frowned, her gaze darkening. "Blood magic? That was banned before the fall."

"I know," Anya said, voice grim. "It's not just the scrolls. She's written notes in the margins, analyzing how bloodlines connected to certain rituals. There are references to 'restoration' throughout."

Max rose from the bed, crossing the room slowly to stand beside Gwen. His eyes flicked to the torn letter on the table, brow furrowed. "Restoration of what?" he asked quietly. The question felt heavy in the air.

Gwen set the letter down, her fingers trembling. "Restoration of magic?" she whispered, as though the words might make them real. "That's insane."

Anya hesitated. "I don't know. But there's more. I found a collection of reports—on us, on other royals. Spies have been feeding her information on everyone. Well, everyone except the Lovells, of course."

"Spies?" Alric's sharp voice cut through the tension. He had remained silent until now, but the tension in his posture was unmistakable. "What kind of information?"

Anya hesitated, cheeks flushing bright pink. She glanced at Max, then back at Gwen, chewing on her bottom lip. "About me—about my lack of interest in men and heirs," she said, her voice tight. "About you and Tyreal too. Rumors you've been together for years."

Gwen's expression darkened with protectiveness. "What would she gain from this? Leverage? To what end?"

"There's more," Anya continued. "She's obsessed with Eliana. Most of the reports focus on her—tracking her movements, her actions. There are notes questioning her right to magic. She sees Eliana as an affront to the Sisterhood, claiming it undermines the 'purity' of our traditions."

Tyreal's fists clenched at his sides. The earlier dread solidified into a searing rage. Gathering intelligence on potential enemies was one thing—it was a necessary tactic. But this? This felt personal. Sinister.

"She's manipulating everyone," Gwen muttered bitterly, pacing the room. "And she'll retaliate if she knows we're investigating."

"She knows. Or she will soon enough," Anya admitted, her face shadowed with guilt. "I wasn't careful enough. Someone came into the office while I was there. I hid, but they knew someone had been there."

A low curse escaped Alric. "Then we've run out of time. She'll come for you."

"And soon," Tyreal added grimly. "We need to act now. These fragments and scrolls point to something huge. But we need more proof."

Alric straightened, voice calm but firm. "You don't need proof. You need to end her. Now."

Tyreal turned to Alric, meeting his gaze. Alric gave a resigned shrug, hands lifted in a gesture of inevitability. Tyreal returned the shrug, nodding in agreement. Gwen sighed and turned away, eyes locking with Max's in a silent exchange.

Max shook his head. "No," he said firmly. "We need to show the other families we sought peace first. If this turns into open conflict, they'll need to see that Tavia acted responsibly."

"It's my country, Max. If she's plotting to destabilize my throne or harm my friends, I shouldn't have to justify my actions to anyone," Gwen snapped.

Max raised his hands, a placating gesture. "I'm not disagreeing. I'm looking at the bigger picture. You've only been queen a short time. We're working from incomplete information. Diplomacy might buy us time."

The room fell into heavy silence as Gwen weighed her options. "Diplomacy gives her the opportunity to strike first," Tyreal cut in, his voice sharp. "I agree with Alric. Let me handle her and be done with it."

Gwen shook her head. "And if she kills you because you don't have magic to defend yourself? Where does that leave me? No. We will go together. I'll confront her, and if there's any shred of decency left, I'll appeal to it. But if not, or if she attacks—" Her voice trailed off, the unspoken threat hanging in the air.

Tyreal ground his teeth. "I don't approve of this plan."

Gwen smiled, though it didn't reach her eyes, and stood on tiptoe to kiss him gently. "I knew you wouldn't. But I am the queen. Like it or not. You can lecture me later." She stepped back, pointing to the key on the table. "Get this back to Sara in the kitchens. I don't want to put her at unnecessary risk. We'll come up with a plan to confront the High Sister after you return."

Tyreal inhaled sharply, nodding, but shot her a sideways look of frustration that conveyed his displeasure. His gaze shifted to Alric, who inclined his head slightly in silent agreement to watch over Gwen in his absence.

Without another word, Tyreal strode toward the door. His footsteps echoed through the corridors, the thud of his boots reverberating against the stone walls. His mind churned with worry and anger—worry for Gwen and what lay ahead, and anger at the High Sister's growing threat.

The halls of Mist Castle felt darker than they should have. The silence pressed in around him, and unease prickled at the back of his neck.

His hand instinctively brushed the hilt of his sword as he exited the wing, crossing the courtyard toward the kitchens. His eyes flicked to the chapel, its stained-glass windows glinting in the dim light, and to the garden where he and Seraphina had spoken earlier.

The warmth of the kitchen hit him as soon as he entered, the chatter and clatter of servants soothing some of his unease. It reminded him of Thorncliff's kitchen, where Cook's loud voice often echoed. Instead, he spotted Sara, kneading dough with more force than necessary, her brows furrowed in concentration. He approached, grumbling about the lack of decent food, grabbing a carrot and biting into it. Nearby servants scattered, startled by his loud presence.

"Captain Blackbane!" Sara exclaimed, eyes widening. "What are you doing in the kitchens?"

"Looking for food," Tyreal responded, his voice carrying across the room. "Impossible to find a decent meal here."

Sara blinked, taken aback by his theatrics, but quickly motioned for him to follow her to a quieter corner where cooling trays of food were laid out. Once out of earshot, she wiped her hands on her apron, glancing over her shoulder before opening her palm. "Did everything go...?"

"According to plan," Tyreal assured her, voice low. He pressed the key into her hand. "But keep your head down. It may get worse before it gets better. Just stick to your routine."

Sara's eyes widened slightly, but she nodded, clutching the key tightly. "Be careful," she whispered, her voice trembling.

Tyreal gave a curt nod and turned to leave, grabbing a meat hand pie on his way out. As he exited, his thoughts returned to the castle's ominous silence. His senses were on high alert, and his mind raced with images of what might be unfolding.

As he passed the chapel, something caught his eye—a faint movement in the shadows near the garden. He paused, setting the pie down on a bench and resting his hand on his sword hilt.

"Captain Blackbane?" A novice stepped from around the corner, clutching a small basket tightly.

"What do you want?" Tyreal's voice was sharp. He had no time for pleasantries.

"I—I was sent to find you," she stammered, her voice trembling. "The High Sister wishes to speak with you."

Tyreal's jaw tightened. "With just me? That's odd," he said evenly, his gaze narrowing. "What does she want?"

"I don't know," the novice stuttered. "I was only told to find you and bring you to her in the library."

Tyreal shook his head. "Tell the High Sister I'll meet with her tomorrow," he said coldly. "I'm needed elsewhere."

The novice shifted uneasily, her fingers twisting around her basket. "She insisted it was urgent, Captain. About the queen. Please, I don't want to anger her." Her voice broke, and Tyreal saw the sheen of tears in her eyes.

He paused, scrutinizing her. The fear seemed genuine, but it was too convenient. "You're trembling," he said, his voice hard. "Are you afraid of me or her?"

The novice hesitated, then whispered, "Both."

Tyreal's grip on his sword tightened. "Where is the High Sister?"

"In the library," she answered quickly, glancing nervously at the building. "She said she'd wait for you."

Part of him wanted to confront the High Sister now, but he couldn't risk leaving Gwen unprotected. "Tell her I'll come in the morning," he said, tone final. "And if you're lying to me, I'll know."

The novice nodded quickly, fear wide in her eyes. "Yes, Captain. I'll tell her." She turned and hurried back into the castle.

Tyreal watched her go, unease settling deeper in his gut. Something wasn't right. He took a deep breath and continued on his way toward the guest wing, quickening his pace, praying his instincts were wrong.

Turning the corner into the wing, the sight that met him hit like a physical blow. The door hung ajar, splintered as if struck by immense force. His heart pounded as he pushed it open. The room was chaos. Scorch marks marred the walls, papers and books lay shredded across the floor, and furniture was overturned.

And amidst the destruction, Alric lay motionless, gasping for air, a bloodied billhook lodged in his chest.

"Alric," Tyreal whispered, rushing to his side. Blood pooled beneath the man, a grim testament to the attack.

Alric's weak voice was barely a whisper. "High Sister... bad... catacombs..." Another coughing fit wracked his body.

Without hesitation, Tyreal yanked the billhook free, but Alric's blood poured out in dark torrents. Tyreal pressed his hands to the wound, trying to heal him with every ounce of magic he could summon. But nothing came.

Alric shook his head weakly. "Not a royal... tell Max... wouldn't change a thing..." His breath faltered, and his head slumped to the side, his eyes vacant.

"No!" Tyreal cried, grief and fury mixing in a raw sob. He swallowed the pain, forcing it down as he secured Alric's daggers. Vengeance burned in his veins. He stormed from the room, racing through the castle, fueled by a rage that would not be quelled.

His steps echoed through the eerie silence of the hallways. No signs of struggle, no further chaos—could Gwen and Anya be unconscious, or worse? He shut down the thought, unwilling to entertain the darkness it invited.

He burst into the great hall, his eyes locking onto a young servant girl. Without hesitation, he crossed the space and grabbed her arm. "Where are the catacombs?" he barked. "Now! The queen's life depends on it!"

The girl gasped, her face pale with fear. "Under the chapel!" she blurted. "Trapdoor in the pulpit!"

Tyreal let go, already turning toward the exit. He broke into a sprint, the pounding of his boots matching the relentless pace of his thoughts. Whatever waited in the catacombs, he had to get there before it was too late.

The chapel doors groaned as Tyreal pushed them open, their weight resisting his urgency. Inside, the silence was oppressive, broken only by the faint creak of the hinges. His eyes swept the room, heart pounding. The altar was askew, its usual alignment disrupted. With a grunt, he shoved it aside, revealing the trapdoor hidden beneath.

Wasting no time, he yanked it open and descended into the catacombs. The air was cold and damp, the scent of earth and stone thick around him. The faint echo of voices reached his ears, distant but growing clearer with each step. He pressed himself against the wall, slipping into the shadows as he moved closer, his every sense on edge.

CHAPTER THIRTY-FOUR

G wen's consciousness clawed its way back through a haze of pain. A relentless throb pulsed in her head, each heartbeat sending sharp spikes through her skull. The scant light that pierced the darkness forced her to squint, as if she were staring into the midday sun. When she tried to move, she found her hands bound tightly behind her, rough rope cutting into her skin, woven through the wooden slats of the chair that held her captive.

The air was damp and cold, carrying the faint, earthy scent of moss mingled with the unmistakable odor of decay. Somewhere in the distance, water dripped rhythmically, its sound echoing off the stone walls. She was under-ground—deep within the catacombs.

A memory flickered to life: Anya's scream, something about the catacombs, just before her vision blacked out. It bubbled to the surface of her mind, too murky to decipher. Everything felt fuzzy, a tingle running from her spine to her extremities. She knew the High Sister had attacked them, but the details eluded her. Squeezing her eyes shut, she willed the memories to return. She dimly recalled sending Tyreal to return something to someone, a servant, maybe? From there, only flashes emerged: a door bursting open, fireballs hurling through the air, Max shouting for Alric. *Where was Alric?*

Shaking her head, she immediately regretted the motion as another wave of excruciating pain rolled over her, black spots clouding her vision. When she reopened her eyes, she was grateful to see her surroundings clearer, but the dire reality snapped into focus. Max lay a few feet away, restrained on a table, his chest rising and falling with shallow breaths. Anya's body lay crumpled on the floor beside the table, a dark patch of blood matting her golden hair. Gwen craned her neck, desperate to see if Anya still breathed, but she couldn't. Her heart clenched at the realization, fear and helplessness warring within her as she strained against her bonds.

Desperately, she scanned the dim chamber for something—anything—that could help her escape. But there was no fire, no water. She'd never been adept at manipulating air without Anya's aid, and the pain in her head made it impossible to focus on the earth and stone around them.

The chamber felt like a scene from a dark, terrifying tale. Across from Max's table stood another large, ancient table in the center of the room, a tome lying open as if waiting to be read. Thick beeswax candles, their wicks unlit, were scattered nearby. The High Sister, it seemed, wasn't foolish enough to light them with Gwen and Anya present. Without the flame, shadows filled the space, illuminated only by the faint glow of bioluminescent algae clinging to the walls.

Near the table with the tome, the High Sister stood, her ceremonial silver and blue robes glowing in the dim light. Her back was turned as she conversed with five other sisters. Gwen couldn't make out their faces from this distance, but they must have been complicit in the attack. There was no way the High Sister could have taken them all down alone.

As if sensing Gwen's gaze, the High Sister turned. Her triumphant smile sliced through the darkness. Her eyes were wide, shiny with an unsettling madness. "Ah, you're awake. Good," she said, her voice strangely warm. "I'm eager to begin. I've spent years preparing for this moment."

Gwen's mind raced, grasping at fragments of information. What could be so crucial that she'd risk kidnapping a queen in a castle full of people? "What are you planning?" she demanded, her voice steady despite the pounding in her head and the panic at the growing pool of blood in Anya's hair.

The High Sister glided toward Max, trailing her fingers over his doublet as she circled the table. "I'm going to correct an error that has lingered for over five hundred summers. For too long, we've been forced to marry royal families to keep the embers of magic alive. We've diluted the bloodlines with royal filth, just scraping by on scraps of power."

Gwen shook her head, confusion swirling. "How do you intend to correct Myaessa's spell? We don't possess the magic to do anything close to that anymore." She kept her voice steady, hoping to stall, clinging to the certainty that Tyreal was on his way. If she could just delay the High Sister, perhaps he would intervene in time.

"Myaessa didn't enact a spell," the High Sister hissed, her eyes narrowing with disdain. "She enacted a curse. It stripped good families of their birthrights. It ended the war, but if she had confined the magic to one family, that alone would've stopped the conflict."

Gwen shifted in her chair, uncomfortable, her shoulder aching from the strained position. "But who would choose that family? Who has the right to judge worthiness?"

The High Sister raised her hands, palms upturned as if invoking the heavens. "The gods, of course! You can tell which family is pure. We Lovells are free of filth." Her voice twisted with venom. "We do not tolerate men masquerading as women, nor those who lie with their own sex, or women who allow common filth to defile them outside of their marriage bed. We adhere to the old ways. We deserve to reclaim our magic, and only we!"

Gwen struggled against her bindings, the rope biting deeper into her skin. "You're mad," she spat. "Magic isn't yours to control. It belongs to everyone."

The High Sister's laugh echoed, bitter and hollow. "Fate has delivered you to me. With my fellow sisters here," she gestured to the four behind her, "and once Captain Blackbane inevitably joins us, I will have a member from every founding family present. I will channel the essence of the original spell and redirect its power. I will restore magic to the Lovell line, and we shall reign as we were destined to—supreme and unchallenged."

Gwen's stomach churned. The High Sister didn't just want Tavia's throne; she was lost in her delusions, interpreting divine signs to justify her twisted plan. "But you were angry about Tyreal," Gwen breathed, torn between hoping for his arrival and fearing what it might mean for them both. "When I told you who he was."

The High Sister picked up a large dagger, trailing the tip of the blade over her fingers as she examined it. "I was, initially. The gods revealed something to me that I didn't comprehend. I feared that if he was indeed who you claimed, it would mean the gods were turning away from me. That if you wed, merging a new line, it would disrupt my plans. But I didn't show enough devotion. I spent last night in flagellation and prayer." She sliced the blade across her palm, watching the blood pool and drip into a chalice. When she looked back at Gwen, her eyes were unfocused, a wide smile stretching across her face. "Then the brilliance of their plan became clear. Your arrival provided everything I need to enact the spell that has eluded me for years."

Gwen's heart pounded, panic igniting within her. "You cannot truly believe the gods condone this—this perversion of their gifts."

The High Sister sneered, her eyes narrowing with contempt. "The gods choose their vessels, Gwendolyn. They chose the Lovells. Who are you—a mere child playing at queen—to question their will?" Her voice dripped with venom. "Myaessa's curse was blasphemy, an affront to the divine order. I am merely the hand restoring balance."

The air felt colder, heavier. Shadows deepened, and Gwen shivered, reaching out desperately, trying to grasp the air with her magic. It slipped through her fingers like sand. Why hadn't Anya moved? Where were Tyreal and Alric? Panic clawed at her mind. *Not now. Not now. I must find a way out of this. For Pip. For Tavia.*

"So, you believe the gods will simply hand you power once you spill our blood?" Gwen asked, her voice shaking but determined. She needed to keep the High Sister talking. If she could delay her long enough...

A cruel smile spread across the High Sister's face. "Not merely hand us power, your majesty." She sneered. "They will anoint us as the rightful rulers, purifiers of this tainted land. It's ironic, really. Your ancestor started all of this, and you and King Lorne will end it."

Gwen froze, locking eyes with the High Sister. "What does my father have to do with any of this?"

The High Sister laughed again, a sound devoid of warmth. "Why, everything, my dear! He conspired with other leaders to limit our powers and remove the rules surrounding marriage. I didn't understand why at first; I only knew he was a threat. But now, I see he was doing it for you. So you could wed whom he thought was a commoner. It's why he rejected my dear nephew's proposal. More evidence that you Thorncrests are nothing but filth."

Gwen's chest tightened. "What did you do to my father?" she whispered, her voice trembling.

The High Sister paused, moving to Max's side. She cut a shallow slit down his arm, letting his blood mingle with hers in the chalice. "I have no desire to harm this one if I can avoid it. His family seems reasonably pure, and he possesses a knack for diplomacy. Though their closeness with yours gives me pause."

Kneeling beside Anya, the High Sister roughly flipped her onto her back. Anya let out a small, pained sound. Relief surged through Gwen. But the High Sister raised her blade high, poised to plunge it into Anya's belly. "This one is a different matter—"

"WHAT DID YOU DO TO MY FATHER?" Gwen screamed, her voice raw, part distraction, part desperation.

The High Sister looked up, blinking in surprise. The other sisters closed in, moving closer, forming a half-circle around the table. Gwen locked eyes with the High Sister. "Why, I had him killed, of course. We believed you, as a former sister, would be easier to control. That you would marry Grigor and see reason."

Rage surged within Gwen, and she squeezed her fingers, struggling once more to grasp the elusive air. She closed her eyes, willing the pain in her head to subside as memories of her Papa's face—before the illness—flickered in her mind. But instead, a different image came to her: a sister, arriving at the castle with books and ancient records her father had requested, and a jar of mountain herb tea, a gift for their ruler.

When Gwen opened her eyes, the sister stood before her, across the large table. Xyndra—Princess Eliana's cousin. Tall, like the Princess, but with a face forever twisted in disdain, as though perpetually sucking on a lemon. It robbed her of beauty. A few years older than Gwen and Anya, she had delighted in tormenting them, finding ways to make their lives unbearable.

And now, she smiled at Gwen, her expression one of pure, wicked satisfaction.

Gwen's fist clenched, and she envisioned the air stream connecting her fingertips to Xyndra's throat. With all her might, she pulled. Xyndra's eyes widened, her hands clawing at her neck, gasping for breath.

The High Sister cocked her head, her gaze sick with fascination as Xyndra struggled. "Restrain her. The Queen deserves this kill. I am nothing if not fair. Besides, her line is tainted, and I have no use for someone so easily swayed to murder a king," she ordered the other sisters.

Gwen's mind reeled back to her father—strong, brave, and confident—how he had wasted away before their eyes, all because he loved her, because he wanted her to marry Tyreal. A primal scream tore from her throat, tears streaming down her face, mingling with the sweat pouring from her brow. She fought to maintain control of the air, to strip it from Xyndra's lungs, but the struggle was tearing her apart.

The other sisters obeyed, holding Xyndra down as the High Sister stepped forward with a blade. She slashed Xyndra's wrist, letting the blood pool in a chalice. "See? I'm benevolent. I'll even refrain from delivering the killing blow," she taunted, one of the sisters nodding eagerly in agreement.

Xyndra collapsed, lifeless. Gwen slumped in her chair, her vision dimming as unconsciousness crept closer. The High Sister smirked at her. "I'd be concerned about your air control, but let's face it—you've always been hopeless at it. I doubt you'll conjure anything now, so this works out nicely." She turned to her sisters. "Light the candles and offer your lifeblood to the chalice."

Numbness spread through Gwen's limbs, her head spinning as blurred sounds and images twisted around her. The air grew thick, and she struggled to stay conscious. Ironically, her breath came in short, ragged gasps, each one failing to fill her lungs. The High Sister cut into her skin, and Gwen gasped, her body recoiling in pain.

The High Sister seized some of Anya's bloody hair, letting it coat her fingers. "I'll deal with both of you once my magic returns," she said, her voice dripping with malice. "The Princess will make wonderful practice." She swirled her bloody finger into the chalice, mixing its contents with sickening satisfaction.

Heavy, unyielding footsteps echoed along the corridor leading to the chamber. The High Sister smiled, turning as her robes swirled around her ankles. As she did, several blades of various sizes rose from the table, controlled by the air as though it were an extension of her will. The blades pointed toward the entrance.

"Hello, Captain Blackbane! How wonderful of you to join us!" the High Sister called, her voice echoing with mocking joy. "You're just in time to witness the dawn of a new era."

CHAPTER THIRTY-FIVE

Tyreal's pulse thundered in his ears as he navigated the twisting catacombs beneath the chapel. He moved as quickly and as quietly as he could, but dread made his stomach churn. Dark stains marred the ground—a grim trail that only deepened his fear. His mind raced with questions, each more harrowing than the last. When he reached the High Sister and Gwen, would he be too late? Would he even be enough to save them? He had to try; Gwen wasn't just his queen—she was the love of his life, his reason for every duty he'd ever sworn to uphold.

The corridor opened into a broad arch-way, faint light spilling out and casting uneven shapes across the stone walls. Tyreal pressed himself against the edge, moving silently as he peered cautiously into the chamber beyond. Gwen was the first thing his eyes found—sweaty, slumped in a chair, her body bound. Her head swayed weakly as though teetering on the edge of unconsciousness. The sight of her, vulnerable and broken, sparked a rage deep within him—an anger so fierce it threatened to swallow him whole. But he couldn't afford to lose control. Not now. He buried it deep, alongside the pain of Alric's death. *Later. I'll deal with it later.*

The High Sister stood in the center of the room, blades at the ready. Her robes billowed as she turned to face him, her expression cold and unflinching. "Ah, Captain Blackbane. How wonderful of you to join us. You're just in time to witness the dawn of a new era," she purred, her voice echoing off the cold stone walls.

Tyreal's mind raced, calculating his options. There was no way to approach without facing her blades. With a deep breath, he stepped into view. "I don't take pleasure in hurting women. But I'm afraid none of you will leave this chamber alive."

The High Sister snorted in derision. "Don't take pleasure in hurting women? Don't make me laugh. The Ardiennes may have worn crowns, but they were brutes long before magic fell. For five hundred summers, you've been nothing but filthy commoners. There's nothing royal about you—you're just the final piece of this puzzle."

Before Tyreal could retort, she flicked her wrists, sending the blades spiraling toward him. Instinct and training kicked in. He dove to the side, rolling across the damp floor as the blades buried themselves in the stone where he had just stood. He scrambled to his feet, drawing his sword. The metal sang as it left its sheath, and chaos erupted in the chamber. The other sisters moved to attack, casting grotesque spells that flickered and distorted the shadows on the walls.

One sister hurled fire at him. He ducked just in time, feeling the heat graze his cheek, singeing the hair at his temple. He charged forward, his blade finding its mark. It sliced through the sister's torso from shoulder to navel, her pained cry of disbelief ringing in the air as she crumpled to the floor.

A fireball exploded against his back, the leather of his cuirass searing uncomfortably. If he didn't deal with the caster quickly, it would burn through to his flesh. Spinning on his heel, he drew one of Alric's daggers from his thigh and hurled it at the sister responsible. The blade struck her throat, blood spurting as she fell. The fireball's grip on him released, but the burns beneath his armor throbbed painfully.

"Enough!" the High Sister shouted, raising her fist. The air around Tyreal constricted, binding him as tightly as rope. He struggled, but movement was impossible. Without killing her, he had no escape. He closed his eyes, silently pleading with any god who would listen to end this, or at least show him a way forward.

The other sister approached, slicing open his hand to collect his blood in a chalice before returning it to the High Sister. She laughed, a sound devoid of humanity, watching the liquid swirl inside. "Perfect. I'm glad you left him alive, Sister. Since everyone else is unconscious, it's good to have a witness to my ascension." Her eyes locked onto Tyreal, and he felt his heart sink at the madness reflecting in them.

She dipped her finger into the chalice and painted a line of blood across her forehead. As she began to chant, the air vibrated with a rising hum. Tyreal swore he could feel it deep within himself. The pitch escalated, ringing painfully in his ears. He fought against the binding, struggling futilely. The High Sister began to float, her voice rising in rapid, incomprehensible words. The other two sisters knelt in worship, their arms raised, their voices blending with the High Sister's chant.

Tyreal felt the bindings around him weaken, the force holding him slackening as the High Sister's focus wavered. Seizing the moment, he broke free, his sword flashing as he surged forward. His chest burned with desperation—not just for the fight, but for Gwen. He had to reach her, had to stand by her side, even if it meant dying with her.

The nearest sister turned as he approached, her chant cutting off with a gasp. Tyreal struck swiftly, the blow precise and final. The second sister rose, hands reaching for him in some spellbound fury, but she fell just as quickly under his blade.

As he closed the distance to the High Sister, her scream shattered the air. "RELEASE!" she bellowed, her voice reverberating like a crack of thunder.

A blast of energy hurled Tyreal against the wall, knocking the air from his lungs as pain tore through him. He cried out, his body convulsing as the force ripped through his very being, burning and reshaping him all at once. His burned flesh knitted back together, but the agony was so consuming that his mouth opened in a silent scream.

When the torment finally subsided, Tyreal forced his eyes open. Gwen and Anya stood together, Anya's blade slicing through the last of Gwen's restraints. Gwen rose to her full height, her golden eyes blazing with a light that illuminated the dim chamber. Power radiated from her, tangible and commanding, unlike anything Tyreal had ever seen.

The High Sister screeched, her voice trembling with disbelief. "This cannot be happening! How is this possible?"

Tyreal pushed himself upright, the energy coursing through him still terrifying, overwhelming, yet strangely familiar. Was this magic? It felt like the force he'd used to heal Max, but magnified to a degree he could barely comprehend. He glanced at Max, who strained against his restraints, as though the same power was surging through him.

Flexing his hands, Tyreal felt the last remnants of pain fade as Gwen and Anya helped free Max. Before he could catch his breath, Lila burst into the chamber, her form flickering uncontrollably. One moment she was a majestic wolf, the next an enormous owl, before finally settling back into her human shape.

Disoriented, she shook her head, and Tyreal caught her hand, steadying her. "With me," he said firmly, pulling her toward Gwen, Anya, and Max as they regrouped in the midst of the chaos.

Kelra appeared beside Tyreal, slipping through the shadows with unnerving ease, vanishing and reappearing like a phantom. Across the chamber, Seraphina summoned a shield of light, intercepting the High Sister's relentless fireballs. Her disgust was evident, her lips curling as she faced the woman she had once followed.

"You've ruined everything!" the High Sister bellowed, her voice dripping with fury. "None of you are worthy of magic! I will kill you all!" With a feral scream, she hurled another fireball at Seraphina, the heat of it searing the air.

Gwen stepped forward, drawing the High Sister's attention. "You killed my father, you mad bitch," she spat. "The only other person who will die in this chamber is you."

Tyreal had never heard Gwen speak with such venom. He charged to her side, ready to protect her, but she shook her head forcefully. Her golden eyes blazed brighter, and he understood her silent message. She needed to handle this on her own. She was more than capable.

"This ends now!" Gwen roared, her voice reverberating through the chamber.

Kelra darted to Max, grabbing his hands. In an instant, they disappeared into the shadows, leaving Gwen, Anya, and Tyreal to confront the High Sister. The High Sister screamed in fury, unleashing a cascade of fire toward them. But Gwen and Anya didn't flinch. Gwen lifted her hands, her magic surging as she redirected the flames into a spiraling vortex of heat and light. Anya stepped forward, her own power binding the fire in place, trapping the High Sister within.

Gwen raised her left hand, summoning a sphere of blinding light, and hurled it into the vortex. The High Sister's screams tore through the chamber as the light shattered her focus, her spells unraveling into nothingness.

The glow of Gwen's magic lit her face, and the pain in her eyes tightened Tyreal's chest. "In Tavia, we demand justice for crimes," she said, her voice thick with emotion. Anya moved to her side, taking her hand, while Tyreal placed a steadying hand on her shoulder.

"This is for every soul you tormented," Gwen said, her voice raw but steady. "But most of all, in the name of King Lorne Thorncrest—a good and kind man, and the best father anyone could have asked for—this is the justice you deserve."

With a flick of her wrist, she extinguished the orb. The High Sister's body crumbled to ash, leaving the chamber in heavy silence.

Gwen turned to Tyreal, and without hesitation, he opened his arms. She flung herself into his embrace, sobbing uncontrollably. He pressed his lips to her temple, silently thanking the gods for bringing him to her in time.

As they held each other, the others gathered around, their faces a mixture of relief and sorrow. Gwen pulled back, her eyes red from tears. "Where's Alric?" she whispered, her voice trembling.

Max's shoulders slumped as he struggled to hold back his tears. "I... I think he's dead. She stabbed him when he stepped in front of me. It's my fault."

Tyreal placed a comforting arm around Max's shoulders. "He is. I'm so sorry. But he wanted me to tell you something. That was how he would've wanted to go—not in vain. He's in the Everafter, celebrating his hero's death. You're alive because of him."

Max choked back a sob, absorbing Tyreal's words but drowning in grief. "His last act was to keep protecting you," Tyreal continued. "Please, don't feel guilty. He wouldn't want that."

Seraphina's gaze softened as she surveyed the group. "Let us leave this place of darkness behind. The sunlight above will do us all good. I'll make arrangements for the aftermath," she said gently, her eyes lingering on the grim scene.

Gwen turned to Tyreal, a small smile breaking through her tears. "Ready for your first round of 'unofficial official King Consort duties'?" she asked as they walked toward the chapel.

Tyreal exhaled deeply. "No, but do you remember what I said about fate that day by the spring?"

She slipped her hand into his, squeezing it gently. "That it's the one thing in life we cannot escape."

-To Be Continued-

AFTERWORD

I hope you enjoyed "Embers of Fate"! Tyreal and Gwen's story will continue in the next book, expected to release in Fall 2025. In the meantime, if you'd like to stay in Tavia a little longer, you can get a free short story about Myaessa and Mist Castle by signing up for my newsletter at my website, https://www.danilo ughary.com

THANKS

There are so many people I need to recognize that helped Embers get to publication.

To my husband—my anchor and Tyreal's inspiration. Thank you for believing in me even on the days I didn't believe in myself. Your unwavering love and endless encouragement made this dream possible. This story, and every chapter of my life, is better because of you.

To Katie, Cara, Cassie, Aarika, and Emily—my incredible cheerleaders. Thank you for listening to my panicked rambles, offering your support, and letting me bounce ideas off you until the plot holes finally made sense. An especially big thanks to Cassie for pointing out the copious amounts of times I started a sentence with the word *but*.

Brittany- thank you for being an amazing Alpha AND Beta reader. Your unhinged comments, edits, and suggestions definitely improved me as a writer and fleshed this story out.

And finally, my BBPR gremlins- your chaos has been my favorite part of this author journey by far.

ABOUT THE AUTHOR

Dani is an indie author that made her debut on the romantasy scene with the novel you are now reading.

Ever since she got pulled into the principal's office for writing stories instead of doing math, she's been obsessed with writing about love and magic.

Embers started as an email story to her husband back in 2012. As a 40th birthday present to herself, Dani set out to finish and publish her first novel.

She lives in Missouri with her husband, two teenagers, and far too many animals. She works a day job in the non-profit sector. Otherwise, you can usually find her with her nose in a book, on social media, or playing The Sims 4 on her overpowered gaming computer.